WARD METHOD PUBLICATIONS

MUSIC INSTRUCTION FOR CATHOLIC SCHOOLS

BY

JUSTINE WARD

LOOK AND LISTEN

BOOK TWO – TEACHER'S MANUAL

Revised Edition – 1981

Revised by an International Committee of Teachers of the

WARD METHOD

New American Edition Prepared by

Theodore Marier

Printed for

THE CENTER FOR WARD METHOD STUDIES

Washington, D.C. 20064

ACKNOWLEDGMENTS

Permission to use the following copyrighted materials in this book is hereby acknowledged with thanks:

Boosey and Hawkes, Music Publishers, London
A Day in the Cornfield (Islay Reaper's Song) Horo Haradal—Dance to Your Shadow, from "Ten Selected Songs of the Hebrides."

J. Curwen and Sons, Ltd. London
Bohemian Dance Melody *Johnnie, I Love You* from "Twelve Czech Songs."

B. Feldman and Co., Ltd. London
Basque Melody from "University Carol Book 123."

Oxford University Press, London
To Thee Who Makest All – Drumcondra, Irish Hymn Melody. Text by P. Dearmer in "Songs of Praise."
Were You Ever in Quebec? Canadian Folk Song in "Oxford Song Book 2." collected by Thomas Wood.

Paterson's Publications, Ltd. London
The Sandman Text by J. Michael Diack from "Hundred Best Short Songs."

Trustees for the Society for the Promotion of Christian Knowledge, London
Tho' at Yule it Bloweth Cool Text by George R. Woodward in "The Cambridge Carol Book."

Theodore Marier, Belmont, Massachusetts
Chants from Order of Mass taken from "Hymns, Psalms and Spiritual Canticles."

Illustrations by

Fran and Shu Dick Ju

INTRODUCTION

LOOK AND LISTEN is the second book in the Ward Method of Music Instruction Series. This book contains material for the second year of the children's study and assumes that they have already assimilated the content of Book One.

Work units in the areas shown below are provided in the 24 chapters of LOOK AND LISTEN. Each chapter contains material for approximately five classes, each of 20 to 25 minutes' duration. Chapter summaries in the form of charts are given in the Appendix.

Vocal Training. From the simple vowel preceded by N, as in NU which was used exclusively in Book One, the vocal drills here progress to the use of four other vowels, namely: o, a, e, i (pronounced as Latin vowels), in both the upper and lower vocal ranges of the major and minor modes. In the last few chapters, a few vocal drills are given to introduce the labial, dental and guttural consonants.

Intonation. The plagal range of the DO Mode is here explored as are the authentic and plagal ranges of the Modes of SOL and LA (natural minor). Drills on the scale lines, the chord lines and auxiliary tones of each are presented.

Rhythm. Coordination of gestures to binary and ternary musical rhythms continues. This study progresses to free rhythm and to the techniques for beating time in duple and triple meters. The divided pulse, that is, eighth notes, and dotted quarter plus eighth notes, is treated extensively.

Staff Notation. The DO Clef is studied in four positions on the five-line staff as are the notation signs for divided pulses, triplets and tied notes. The students are also introduced to the concepts of key signatures, the use of sharps and flats, and leger lines.

Creative Activity. Musical "conversations" on the tones of the scales and in various rhythmic structures continue in this book from the simple beginnings found in BOOK ONE. Experience in setting poetic texts to music is provided as well as a consideration of such compositional techniques as repetition, sequence and inversion, of melodic designs.

Repertoire. The melodies included in LOOK AND LISTEN have been selected from a vast literature of folk and classical music. 148 in number, these melodies – some with and some without words – serve to illustrate the technical points under discussion in each chapter and, in addition, provide rich musical experiences in ensemble singing for the classroom children. Chants and hymns for the celebration of liturgies in the vernacular tongue of English are included as are examples of the classical hymnody of the Christian church.

Translations of the revised books are being made for use in the various European countries where the Ward Method is used. Among them are Portugal, France, Switzerland (French and German), and Holland.

Special acknowledgment is made here of the assistance given by Miss Olga Wilson of the Cambridge (England) Ward Center, in the disposition of the chapter content for these revised books.

Information concerning courses in the Ward Method and other matters should be directed to the Ward Center, School of Music, The Catholic University of America, Washington, D.C. 20064.

ABOUT THE AUTHOR: JUSTINE BAYARD WARD

FAMILY BACKGROUND

Justine Bayard Ward, the former Justine Bayard Cutting, creator of the Ward Method of Music for school children, died on November 27, 1975 at 5:50 p.m. at her residence at 2500 30th Street, N.W., Washington, D.C. She was born in Morristown, New Jersey on August 7, 1879. Her parents were William Bayard Cutting, one of the founders of the Metropolitan Opera Company, and Olivia Murray Cutting. Her marriage on July 2, 1901 to George Cabot Ward was later annulled. The residence of her parents at Westbrook, Oakdale, Long Island, New York, where she lived as a child, is now open to the public as the W. Bayard Cutting Arboretum. Her brother, Bronson Cutting, was a United States Senator from New Mexico at the time of his death on May 6, 1935 in a plane crash. Mrs. Ward's niece, Iris Cutting Origo, only child of another deceased brother, W. Bayard Cutting, is a biographer and historian and resides in Italy.

PROFESSIONAL CAREER

From an early age Mrs. Ward was interested in music, and was an accomplished pianist. She was educated by tutors and at the Brearley School, New York. Mrs. Ward was converted to Roman Catholicism in 1904 and devoted the rest of her life to the cause of liturgical music of the Catholic Church. During the years 1921 to 1929 she studied under Reverend Dom André Mocquereau, O.S.B., living at Sablé sur Sarthe, near the famous French Benedictine Abbaye St. Pierre de Solesmes. In 1910 Mrs. Ward was requested by Reverend Thomas Edward Shields, the head of the Department of Education of the Catholic University of America, to write a series of music books for the teaching of children in Catholic schools, which later became known as the Ward Method of School Music. Her books have been translated in French, Dutch and Portuguese and are now being used in France, Holland, England, Switzerland and Portugal as well as the United States and Philippine Islands. She founded the Dom Mocquereau Foundation in 1928, a New York charitable corporation organized for the purposes of the teaching and dissemination of Gregorian chant. Mrs. Ward wrote several books in addition to her music series, including a biography of *Thomas Edward Shields.* In 1962 at the opening session of the Fifteenth National Convention of the National Catholic Music Educators Association Mrs. Ward was cited as a "tenacious pioneer," who for years "devoted herself untiringly to music education in our elementary schools." In 1967 the Catholic University of America named its music building, Ward Hall, in her honor.

Mrs. Ward received high civilian awards in both Italy and Holland, having received the Benemerenti Medal for exceptional civil service, and the Order of William of Orange, the highest civilian honor in Holland. She was honored in 1944 by the Order of Malta with the "Croce di Benemerenza" of the Sovereign Military Order of Malta, and Pope Pius XII with the Cross Pro Ecclesia and Pontifical Medals. She received the Honorary Degree of Doctor of Gregorian Chant from the Pontifical Institute of Sacred Music, Rome, Italy, an Honorary Degree from Annhurst College, and was awarded the degree of Doctor of Music, Honoris Causa, in 1971 by the Catholic University of America.

PERSONALITY

No description of her work, however, would be complete without a reference to the quality of spirit which made her achievements possible. Her deep faith and undaunted enthusiasm, enhanced by a vitality and gaiety which she communicated to all her pupils at their lessons, from the smallest children in the first grade, was an inspiration and a delight. She maintained that there was no such thing as a totally unmusical child: "they could be taught to communicate with each other in song, like young birds." That, indeed, in the purity and lightness of tone achieved, was what her younger classes sounded like. No musician who has ever come into touch with her has failed to speak of both her gifts and her Method with admiration and respect.

INDEX

Each chapter contains a section on Vocal training, Intonation, Rhythm, Staff Notation, Creative Activities, and Songs.

Chapter One

Vocal Training

Review exercises of Book One

Vocal Exercise 1

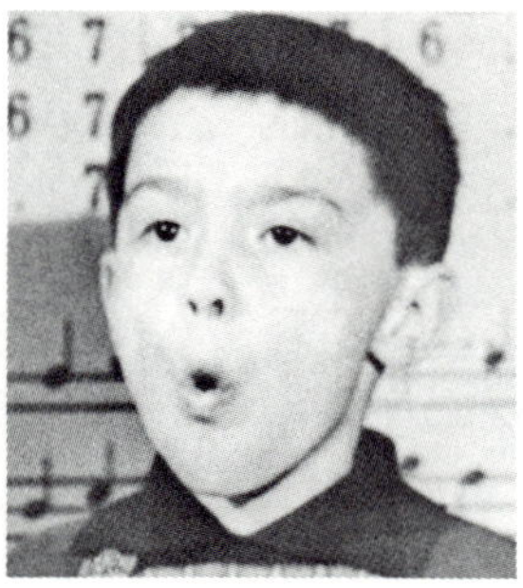

$1 = B^b$ F D

|| 1 ——————
Nu —————— ||

Stand with knees together and weight of body on both feet.
Sustain tone for 8 slow counts ♩ = 60.
Notice position of lips. Mouth open wide inside.
With finger-tips on forehead feel vibration of Nnnn inside cranium.

Vocal Exercise 2

$1 = B^b$ F D

|| 1 | 1 1 | 1 1 | 1 . | . ||
Nu Nu Nu Nu Nu Nu ——

> The group that has not developed to the point of matching tones accurately still does not participate in vocal exercises. Off-key droning must not be tolerated. Droners continue to participate in all other class activities that do not demand pitch accuracy. As soon as they find their "singing voices," they are promoted to the next group.

Intonation

Review Compass Exercises *of* Book One.
If a more basic review of the scale line seems to be called for, Intonation Exercises 11, 12, 27, *and* 31 *with* Intonation Diagram 6, *as found in* Book One, *may be used.*

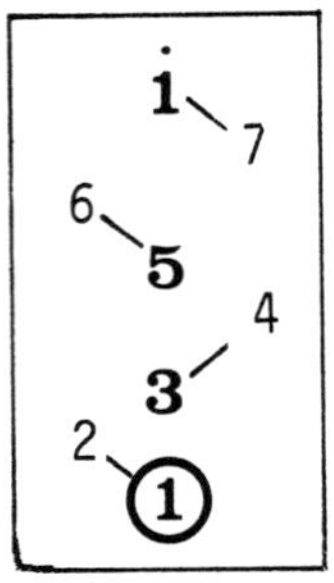

Intonation Diagram 1

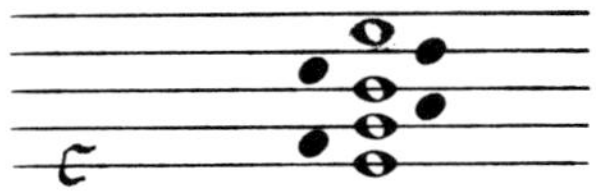

Staff Diagram 1a

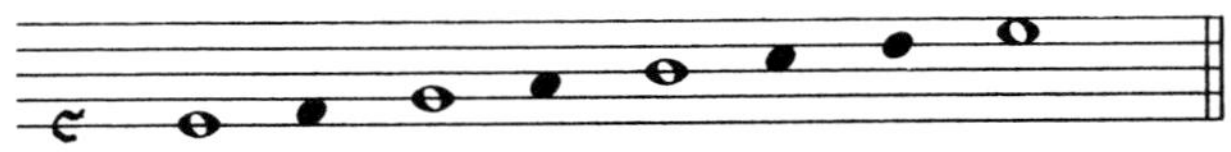

Staff Diagram 1b

Intonation Exercise 1 - First Compass Exercise *With* Int. Diagram 1 *and* Staff Diagrams 1a *and* 1b

N.B. Italicized numbers represent "think" tones and are not to be sung.

a) →

| 121 *123* 343 *345* 565 *5671̇* 1̇71̇ | 1̇71̇ *1̇765* 565 *543* 343 *321* 121 |

| 121 343 565 1̇71̇ | 1̇71̇ 565 343 121 |

b) →

| 121 343 565 1̇71̇ | 1̇71̇ 565 343 121 |

| 121 *343* 565 1̇71̇ | 1̇71̇ 565 *343* 121 |

| 121 343 *565* 1̇71̇ | 1̇71̇ *565* 343 121 |

| 121 *343* *565* 1̇71̇ | 1̇71̇ *565* *343* 121 |

1̇ = E♭ for all drills
(5 = B♭)

Intonation Exercise 2 - Second Compass Exercise *With* Int. Diagram 1 *and* Staff Diagrams 1a *and* 1b

a) →

| 121 343 565 1̇71̇ | 1̇71̇ 565 343 121 |

| 1*21* *343* *565* 1̇*71̇* | 1̇*71̇* *565* *343* 1*21* |

b) →

| 1 3 5 1̇ | 1̇ 5 3 1 |

| 1 *3* 5 1̇ | 1̇ 5 *3* 1 |

| 1 3 *5* 1̇ | 1̇ *5* 3 1 |

| 1 *3* *5* 1̇ | 1̇ *5* *3* 1 |

Continue to use pointer painted with two colors:
GREEN means "sing"
RED means "stop - think"

Intonation Exercise 3 - Third Compass Exercise *With* Int. Diagram 1 *and* Staff Diagrams 1a *and* 1b

| 121 343 565 1̇71̇ | 1̇71̇ 565 343 121 |

| *121* *343* *565* *1̇71̇* | *1̇71̇* *565* *343* *121* |

Intonation Exercise 4 - Compass Exercises Combined *With* Int. Diagram 1 *and* Staff Diagrams 1a *and* 1b

| 12345 | 1 3 5 *121* *343* *565* | 5 3 1 *565* *343* *121* |

| 13135 *121* *343* 565 | 53531 565 *343* *121* |

| 135313 43 *565* | 531353 565 3 21 |

> It is advisable from time to time to practise the "think" tones by humming them to make sure that students are not guessing at the distances between the notes of the exercise.

Dictations

Eye and Ear Tests *Look and Listen!*

1̇ = Eb

The students' powers of concentration are becoming stronger at this stage of their development. It is well, therefore, to follow the Intonation Exercise *in each lesson with two or three* Ear and Eye Tests.

Review: Arm Gesture *and* Finger Notation *for indicating scale tones*
Visual tests written on blackboard and erased
Tonal fragments flashed on screen for a few moments and turned off

151 1 121 | 21 343 | 1 21 43 65 | 1̇71̇ 65 71̇ | 1 3 5 1̇
115 51 343 | 43 565 | 65 21 43 | 1 5 65 51 | 21 43 65 71̇

121 1̇71̇ 1 | 2211 443 | 1̇71̇ 65 43 | 51 115
1 1 343 | 44 3 665 | 43 665 71̇ | 53 665 71̇

Rhythm

Review: Up-pulse Beginning of Binary Groupings (Measures)

Review Rhythmic Gestures I *and* II *to the accompaniment of the cassette recording provided for these gestures or of a song with this rhythmic structure that the children learned in Book One, such as, "O HOLY SPIRIT, LORD OF GRACE," or "O COCK-DOODLE-DOO."*

Rhythmic Gesture I

Rhythmic Gesture II

Review Rhythm Patterns - Series 1

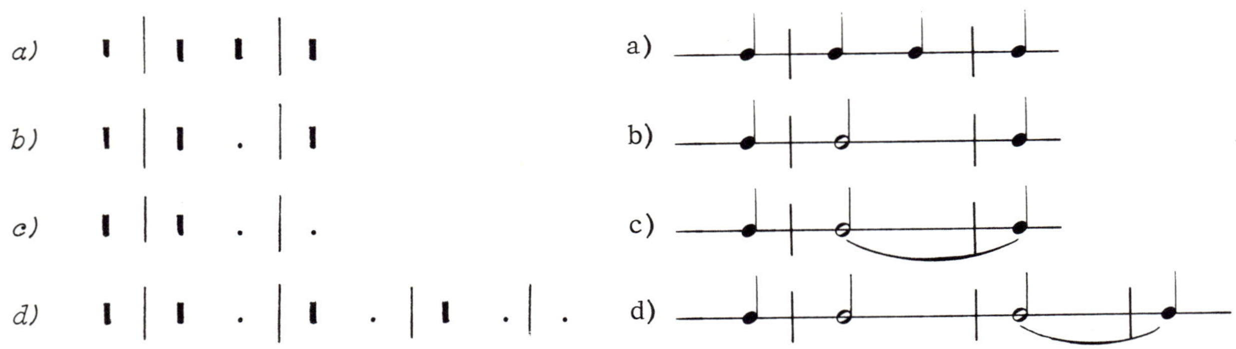

Metrical Gesture I

1. *Sing each pattern using:*

   Metrical Language   la = ❙ long = ❙ . *or* ❙ . | .

   Metrical Gesture I

2. *Form longer rhythms by combining patterns and improvising melodies for each new combination. Teacher writes two or four lines of rhythms on board and invites students to provide a melody for each. Examples given may serve as models.*

Repetition of patterns

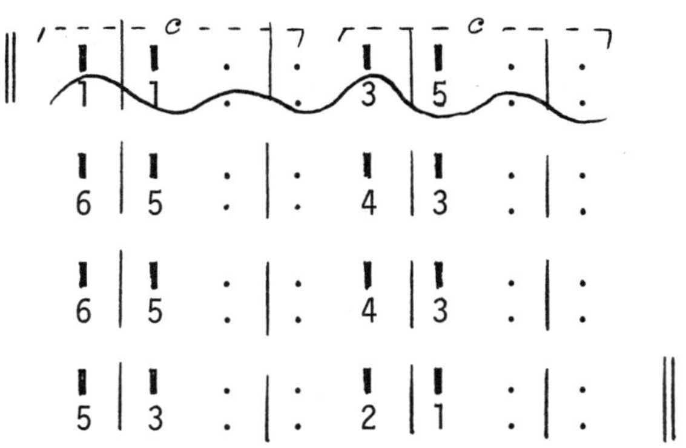

Combining and alternating patterns

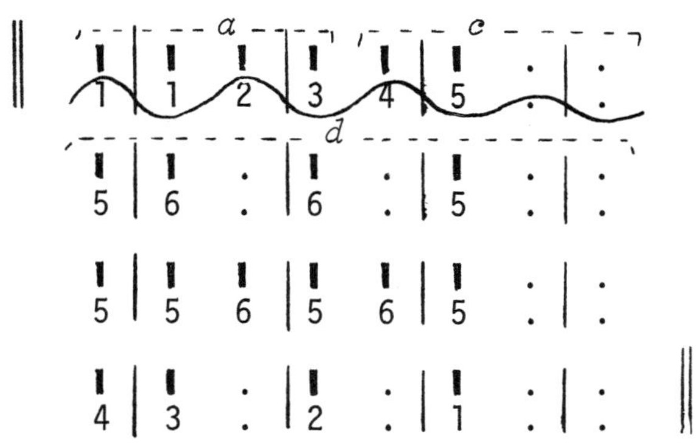

Students sing final version of melody with appropriate gesture.

3. Rhythmic Dictations

- *With patterns in full view of class, teacher sings a line of melody taken from one of the songs to be learned while making appropriate rhythmic gesture.*
- *Students identify combination of patterns used. One student is invited to board.*
- *Teacher repeats melody while student pretends to write correct rhythm strokes with finger; other students write rhythm "in the air."*
- *If student has sketched rhythm correctly he is allowed to use chalk. All repeat melody as he writes rhythm strokes while singing the melody in strict time.*
- *Student adds bar-lines beginning with long note.*
- *Another student is invited to add melody; a third student adds rhythm wave.*
- *All stand and sing melody while making appropriate gesture.*

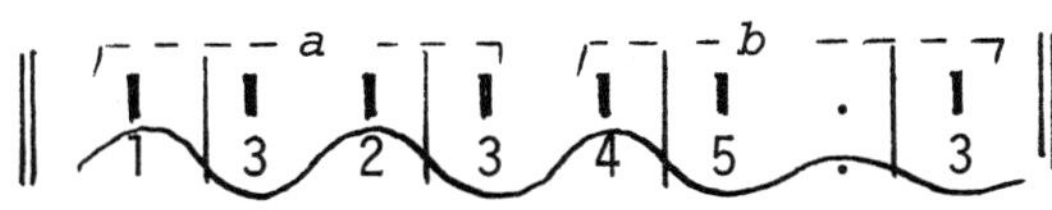

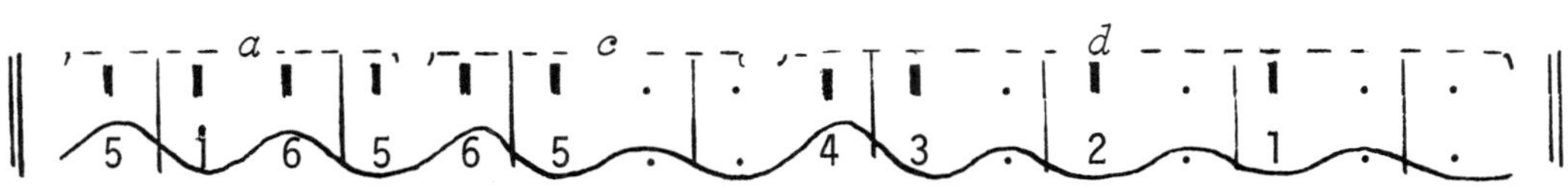

> Continue to use colored chalk for dictations. A suggested plan could be the following:
>
> | | |
> |---|---|
> | YELLOW | for rhythm strokes |
> | RED | for bar-lines |
> | BLUE | for rhythm wave |
> | WHITE | for melody |

Notation

Review 5-line Staff, DO Clef (Bottom Line)
Mode of DO - Authentic Range
Single and 2-Pulse Notes, Ties

1. *On* 5-Line Staff *teacher writes a quotation from* First Compass Exercise. *A student is invited to transcribe notes from staff to* Number Notation *up to double-bar. A second student transcribes up to second double-bar, and a third finishes line. When completed all sing pitches from staff using correct* Arm Gesture *for each tone.*

Given:
To be transcribed:

Another example with same procedure but transcription is from Number Notation *to* Staff Notation.

To be transcribed:
Given:

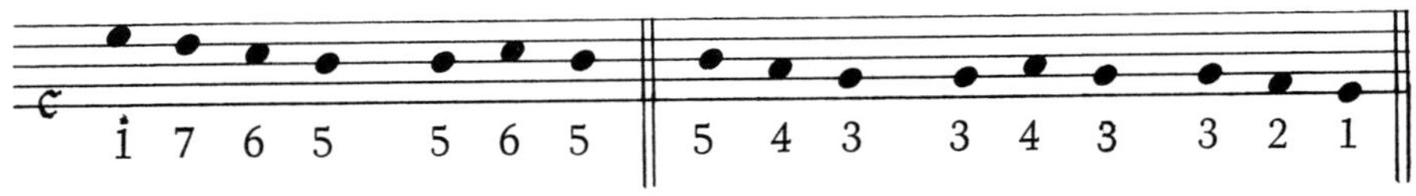

2. *Teacher combines two rhythm patterns on board from series being studied. Students are invited to transcribe rhythm strokes to* Staff Notation *equivalents.*

Given:
To be transcribed:

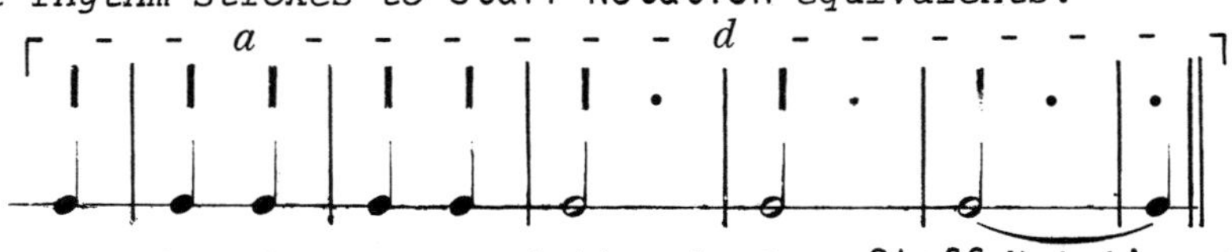

Another example with same procedure but transcription is from Staff Notation *to rhythm strokes.*

To be transcribed:
Given:

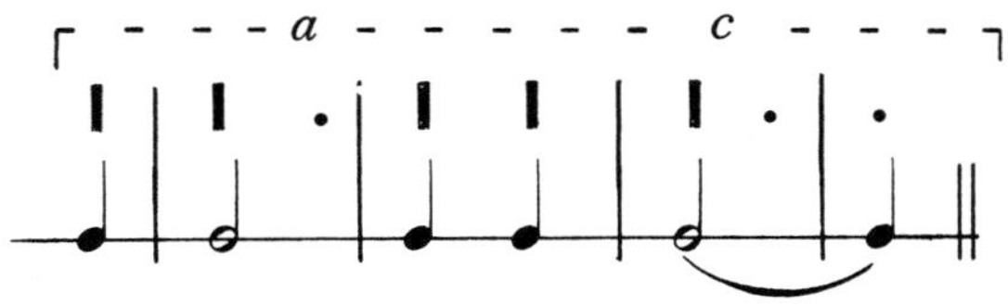

3. *Student at board transcribes fragment of song to be studied to* Staff Notation.

To be transcribed:
Given:

Another example but transcription is to Number Notation.

Given:
To be transcribed:

Creative Activity

Review: Musical Conversations
Improvising Melodies for Verbal Phrases

In study of Rhythm *in this chapter, the technique of* Melodic Application *to rhythm patterns is reviewed. Two other types of improvisation are here reviewed.*

1. Musical Conversations

Teacher begins by establishing rhythm pattern to be used. Bluebirds - one at a time - continue the "conversation" using the same rhythm but different scale tones. All make appropriate gesture during the conversation. (Try not to end on DO *until end!)*

Suggestions for initiating conversation:

	d
Teacher:	1 | 1 . | 2 . | 3 . | .
First Student:	3 | 3 . | 4 . | 5 . | .
Second Student:	*etc...... Third Student.... until some one ends on* DO.

	a c
Teacher:	1 | 1 2 | 3 2 | 3 . | .
First Student:	*etc.....*

2. Improvising Melodies for Verbal Phrases

Teacher writes one line of text on board syllabicating all words of more than one syllable.
Students try to guess which rhythm patterns apply to text recited.
Correct rhythm is placed beneath syllables.
Students then improvise a melody for the text. (Melodies given are suggestions.)

Examples:

Given: (a, c)	I	wait-	ed	for	the	Lord	.	.				
To be added:	(3	5	3	1	2	3	.	.)				
Given: (b, b)	The	Lord	.	is	my	shep-	.	herd.				
To be added:	(5	6	.	5	4	3	.	1)				
Given: (a, a, c)	I	saw	a	snail	come	down	the	gar-	den	walk	.	.
To be added:	(3	5	6	5	3	2	4	3	2	3	.	.)

> Rhythm patterns must be in full view of class during improvisations.

Additional texts may be selected at discretion of teacher.

SIGHT SINGING DRILLS

To be used in song preparation

1. *Sing each segment several times*

   1̂ = E♭

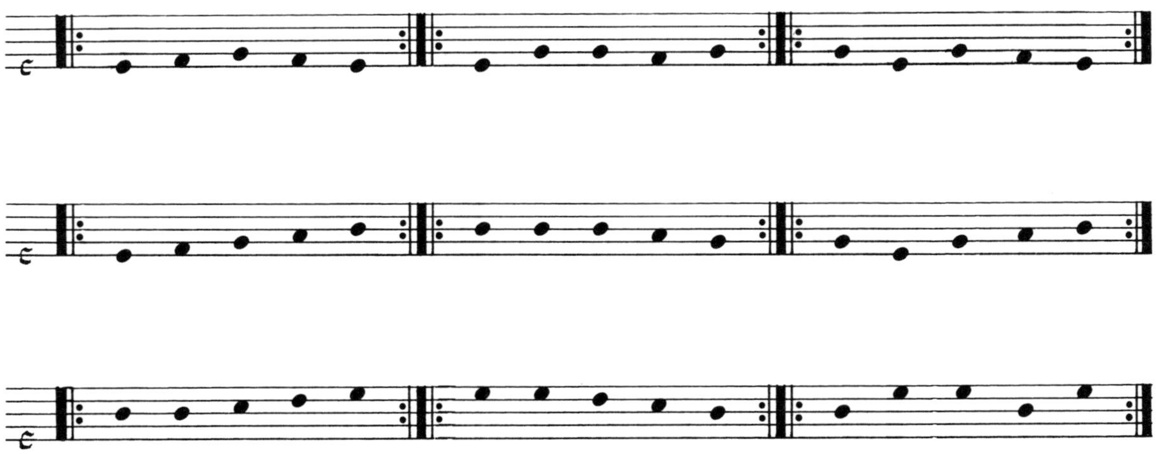

2. Visual Memory Tests *Written on blackboard and erased or flashed momentarily on screen*

a) 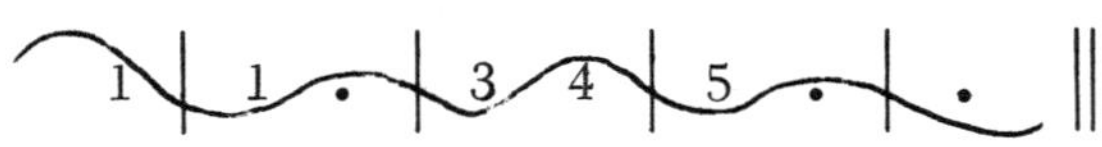

b) 

c) 

d) 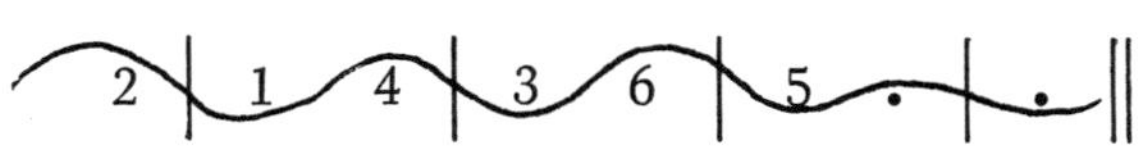

e) 

Songs

Mode of DO - Authentic Range
Binary Rhythm Beginning on Up-pulse
Rhythm Gestures I and II

Review (Book One) Same rhythm and tonal range as songs of this chapter:

O COCK-A-DOODLE-DOO

O HOLY SPIRIT

Presenting a New Song

The aim of each lesson should be to learn a new song. This means that from the pitch given for the Vocal Exercise with which the lesson begins through each succeeding lesson segment such as Intonation, Rhythm, Notation, etc., the groundwork for the new song should be prepared. Consistent use of the same pitch for DO will help to unify the presentation of the materials of a given lesson.

PROCEDURE

Song Without Words:

1. *All students say rhythm with* Metrical Language *and* Metrical Gesture I
2. *All students name notes while making* Metrical Gesture I
3. *Teacher gives pitch*. Bluebirds and Robins sing note names and Sparrows repeat gesture -* Metrical Gesture I
4. *Repeat adding* Rhythm Gesture I *or* II *to sung pitches*

Song With Words:

5. *All recite words according to rhythm of the song*
6. *Bluebirds and Robins sing words while Sparrows make appropriate gesture*

MELODY No. 1a "Scale Song" *Anonymous*

Melodic Application of Rhythm Patterns

i̇ = E♭
(5 = B♭)

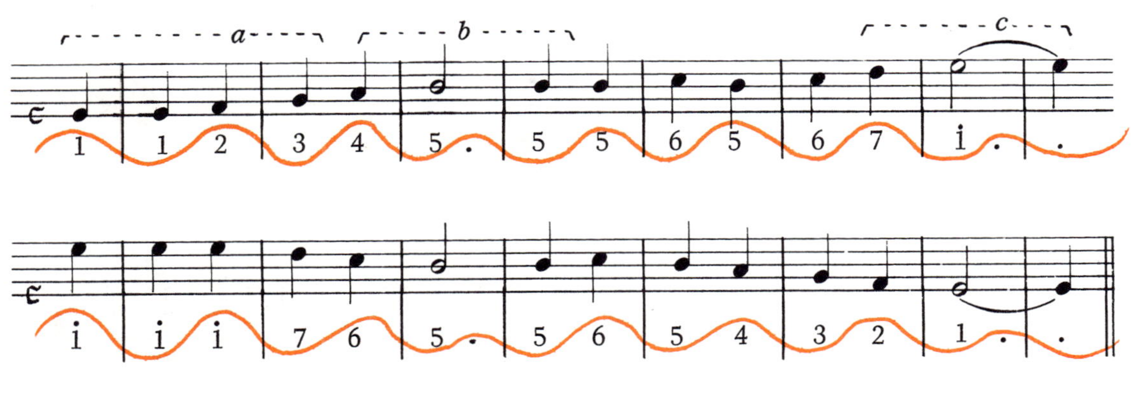

* *If pitch given for song is E^b and this tone is not on pitch pipe, teacher sounds B^b as SOL and sings down to DO. i̇ = Eb may also be used.*

MELODY No. 1b "Compass Song" *Anonymous*

I HEAR YOU WIND *Melody:* French Folk Song *Text:* JBW

MELODY No. 2 German Chorale "O Morning Star"

i̇ = E♭
(5 = B♭)

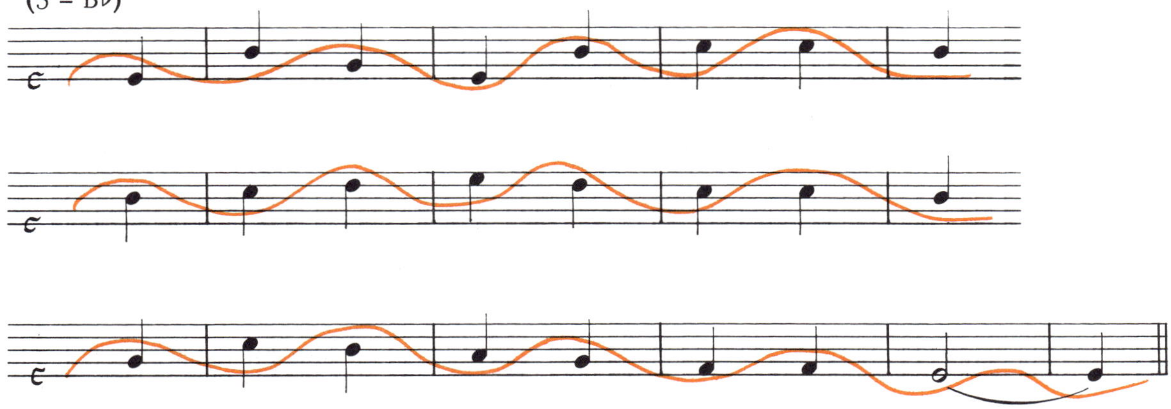

COLUMBUS *Melody:* 15th Century Air *Text:* JBW

1 = F or G
(5 = C or D)

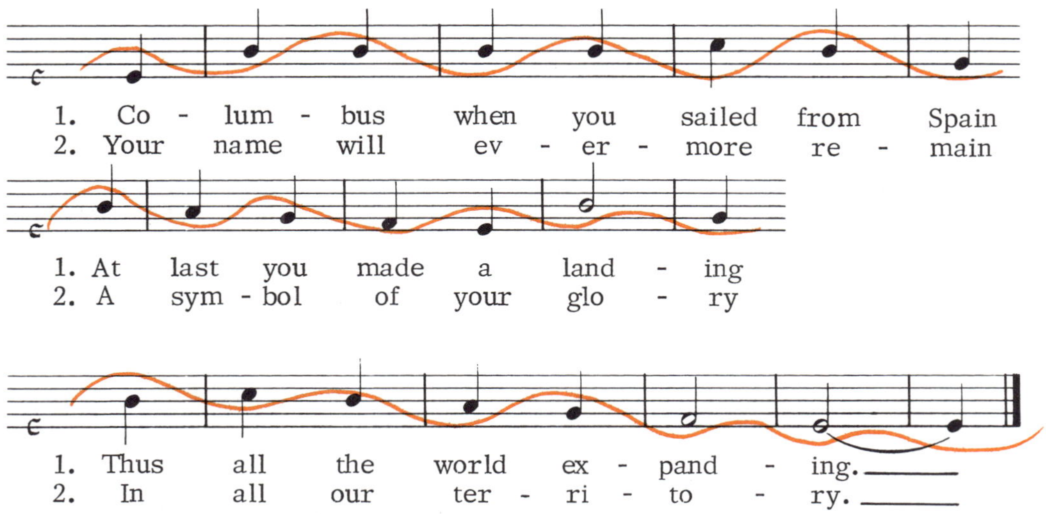

O LORD, I AM NOT WORTHY *Melody:* Mediaeval Folk Song
Text: Adapted from liturgical text

*TI in final cadence anticipates study of Plagal Range in Chapter Three.

i̇ = E♭ (5 = B♭)

Suggestions for

LESSON PLANNING

Elements to be included in a 20 or 25-minute lesson:

Stand	VOCAL TRAINING	- Long tones on given vowels in various registers of the singing voice. Suggestions for pitches are given in each lesson.
Sit	INTONATION	- Exercises with number and/or staff diagrams. Ear and eye tests.
Stand	RHYTHM	- Practise for correctness of posture and coordination of body movement with a known song as an accompaniment.
Sit	NOTATION*	- Transcriptions of musical materials of the lesson.
Stand	VOCAL TRAINING	- Melodic vocalises with accompanying gestures.
Sit	RHYTHM	- Study of patterns with metrical language and metrical gesture. Improvising melodic applications of rhythm patterns. Dictations.
	CREATIVE ACTIVITY*	Conversations with tones on rhythm patterns. Improvising melodies to rhythm patterns and/or words.
Sit *Stand*	SONGS	Study of musical elements separately and in combinations as shown on Page 9. If time permits, songs of previous chapters or from BOOK ONE may be reviewed.

*May be alternated from day to day according to available time. All other elements ought to be included daily if possible.

Chapter Two

Vocal Training

Review Exercises of Book One

Vocal Exercise 1

1 = B♭ / F / D

‖ 1 ———
Nu *(oo as in noon)* ——— ‖

Good posture and good breathing
Every student should feel vibration of the Nnnnnn by pressing finger-tips on forehead while singing long tone

Special attention should be given to Group III (Sparrows) in these exercises

Vocal Exercise 3

1 = F / G / A♭

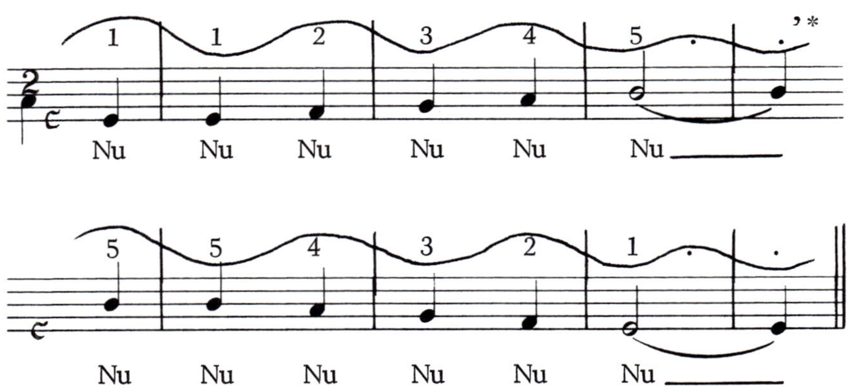

Begin each tone with a strong Nnnnn.
Take breath at end of line.

* *A comma (’) placed above staff indicates a place for taking breath*

Intonation

Review Mode of Do - Authentic Range
Fourth Compass Exercise

	6
5	
	4
3	
	2
1	

Int. Diagram 2

Intonation Exercise 5 - Fourth Compass Exercise

With Intonation *and* Staff Diagrams 2

1 = E♭ or F
(5 = B♭ or C)

121 21 43 65	65 43 21 121
121 21 43 65	65 43 21 121
121 2 4 6	6 4 2 121

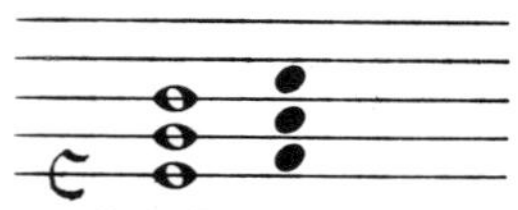

Staff Diagram 2

Intonation Exercise 6

With Intonation *and* Staff Diagrams 2

| 1 3 5 6 5 4 3 2 1 | 2 1 4 3 6 5 5 3 1 |
| 1 3 5 6 4 2 | 2 4 6 5 3 1 |

$\dot{1}$	
	6
5	
	4
3	
	2
1	

Int. Diagram 3

Intonation Exercise 7

With Intonation *and* Staff Diagrams 3

$\dot{1}$ = E♭
(5 = B♭)

| 1 3 5 5 $\dot{1}$ $\dot{1}$ 5 6 5 4 3 2 1 | 1 2 3 4 5 6 5 $\dot{1}$ $\dot{1}$ 5 3 1 |
| 1 3 5 5 $\dot{1}$ $\dot{1}$ 6 4 2 1 | 2 4 6 $\dot{1}$ $\dot{1}$ 5 3 1 |

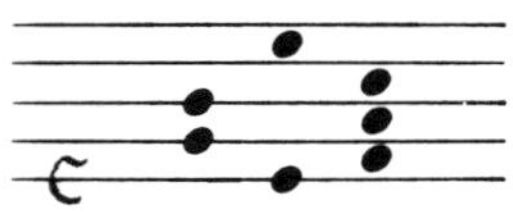

Staff Diagram 3

> Do not attempt all Intonation Exercises in one lesson. It is better to vary form Number Diagram to Staff Diagram and from group to group using same exercise.

Intonation Exercise 8 - *With* Intonation *and* Staff Diagrams 2

1 = E^b or F
(5 = B^b or C)

1 3 5	4 5 6	5	6 5 4 3 5
1 3 5	4 5 6	5	6 5 4 3 5
1 5 3	4 3 2	3	2 3 4 3
1 5 3	4 2	3	2 4 3

> Intonation Exercises should be followed by Eye and Ear Tests. Tones selected for dictation should be chosen from those used in preceding exercise. Dictations given may also be used

Ear Tests

1 3 5 6 4 2 1 | 1 2 3 4 2 1 | 1 3 5 4 6 4 5
5 3 1 2 4 6 5 | 1 2 3 2 4 2 3 | 5 3 5 4 4 6 6 5

5 6 1̇ 5 6 4 5 | 1 3 5 4 6 5
5 1 5 5 4 6 5 | 3 3 5 4 2 1

Eye Tests

1 2 3 4 5 4 6 5 | 1 5 4 3 2 4 2 3
1 2 3 4 5 6 4 5 | 1 5 4 3 4 2 4 3

1 3 5 6 4 6 5 | 5 6 5 3 5 4 2 3
5 6 5 4 5 4 6 5 | 1 3 5 4 2 4 3

1̇ 5 4 6 5 5 1̇

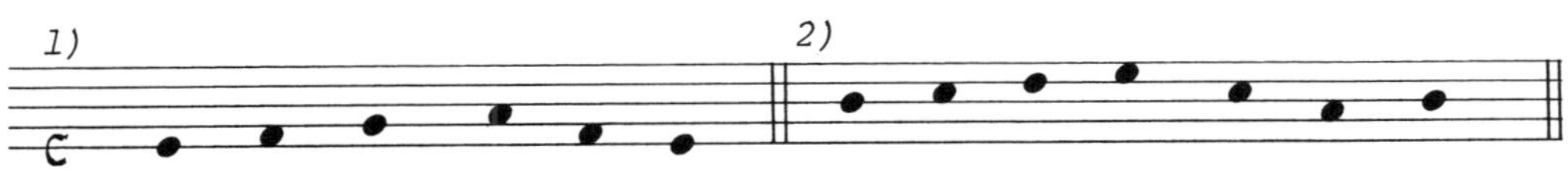

Rhythm

Review Down-pulse Beginnings in Binary Rhythm (Duple Time)
Arsis-Thesis Gesture

Rhythm Patterns - Series 2

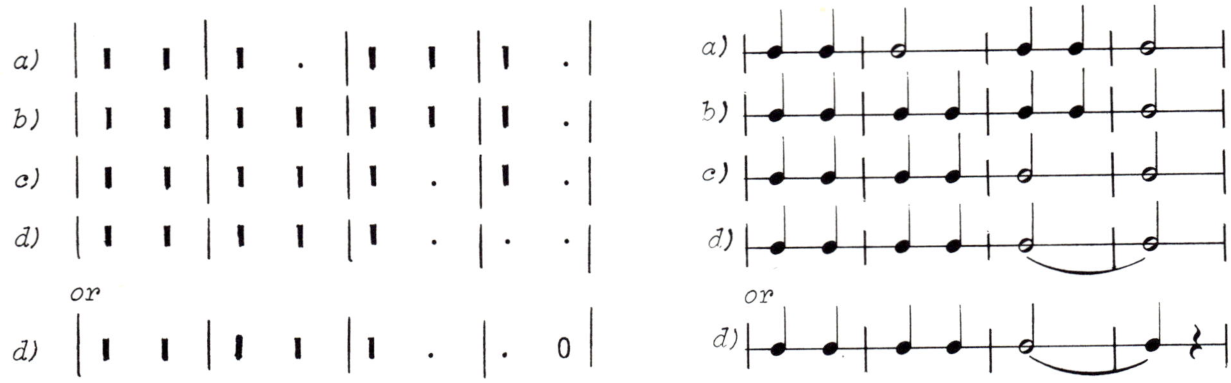

With patterns in full view of class, all sing rhythms using Metrical Language *and* Metrical Gesture 1.

Guessing Game *Teacher sings melodic application of a Rhythm Pattern. Students guess which pattern was used.*

A student is invited to improvise a melody to a pattern. Others guess which pattern was used.

Arsis-Thesis Gesture - Rhythm Gesture IV

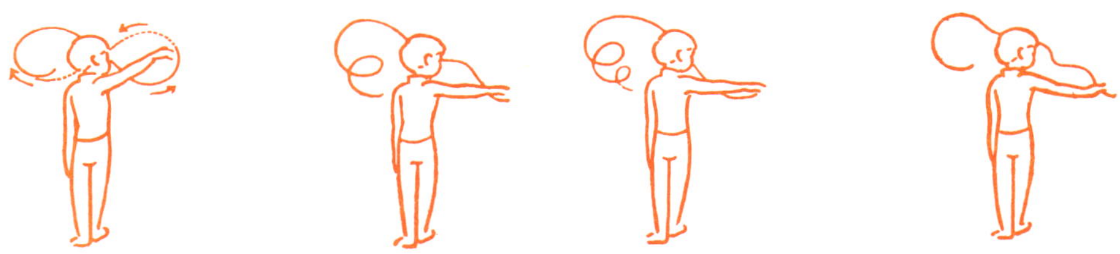

A T A T *A A T T* *A A A T* *A T T T*

All make gesture. Wrists loose. Back erect.

Practise gesture to cassette recording or to a known melody such as, "FOR THE GIFT OF DAILY BREAD", or "THE FATHER'S LOVE".

Improvise melodies for each set of four rhythm gestures:

A T A T *A A T T* *A A A T* *A T T T*

A = At beginning and for rise in melody
T = For descent of melody and at the end

MELODIC APPLICATIONS to ARSIS-THESIS GESTURE:

(1 = G)

a) 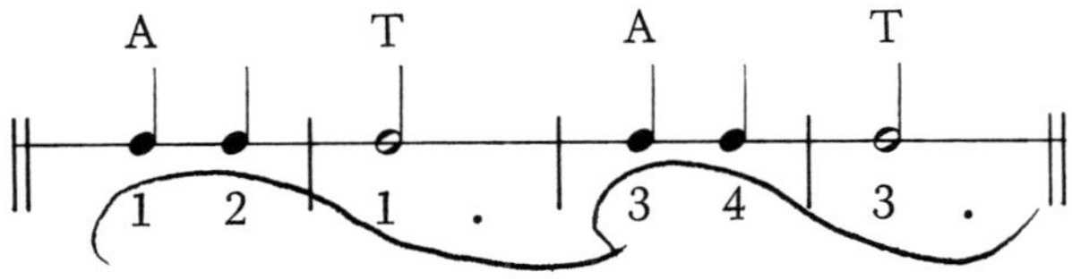

b) 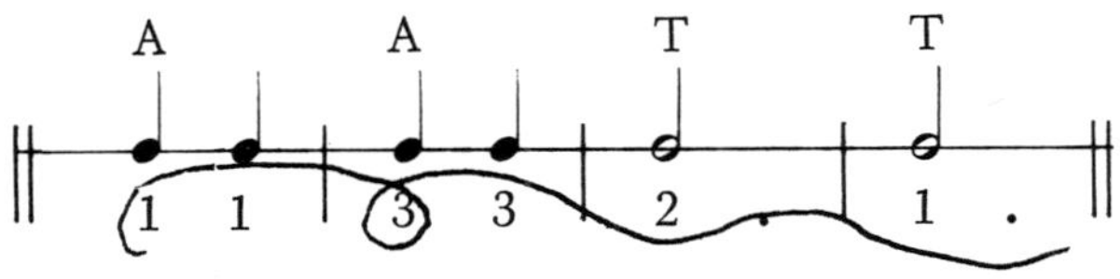

c) 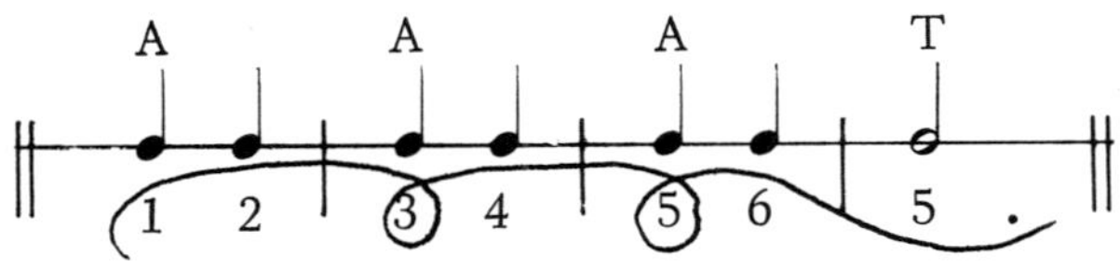

d) 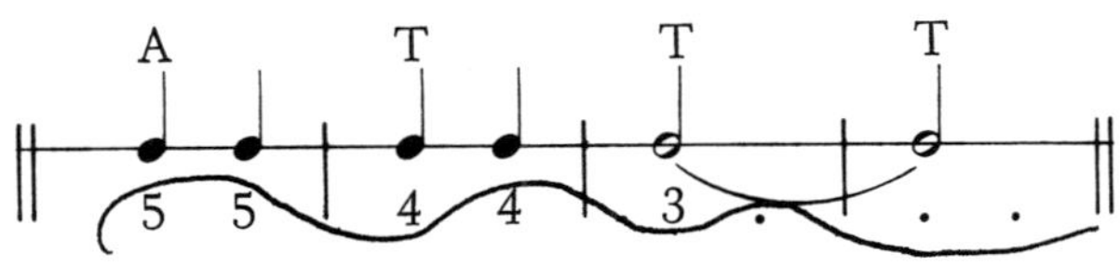

or

d) 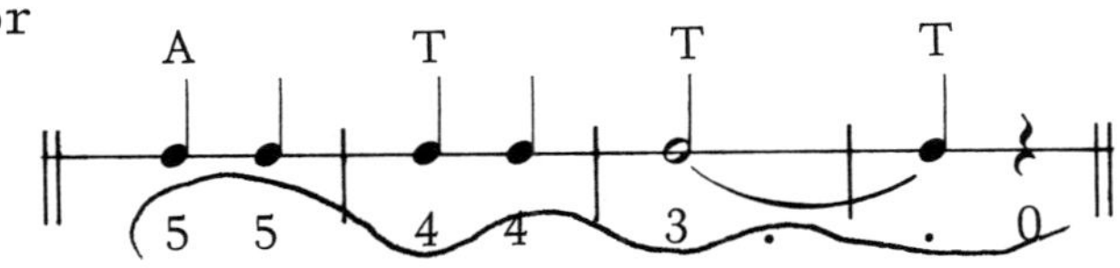

Aural Training in Rhythm - Step 1

Problems in Duple Time - Binary Rhythm
Rhythm determined by final cadence (repose)

Suggested lines for tests: *(See next page for procedure)*

3 1 3 5

1 3 3 2 3

3 2 3 4 2 1

5 5 1̇ 5 6 6 5

1 5 3 1 5 6 6 5

<u>*PROCEDURE:*</u>

1. *Place series of single-pulse notes on board. Children sing them*

   3 1 3 5

2. *Place bar-line before last note*

   3 1 3 | 5

3. *Count back by twos to place remaining bar-lines*

   3 ¦ 1 3 | 5

4. *Discover up-pulse or down-pulse beginning,* Arsis-Thesis *or* Rhythm Gesture II.

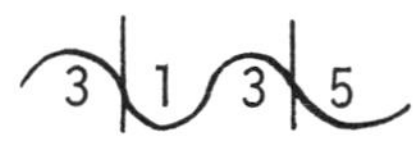

5. *Add length to last note plus other necessary bar-lines*

6. *Add double-bars at beginning and end. Sing complete melody with appropriate gesture.*

Repeat using other lines - a new line for each lesson

<u>RHYTHMIC DICTATIONS</u> *Rhythm Patterns must be in full view of class.*

(1 = E^b *or F)*

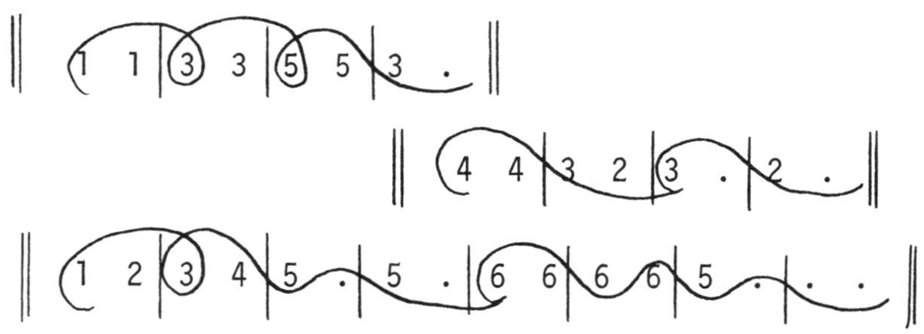

Select lines from songs to be studied at end of chapter.

Notation

Review: Single-pulse Notes = Quarter Notes
Two-pulse Notes = Half Notes
Ties
One-Pulse Rest (Silence)
Time Signature 2/♩

Notation Signs and Time Values

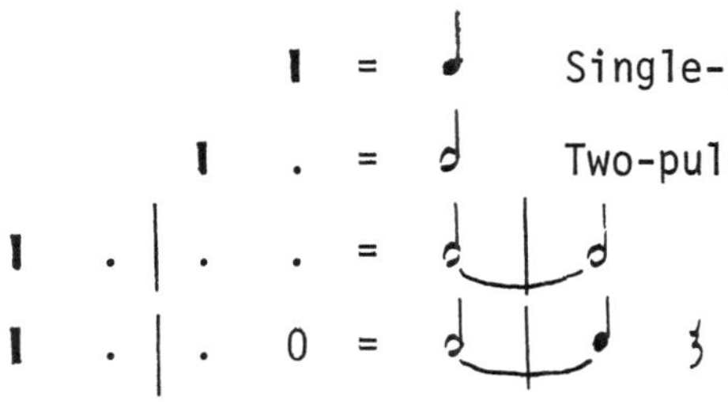

Single-pulse Note (Quarter Note)
Two-pulse Note (Half Note)
Half Notes Tied
Ties with One-pulse Rest

NEW - Time Signature 2/♩

2 = *Two pulses in a measure*

♩ = *Quarter Note receives one pulse*

PRACTISE TRANSCRIBING TONAL AND RHYTHM VALUES

Unfinished transcription is prepared or projected on blackboard.

1) From Number Notation *to* Staff Notation

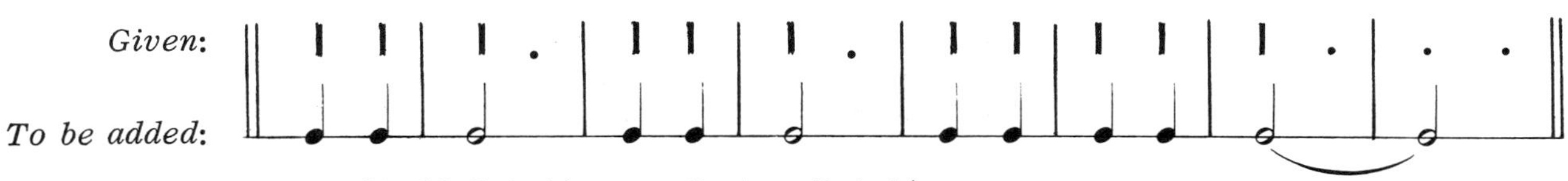

2) From Staff Notation *to* Number Notation

3. From Number Notation *to* Staff Notation

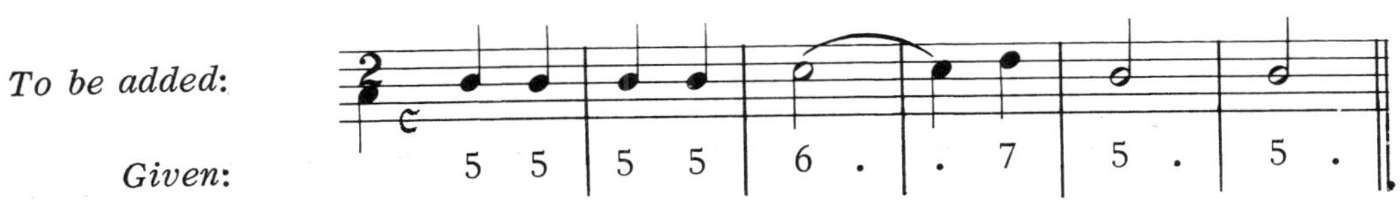

Creative Activity

Review: Improvising Melodic Application to Rhythm Patterns
Duple Time
Mode of DO - Authentic Range
Musical Conversation

1) Single pattern is placed on board. Students invited to provide melody for it.

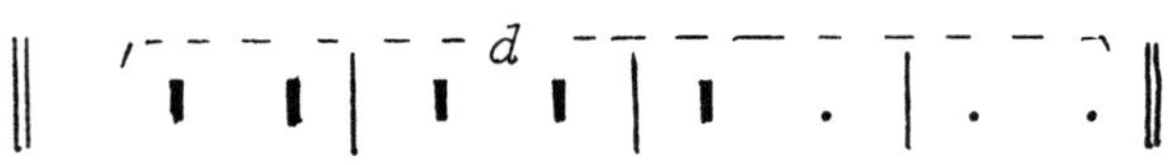

2) Same for combination of two patterns

a + b
c + d

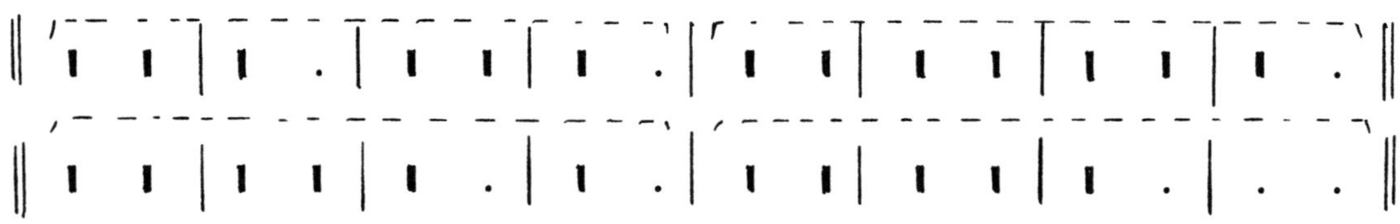

3) Musical Conversations. Students, one at a time and in continuous sequence, are invited to converse on the following rhythms using note names:

First Student -

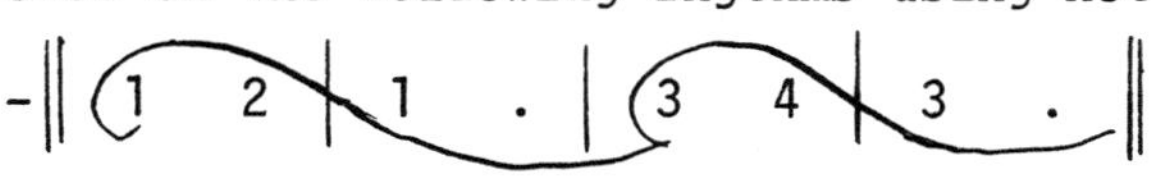

Second student responds on same rhythm but with different notes. Third follows, etc.

Same for another rhythm:

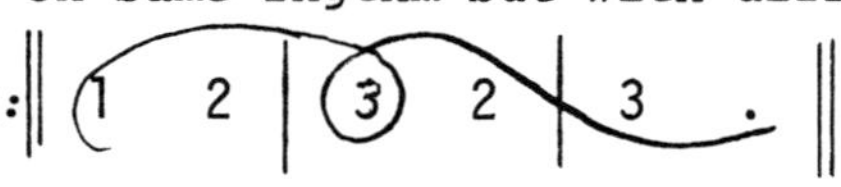

Preparation for Singing Staff Notation Songs

Sing each segment several times

(1 = E♭)

Songs

Selected according to matter studied in this chapter

MELODY No. 3 French Carol

1 = F

|| 3 3 | 5 5 | 4 . | 2 . | 1 2 | 3 4 | 2 . | . 0 |

| 4 4 | 3 3 | 6 . | 5 . | 5 4 | 3 2 | 1 . | . 0 ||

AUTUMN LEAVES *Melody:* Catalan Folk Song *Text:* JBW

$\dot{1}$ = E♭ Prep. $\dot{1}$765

|| 5 5 | 5 5 | 6 . | . 7 | 5 . | 5 . |
Au - tumn leaves are fall - ing, fall - ing,

| 5 5 | 5 5 | 6 . | . 7 | 5 . | . . |
On the ground they swirl ___ and play. ___

| 5 $\dot{1}$ | 7 5 | 6 . | . 4 | 3 . | 3 . |
Au - tumn winds are call - ing, call - ing,

| 5 $\dot{1}$ | 7 5 | 6 . | . 4 | 3 . | . . ||
Sum - mer birds have flown ___ a - way. ___

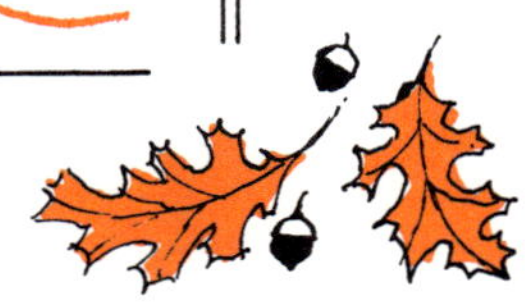

MELODY No. 4 Basque Folk Song

$\dot{1}$ = E♭ Prep. $\dot{1}$765

THIS IS JESUS' BIRTHDAY *Melody:* French Noel *Text:* JBW

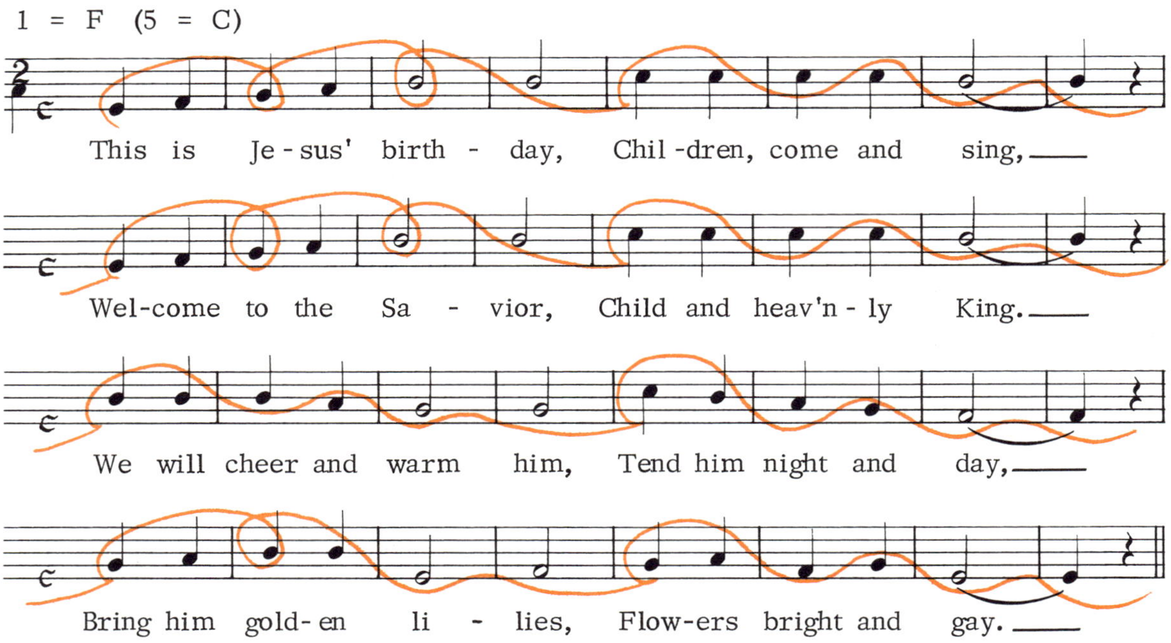

FLAG OF OUR NATION *Melody:* Basque Folk Song *Text:* JBW (alt.)

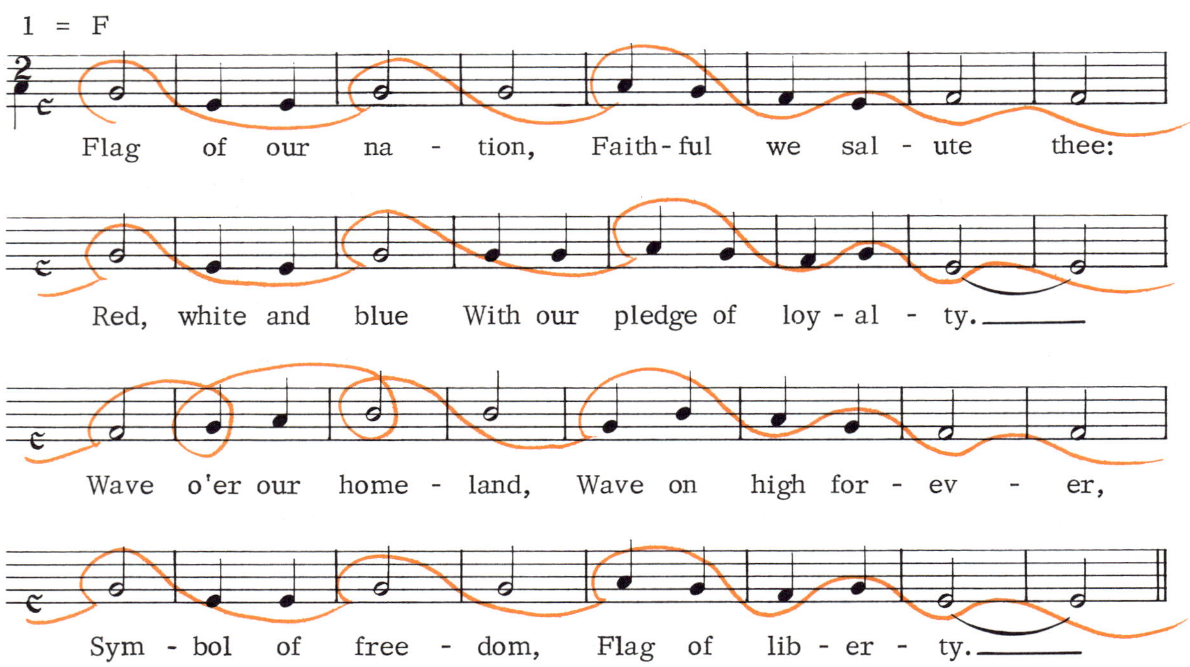

Chapter Three

Vocal Training

Placement of Vowel "o"
Slurs

Vocal Exercise 4

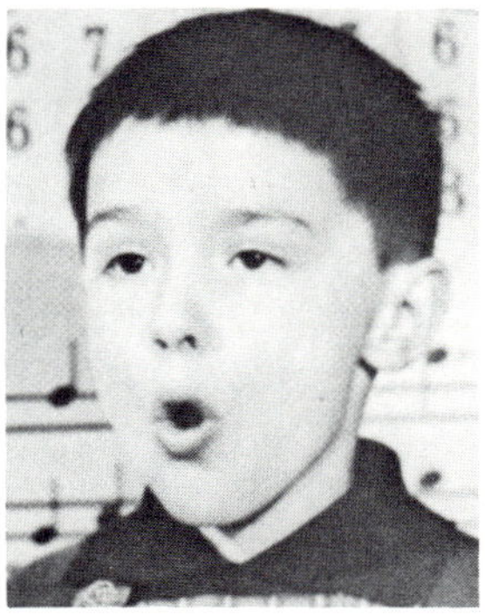

1 = G B D

|| 1 Nu ___ o ___ u ||
(Noo oh oo)

Take deep breath (shoulders down). Sustain "oo" momentarily then open lips slightly for "oh"

Return to "oo" without stopping for breath

Practise first with Bluebirds on comfortable pitches

Vocal Exercise 5

1 = F G

Same exercise as No. 4 *but "slurs" are added. "Slur" means: two notes are sung on same vowel.*

> The same full resonance must be achieved for "oh" as for "oo" on all pitches. The jaw drops slightly and the lips open more for 'oh" than for "oo". When original position of mouth is resumed there should be no change in the quality of the sound.

Intonation

Presenting Plagal Range of DO Mode

Up to now all scale-line drills have been in the Authentic Range, that is, DO (1) *to* DO (1̇)
In this lesson the scale is extended to SOL *below* DO.
Introduce extension by singing scale as follows: 1 2 3 4 5   5 4 3 2 1 7̣ 6̣ 5̣ 6̣ 7̣ 1

Tones of the scale that come below DO (1) *are shown with dots beneath them.*
Use either Diagram 4a *or* 4b *at first. Later* Intonation Exercises 9 *and* 10 *should be given with* Staff Diagram 4.

> Notice that DO is still the home tone of the scale even though it is not the lowest tone. It is known as the FINAL of the Mode.

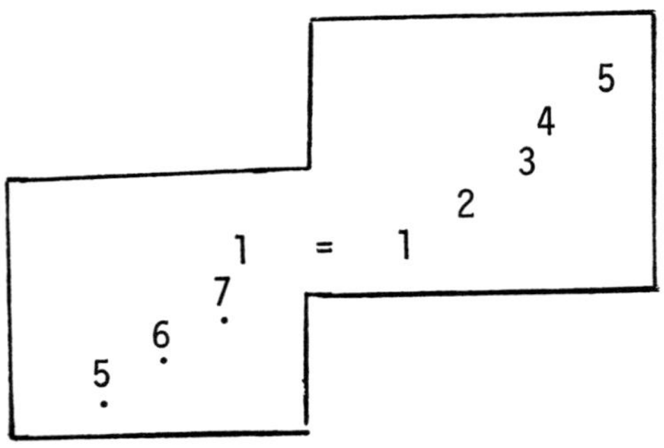

Int. Diagram 4a

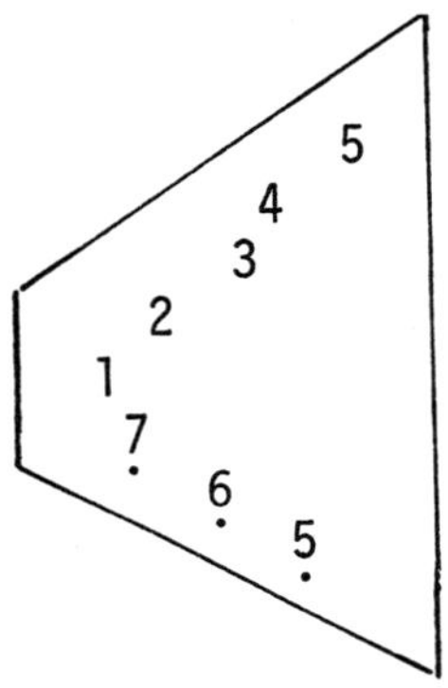

Intonation Diagram 4b

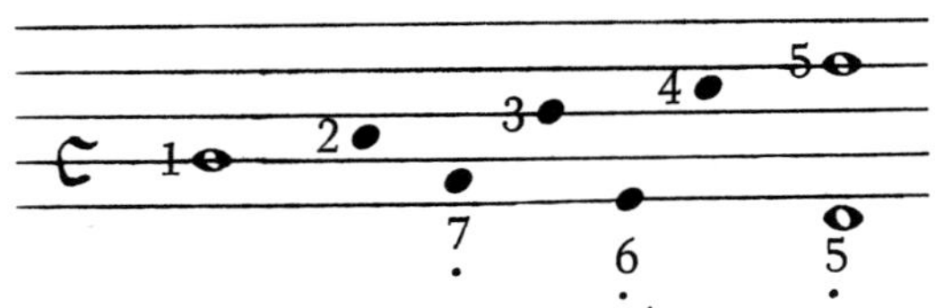

Staff Diagram 4

Intonation Exercise 9

1 = G
(5 = D)

| 1 5   5 4 3 2 1 7̣ 6̣ 5̣ 6̣ 7̣ 1   5̣ 1 |
| 1 5̣   5̣ 6̣ 7̣ 1 2 3 4 5 4 3 2 1   5̣ 1 |
| 1 5̣   5̣ 6̣ 7̣ 1 2 3 4 5   5 1 |
| 1 5   5 4 3 2 1 7̣ 6̣ 5̣   5̣ 1 |

Intonation Exercise 10

1 = G
(5 = D)

| 1 2 3 4 5   5 4 3 2 1   1 7̣ 6̣ 5̣   5̣ 6̣ 7̣ 1 |
| 1 2 3 4 5   4 3 2 1   1 7̣ 6̣ 5̣   6̣ 7̣ 1 |

DO

The Arm Gesture *for measuring distances between tones can still be useful. Position of* DO *has changed to accommodate the lower tones of the* Plagal Range.

Finger Notation *likewise is useful. Teacher's right hand, palm facing children, little finger upright shows* DO. *Left hand crosses over with thumb for* TI (7̣), *index finger extended for* LA 6̣ *and middle finger extended for* SOL (5̣)

1

7̣

6̣

5̣

Eye and Ear Tests *(1 = G)*

1 5̣ 1 2 3 2 1	1 2 3 2 1 1 7̣ 6̣ 5̣	1 7̣ 6̣ 5̣ 5̣ 6̣ 7̣ 1	5̣ 6̣ 7̣ 1 2 3 1
1 5̣ 5̣ 5̣ 6̣ 7̣ 1	1 5 5 4 3 2 1 5̣ 1	5̣ 5̣ 1 1 1 1 7̣	1 1 7̣ 6̣ 5̣ 5̣ 5̣ 1

Flash momentarily on screen:

Rhythm

Review Up-pulse Beginnings in Ternary Rhythm - Triple Time
Rhythm Gesture III

Review Rhythm Gesture III *to accompaniment of cassette recording or song studied in Book One, such as "I SAW A SHIP."*

Rhythm Patterns - Series 3 *Review*

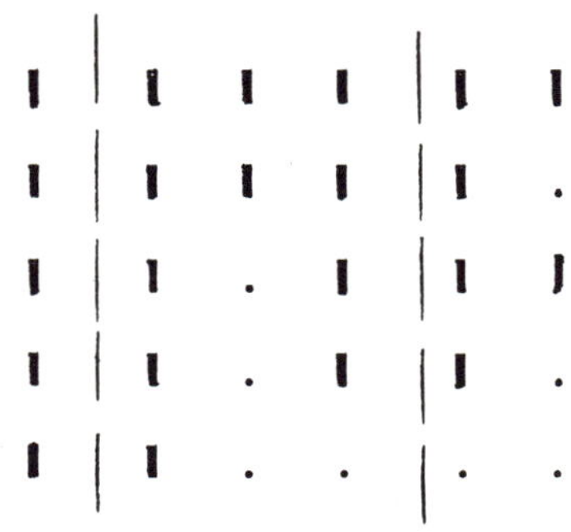

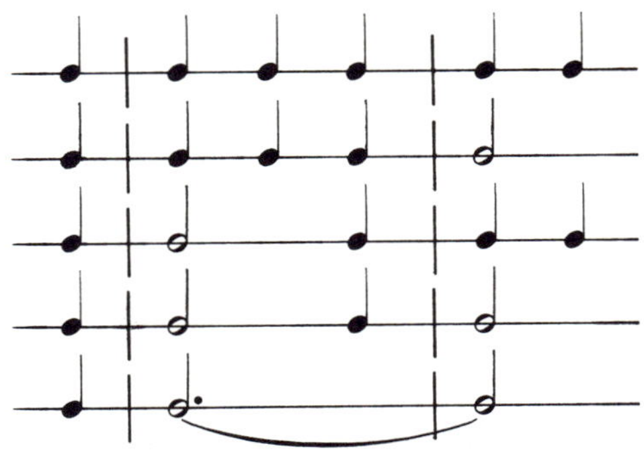

1. *Sing patterns with* Metrical Language *and* Metrical Gesture I.
2. *Students identify pattern(s) when sung by teacher to melodic application.*
3. *Combine patterns and students invited to improvise melody for each:*

c + d *a + e* *b + b*

Rhythmic Dictations

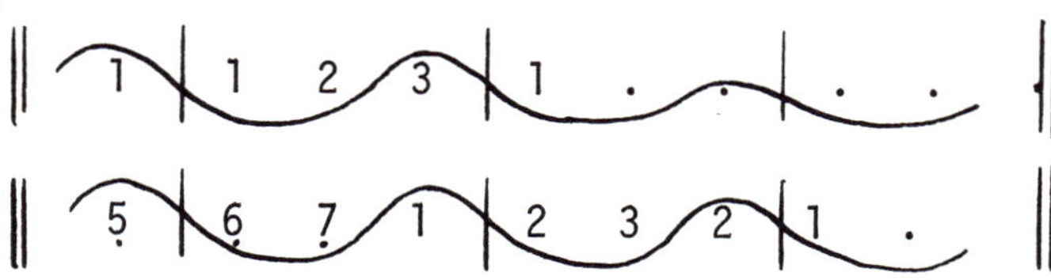

Select lines from song to be studied.

Notation

DO Clef on Second Line
Three-Pulse Notes
Time Signature 3
Repeat Sign

I. "Moving Day" on Staff

A. DO Clef moves from first line to second

Tones of Plagal Range *need a home on the Staff and so* DO *moves upstairs.*

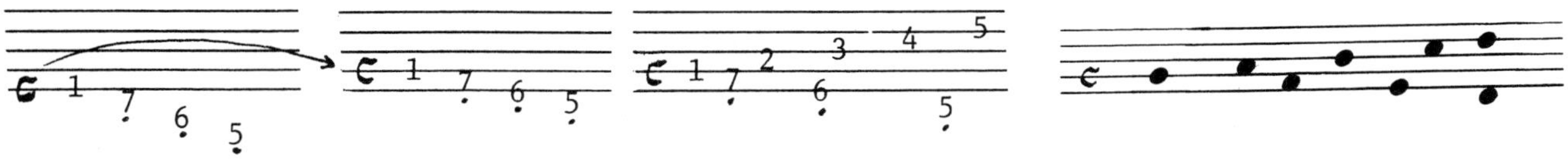

B. Exercises

1. *Transcribe first line of* Intonation Exercise 9 to Staff Notation.

Given: 1 5 5 4 3 2 1 7 6̣ 5̣ 6̣ 7̣ 1 5̣ 1

2. *Transcribe first line of* Intonation Exercise 10 to Number Notation.

Given:

1 2 3 4 5 5 4 3 2 1 1 7̣ 6̣ 5̣ 5̣ 6̣ 7̣ 1

C. Staff Game

"Where will DO Clef *be placed if we wish to write the following notes on the Staff?"*

A staff segment with DO Clef *on bottom line and another staff segment with* DO Clef *on second line should be in full view of class.*

1. 1 3 5 1̇ — *Answer: First line. All tones above* DO.
2. 1 5̣ 1 3 5 4 3 2 1 — *Answer: Second line.* SOL *below* DO *needs a proper place on staff.*
3. 1 5 4 3 2 1 7̣ 6̣ 5̣ 1 — *Answer: Second line. Some notes below* DO.
4. 1̇ 7 1̇ 5 6 5 3 4 3 1 — *Answer: First line. All notes above* DO.

Continued

II Review - Time Values of Staff Notes

A. Single-pulse, two-pulse and three-pulse notes and ties

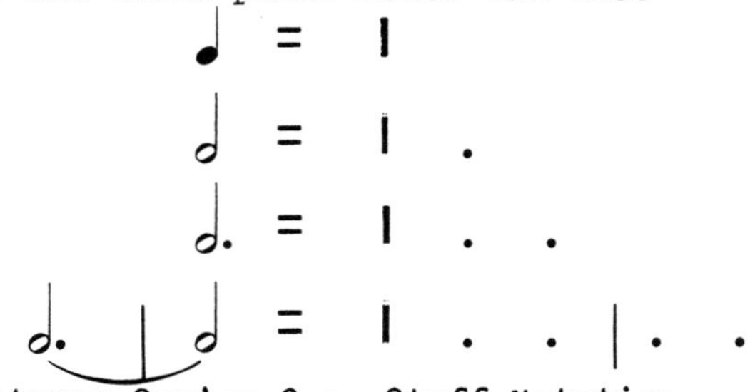

B. Transcribe Rhythm Patterns Series 3 *to* Staff Notation

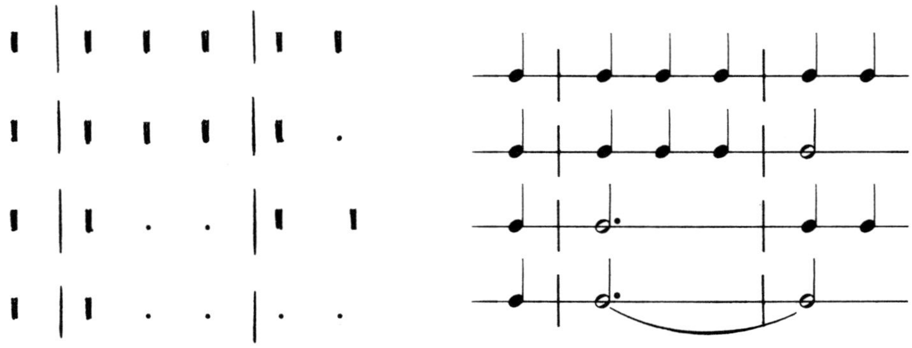

C. Staff Notation - *Special Signs*

1. *NEW*  *Time Signature which means:* *three pulses in a measure; quarter note* ♩ *receives one pulse.*

   See Staff Notation Songs *at end of chapter.*

2. *Repeat Sign:* 

   See SONGS at end of Chapter

3. *Slur: Two or more notes sung to one syllable of text.*

   See SONGS at end of chapter.

III. Combining Pitch and Rhythm values in melodies

A. Exercise *Transcribe the following melody to* Staff Notation

Creative Activity

Conversation: Statement-Response
Duple Time Beginning on Down-Pulse
Slur

I. Conclusive and Inconclusive Responses

A. Teacher or student sings a line of a melody. Another makes a response using same rhythm.

NOTE: Conclusive Response is one that ends on DO

Inconclusive Response ends on some other note

1. Examples:

Statement:	1 .	7̣ 6̣	5̣ 6̣	5̣ .
Conclusive Response:	5̣ .	6̣ 7̣	1 7̣	1 .
Inconclusive Response:	1 .	7̣ 1	2 3	2 .

2. Theme for study:

Statement:	1 .	5̣ .	6̣ 7̣	1 .	2 .	. .
Inconclusive Response:						
Conclusive Response:						

II. Repetitive and Complementary Responses

A. Same as above

1. Examples:

Statement:	5 4	3 2	1 .	5̣ .
Repetitive Response:	5 4	3 2	3 .	3 .
Complementary Response:	1 7̣	6̣ 5̣	6̣ .	5̣ .

2. Theme for study:

1 3	5 3	1 5̣	5̣ .

NOTE: Repetitive Response is one that repeats a phrase note for note but but admits some slight change usually at the end.

Complementary Response is one that imitates the design of a melody at a different pitch level from that of the statement, or imitates only the rhythm of the statement.

III. Find Repetitive and Complementary Responses in SONGS at end of chapter.

SIGHT SINGING DRILLS

Preparation for Staff Notation Songs

Sing each segment several times

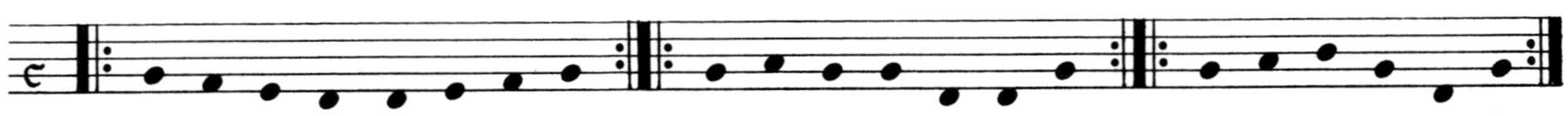

Visual Memory Tests - Flash momentarily on screen or write on blackboard and erase.

Songs

Selected according to matter studied in this chapter:

Mode of DO - Plagal Range

Ternary Rhythm (Triple Time) Beginning on Up-pulse

DO Clef on Second Line
Rhythm Gesture III
Time Signature 3
♩

N.B. 3 = three pulses in a measure
♩ = quarter note = one-pulse note

MELODY No. 5 Anonymous

1 = G (5 = D)

‖: 5 | 1 2 3 | 2 . 5 | 3 . 2 | 1 . :‖

5 | 2 . 5 | 3 . 5 | 4 3 2 | 3 1

5 | 2 . 5 | 3 . 5 | 4 3 2 | 1 5 5 | 1 . ‖

THE NORTH WIND DOTH BLOW English Folk Song

1 = B♭ (5 = F)

‖ 5 | 5 1 1 | 1 7
The north wind doth blow—

1 | 3 2 2 | 2 3
And we shall have snow—

4 | 3 2 1 | 1 7 1 | 2 . 5 | 5 .
And what will the rob - in do then, poor thing?

5 | 5 1 1 | 1 7
He'll sit in the barn—

1 | 3 2 2 | 2 3
And keep him-self warm—

4 | 3 4 3 | 2 1 2 | 3 . 1 | 1 . ‖
And hide his head un - der his wing,— poor thing.—

MELODY No. 6 English Carol

1 = G (5 = D)

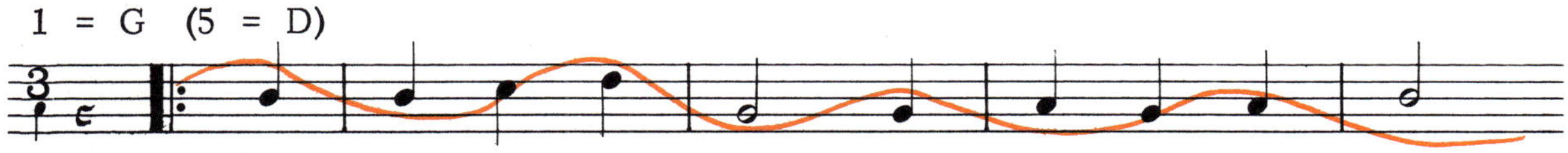

Inconclusive Response

Conclusive Response

WHEN CHRIST WAS BORN TO SET US FREE *Melody:* German Carol *Text:* JBW (alt.)

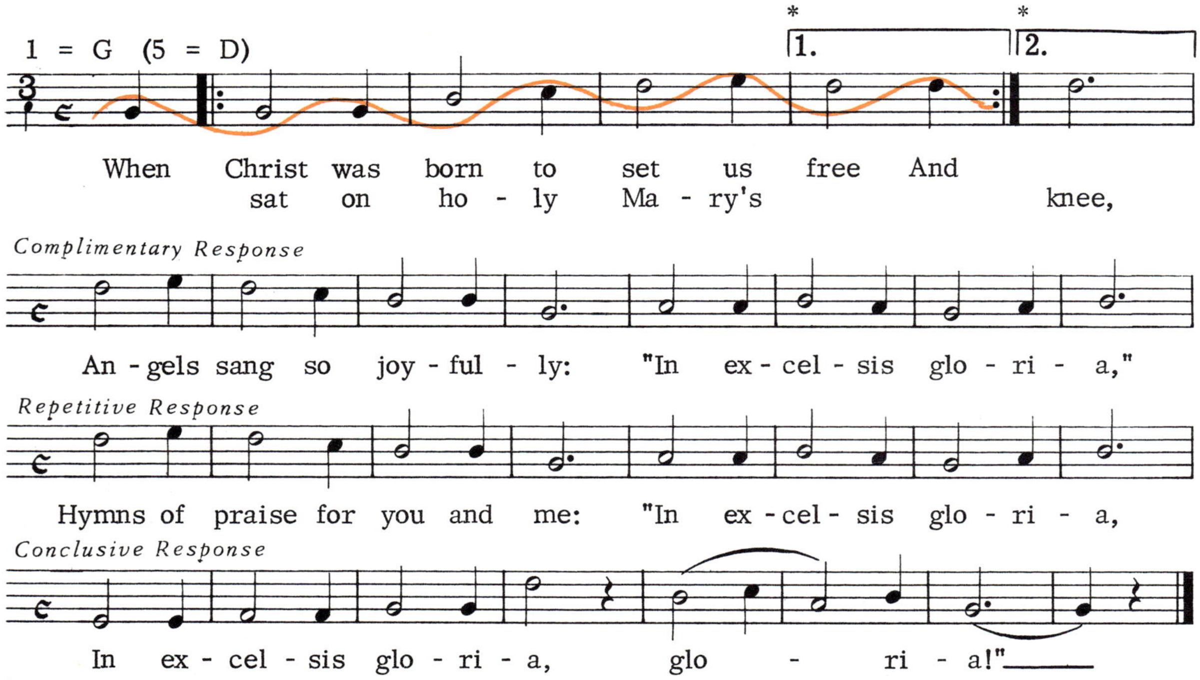

* *First and second endings. Cf. Bk. I, Chapter 19, P. 159*

HALLOWEEN SONG *Melody:* Air 1592 *Text:* JBW

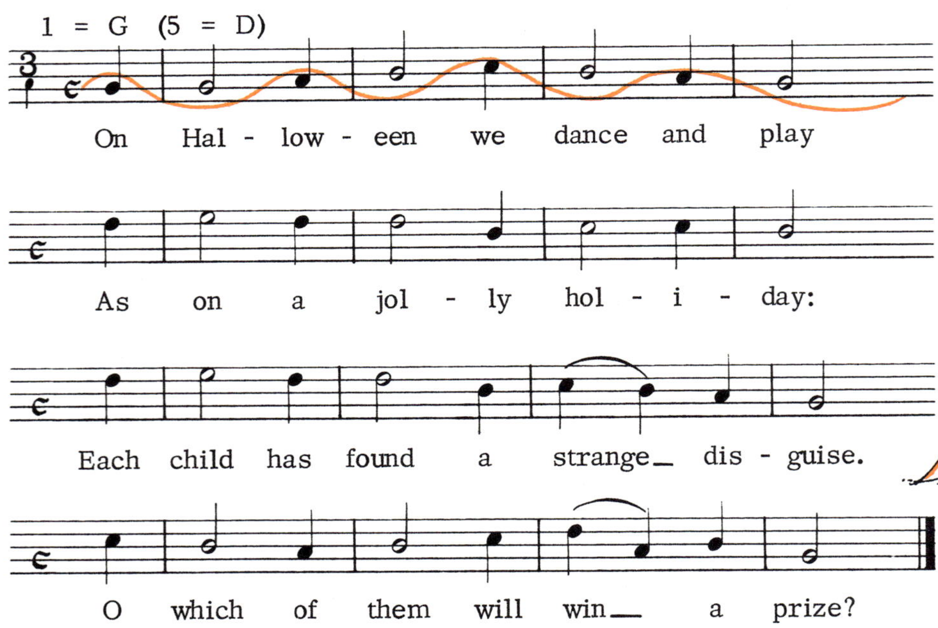

Chapter Four

Vocal Training

Drills on "o" Vowel Continued
Vocalises in Plagal Range - Binary and Ternary

Review Vocal Exercise 4

1 = A D F

|| 1 ——————————— ||
|| Nu ———————— o —— u ——— ||

High pitches should be used only for Bluebirds, i.e., Group I

Daily tests on lower pitches for Groups II and III

Vocal Exercise 6a

1 = G A

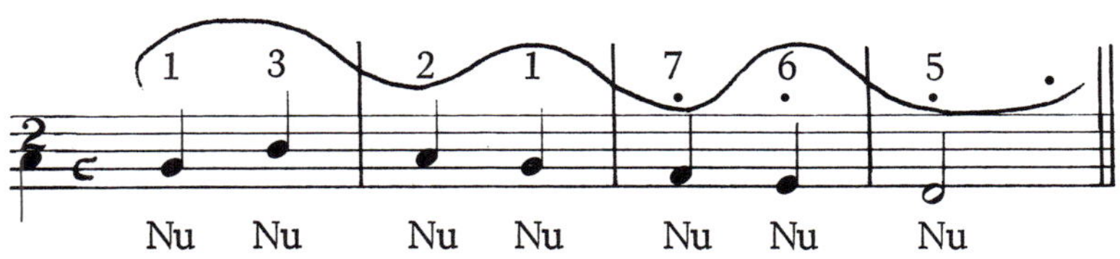

Vocal Exercise 6b

1 = G A

Note Time Signatures 2 *and* 3 *in above vocalises*

As an additional exercise, Groups I and II are invited to sing the syllable Nu *on the melody of a known song, e.g., "O LORD, I AM NOT WORTHY." Group III meanwhile makes appropriate* Rhythm Gesture I *or* II

1 = Eb

Intonation

Plagal Range - Chord Line - 5 1 3 5
Compass Exercises I, II, III

1 = G for all drills

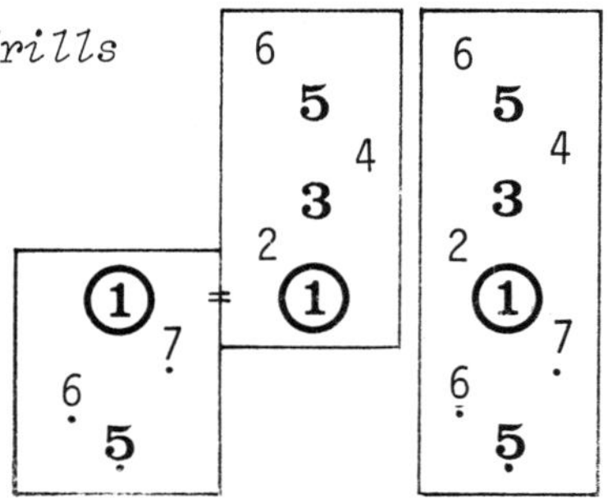

Int. Diagram 5 Int. Diagram 6

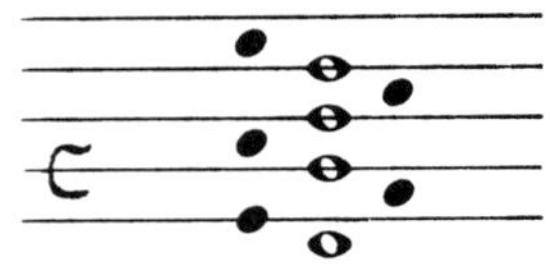

Staff Diagram 6

Intonation Exercise 11 - *With* Intonation *and* Staff Diagrams 6

C. Ex. I | 1 2 1 3 4 3 5 6 5 5 6 5 3 4 3 1 2 1 1 7 1 5 6 5 1 7 1 |

| 1 3 *4 3* 5 *6 5* 5 *6 5* 3 *4 3* 1 *2 1* 1 *7 1* 5 *6 5* 1 *7 1* |

C. Ex. II | 1 3 5 5 3 1 1 5 1 |

Allow plenty of time for "think" tones.

Intonation Exercise 12 - *With* Intonation *and* Staff Diagrams 6

| 1 2 1 3 4 3 5 6 5 5 6 5 3 4 3 1 2 1 1 7 1 5 6 5 1 7 1 |

| 1 3 5 5 3 1 1 5 1 |

C. Ex. III | 2 1 4 3 6 5 6 5 4 3 2 1 7 1 6 5 7 1 |

Eye and Ear Tests *Use pointer, fingers and arm gesture*

1 2 1 5 6 5 1 2 1 | 1 5 1 3 5 1 | 6 5 7 1 4 3
2 1 6 5 5 6 7 1 | 5 5 1 2 3 4 5 3 1 | 1 5 1 3

1 6 5 2 1 | 1 5 7 1 4 3
1 6 5 7 1 | 1 5 2 1 7 1

Rhythm

Review Arsis-Thesis in Ternary Rhythm (Triple Time)
Down-pulse Beginning
Rhythm Gesture IV - Ternary

1. *Review* Rhythm Gesture IV - *Ternary. Use "How do You like to Go up in a Swing?" BOOK ONE.*

2. *Study with* Metrical Language *and* Metrical Gesture I
Students identify patterns from melody sung by teacher

Rhythm Patterns - Series 4 *Review*

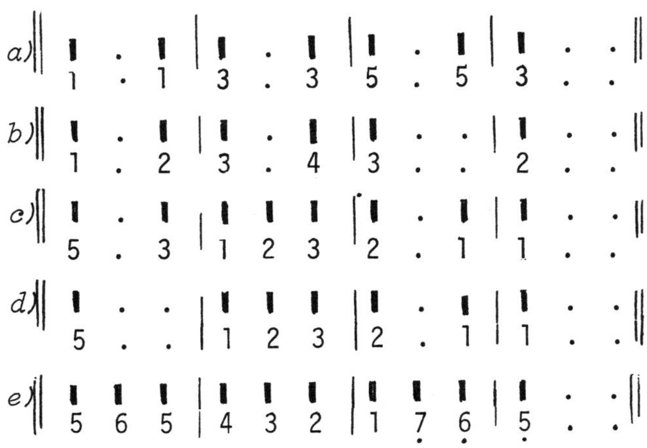

Rhythmic Dictations

Show all patterns on blackboard or screen during dictations

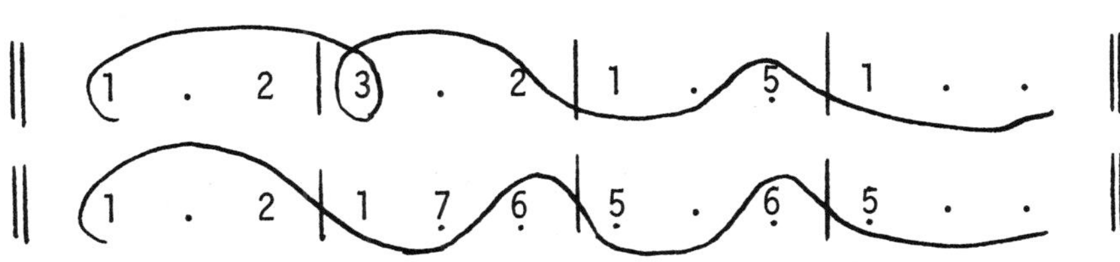

Use also single lines from songs studied in this chapter

REVIEW: Note names for identifying rhythm values:

One-pulse note = *Quarter Note*

Two-pulse note = *Half Note*

Three-pulse note = *Dotted Half Note*

Aural Training in Rhythm - Step 2

Continued from Chapter Two

Problems in Triple Time - Ternary Rhythm
Rhythm determined by final cadence (repose)

Suggested lines for tests:

5̣ 1 2 3 2

5 4 3 2 1 5̣ 5̣ 1

3 2 3 1

3 4 3 2 1 2 1

1 3 4 5 6 5 4 3 2 1

2 3 4 5 3 2 1 2 1 7̣ 1

PROCEDURE:

1) *Place series of single-pulse notes on board. Students sing them.*

5 4 3 2 1 5̣ 5̣ 1

2) *Draw bar-line before last note.*

5 4 3 2 1 5̣ 5̣ | 1

3) *Count back by threes for each remaining bar-line*

5 ⁞ 4 3 2 ⁞ 1 5̣ 5̣ | 1

4) *Discover up-pulse or down-pulse beginning*
Arsis-Thesis *or* Rhythm Gesture III

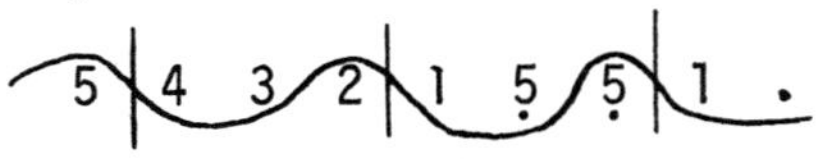

5) *Add length to last note and bar-lines as needed*

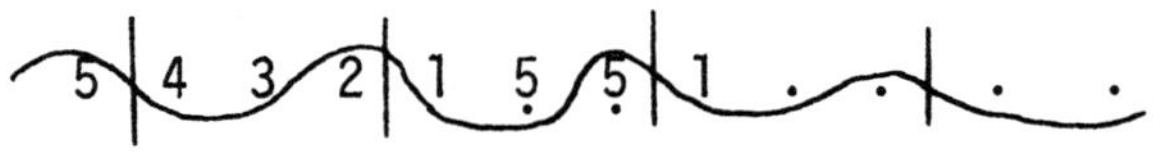

6) *Add double-bars at beginning and end. Sing complete melody with appropriate* Rhythm Gesture IV (Ternary)

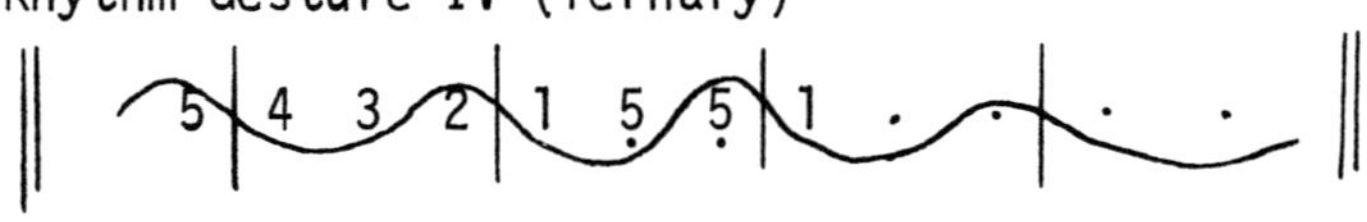

Notation

Review: DO Clef on Second Line
3 Time Signature

Transcriptions *Solutions are given here as aids to the teacher*

1. *Numbers to Staff*

To be added:

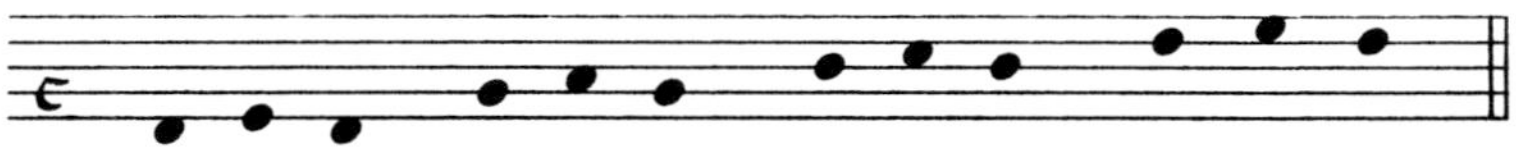

Given: 5 6 5 1 2 1 3 4 3 5 6 5

2. *Staff to Numbers*

Given:

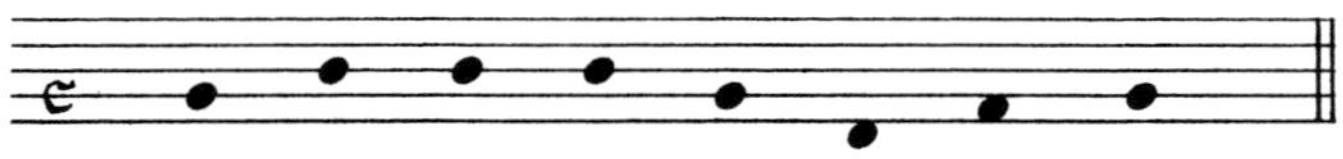

To be added: 1 3 3 3 1 5 7 1

3. *STAFF GAME* – *Continued from Chapter Three*

"Where will DO Clef *be placed for the following notes?"*

1 5 1 2 3 *(Second line because of 5)*

1 3 5 1 *(First line because of 1)*

1 5 6 7 1 3 5 *(Second line because of 5 6 7)*

1 7 1 5 6 5 3 4 3 *(First line because of 1 7 1)*

4. *Rhythm Patterns*

Given:

To be added:

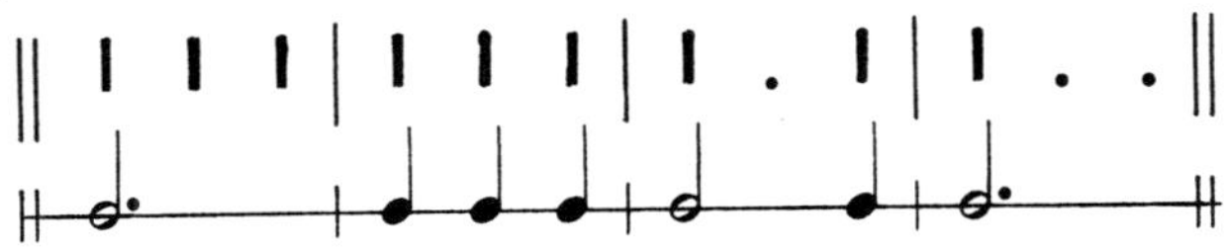

5. *Melody – Staff to Numbers*

Given:

To be added: 3 . . | 1 2 1 | 7 . 6 | 5 . .

6. *Melody – Numbers to Staff*

To be added:

Given: 6 7 1 | 5 . 5 | 4 . 4 | 3 . 2 | 1 . .

Creative Activity

Conversations: Statement - Response in Triple Time
Melodic Applications of Rhythm Patterns

Conversations

1 = G

Conclusive Responses end on DO. *Inconclusive Responses end on some other note. Same rhythm is used for Statement and Response.*

Examples of possible student responses are given.

1 *Teacher:* || 1 . 3 | 5 . 3 | 1 7̣ 1 | 2 . . |

Student: | 2 . 7̣ | 5̣ . 6̣ | 5̣ 6̣ 7̣ | 1 . . ||

2 *Teacher:* || 1 . 5̣ | 5̣ . 5̣ | 6̣ 7̣ 1 | 5̣ . . |

Student: | 5̣ . 1 | 3 . 5 | 4 3 2 | 1 . . ||

3 *Additional statements to which students improvise responses:*

a) || 1 . . | 7̣ . 6̣ | 5̣ . 6̣ | 5̣ . . ||

b) || 1 . 1 | 5̣ . 5̣ | 6̣ 7̣ 1 | 2 . . ||

c) || 5 . 4 | 3 . 2 | 1 7̣ 6̣ | 5̣ . . ||

Improvise Melodies to Rhythm Patterns - Series 4

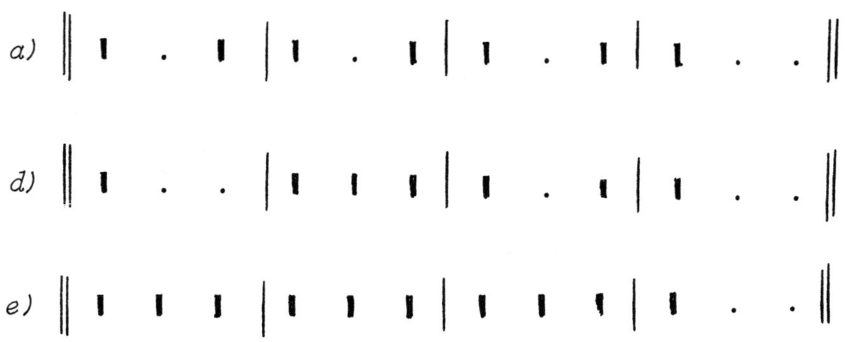

Combinations of patterns may be used if students are making ready responses to single patterns

SIGHT SINGING DRILLS

Preparation for Staff Notation Songs

Sing each segment several times

1 = G (5 = D)

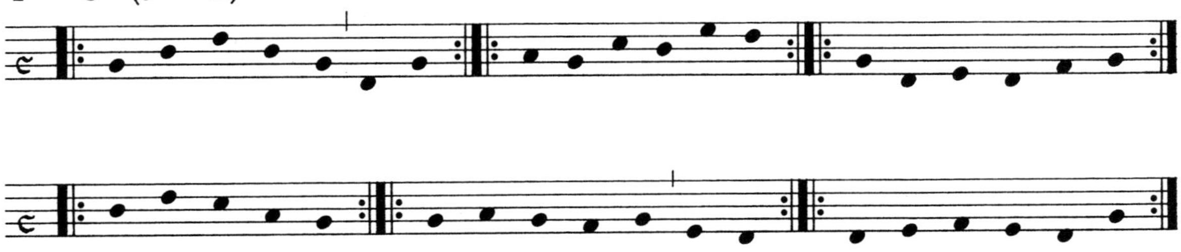

<u>*Visual Memory Tests*</u> - *Flash on screen or write on board and erase*

1 = G (5 = D)

a)

b)

Songs

Selected according to matter studied in this chapter:

<u>Mode of DO - Plagal Range</u>
Special attention to skips along chord line

<u>Ternary Rhythm (Triple Time) Beginning on Down-pulse</u>
Arsis Thesis - Rhythm Gesture IV

<u>DO Clef on Second Line</u>

<u>Time Signature:</u> 3 ♩

REVIEW: <u>*How To Study a Song - Chapter 1, Page 9*</u>

See bottom of preceding page for indications of correspondence between songs given below and the matter of this chapter.

MELODY No. 7 Catalan Folk Song

1 = E

‖: 3 1 5 | 6 . 4 | 5 . 5 | 3 1 5 | 6 . 4 | 5 . . :‖

| 3 5 6 | 4 . 2 | 1 . 1 | 5 5 1̇ | 6 . 4 | 5 . . |

| 3 5 6 | 4 . 2 | 1 . 1 | 5 5 1̇ | 6 . 7 | 1̇ . . ‖

MELODY No. 8 French Folk Song

1 = G (5 = D)

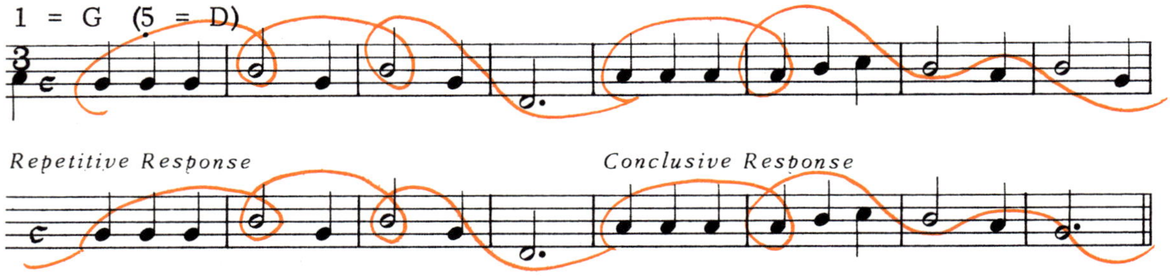

LONDON BRIDGE English Folk Song

1 = G (5 = D)

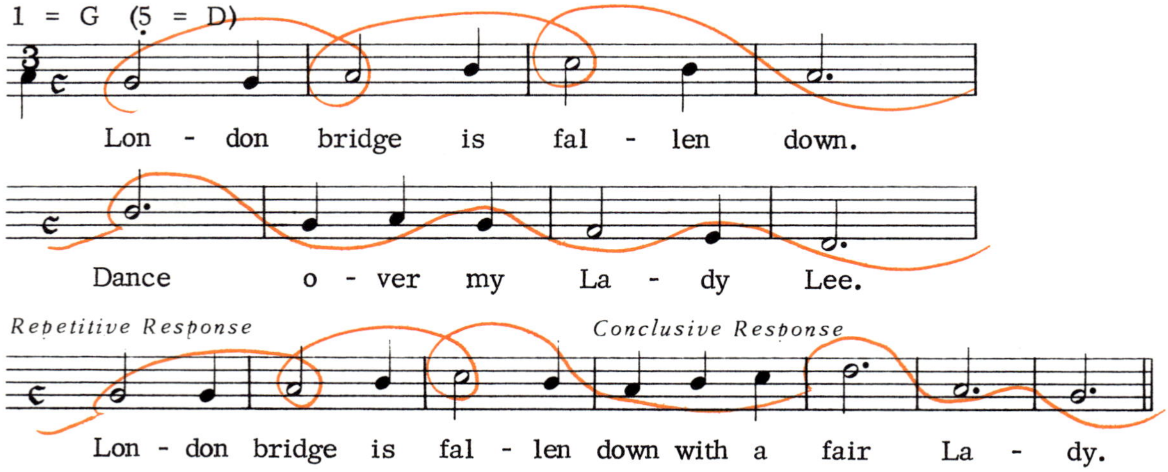

BRING A TORCH, JEANNETTE ISABELLA Traditional Carol

* *Interval of 7th. Prepare as follows:*

5̣	1	3	5	4
5̣	*1*	*3*	5	4
5̣	*1*	*3*	*5*	4

DRAW A BUCKET OF WATER English Folk Melody

1 = G

|| 1 . 2 | 3 4 3 | 2 . . | 1 . . |
Draw __ a buck - et of wa - ter ______

Repetitive Response

| 1 . 2 | 3 . 4 | 3 . . | 2 .
For ___ my la - dy's daugh - ter. __

5̣ | 1 1 2 | 3 3 4 | 3 3 2 | 3 .
My fa - ther's a king and my moth - er's a queen, __

Complementary Response

5̣ | 1 3 4 | 5 6 5 | 4 3 2 | 1 . . ||
My two lit - tle sis - ters are dressed up in green. _____

ANGEL, MY GUARDIAN *Melody:* Anonymous *Text:* JBW

1 = G

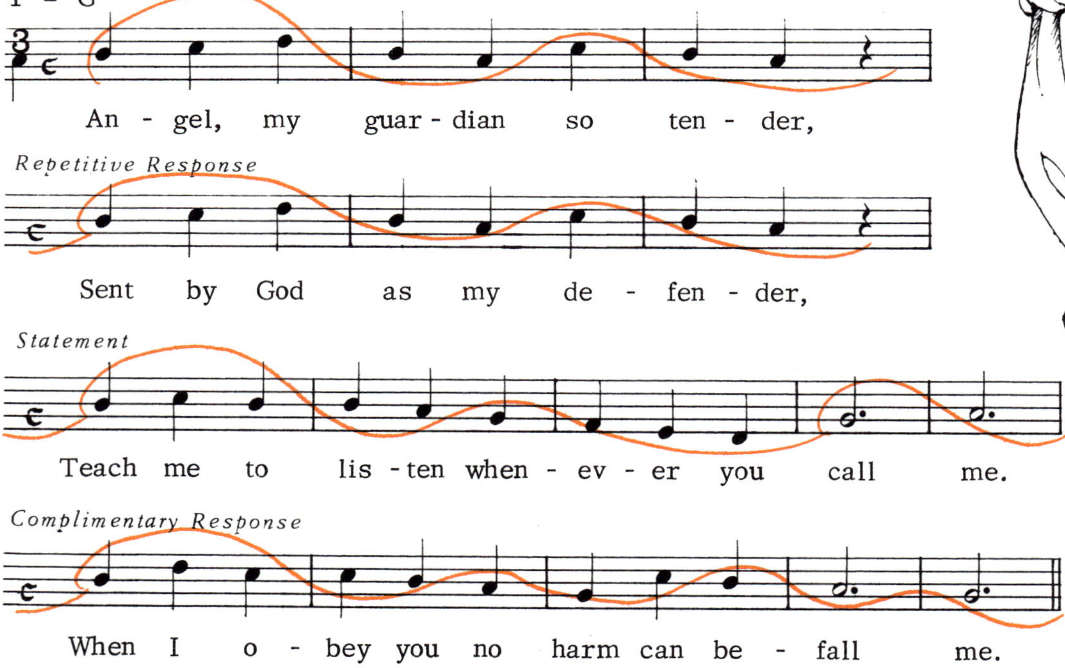

Review Songs: (Book I)
"Near to My Woodland Cottage"
"Children of Your Heavenly King"

Chapter Five

Vocal Training

Placement of Vowel "a"

A new vowel is introduced in this lesson. It is the "a" - pronounced as "ah". Tongue remains down. Jaw drops slightly. Lips open wider than for "oh".

Practise sustaining tone as shown from "oo" through "oh" to "ah" and back to "oo". Sing on one breath. Resonance for "ah" should be felt at the top of the head - same as for other vowels.

Vocal Exercise 7

1 = G/D

‖ 1 ______________________________ ‖
Nu ______ o ______ a ______ u
(Noo oh ah oo)

Note shape of lips for vowels: oo oh ah

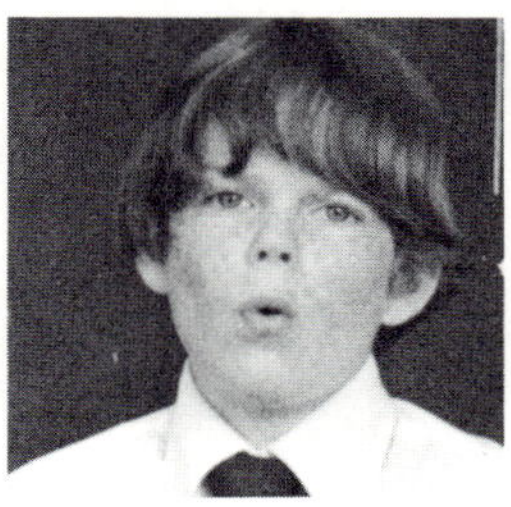

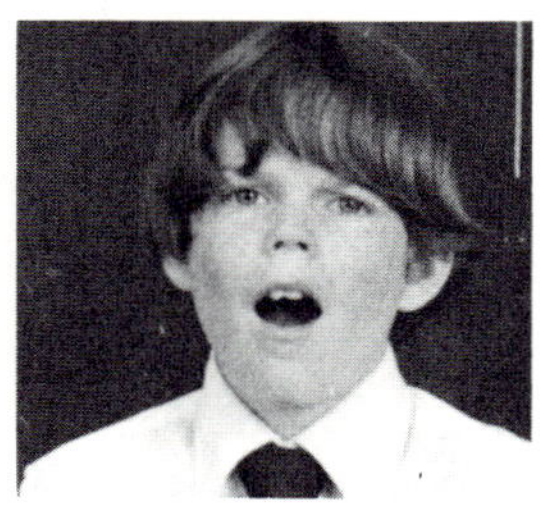

Vocal Exercise 8a

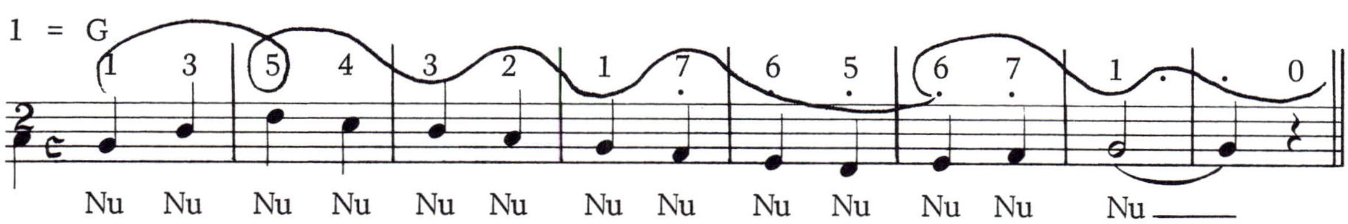

Vocal Exercise 8b

Intonation

Compass Exercises II and III Plagal Range
Assimilation of Compass Exercise III

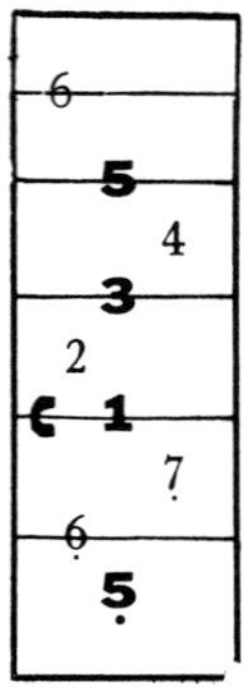

Int. D. 6

Intonation Exercise 13 - *With* Intonation *and* Staff Diagrams 6

Segments of
Compass Ex. II *and* III
with scale passages

a) ⟶

| 1 7̣ 6̣ 5̣ 1 | 1 5̣ 1 1 3 | 3 2 1 |

| 1 5̣ 1 3 | 3 2 1 6̣ 5̣ 7̣ 1 |

1 = G | 1 2 3 | 3 1 1 5̣ 5̣ 1 | 1 7̣ 6̣ 5̣ 1 2 3 |

| 3 1 5̣ 1 | 1 2 3 2 1 7̣ 6̣ 5̣ 1 |

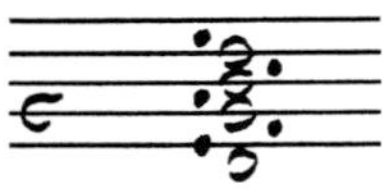

Staff D. 6

Intonation Exercise 14

a) ⟶ *b)* ⟶

c) ⟶

1 = G
(5 = D)

| 1 5̣ 1 1 3 5 | 5 3 1 1 5̣ 1 |

| 1 5̣ 1 3 5 | 5 3 1 5̣ 1 |

| 1 5̣ *1* 3 5 | 5 3 *1* 5̣ 1 |

| 1 5̣ *1 3* 5 | 5 *3 1* 5̣ 1 |

Free use of
Compass Exercise II

> CAUTION: Do not try more than one exercise in a lesson.

Intonation Exercise 15

1 = G *On blackboard* *Solution (Not shown)*

On blackboard	Solution (Not shown)
1 *5 *1	1 6 5 2 1
1 *5 *1	1 6 5 7 1
5 *1 *3	5 2 1 4 3
5 *1 *3	5 7 1 4 3
3 *1 *5	3 2 1 6 5
3 *1 *5	3 7 1 6 5
1 *5 *1 *3	1 6 5 2 1 4 3
1 *5 *1 *3	1 6 5 7 1 4 3
3 *1 *5 *1	3 2 1 6 5 2 1
3 *1 *5 *1	3 7 1 6 5 7 1

Assimilation of Compass Exercise III

Eye and Ear Tests

1 7 6 5 5 1 | 1 2 3 3 1 5 1 | 1 5 1 1 3 5
1 5 1 1 3 5 | 1 7 6 5 1 2 3 | 3 1 5 1

1 2 3 2 1 7 6 5 | 3 3 1 1 5 5 1 1
1 7 6 5 1 1 3 1 | 1 3 5 5 1

6 5 7 1 2 1 | 1 2 1 6 5 7 1
7 1 6 5 7 1 | 1 5 1 1 3

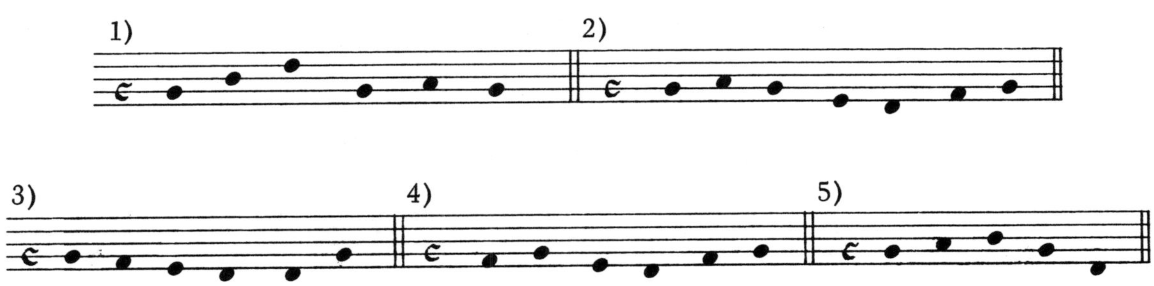

Rhythm

Presenting Half-pulse (Eighth) Notes
Binary Rhythm (Duple Time) Beginning on Up-pulse

Half-pulse or divided beat, means two notes are sung to one pulse. Half-pulse notes in Number Notation *are shown with a bar above the numbers:*

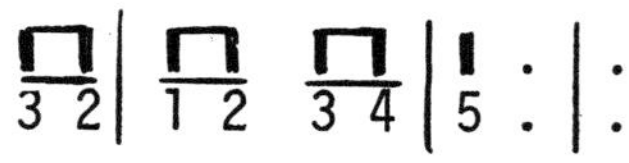

In Staff Notation *half-pulse notes are shown with bars connecting note-stems above or below notes:*

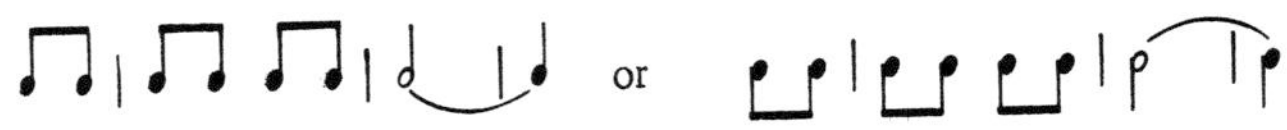

Metrical Language *for half-pulse notes is:*

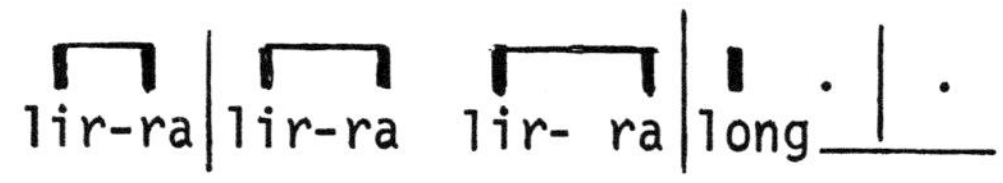

Rhythm Patterns - Series 5 *With and without final repose*

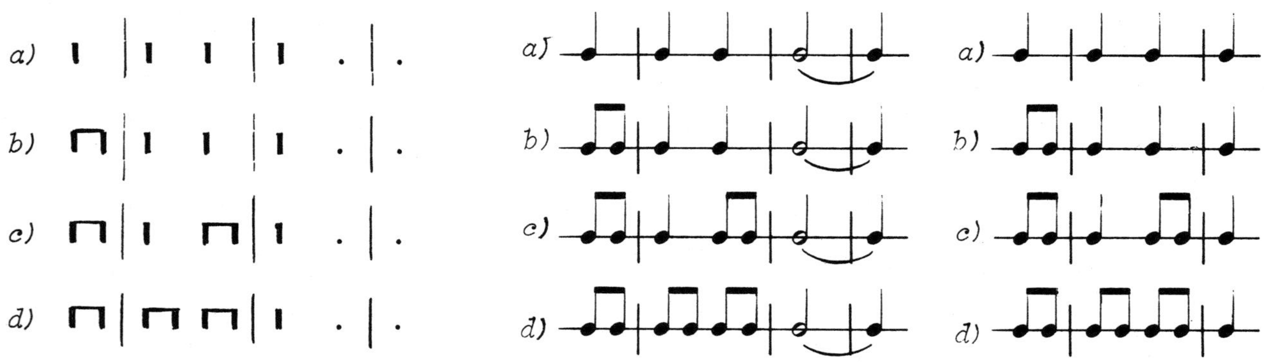

Study Rhythm Patterns with: Metrical Gesture I, Metrical Language, Rhythm Gesture II.

Same study procedure for Melodic Application - "Eighth-Note Song" *given below:*

a) ‖ 3 | 1 3 | 5 . | .
d) 3 2 | 1 2 3 4 | 5 . | .
a) 5 | 5 3 | 5 . | .
d) 5 6 | 5 4 3 2 | 1 . | . ‖

Rhythmic Dictations

‖ 1 2 | 3 3 4 | 3 . | . ‖
‖ 5 4 | 3 3 2 | 1 7 6 | 5 . | . ‖
‖ 6 6 | 5 5 | 4 3 | 2 . | 1 . | . ‖

Notation

Study of Half-Pulse Notes (Eighth Notes)
DO Clef on Line 2 of Staff

Transcriptions

Half-pulse Notes *are shown with bars connecting stems:*

1) Transcribe to Staff Notation:

Given:
Solution:
Given:
Solution:

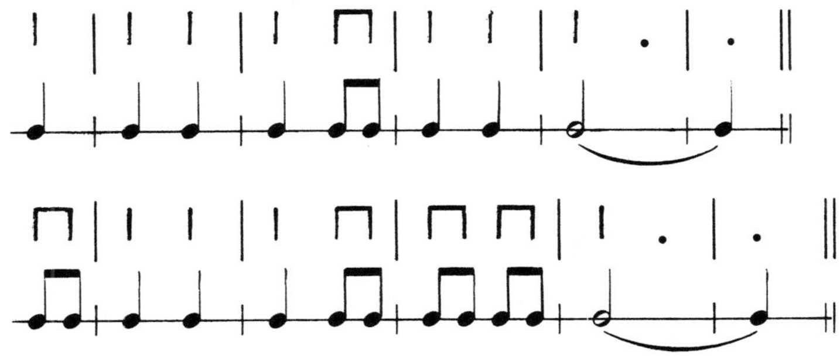

2) Transcribe to Number Notation:

Given:
Solution:

3) Transcribe to Staff Notation:

Solution:
Given:

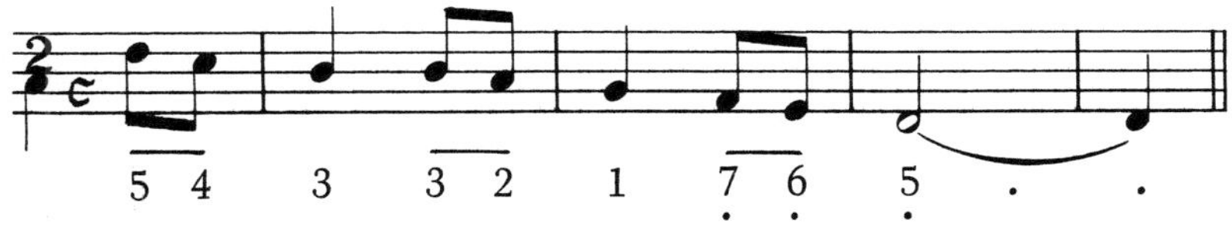

For additional transcriptions use lines from songs studied in this chapter.

Creative Activity

Composing Two-Line Songs from Rhythm Patterns
Statement- Response for Balanced Phrasing

Compose Two-Line Song from Rhythm Patterns Given

Teacher writes patterns on board. Students improvise responses as follows: Line 1 - Inconclusive Response; Line 2 - Conclusive Response.

1\.

Inconclusive:

Conclusive:

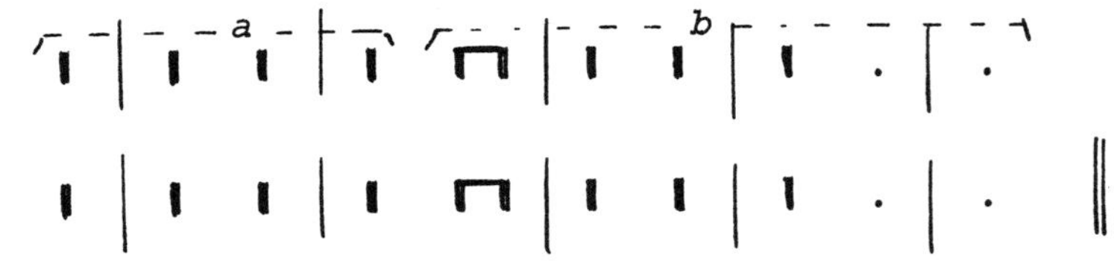

2\.

Inconclusive:

Conclusive:

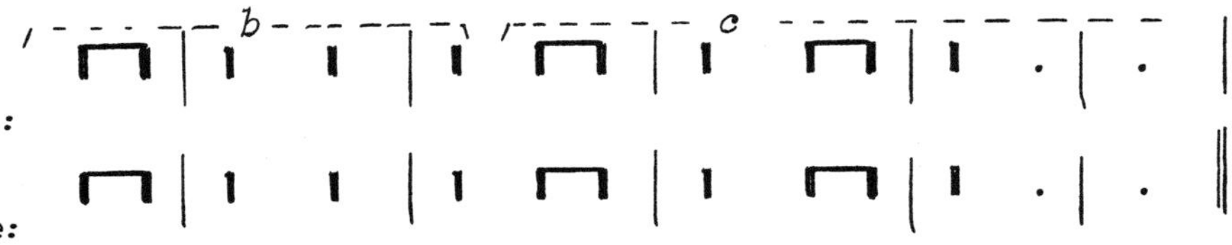

Compose Missing Line of Each Song Given - *Inconclusive Response*

1\.

5 5 | 1 2 2 | 3 5 5 | 1 2 2 | 3

Inconclusive Response: (Same rhythm as in line 1)

| | | |

5 5 | 1 2 2 | 3 1 1 | 3 4 4 | 5

5 5 | 6 5 4 | 3 5 5 | 5 5 5 | 1 . | . ||

2\.

Inc. Resp. (Different rhythm)

Songs

Mode of DO - Plagal Range
Do Clef on Second Line

Binary Rhythm (Duple Time) Beginning on Up-pulse
With Half-pulse notes
Rhythm Gesture II
Time Signature 2

JESUS, THE VERY THOUGHT OF THEE *Melody:* Old German
Text: Mediaeval Hymn "Jesu, Dulcis Memoria." Trans. E. Caswall

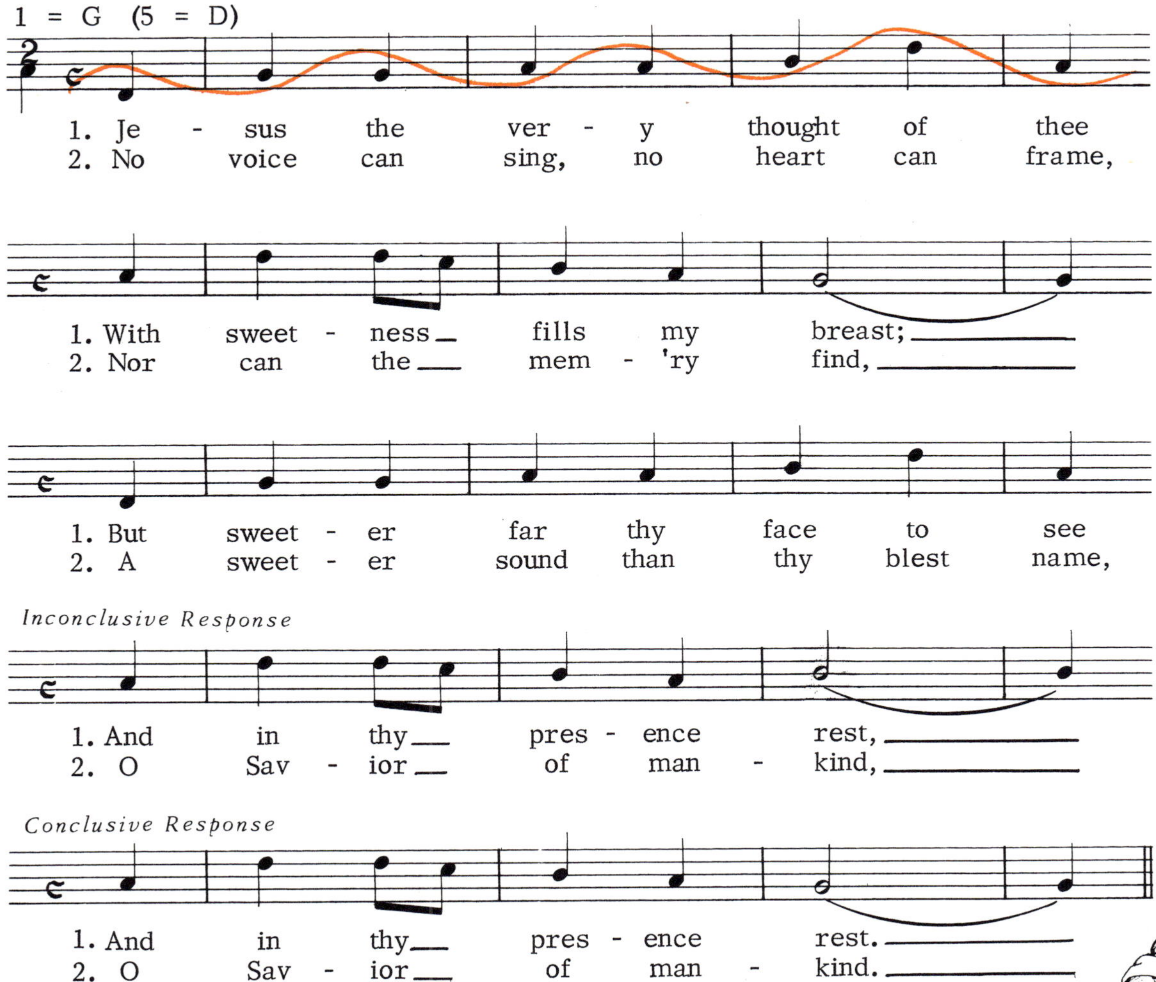

MELODY No. 9 Anonymous

1 = D (5 = A)

‖ 3 2 | 1 3 4 | 5 . | . 3 4 | 5 6 | 5 . | .

3 4 | 5 1 | 5 . | . 5 6 | 5 4 3 2 | 1 . | .

3 | 1 3 | 5 1 | 5 6 | 5

3 | 1 2 | 1 . | . ‖

MELODY No. 10 "Staff Song" *Anonymous*

1 = G (5 = D)

GOD'S MESSENGER *Melody:* 14th Century Air *Text:* JBW (alt.)

1 = G (5 = D) R.G.II

‖ 1 | 1 1 | 3 3 | 6 6 | 5 5 | 3 2 | 1 . | .
There came one star - ry night an an - gel clothed in white. ___

1 | 1 1 | 3 3 | 6 6 | 5 5 | 3 2 | 1 . | . . |
His name was Ga - bri - el. He came good news to tell. ___

R.G. IV-B

| 7 . | 1 1 | 3 3 | 2 2 | 6 6 | 5 . | .
"Hail,__ Ma - ry, full of grace, God comes to thee. ___

5 | 3 2 | 3 4 | 5 6 | 5 4 | 3 1 | 7 1 |
Of all the hu - man race God choos-es thee his Moth - er

| 3 . | 2 . | 1 . | . ‖
soon ___ to ___ be." ___

THE CIRCUS *Melody:* Anonymous *Text:* JBW

1 = G (5 = D)

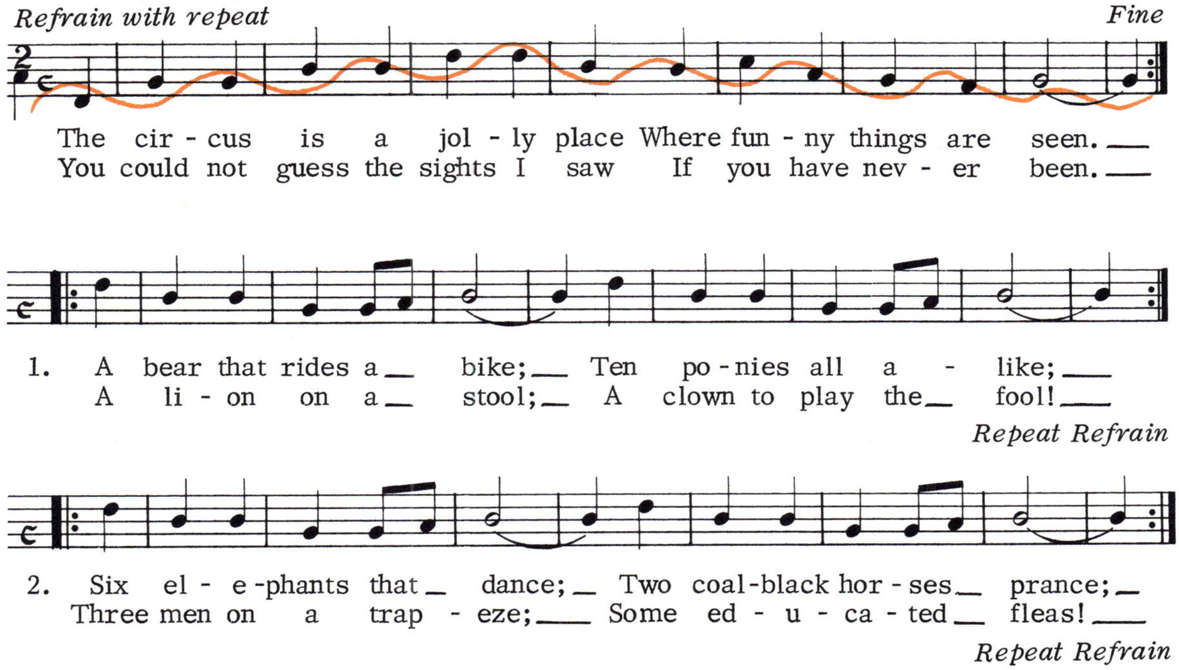

AH! MY CASTLE FINE *Melody:* French Folk Song *Text:* Anonymous

1 = G (5 = D)

CHAPTER SIX

LESSON PLAN

In preparing a lesson for teaching a song, the teacher ought to make use of the resources of the chapter that effectively lead up to a song. At the same time that a song is being learned a set of new techniques is also being learned.

It is perhaps not necessary to make a lesson plan for each and every song. Some melodies are easier to grasp than others and can readily be taught from a brief sight-singing review.

In the chapters that follow, a brief summary of the musical techniques taught in that chapter is given at the beginning of the SONGS section. This commentary will indicate the correspondence between the songs and the matter of the chapter.

As has been suggested elsewhere, it is good pedagogy to maintain the same pitch for DO in a lesson wherever possible.

"Place the bar-line before the long note!"

Chapter Six

Vocal Training

Review: Vocal Exercise 7 Sustained sound on each of three vowels

1 = F/G

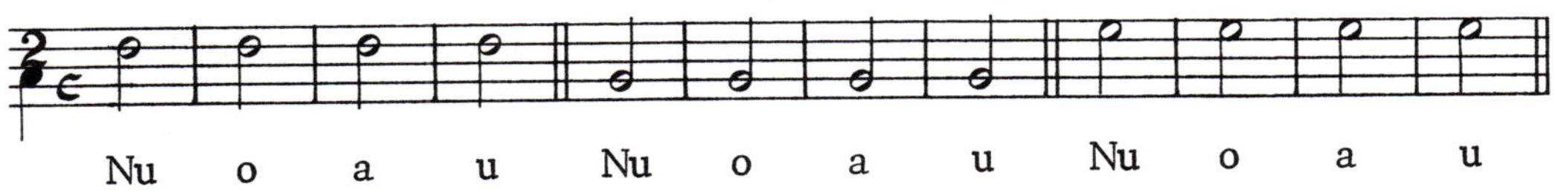

Vocal Exercise 9a Change of pitch with change of vowel

1 = G/C
(5 = F/G)

Vocal Exercise 9b

Vocal Exercise 9c

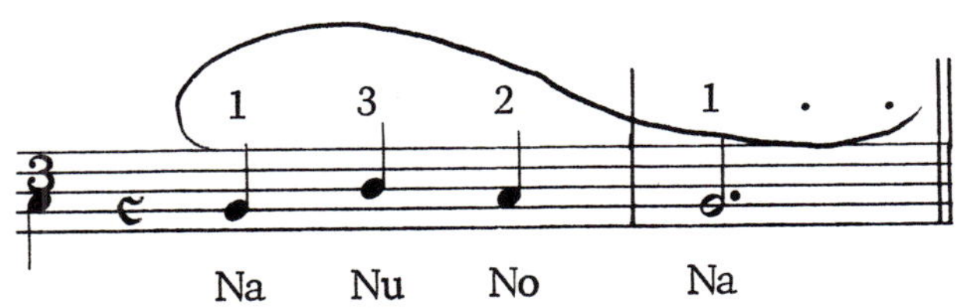

Vocal Exercise 10a

1̇ = B♭/C

Vocal Exercise 10b

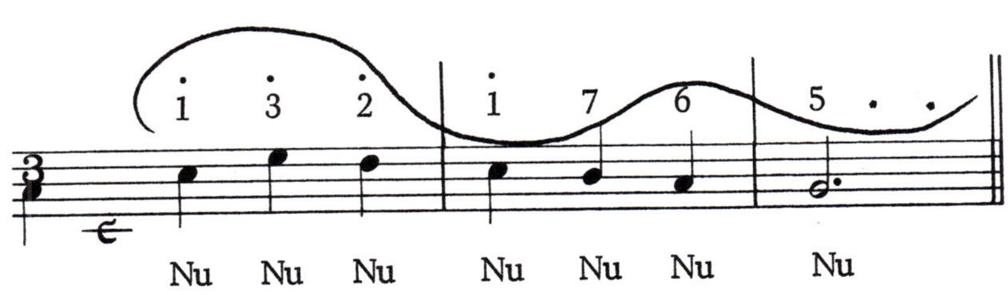

Intonation

Extension of Scale Line Above Upper Tetrachord

Notice that the dots in this set of exercises are __above__ the numbers. As a rule dots are placed above the numbers when most of the melody is below DO - 1. *When, however, the greater part of the melody is above* DO - 1 - *as was noticed in the* Plagal Range - *the dots are placed __below__ the numbers. There is no difference in the relationship of the scale tones to each other. The difference is only a matter of notation.*

For example: 1̇ = *Bb* 1̇ 3̇ 2̇ 1̇ 7 6 5 *sounds the same as* 1 = *Bb* 1 3 2 1 7̣ 6̣ 5̣

Work for pitch accuracy on the highest tones.

Intonation Exercise 16 - *With* Intonation Diagram *and* Staff Diagram 7

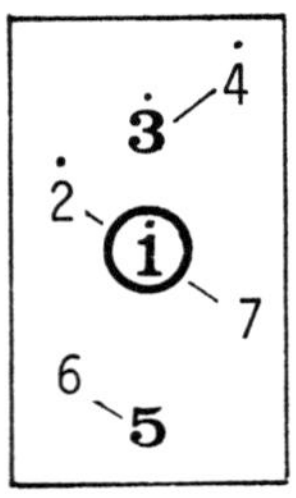

Int. Diagram 7

1̇ = *Bb or G* *Notes of Tonic Chord with scale passages*

a) | 1̇ 2̇ 3̇ 3̇ 1̇ 5 1̇ 3̇ b) | 5 1̇ 3̇ 1̇ 5 5 6 7 1̇ 2̇ 3̇ |

| 3̇ 1̇ 5 1̇ 3̇ | 5 1̇ 3̇ 1̇ 5 5 6 7 1̇ 2̇ 3̇ |

| 3̇ 5 1̇ 3̇ 1̇ | 5 3̇ 5 1̇ |

Intonation Exercise 17 - *With* Intonation Diagram *and* Staff Diagram 7

Drill on the interval 2̇ 5

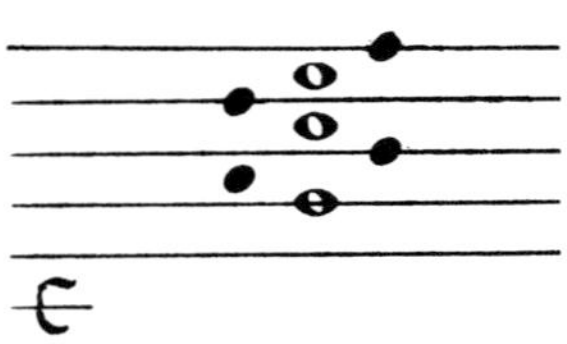
Staff Diagram 7

1̇ = *Bb or G*
(5 = *F or D*)

| 1̇ 5 1̇ 1̇ 3̇ 1̇ 2̇ 1̇ 2̇ 1̇ 5 1̇ |

| 1̇ 5 1̇ 1̇ 3̇ 1̇ 2̇ 1̇ 2̇ 1̇ 5 1̇ |

| 1̇ 5 1̇ 3̇ 1̇ 1̇ 2̇ 1̇ 5 1̇ |

| 1̇ 5 3̇ 2̇ 5 1̇ |

Intonation Exercise 18 - *Notes of the Tonic Chord with groups from* Third Compass Exercise

$\dot{1}$ = *Bb*

On blackboard	*Solution (Not Shown)*
$\dot{3}$ $\dot{1}$ *5	$\dot{3}$ $\dot{1}$ 65
$\dot{3}$ *$\dot{1}$ *5	$\dot{3}$ $\dot{2}\dot{1}$ 65
5 $\dot{1}$ *$\dot{3}$	5 $\dot{1}$ $\dot{4}\dot{3}$
5 *$\dot{1}$ *$\dot{3}$	5 $\dot{2}\dot{1}$ $\dot{4}\dot{3}$
$\dot{3}$ 5 *$\dot{1}$	$\dot{3}$ 5 $\dot{2}\dot{1}$
$\dot{3}$ *5 *$\dot{1}$	$\dot{3}$ 65 $\dot{2}\dot{1}$
$\dot{3}$ *$\dot{1}$ *5 *$\dot{1}$ *$\dot{3}$	$\dot{3}$ $\dot{2}\dot{1}$ 65 $\dot{2}\dot{1}$ $\dot{4}\dot{3}$

Finding Tones Above DO on Fingers

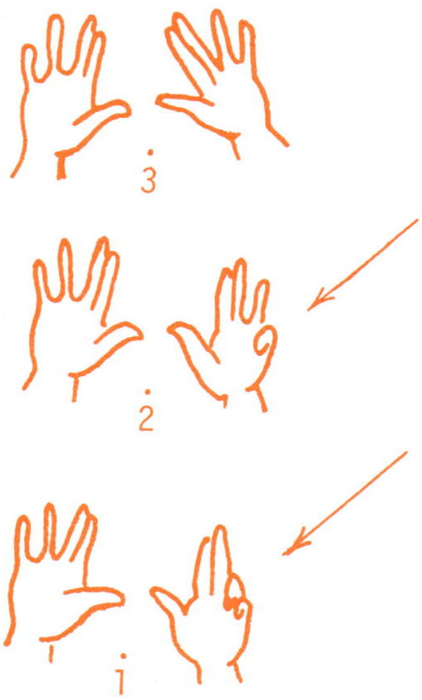

Ear and Eye Tests

$\dot{1}$ = *Bb*
(5 = F)

Use Pointer; Syllable "Nu"; Finger Notation.

$\dot{1}$ $\dot{2}$ $\dot{3}$ $\dot{3}$ $\dot{1}$ 5 $\dot{1}$ $\dot{3}$	$\dot{1}$ $\dot{2}$ $\dot{3}$ $\dot{3}$ $\dot{2}$ $\dot{1}$ 5 $\dot{1}$	$\dot{1}$ 6 5 $\dot{2}$ $\dot{1}$
5 $\dot{1}$ $\dot{3}$ $\dot{1}$ 5	$\dot{1}$ 5 $\dot{2}$ $\dot{1}$ $\dot{2}$ $\dot{1}$	$\dot{3}$ $\dot{1}$ 6 5 5 $\dot{1}$

$\dot{1}$ $\dot{3}$ $\dot{2}$ 5	$\dot{1}$ $\dot{3}$ $\dot{2}$ $\dot{1}$ 7 $\dot{1}$
$\dot{1}$ $\dot{2}$ $\dot{3}$ $\dot{1}$	$\dot{1}$ 7 $\dot{1}$ 6 5 $\dot{1}$ 5

Rhythm

Half-pulse Notes With Rhythm Gesture II *Continued*
Repeating and Combining Patterns

Rhythm Patterns - Series 6

Study with Metrical Gesture I *and* Metrical Language

Sing with melodic application of 1 3 5 3 *as shown*

Use Rhythm Gesture II

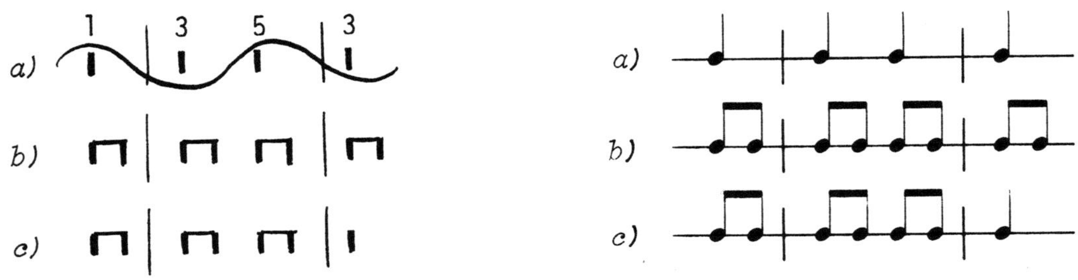

Derive rhythm pattern from songs at end of chapter. For example, the French folk melody "Sur le Pont" could give us a new pattern:

d) 

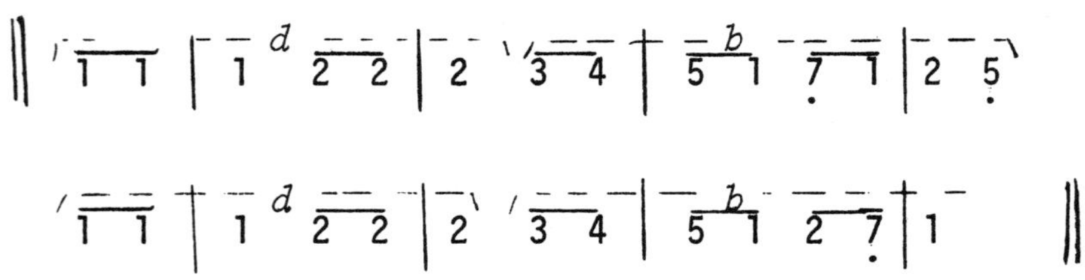

Study Melody 11 *and* Coming Back From Fremley Fair Ground *to discover new patterns*

NEW TERMINOLOGY: Half-pulse notes are called EIGHTH NOTES.
Sometimes they are shown with one flag:
or are tied together in pairs with a bar:

Aural Training in Rhythm *Continued*

Rhythm determined by long notes

GAME: Find correct rhythm gestures for melodic designs given:

1) $\dot{1}$ = C $\dot{1}$. $\dot{2}$ $\dot{1}$ 7 . $\dot{1}$.

2) 1 = G   3 . 1 1 3 . 3 .
4 3 2 1 2 . 2 .

3) $\dot{1}$ = E♭   3 1 3 5 . $\dot{1}$. 5 6 5
3 3 2 3 . 5 . 2 3 1

4) $\dot{1}$ = C $\dot{1}$ $\dot{1}$. 5 $\dot{1}$. $\dot{1}$ $\dot{2}$. $\dot{2}$ $\dot{1}$.

5) 1 = G   1 . 1 3 . 3 5 5 5 3 . .
5 5 5 3 . . 5 5 3 2 . .

6) 1 = G   5 . 5 6 . 5 4 . 3 5 . . 3 . .

Steps:

Place one of the above lines on board. Students sing notes while making simple Metrical Gesture

Draw bar-line before the last note and before each long note. Binary and ternary groupings will be noted

Draw remaining bar-lines and complete the example by adding double-bar at end

Sing complete melody with appropriate gesture

Rhythmic Dicatations

1 = G

|| $\overline{1\ 3}$ | $\overline{5\ 5}$ $\overline{5\ 5}$ | $\overline{3\ 1}$ $\overline{1\ 2}$ | $\overline{3\ 4}$ $\overline{3\ 2}$ | 1 ||

|| $\overline{1\ 2}$ | 3 $\overline{3\ 2}$ | 1 $\overline{3\ 4}$ | 5 $\overline{5\ 4}$ | 3 ||

Use additional lines from songs studied

Notation

DO Clef on Line Below Staff (Leger Line)

"Moving Day again!" DO Clef *moves to line below staff to make room on staff for notes that go above high* DO (1̇).

Mode of DO *with upper tetrachord extensions appears on staff as follows when clef is placed on line below staff:*

Teacher places numbers on staff as follows:

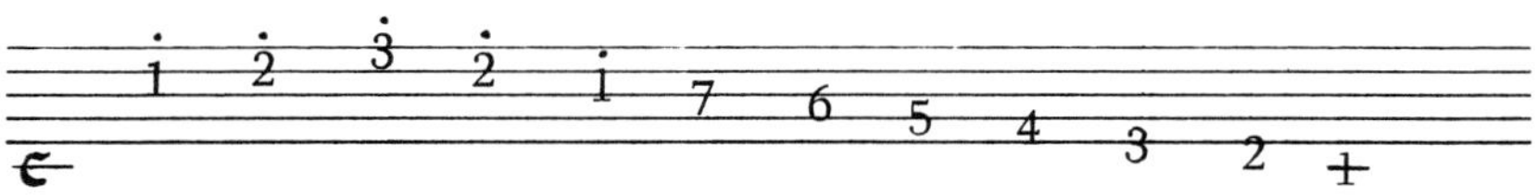

Then chalks over numbers to show notes on staff:

Transcriptions *Solutions are offered as an aid to the teacher*

1) Transcribe numbers given to correct staff notation:

To be transcribed:

Given:

2) Students must identify notes given with correct numbers:

Given:

To be transcribed:

3) Transcribe numbers given to correct notes on staff:

Given:

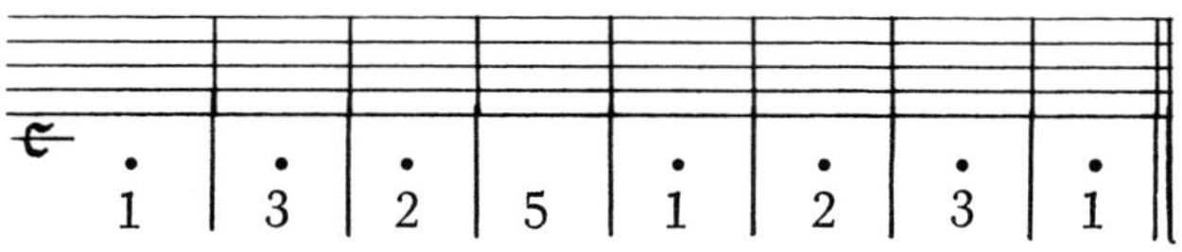

4) Transcribe numbers given to correct notation on staff:

Given:

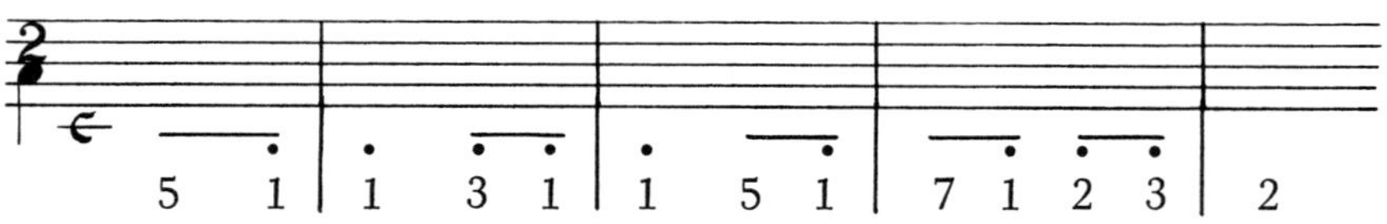

N.B. Half-pulse Notes *may be transcribed as* 

Creative Activity

Review Study of Rhythmic Enlargement
(See BOOK ONE - Closing Chapters)

Teacher places rhythm pattern combination on board:

Children suggest tune for rhythm given:

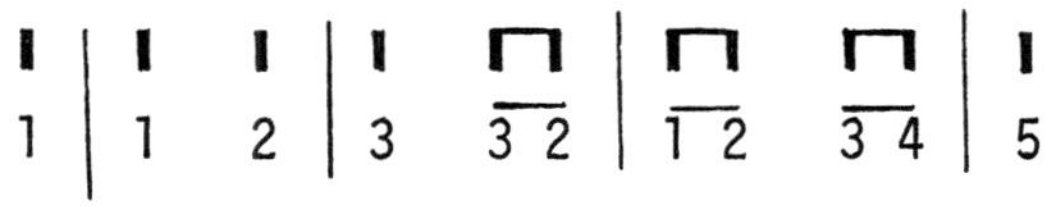

Teacher suggest several notes for enlargement - shown with cross

```
      +   +   +
1 | 1   2 | 3   3 2 | 1 2   3 4 | 5
```

Resulting melody is the following:

```
1 | 1  .  | 2  .  | 3   .  |  .  3 2 | 1 2   3 4 | 5
```

Notice how this happened in "DRAW A BUCKET OF WATER" - Chapter Four

```
                      +       +
1st Line -|| 1  .  2 | 3   4   3 | 2  .  . | 1  .  . |
                      +         +
2nd Line -|  1  .  2 | 3   .   4 | 3  .  . | 2  .  . ||
```

<u>*Assignment*</u> *Complete second line of melody given using rhythmic enlargement*
Improvise melodies for lines 3 and 4 to finish the song

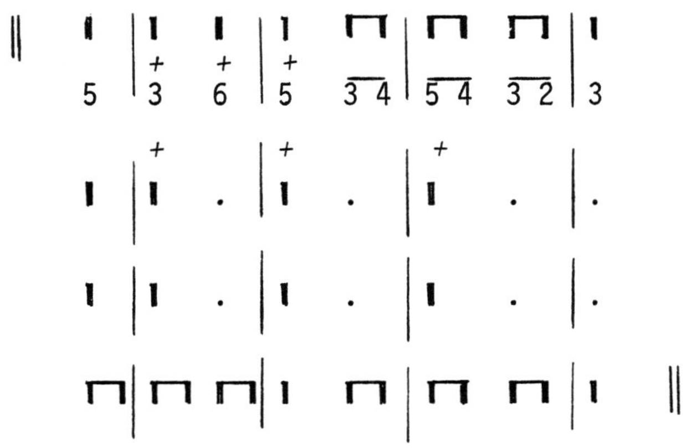

SIGHT SINGING DRILLS

Preparation for Staff Notation Songs

1. *Sing each segment several times*

$\dot{1}$ = B♭

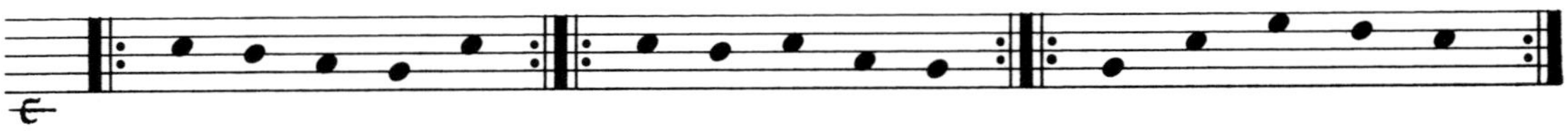

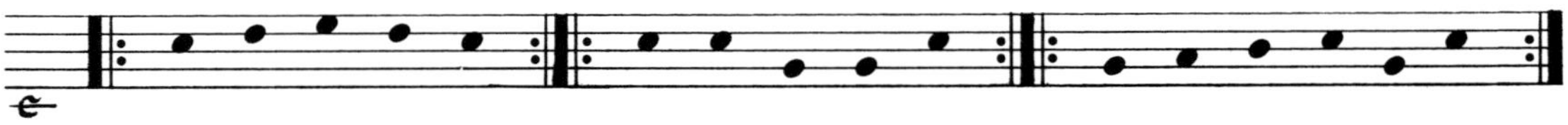

2. *Repeat line given several times: Bluebirds; Robins; individual students; numbers; staff notes.*

$\dot{1}$ = B♭

3. *Flash segments on screen and cover up or write on board and erase after a few moments to give students time to grasp the whole line of music*

1 = G

$\dot{1}$ = C

Songs

Mode of DO - Extension of Upper Tetrachord
DO Clef on Leger Line Below Staff
Notes of Tonic Chord
Binary Rhythm (Duple Time) Beginning on Up-pulse
Rhythm Gesture I or II
Time Signature 2/♩

MELODY No. 11 "Invention" *by J. S. Bach*

1 = E (5 = B)

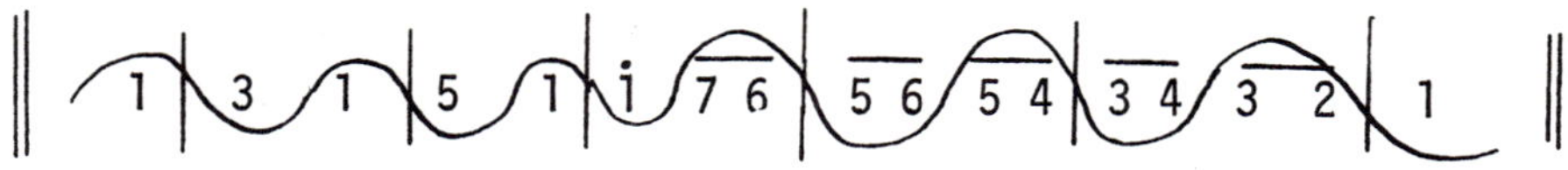

MELODY No. 12 "Sur le Pont d'Avignon" *French Folk Song*

1 = G
(5 = D)

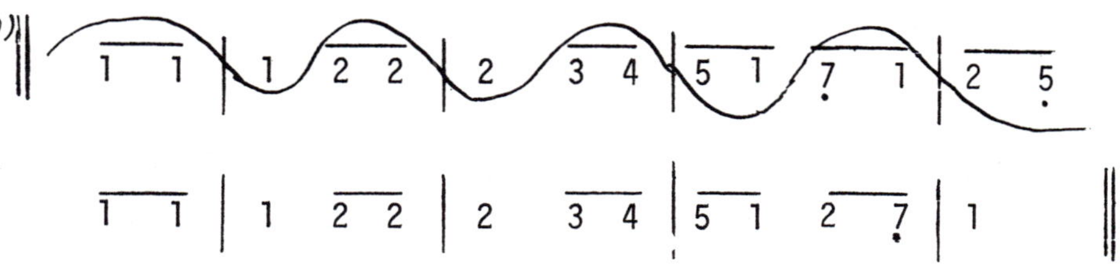

MELODY No. 13 "Staff Song" *Anonymous*

1̇ = B♭ (5 = F)

WESTMINSTER CHIME English Folk Melody

$\dot{1}$ = B♭ (5 = F)

|| $\dot{1}$ | $\dot{3}$ $\dot{2}$ | 5 . | .
All through the hour ______

$\dot{1}$ | $\dot{2}$ $\dot{3}$ | $\dot{1}$. | .
Lord, be my guide ______

$\dot{3}$ | $\dot{1}$ $\dot{2}$ | 5 . | .
And with thy pow'r ______

5 | $\dot{2}$ $\dot{3}$ | $\dot{1}$. | . ||
Stay by my side. ______

ALL GLORY, LAUD AND HONOR *Melody:* M. Teschner *Text:* "Gloria, Laus et Honor" from Palm Sunday Liturgy. Translated by J. M. Neale

$\dot{1}$ = C (5 = G)

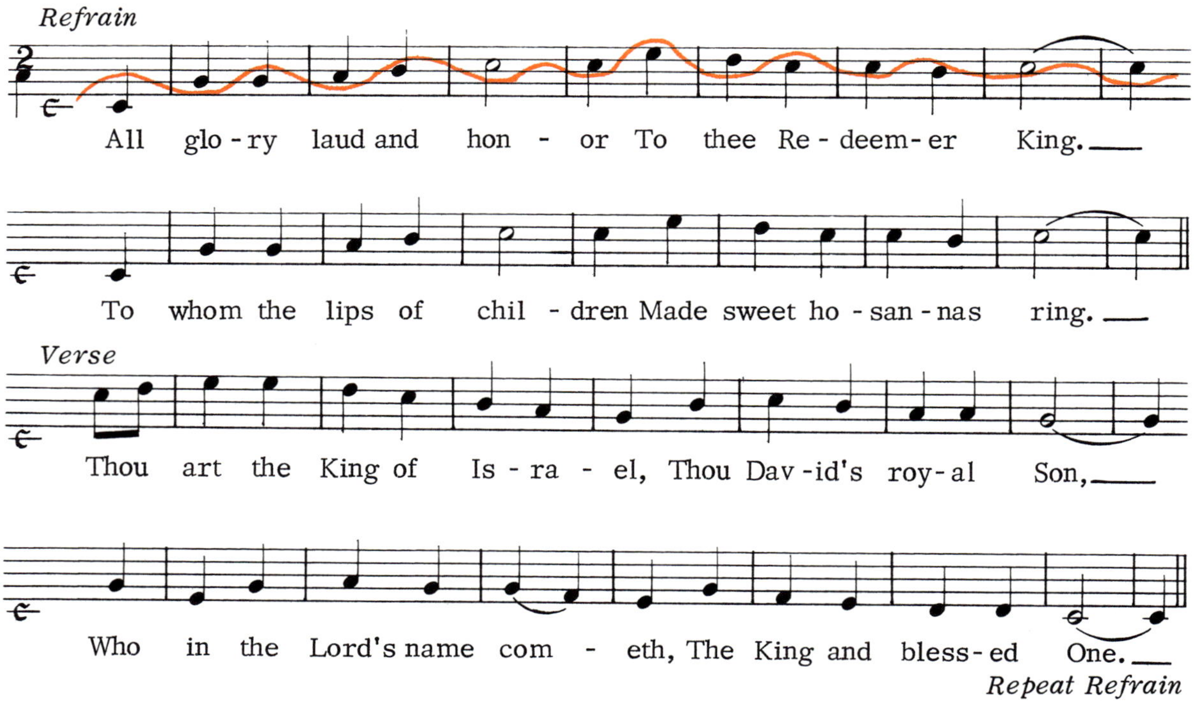

COMING BACK FROM FREMLEY FAIR GROUND English Folk Song

1 = G

‖ 1 3 | 5 5 5 5 | 3 3

1. Com - ing back from Frem - ley fair ground,
2. Then I asked of that old wom - an
3. So I asked of that old wom - an

1 2 | 3 4 3 2 | 1

1. From the town I took my way.
2. Where her hus - band was that day:
3. If her chil - dren were her stay:

1 3 | 5 5 5 5 | 3 3

1. On the road I met a wom - an
2. "He's been dead these thir - ty win - ters",
3. "They are grown and gone to Lon - don,

1 2 | 3 4 3 2 | 1 ‖

1. Rid - ing on a don - key grey.
2. That old dame did sad - ly say.
3. Stop your ques -tions, Sir, I pray!"

Refrain

‖ 1 2 | 3 3 2 1 | 5 5 6 | 5 4 3 2 | 3 1

Then I saw her crack her whip, Poor old don - key, poor old don -key,

1 2 | 3 3 2 1 | 5 5 6 | 5 4 3 2 | 5

Then I saw her crack her whip, Poor old don - key, don- key grey,

5 6 | 5 4 3 2 | 1 . | . . | . ‖

Poor old don- key, don - key grey. ——————

RAMPONEAU ISN'T DEAD French Folk Song. Translation anonymous

$\dot{1}$ = B♭ (5 = F)

Chapter Seven

Vocal Training

Review <u>Vocal Exercise 7</u> Sustained Vowels "u" "o" "a"

Review <u>Vocal Exercise 10a</u>

<u>Vocal Exercise 11a</u> Various Tones and Slurs on "u" "o" "a"

> Remember: good posture
> deep breathing
> maximum vowel resonance

Intonation

Major Mode (DO) 3 - 3̇ Range
Tonic Triad in Root Position and First Inversion

Intonation Exercise 19 - *With* Intonation Diagram 8 *and* Staff Diagram 8

4̇
3̇
2̇
(1̇)
7
6
5
4
3

Int. Diagram 8

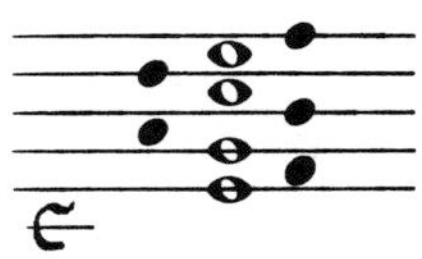

Staff Diagram 8

1̇ = Bb or C

Drills on 3 *to* 3̇ *range*

a)		b)	
1̇ 7 6 5 4 3	3 4 5 6 7 1̇	3 5 1̇ 3̇	3̇ 1̇ 5 3
1̇ 5 3	3 5 1̇	3 5 1̇ 3̇	1̇ 5 3
1̇ 5 3	5 1̇	3 4 5 6 7 1̇	

Intonation Exercise 20 - *With* Intonation Diagram 9a *and* Staff Diagram 9b

1̇ = Eb

6
5
4
3
2
(1)

(1̇)
7
6
5
4
3

Int. Diagrams 9a and 9b

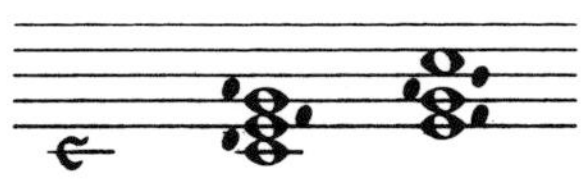

Staff D. 9a 9b

Different ranges of
First Compass Exercise

a)

121 343 565	565 343 121
121 *343* 565	565 *343* 121

b)

1̇71̇ 565 343	343 565 1̇71̇
1̇71̇ *565* 343	343 *565* 1̇71̇

Eye and Ear Tests

1̇ 7 1̇ 3 4 3 1̇ 7 1̇	3 5 1̇ 3̇ 3̇ 1̇ 5 3
1 2 1 5 6 5 1 2 1	5 6 7 1̇ 1̇ 2̇ 3̇

1̇ 5 3 5 1̇	3 2 3 1 5
1̇ 1̇ 5 5 3 3	1̇ 5 1̇ 1̇ 1̇ 5 1̇

Rhythm

Half-Pulse Notes in Duple Time
Arsis-Thesis in Binary Groupings Beginning on Down-Pulse
Conducting with Metrical Gesture II (Beating Time in 2)

Rhythm Patterns - Series 7

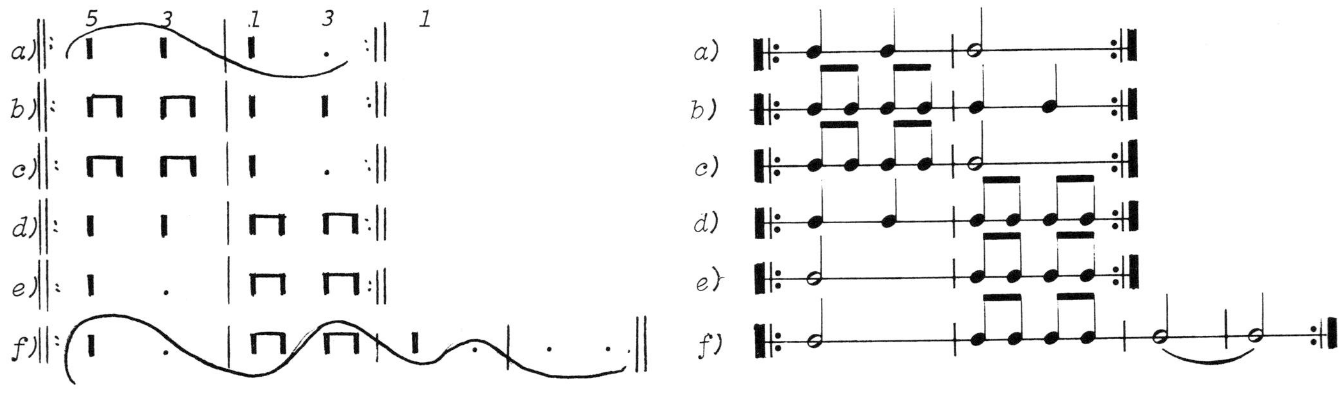

1) *Sing first with* Metrical Gesture I *and* Metrical Language
2) *Repeat with* Arsis *and* Thesis *as shown*
3) *Repeat while making* Metrical Gesture II - *beating time in Duple Time*

4) *Sing patterns on notes suggested at the head of the columns*
For example:

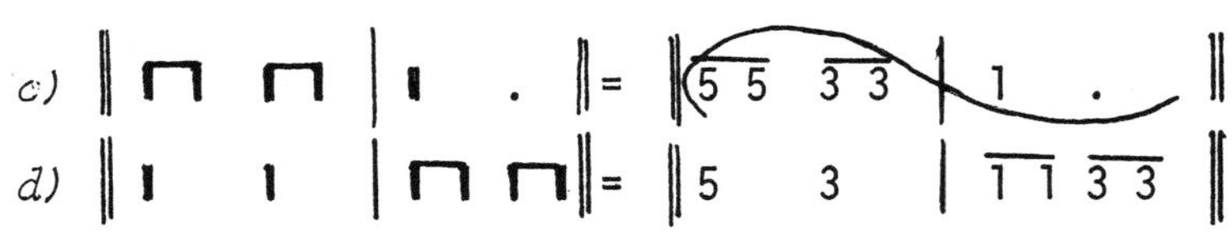

5) *Sing patterns with "help notes" between the notes 5 3 1 3 when half-pulse rhythms are given. For example:*

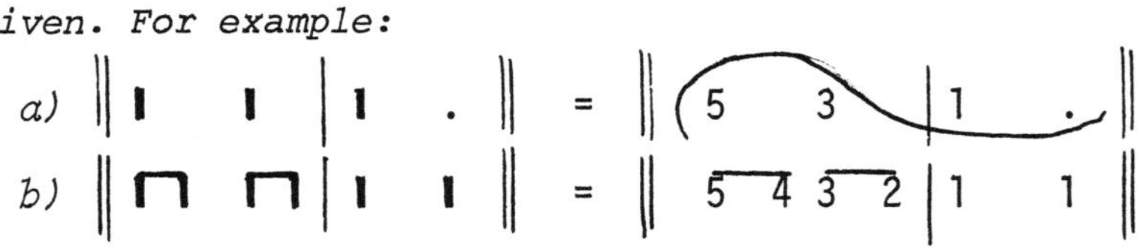

Rhythmic Dictations - Metrical Gesture II

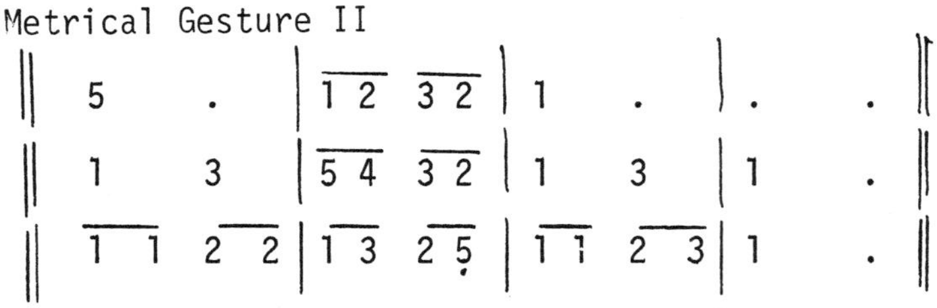

Aural Training in Rhythm — Rhythm Determined by Melodic Line - Step 3

Examples of melodies to be studied placed on board with bar-lines. Teacher invites children to sing example and shows them how rhythmic grouping of notes depends upon certain types of melodic patterns:

1. Repeated Notes

2. Repeated Short Motifs

1. Repeated Notes

‖ 1 1 | 5 5 | 6 6 | 5 . |
| 4 4 | 3 3 | 2 2 | 1 . ‖

("Twinkle, Twinkle" Book One Chapter 20)

‖ 1̇ 1̇ 1̇ | 7 7 7 | 6 7 1̇ | 5 . . |
| 4 4 4 | 3 3 3 | 2 2 2 | 1 . . ‖

(Melody No. 20, Book One Chapter 19)

Unbarred melodies are placed on board. Before singing them children must discover correct place for bar-lines

Examples:

a) ‖ 1 1 | 3 3 | 5 5 | 3 . |
| 4 4 | 2 2 | 3 3 | 1 . ‖

b) ‖ 1 1 1 | 3 3 3 | 5 . . |
| 4 4 4 | 2 2 2 | 1 . . ‖

Children invited to finish melody begun by teacher:

Examples:

a) ‖ ı ı | ı ı | ı ı | ı . |
5 5 4
| 4 4 | 3 | | ‖

GAME *Teacher sings short melody without making rhythmic gesture. Students listen for clues as to the rhythm (time). After several renditions by teacher, a student is invited to repeat melody and make the appropriate gesture.*

Examples:

a) ‖ 3 3 | 1 1 | 3 3 | 5 . |
| 4 4 | 2 2 | 1 . | 1 . ‖

b) ‖ 1 | 1 1 | 3 3 | 6 6 | 5 5 | 3 2 | 1 . | . ‖

2. *Repeated Short Motifs*

Examples for observation:

a) ‖ 1 3 | 1 3 | 1 3 | 2 . |
| 7 2 | 7 2 | 7 2 | 1 . ‖

b) ‖ 1 2 3 | 1 2 3 | 1 2 3 | 4 . . |
| 2 3 4 | 2 3 4 | 2 3 4 | 5 . . ‖

Unbarred examples for students to study:

a) 5 3 5 3 5 3 1 .

b) 4 3 2 4 3 2 4 3 2 1 . .

Melody to be completed and sung:

‖ 1 | 3 2 1 | 3 | | .
| 7 | 2 1 7 | 2 | | ‖

Melody for aural interpretation. Students must identify pitches and correct place of bar-line from listening to melody sung by teacher.

‖ 1 7 6 | 1 7 6 | 1 7 6 | 5 . . |
| 4 3 2 | 4 3 2 | 4 3 2 | 1 . . ‖

Notice especially repeated notes and motifs in songs studied at end of Chapter Seven.

Notation

Review Three Known Positions of DO Clef

Transcriptions

1. DO Clef *on First Line. Transcribe from notes to numbers.*

Given:
To be added:

2. DO Clef *on Second Line. Transcribe from numbers to notes.*

To be added:
Given:

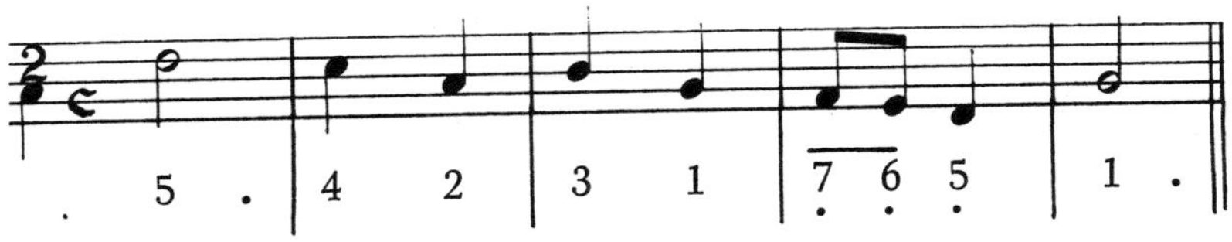

3. DO Clef *on ledger line below staff. Transcribe from notes to numbers.*

Given:
To be added:

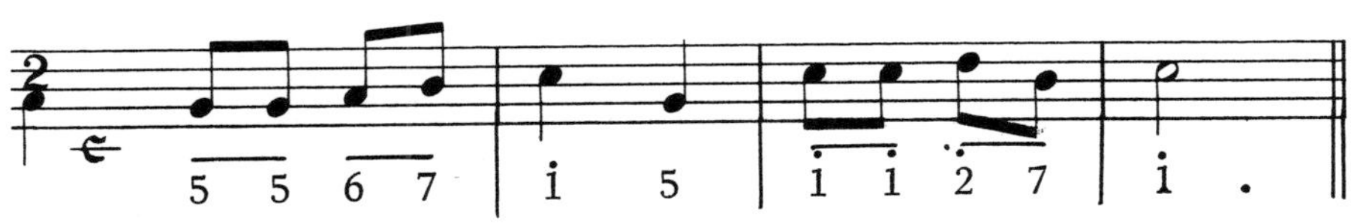

4. DO Clef *on ledger line below staff with extended range of upper tetrachord*

To be added:
Given:

Creative Activity

Contrast and Repetition in Composition

Students' compositions should now make use of musical ideas of contrasting phrases, repeated notes and motifs.

Notice structure of Melody No. 16. *(Theme of Beethoven)*

Scale line of melody is contrasted with skips at end of line.
Line 3 repeats Line 1.

Students invited to compose Line 4 of melody given. End on DO. Added line should imitate rhythm of Line 2, and be a Conclusive Response.

1 = G

Students add responses to each of statements given. Use repeated notes, contrasts, etc.

Given: ‖ 3 2 1 2 | 3 4 | 5 6 | 5 . |
To be added: | | | | ‖

Given: ‖ 1 5 | 1 2 3 4 | 3 . | 2 . |
To be added: | | | | ‖

Given: ‖ 5 5 5 | 1̇ 6 | 5 4 3 | 2 . |
To be added: | | | | ‖

Given: ‖ 5 5 5 | 6 5 | 5 4 3 2 | 1 2 | 5̣ . |
To be added: | | | | | |

S I G H T S I N G I N G D R I L L S

Preparation for Staff Notation Songs

1) Sing each fragment several times

$\dot{1}$ = B♭

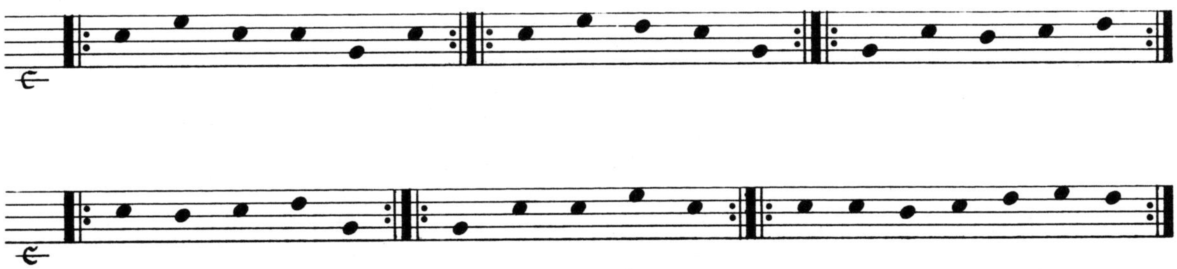

2) Visual memory tests. Each line is shown on screen or on blackboard briefly. Students study it and when it is withdrawn someone is invited to sing it from memory.

a)

b)

c)

Use lines also from songs being studied

Songs

Mode of DO - Tonic chord line extending up to $\dot{3}$
Half-pulse notes in Duple Time beginning on the down-pulse
Arsis-Thesis (R. G. IV) in binary groupings beginning on down-pulse
Metrical Gesture II
Repeated notes and repeated motifs in melodic designs

SONGS *See bottom of preceding page for indications of correspondence between songs given below and the matter of this chapter.*

MELODY No. 14 Basque Folk Song

$\dot{1}$ = B♭ ($\dot{3}$ = D)

‖ $\dot{3}$ $\dot{3}$ | $\dot{1}$ $\dot{1}$ | $\dot{2}$ $\dot{2}$ | $\dot{3}$ $\dot{1}$ | 6 7 | $\dot{1}$ 6 | 5 4 | 3 . |

| $\dot{3}$ $\dot{3}$ | $\dot{1}$ $\dot{1}$ | $\dot{2}$ $\dot{2}$ | $\dot{3}$ $\dot{1}$ | 6 7 | $\dot{1}$ $\dot{1}$ | $\dot{2}$ $\dot{2}$ | $\dot{1}$. ‖

MELODY No. 15 French Folk Song from Lorraine

$\dot{1}$ = C (5 = G)

BROOM DANCE Anonymous

1 = E♭ (5 = B♭)

‖ $\overline{5\ \ 1}$ $\overline{1\ \ 1}$ | $\overline{1\ \ \underset{\cdot}{7}}$ 2 |
One, two, three, four, five, six, sev'n,

| $\overline{5\ \ 2}$ $\overline{2\ \ 2}$ | $\overline{2\ \ 1}$ 3 |
Where's my part - ner, nine, ten, 'levn?

| $\overline{1\ \ 3}$ 5 | $\overline{6\ \ 6}$ 5 |
Too- lay- doo,___ oh- ee- oh,

| $\overline{4\ \ 4}$ $\overline{3\ \ 3}$ | $\overline{2\ \ 2}$ 1 ‖
That's the way we have to go!

MELODY No. 16 "From "Violin Concerto" *L. van Beethoven*

$\dot{1}$ = E♭ (5 = B♭)

‖ 3 4 | 5 $\overline{6\ 7}$ | $\dot{1}$. | 5 . |

| 4 3 | 2 $\overline{3\ 1}$ | 2 . | 5 . |

| 3 4 | 5 $\overline{6\ 7}$ | $\dot{1}$. | 5 . |

| 6 4 | 2 5 | 3 . | . . ‖

HAIL REDEEMER, KING DIVINE *Melody:* Mediaeval Hymn *Text:* "Orientis partibus" Translation anonymous

1 = E♭ (5 = B♭)

|| 1 2 | 3 1 | 2 7̣ | 1 . |
Hail Re - deem - er, King div - ine! __

| 5 5 | 6 4 | 5 5 | 3 . |
Priest and Lamb, the throne is thine, __

| 3 2 | 4 3 | 2 1 | 3 . |
King, whose reign shall nev - er cease, __

| 5 4 | 3 1 | 2 7̣ | 1 . ||
Prince of ev - er - last - ing peace. __

| 0 1 | 2 3 | 2 . | 1 . ||
Al - le - lu - ia. __

TRIUMPH, ALL YE CHERUBIM Traditional

1̇ = B♭ (5 = F)

|| 1̇ 7 | 6 2̇1̇ | 7 6 | 5 . |
Tri - umph, all ye Cher - u - bim! __

| 1̇ 7 | 6 2̇1̇ | 7 6 | 5 . |
Sing with us, ye Ser - a - phim! __

| 1̇ 2̇ | 3̇ 1̇ | 1̇ 7 | 1̇ . |
Heav'n and earth re - sound the hymn: __

| 1̇ 7 | 6 . | 2̇ 1̇ | 7 . | 1̇ 2̇ | 3̇ 1̇ | 2̇ . | 1̇ . ||
Sal - ve, __ sal - ve, __ sal - ve, Re - gí - na. __

(Salve pronounced as *sahl-vay*, means: Hail. Regína, pronounced *Ray-jee-nah*, means: Queen.)

YANKEE DOODLE Traditional American

SHETLAND PONY *Melody:* Air of 1599 *Text:* JBW

1 = G (5 = D)

|| 1 5 | 5 3 | 4 5 6 | 5 . |
Shet- land Po- ny, ti - ny and black,__

| 4 3 | 2 1 | 7̣ 1 2 | 1 . |
How I'd love to ride on your back.__

| 5̣ 2 | 2 3 | 1 2 | 2 1 7̣ | 6̣ 5̣ 6̣ | 5̣ . | . 0 |
Your long mane and tail I love and your pret - ty wee feet.____

| 5̣ 2 | 2 2 | 3 4 5 3 | 4 3 | 2 1 2 3 | 1 . | . 0 ||
Shet - land Po - ny, if you let me ride I prom - ise you a treat.____

Chapter Eight

Vocal Training

Review Sustained Vowels "u" "o" "a"
Plagal Range

Review Vocal Exercise 7

1 = G
(5 = D)

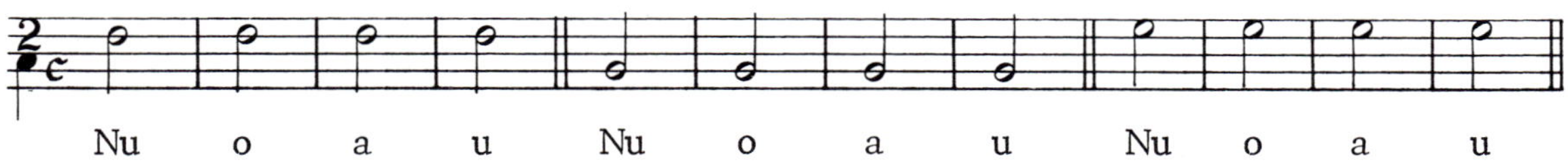

Review Vocal Exercise 8a

1 = G

Review Vocal Exercise 8b

1 = G

Intonation

Discovery of Dominant Triad (5 7 2) in Plagal Range
Appearance of Dominant Seventh
Developing Agility in Approaching 5 and 5

> These exercises must be sung slowly at first. Supply help notes and work for exactness of pitch. Teacher must allow students to discover the notes themselves as this is a necessary step in the child's inner development

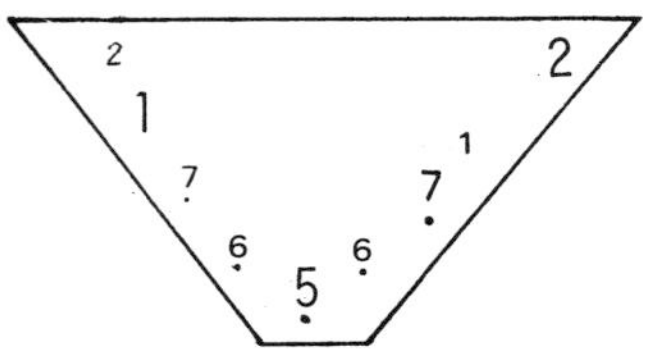

Int. Diagram 10

Staff Diagram 10

1 = G for all drills
(5 = D)

<u>Intonation Exercise 21</u> - *With* Intonation Diagram 10 *and* Staff Diagram 10

a) → b) →

| 1 5 5 1 7 1 2 2 1 7 1 5 5 1 | 1 2 2 1 7 1 5 5 1 7 1 2 | *Notes of Dominant Triad*
| 1 5 5 *1* 7 *1* 2 2 *1* 7 *1* 5 5 1 | 2 *1* 7 *1* 5 5 *1* 7 *1* 2 | 5 7 2
| 1 5 5 7 2 2 7 5 5 1 | 2 7 5 5 7 2 |
| 1 5 5 7 2 7 5 5 1 | 2 7 5 7 2 2 1 |

When necessary, review Compass Exercises for Plagal Range in Chapter Four.

Intonation Exercise 22 - *With* Intonation Diagram 11

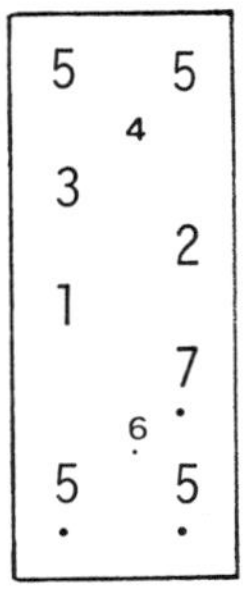

Int. Diagram 11

Notes of Dominant Chord in octave range with addition of 4 (seventh)

a)
| 1 5 5 1 7 1 2 1 5 5 4 3 2 1 5 |
| 5 1 7 1 2 1 5 5 3 1 5 5 1 |

b)
| 1 5 5 1 3 5 5 1 2 1 7 1 5 |
| 5 1 3 5 5 1 2 1 7 1 5 |
| 5 1 3 5 5 4 3 2 7 5 5 1 |

Intonation Exercise 23 - *With* Staff Diagram 11

Agility

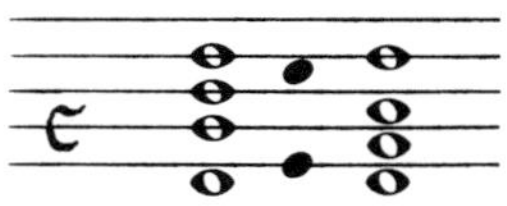

Staff Diagram 11

a)
| 1 5 1 2 5 2 3 5 3 4 5 4 3 5 3 2 5 2 1 5 1 7 5 7 1 |
| 1 5 1 2 5 2 3 5 3 4 5 4 3 5 3 2 5 2 1 5 1 7 5 7 1 |
| 1 5 2 5 3 5 4 5 3 5 2 5 1 5 7 5 1 |

b)
| 1 5 1 2 5 2 3 5 3 4 5 4 3 5 3 2 5 2 1 5 1 7 5 7 1 |
| 1 5 1 2 5 2 3 5 3 4 5 4 3 5 3 2 5 2 1 5 1 7 5 7 1 |
| 1 5 2 5 3 5 4 5 3 5 2 5 1 5 7 5 1 |

Eye and Ear Tests

1 = G

5 1 1 1 1 7 2 | 5 6 5 1 7 1 5 6 5 | 7 1 2 5 1 2 3 5
5 2 2 2 2 1 3 | 1 2 2 1 7 1 5 5 1 | 5 3 1 5 5 1

1 5 5 7 2 7 1 | 5 1 2 1 7 1 5
2 1 7 1 5 5 1 | 5 4 2 7 1 5 1

Rhythm

Half-Pulses with Rhythm Gesture III
Ternary Rhythm (Triple Time) Beginning on Up-Pulse

Rhythm Patterns - Series 8

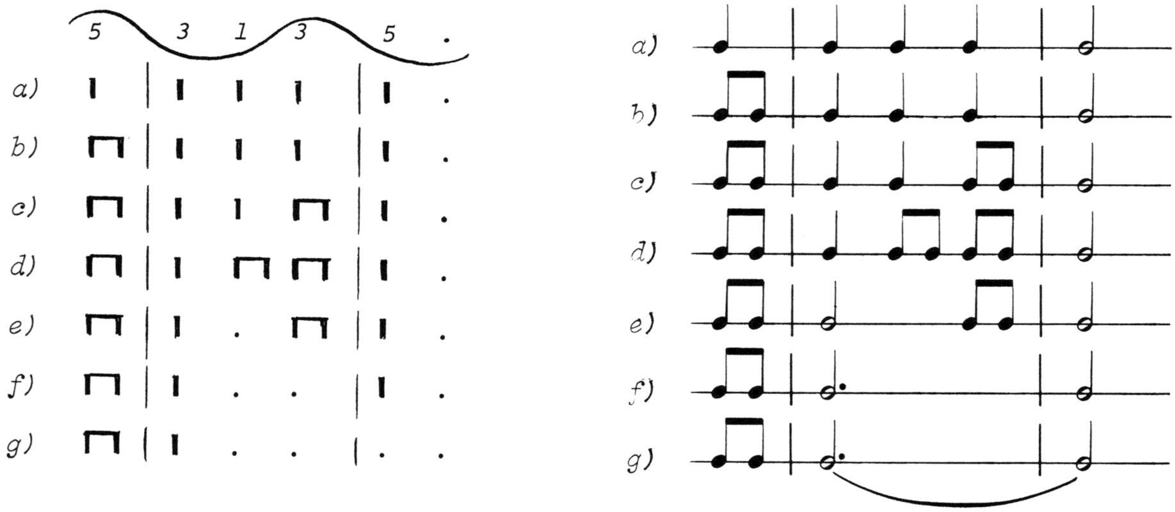

1. *Say each pattern with* Metrical Gesture I *and* Metrical Language

2. *Sing patterns with Melodic Applications indicated above.*
   - *a) Repeated notes where necessary on tones given.*
   - *b) Fill in passing tones between tones of tonic chord.*
   - *c) Use* Rhythm Gesture III;

3. *Combine patterns and compose melodies for the combinations indicated:*

a + b 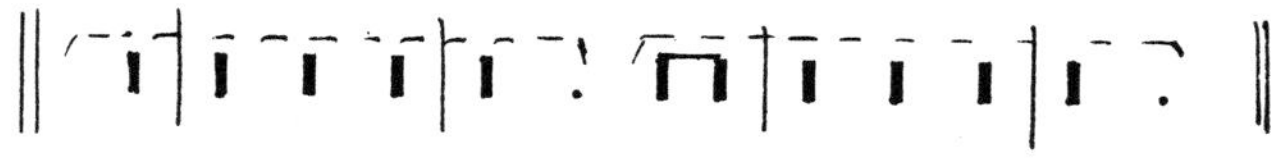

d + e 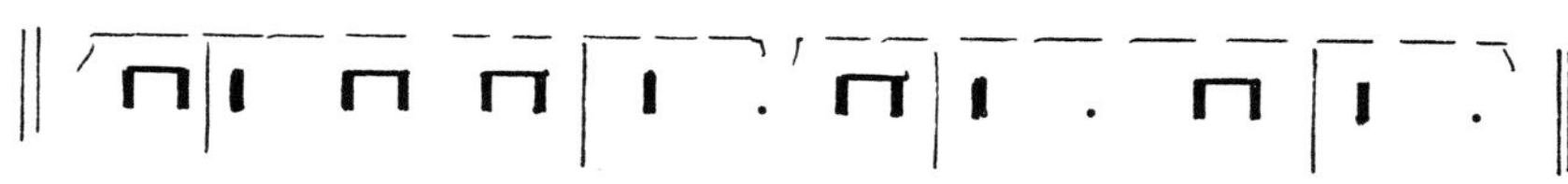

e + g 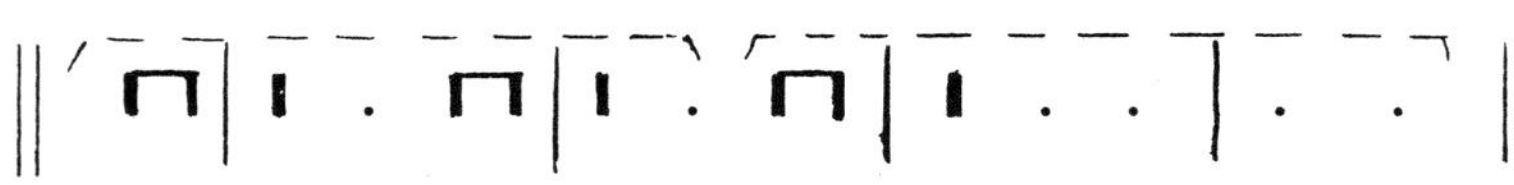

4. *Discover other possibilities in up-pulse ternary rhythm patterns. E.g., Line 3 of "O Where, O Where Is My Little Dog Gone?"*

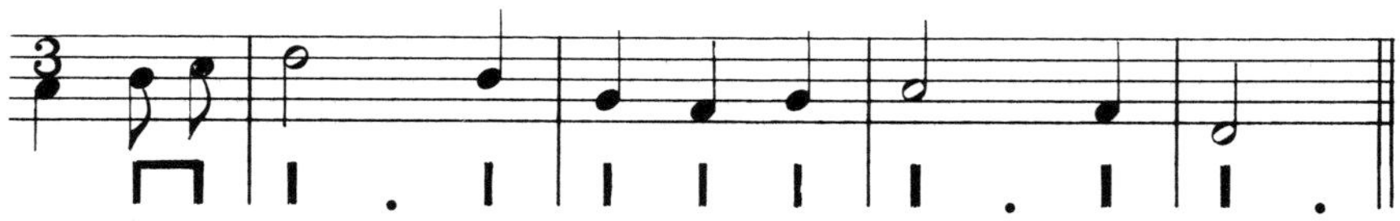

Also "If I Get My Pick of the Three of Them" at end of chapter

Rhythmic Dictations

|| 5 | 6 . 5 | 4 3 2 | 1 . . | . . ||

|| 5 | 1 1 2 | 3 3 3 4 | 5 3 2 | 1 . ||

|| 5 | 1 . 1 | 2 3 4 | 3 . . | 2 . ||

AURAL TRAINING IN RHYTHM - Rhythm Determined by Melodic Line - Step 4 *continued*

3. *Motifs repeated in sequence*

Ex. for observation: || 1 3 | 2 4 | 3 5 | 4 6 | 5 . ||

|| 5 4 3 | 4 3 2 | 3 2 1 | 2 1 7 | 1 . . ||

Identify place where motif repeats and add bar-line at beginning of each repetition:

|| 1 6 ¦ 7 5 ¦ 6 4 ¦ 5 . ||

|| 3 4 5 ¦ 4 5 6 ¦ 5 6 7 ¦ 1 . . ||

Passages to complete (sequence):

|| 5 3 | 4 | | | 1 . ||

|| 1 2 3 | 2 | | | 5 . . ||

Melody for aural interpretation. Teacher sings melody. Students observe sequence.

|| 1 3 | 2 4 | 3 5 | 5 . |

| 4 2 | 3 1 | 2 7 | 1 . ||

4. *Motifs repeated by inversion:*

Ex. for observation:

|| 1 3 | 3 1 | 3 5 | 5 3 | 2 4 | 4 2 | 3 1 | 1 . ||

|| 1 2 3 | 3 2 1 | 3 4 5 | 5 4 3 | 4 3 2 | 2 3 4 | 3 2 1 | 1 . . ||

Identify place where motif is repeated and add bar-line at beginning of each repetition:

|| 5 3 ¦ 3 5 ¦ 4 2 ¦ 2 4 ¦ 3 1 ¦ 1 3 ¦ 2 . ¦ . . ||

|| 4 5 6 ¦ 6 5 4 ¦ 3 4 5 ¦ 5 4 3 ¦ 2 3 4 ¦ 4 3 2 ¦ 1 . . ||

Passage to complete:

|| 5 6 | 6 5 | 4 | | | | | | | . | . . ||

Melody for aural interpretation. Teacher sings melody. Students observe inversion.

|| 3 5 | 3 1 | 3 5 | 3 . |

| 2 4 | 2 7 | 2 4 | 2 . ||

Example containing several features of melodic and rhythmic designs. "How many features can you find?" (Repeated notes; repeated motifs; sequence; inversion.)

|| 1 3 | 3 5 | 4 2 | 2 . | 1 3 | 5 1 | 6 . | 5 . |

| 4 4 | 2 2 | 3 5 | 1 . | 3 2 | 1 7 | 2 . | 1 . ||

Observe song being studied. How many features are found in its design?

Song 17

Song 18

"The Mill Wheel"

Creative Activity

Composition With Words - Two Phrases

Syllabic settings in which regular rhythm patterns are suggested by poetic text

PROCEDURE

1. *Teacher writes poem on board isolating all syllables.*

   The mer- ry bells ring
   To wel- come the Spring. *Blake*

2. *Teacher recites poem with strong emphases on stressed syllables. All repeat.*

   The mér- ry bells ríng
   To wél- come the Spríng.

3. *Rhythm pulse-lines placed beneath syllables and bar-lines before each stressed syllable. Rhythm pattern emerges. Leave space between lines for melody.*

   ‖ The | mér- ry bells | ríng .
   To | wél- come the | Spríng. ‖

   Dot is placed at the end of each line to complete ternary measure structure.

4. *Teacher sounds* DO *(1 = G) All repeat recitation of poem. Students "think" of melody. (Possibility of using* Plagal Range.*)*

5. *Additional texts.*

   a) ‖ A | mán of | wórds and | nót of | déeds
   Is | líke a | gár- den | fúll of | wéeds. ‖ *Nursery Rhyme*

   b) ‖ Lit- tle | Jé- sus we shall | sée .
   And a- | dóre on bend- ed | knée. ‖ *Wm. Grynkiewicz*

Notation

Review Transcriptions With DO Clef on Second Line

1. *Transcribe pitch values only.* Intonation Ex. 21, Line 1, Column a

2. *Transcribe from numbers to staff*

3. *Transcribe from staff to numbers*

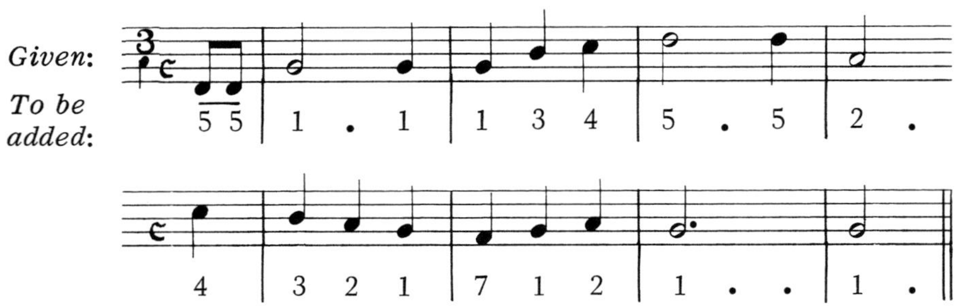

Songs

Ternary Rhythm - Triple Meter Beginning on Up-Pulse
Half-Pulses

Discover in songs: Dominant Triad 5 7 2

Repeated Motifs
Repeated Notes
Sequence
Inversion

Practise Songs With Rhythm Gesture III

MELODY No. 17 Johannes Brahms

1 = G (5̣ = D)

```
‖ 5̣ | 1  .  3 | 5  .  5̣ | 1  .  3 | 5  .
         3 | 1  .  3 | 5  .  3 | 2  .  . | .  .
  5 | 5  .  5 | 6  .  5 | 4  .  4 | 5  .
         4 | 3  .  1 | 4  .  3 | 2  .  . | .  .
  5 | 5  .  5 | 6  .  5 | 4  .  4 | 5  .
         4 | 3  .  1 | 4  .  3 | 2  .
         1 | 2  .  5̣ | 1  .  . | 1  .  ‖
```

IF I GET MY PICK OF THE THREE OF THEM English Folk Song

1 - G (5 = D)

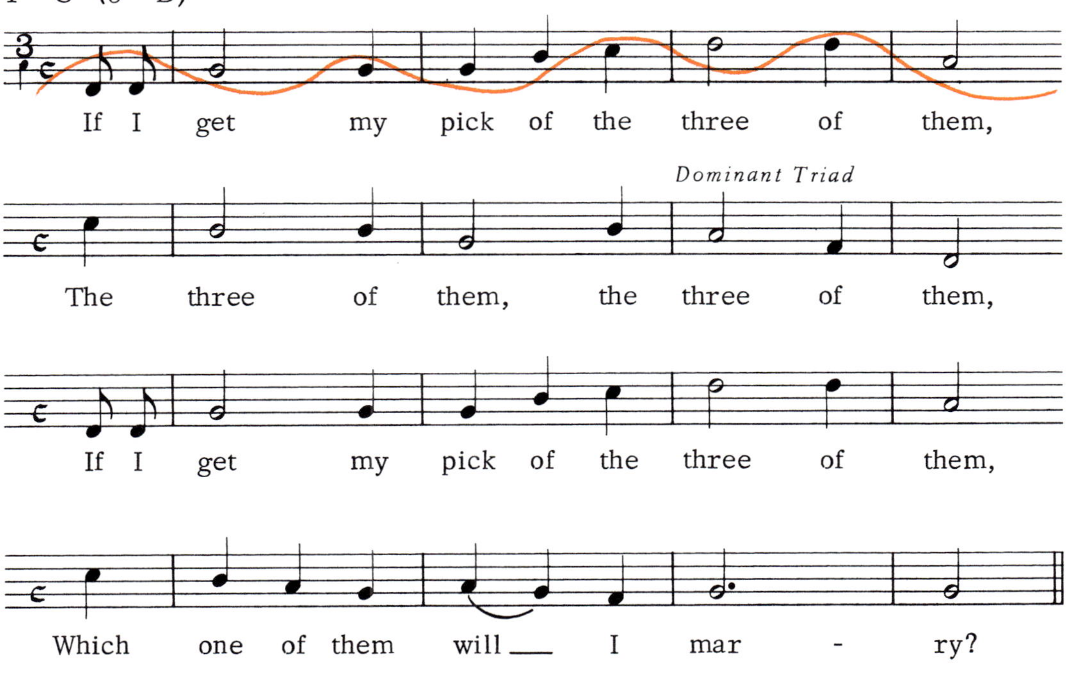

MELODY No. 18 "Intonation Song" TM

1 = G (5̣ = D)

‖ 1 | 1 3 5 | 5 3 1 | 7̣ 1 2 | 5̣ .

5 | 3 4 5 | 5 4 3 | 2 . . | . .

1 | 1 3 5 | 5 3 1 | 7̣ 1 2 | 5̣ .

5 | 5 4 3 | 4 3 2 | 1 . . | . . ‖

MELODY No. 19 "Maria zu Lieben" *German Melody*

1 = G (5̣ = D)

Repetitive Response

Sequence

THE MILL WHEEL English Folk Song

1 = G (5 = D)

‖ 1 | 3 2 1 | 3 2 1 | 3 2 1 | 2 .
The mill-wheel is turn- ing and turn- ing all day, ___

2 | 3 2 1 | 3 2 1 | 2 1 7̣ | 1 .
The mill- stones are grind- ing and grind- ing a- way. ___

1 | 3 4 5 | 5 4 3 | 2 3 4 | 4 3 2
They're grind- ing the flour for the bak- er to bake In- to

| 1 2 3 | 3 2 1 | 5 3 2 | 1 . ‖
new crus- ty bread and a fine yel- low cake. ___

O WHERE, O WHERE IS MY LITTLE DOG GONE? Dutch Folk Song

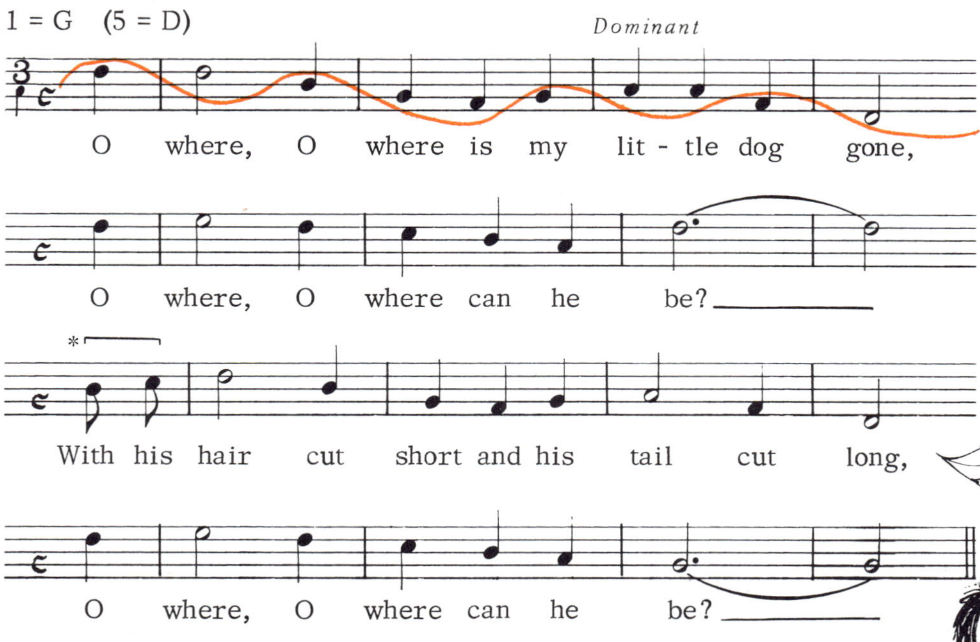

*See bottom of Page 58.

ALTHO' AT YULE IT BLOWETH COOL *Melody:* TM *Text:* G. P. Woodward

1 = G (5 = D)

1	5 .	5	5 .	1	2 . (Dominant)	7̣	5̣ .
Al-	tho'__	at	Yule__	it	blow-	eth	cool__
In	snow__	and	sleet__	we	pace__	the	street,_

5̣	1 .	1	2 ⌒ 3	4	3 . .	2 .
And	frost__	doth	grip__	the	fing-	ers__
Fair	Sirs,__	with	right__	good	rea-	son__

1	5 .	5	5 .	1	2 .	7̣	5̣ .
And	nip__	the	nose__	and	numb__	the	toes__
To	wish__	you	all,__	both	great__	and	small,_

5̣	2 ⌒ 3	4	3 .	2	1 . .	1 .
Of	out-	door	car-	ol	sing-	ers.__
The	bless-	ings	of__	the	sea-	son.__

Chapter Nine

Vocal Training

1 = G (5 = D)

Review Vocal Exercise 7 Sustained Vowels

Review Vocal Exercise 6a

Review Vocal Exercise 6b

Review Vocal Exercise 8a

Review Vocal Exercise 8b

Review Vocal Exercise 9c

Review Vocal Exercise 9b

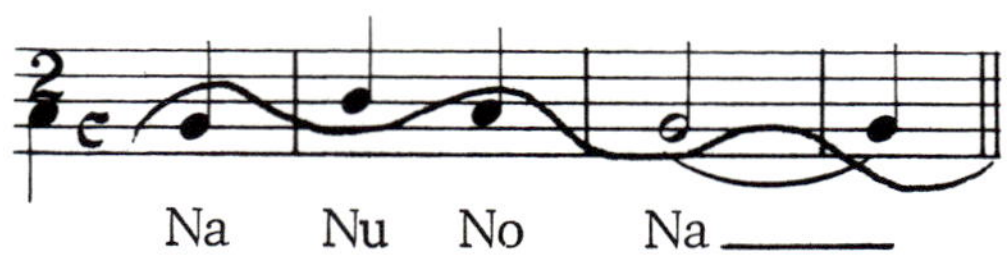

Intonation

Plagal Range: Tonic and Dominant Chords
Octave Interval 5̣ - 5 and 5 - 5̣

Intonation Exercise 24 - *with* Intonation Diagram 11 *and* Staff Diagram 11

5 5
4
3
2
1
7̣
6̣
5̣ 5̣

Int. Diagram 11

1 = G
(5 = D)

Free use of notes of Tonic and Dominant chords

a)

| 1 5̣ 5̣ 1 3 5 5 3 1 5̣ |
| 5̣ 1 *3* 5 5 *3* 1 5̣ |
| 5̣ *1* 3 5 5 3 *1* 5̣ |
| 5̣ *1* *3* 5 5 *3* *1* 5̣ 5̣ 1 |

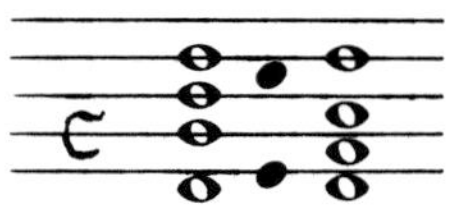

Staff Diagram 11

b)

| 1 5̣ 5̣ 7̣ 2 5 5 4 2 7̣ 5̣ |
| 5̣ *7̣* 2 5 5 4 2 *7̣* 5̣ |
| 5̣ 7̣ *2* 5 5 *4* *2* 7̣ 5̣ |
| 5̣ *7̣* *2* 5 5 *4* *2* *7̣* 5̣ 5̣ 1 |

Intonation Exercise 25 - *with* Staff Diagram 4

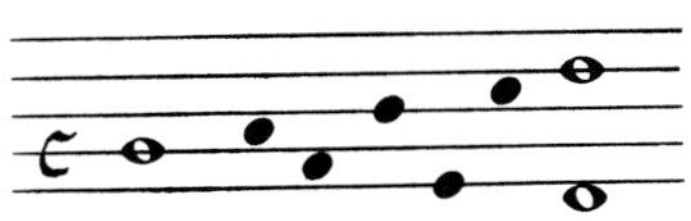

Staff Diagram 4

a)

| 1 5̣ 5 1 2 5̣ 5 2 3 5̣ 5 3 4 5̣ 5 4 3 5̣ 5 3 2 5̣ 5 2 1 5̣ 5 1 7̣ 5̣ 5 7̣ 1 |
| 1 5̣ 5 *1* 2 5̣ 5 *2* 3 5̣ 5 *3* 4 5̣ 5 *4* 3 5̣ 5 *3* 2 5̣ 5 *2* 1 5̣ 5 *1* 7̣ 5̣ 5 *7̣* 1 |
| 1 5̣ 5 2 5̣ 5 3 5̣ 5 4 5̣ 5 3 5̣ 5 2 5̣ 5 1 5̣ 5 7̣ 5̣ 5 1 |

b)

| 1 5 5̣ 1 2 5 5̣ 2 3 5 5̣ 3 4 5 5̣ 4 3 5 5̣ 3 2 5 5̣ 2 1 5 5̣ 1 7̣ 5 5̣ 7̣ 1 |
| 1 5 5̣ *1* 2 5 5̣ *2* 3 5 5̣ *3* 4 5 5̣ *4* 3 5 5̣ *3* 2 5 5̣ *2* 1 5 5̣ *1* 7̣ 5 5̣ *7̣* 1 |
| 1 5 5̣ 2 5 5̣ 3 5 5̣ 4 5 5̣ 3 5 5̣ 2 5 5̣ 1 5 5̣ 7̣ 5 5̣ 1 |

Rhythm

Single-Pulse (Quarter) Notes and Half-Pulse (Eighth) Notes in Triple Time Beginning on a Down-Pulse
Beating Time in 3

Rhythm Patterns Series 9

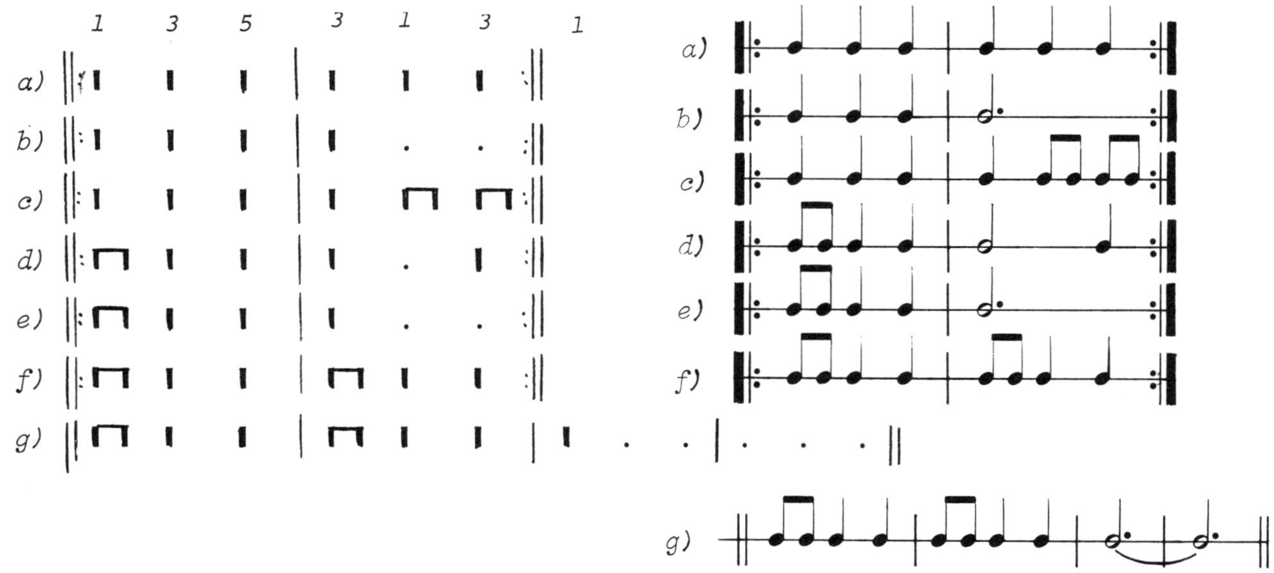

1) Sing each rhythm pattern with Metrical Gesture I *and* Metrical Language

2) Sing each rhythm pattern with Melodic Application indicated above
a) Repeated notes where necessary on tones given
b) Fill in passing tones between tones of tonic chord
c) Use Rhythm Gesture III.

Beating Time in 3 - Metrical Gesture III

Practise making gesture correctly:
hands separately
hands together

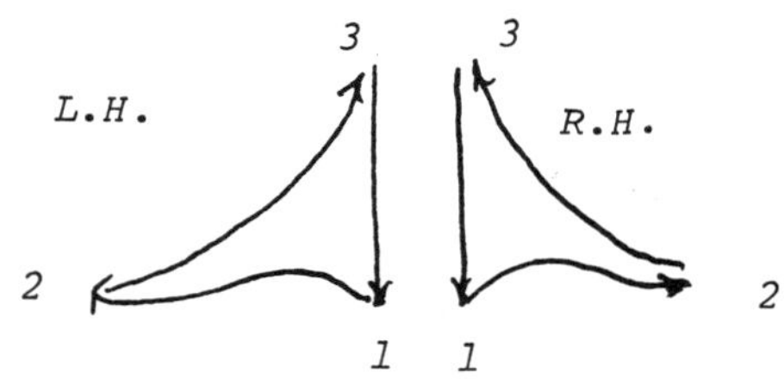

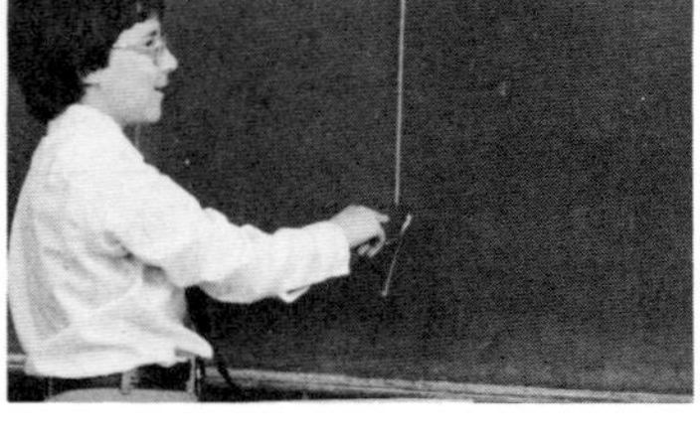

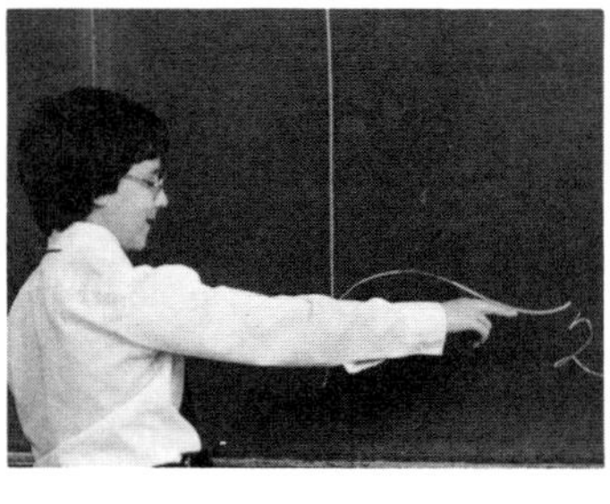

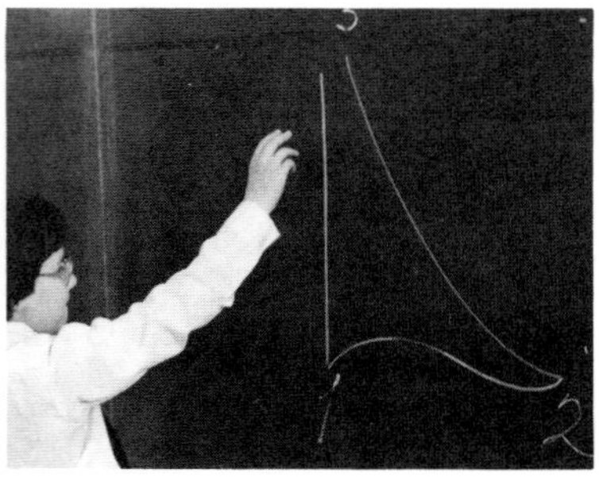

Repeat Rhythm Patterns with Metrical Gesture III

Sing the following melodies based on the Intonation Exercises while making the new Metrical Gesture.

a) ‖ 1 5 5 | 2 5 5 | 3 5 5 | 4 5 5 | 3 5 5 | 2 5 5 | 1 5 7 | 1 . . ‖

b) ‖ 1 5 1 | 2 5 2 | 3 2 1 | 5 . . | 5 4 3 | 2 . . | 5 3 2 | 1 . . ‖

c) ‖ 1 . 5 | 2 . 5 | 3 . 5 | 2 . . | 5 . 4 | 3 2 3 | 2 . . | 5 . . |

| 5 . 4 | 3 2 1 | 5 . 2 | 3 2 1 | 2 . 3 | 4 3 2 | 1 . . | . . . ‖

Aural Training in Rhythm - Step 5 Rhythmic Transformation of a Melody

PROCEDURE -"Guessing Game"

1. *Teacher places a two-line unbarred phrase on board*

3 2 1 7 6 5

5 6 7 1 2 3

2. *Without making a rhythmic gesture, the teacher sings one of the following rhythmed forms of the given phrase. Students must recognize the correct rhythm and repeat while making the appropriate gesture.*

a) ‖ 3 | 2 1 | 7 6 | 5 . | .
5 | 6 7 | 1 2 | 3 . | . ‖

b) ‖ 3 | 2 . 1 | 7 . 6 | 5 .
5 | 6 . 7 | 1 . 2 | 3 . ‖

c) ‖ 3 2 | 1 7 | 6 . | 5 . |
5 6 | 7 1 | 2 . | 3 . ‖

d) ‖ 3 . 2 | 1 . 7 | 6 . . | 5 . . |
5 . 6 | 7 . 1 | 2 . . | 3 . . ‖

3) *The following unbarred phrase may also be used:*

i̇ 7 6 5 4 3 3 4 5 6 7 i̇

A Second "Guessing Game"

1) *Teacher makes a rhythm gesture silently for one of the above rhythmed versions of the phrase. Students must guess which melody fits the gesture.*

Teacher:  *Student:* ‖ 3 2 | 1 7 | 6 . | 5 . ‖

Dictations

Eye and Ear Tests   Intonation Diagram 11 *in full view of class*

1 = G for all tests

1 5 5 1 3 5 5 1 | 1 5 5 3 5 1 1 5 | 5 5 5 3 1 3 5
1 5 5 7 2 7 5 1 | 1 5 5 4 2 7 5 1 | 5 5 5 7 2 7 5

1 2 5 5 5 2 3 | 1 5 5 5 3 4 2 7 1
1 5 5 2 5 5 3 5 5 | 1 5 5 5 6 7 5 5 1

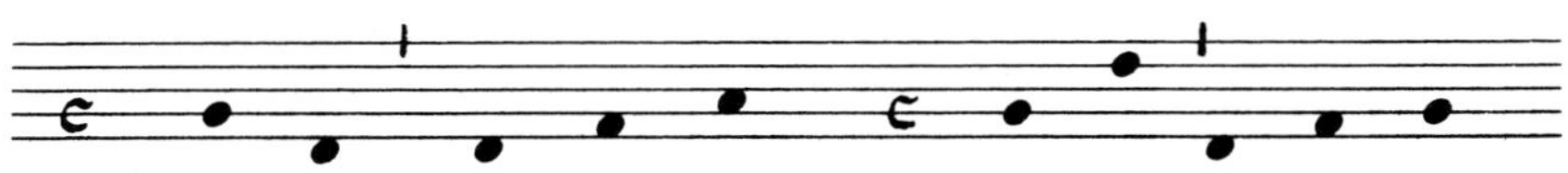

Rhythmic Dictations   *Rhythm Patterns in full view of class*
New Metrical Gesture III

(a + b) ‖ 1 5 5 | 2 5 5 | 3 2 1 | 5 . . ‖

(g + b) ‖ 5 5 1 1 | 7 1 2 5 | 3 2 1 | 5 . . ‖

(c + b) ‖ 1 1 7 6 | 5 5 6 7 1 | 2 2 5 | 1 . . ‖

(g) ‖ 1 2 3 1 | 2 3 4 2 | 1 . . | . . . ‖

Notation

Transcriptions
Interval Drills of Intonation Exercises on Staff
Visual Memory Tests

1. *Transcribe first line of* Intonation Exercise 25 *to staff*

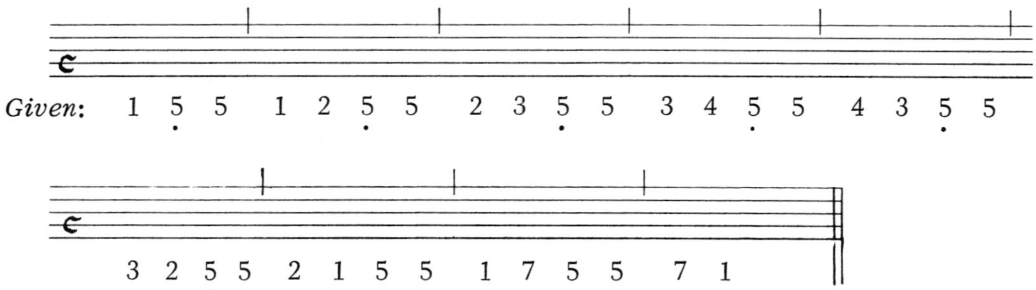

2. *Transcribe song "MORNING" to staff*

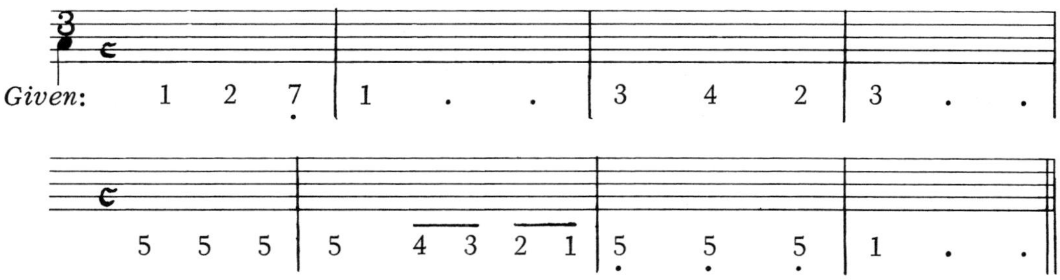

3. *Repeat each segment several times*

4. *Visual memory tests. Flash on screen or write on board and erase.*

Creative Activity

Melodic Application of Rhythm Patterns in Combination
Setting Texts in Ternary Rhythm (Triple Time)

1) *Improvise two-line melody for the rhythm patterns given*

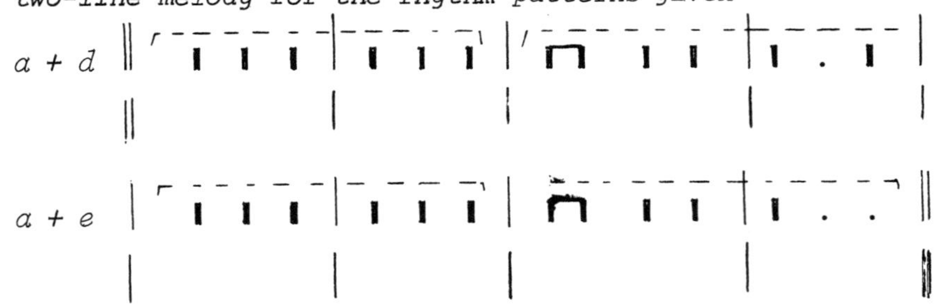

2) *Compose melody for each of the texts given.* Mode of DO; Plagal Range: Ternary Rhythm. *Review "Procedure" given in Chapter Eight.*

a) Shout the glad | tid- ings, ex- | ult- ing- ly | sing! ___
Born is the | Sav- ior, our | heav- en- ly | king. ___

b) Down in the | val- ley, the | val- ley so | low, ___
Hang your head | ov- er and | hear the wind | blow, ___

Songs

Discover Musical Techniques Studied Thus Far

Melody No. 20 — *Intervals of Intonation Exercise. Triple time beginning on down pulse. Conduct with Metrical Gesture III (Beat time).*

Melody No. 21 — *DO Clef on bottom line (review). Repetition of motifs. Arsis and Thesis in ternary rhythm.*

Morning — *Sequence. State-Response. Plagal Range. Half-pulses in ternary rhythm.*

Melody No. 22 — *Repetition. Inversion. Ternary rhythm beginning on down-pulse.*

O Dear What Can the Matter Be? — *Repetition. Sequence. Intervals of tonic chord line. DO Clef on bottom line.*

Holiest Night — *Intervals of Intonation Exercise 24. Sequence. Repetition. Half-pulses in ternary rhythm. Conduct with Metrical Gesture III.*

See preceding page for indications of correspondence between the songs and the matter of the chapter.

MELODY No. 20 TM

1 = G (5 = D)

|| 1 5 5 | 2 5 5 | 3 2 1 | 5 . . |

| 5 4 3 | 2 . . | 4 3 2 | 1 . . |

| 1 5 5 | 2 5 5 | 3 2 1 | 5 . . |

| 5 4 3 | 2 . 3 | 2 5 5 | 1 . . ||

MELODY No. 21 Bohemian Dance Tune

1 = E♭
(3 = G)

MORNING* Traditional

1 = G (5 = D)

|| 1 2 7 | 1 . . | 3 4 2 | 3 . . |
Morn - ing is come; ___ Night's passed a - way; ___

| 5 5 5 | 5 4 3 | 2 1 | 5 5 5 | 1 . . ||
Rise with the sun - rise ___ And ___ wel- come the day. ___

May be sung as a two-, three- or four-part round. The sign + indicates the place where the added voices begin.

MELODY No. 22 German Carol

1 = G (5 = D)

|| | 1 . 2 | 3 . 4 | 2 1 2 | 3 . 1 |

| 1 . 2 | 3 . 4 | 2 1 2 | 3 . 3 |

| 5 . 4 | 3 . 2 | 3 2 3 | 2 . . |

| 5 . 4 | 3 . 2 | 3 2 3 | 2 .

3 1 | 5 6 7 | 1 2 3 | 2 1 2 | 1 . . ||

OH DEAR, WHAT CAN THE MATTER BE? Traditional

1 = E♭ (5 = B♭)

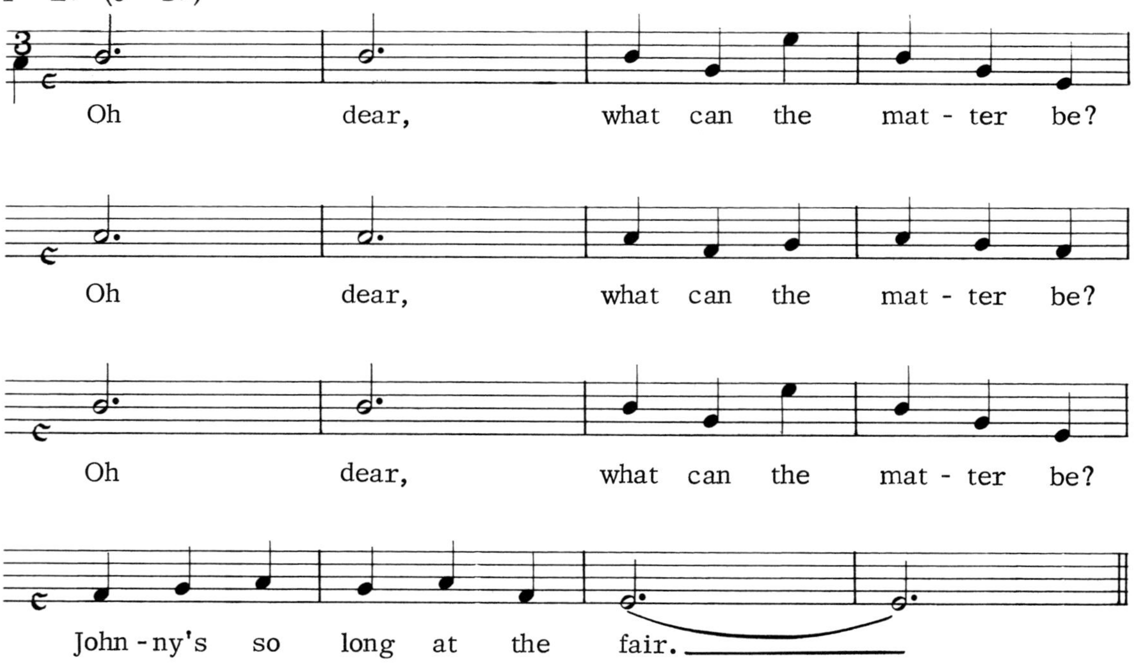

HOLIEST NIGHT *Melody:* German Carol *Text:* Edward Currie

1 = G (5 = D)

Chapter Ten

Vocal Training

Review Vocal Exercise 7 Sustained Vowels "u" "o" "a"

1 = G
(5 = D)

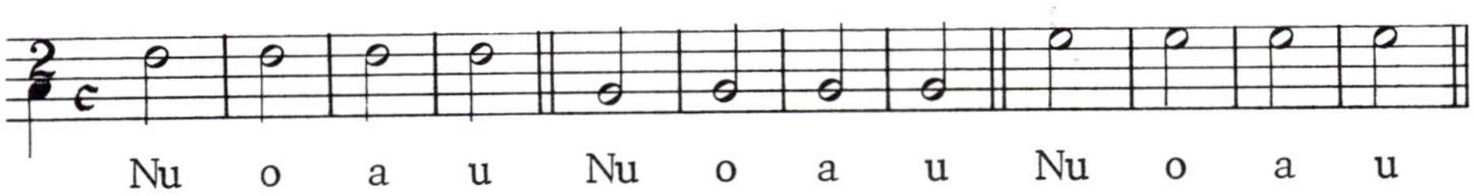

Review Vocal Exercise 11a Various Tones and Slurs on "u" "o" "a"

1 = G F A♭

Vocal Exercise 11b In Context of Mode of SOL

5 = G F A♭

Intonation

Discovery of Mode of Sol

Pentachord: 5 6 7 1̇ 2̇

Special Cadences

Intonation Exercise 26 *Discovery of* SOL *as Final (Tonic)*

1 = G
(5 D)

Sing column a) and pass immediately from Diagram 6 *to* Diagram 12 *to sing column b). Do same when passing from column a) to column c)*

Int. D. 6
6
5
4
3
2
1
7̣
6̣
5̣

a) With Intonation Diagram 6

| 1 3 5 5 3 1 5̣ |
| 1 2 3 4 5 5 4 3 2 1 7̣ 6̣ 5̣ |

Int. D. 12
5
4
3
2
1
7̣
6̣
5̣
4̣

b) With Intonation Diagram 12

| 5̣ 6̣ 7̣ 1 2 2 2 3 4 5 |
| 5 4 3 2 5 2 2 3 4 5 2 5 |
| 2 1 7̣ 6̣ 5̣ 4̣ 5̣ |

c) With Intonation Diagram 12

| 5̣ 5̣ 7̣ 2 2 1 7̣ 6̣ 5̣ |
| 5̣ 7̣ 2 2 5 5 4 3 2 5̣ |
| 5̣ 6̣ 5̣ 4̣ 5̣ |

Intonation Exercise 27 *With* Intonation Diagram 13

Drills on Pentachord range SOL as Final of the mode

1̇ = C (5 = G)

Int. D. 13
2̇
1̇
7
6
5

5 6 7 1̇ 2̇	1̇ 5 6 7 1̇ 5
5 6 7 1̇ 2̇	1̇ 6 7 5
5 6 7 1̇ 2̇	1̇ 6 7 5
5 7 2̇	1̇ 6 7 5
5 7	1̇ 6 5
5 7 6 1̇	1̇ 2̇ 7 1̇ 6 5

Intonation Exercise 28 - *With* Intonation Diagram 4 *and* Staff Diagram 14

2̇	
	1̇
7	
	6
5	
	4

Int. D. 14

1̇ = C (5 = G)

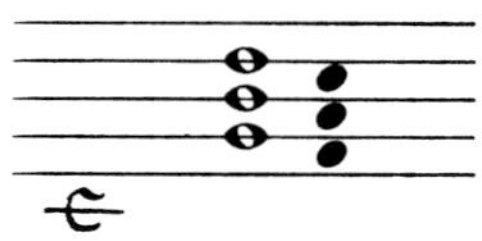

Staff Diagram 14

Prep. 1̇ 7 6 5

a)

| 5 1̇ 7 1̇ 2̇ | 1̇ 5 6 5 4 |

| 5 *1̇* 7 *1̇* 2̇ | 1̇ *5* 6 *5* 4 5 |

b)

| 2̇ 1̇ 7 1̇ 5 | 4 5 6 5 1̇ |

| 2̇ *1̇* 7 *1̇* 5 | 4 *5* 6 *5* 1̇ 5 |

Eye and Ear Tests *With suggested diagram in full view of class*

Intonation Diagram 6 - *1 = G*
1 3 5 5 3 1 5̣ 1 | 1 2 3 4 5 1 7̣ 6̣ 5̣
5 3 1 5̣ 5̣ 6̣ 7̣ 1 | 5 4 3 2 1 5̣ 1 3 5

Intonation Diagram 12 - *1 = G*
1 2 7̣ 6̣ 5̣ 5̣ 1 | 5̣ 6̣ 5̣ 4̣ 5̣
5̣ 7̣ 2 2 5̣ | 5 4 3 2 5̣ 6̣ 6̣ 5̣

Intonation Diagram 13 - *1̇ = C*
5 7 2̇ 1̇ 6 7 5 | 1̇ 2̇ 7 1̇ 6 5
5 6 7 1̇ 1̇ 2̇ 7 6 5 | 5 7 6 5 5 7 2̇

Intonation Diagram 14 - *1̇ = C*
5 7 2̇ 1̇ 5 6 5 4 5 | 4 6 1̇ 5 6 5
2̇ 1̇ 7 1̇ 5 6 5 | 5 7 2̇ 1̇ 6 4 5

Visual Memory Tests *Study each line. Teacher erases line from board and invites student to sing line from memory.*

|| 1̇ 2̇ | 1̇ . | 5 6 | 5 4 | 5 . ||

|| 5 2̇ | 2̇ . | 5 6 | 4 5 | 5 . ||

Rhythm

Presenting Free Rhythm: Irregular Combinations of Binary and Ternary Rhythms

1. *Practise conducting the following phrases with A T T T gesture. Repeated notes serve to identify rhythm groups.*

   a) *Binary rhythms:* ‖ A: 5 5 | T: 3 3 | T: 2 2 | T: 1 . ‖

   b) *Ternary rhythms:* ‖ A: 5 5 5 | T: 3 3 3 | T: 2 2 2 | T: 1 . . ‖

   c) *Mixed rhythms:* ‖ A: 5 5 | T: 3 3 | T: 2 2 2 | T: 1 . ‖

   ‖ A: 5 5 5 | T: 3 3 3 | T: 2 2 | T: 1 . ‖

   ‖ A: 5 5 | T: 3 3 3 | T: 2 2 | T: 1 . ‖

   ‖ A: 5 5 5 | T: 3 3 | T: 2 2 2 | T: 1 . ‖

2. *Study pitch values of melodies given and sing with appropriate Arsis-Thesis gesture*

1 = G   a) ‖ 1 $\underset{\cdot}{5}$ | $\underset{\cdot}{5}$. | 1 2 3 | 5 . | 5 4 3 | 2 . . | 1 $\underset{\cdot}{5}$ | 1 . ‖

1 = G   b) ‖ 1 2 | (3) 5 | 5 . | 5 4 3 | 2 1 2 | 1 . ‖

$\dot{1}$ = C   c) ‖ 5 6 $\dot{1}$ | ($\dot{1}$) $\dot{2}$ | $\dot{2}$. ‖

$\dot{1}$ = C   d) ‖ 5 6 5 | 4 . | 5 . ‖
A- men. ———

$\dot{1}$ = C   e) ‖ 5 $\dot{2}$ $\dot{2}$ | $\dot{1}$. | $\dot{2}$ $\dot{1}$ 6 | ($\dot{1}$) $\dot{2}$ | $\dot{2}$. ‖
Al- le- lu- ia.

Rhythmic Dictations

1. *Teacher: "I am going to conduct four rhythms silently. See if you can guess which of the four rhythms is binary and which is ternary."*

"Here is another set of four rhythms. Guess again which are binary and which ternary."

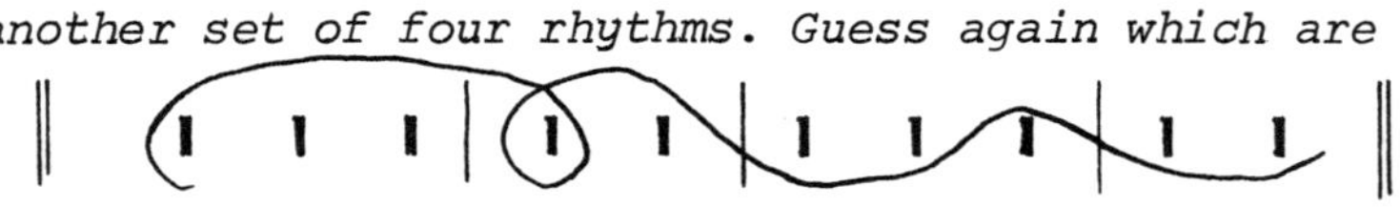

"I shall give two more examples. Then I am going to ask someone else to give us a silent rhythm test to see if we can guess the correct rhythms."

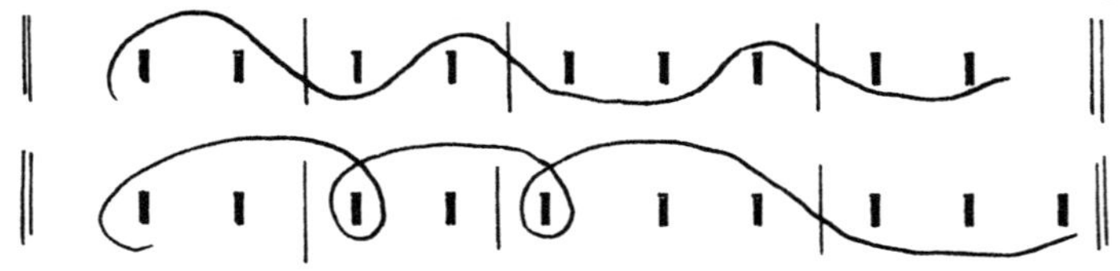

2. *Teacher: "Now I'm going to sing a melody and conduct it at the same time. I shall ask someone to come to the board to write down the melody; someone else to add the correct measure bars; and then someone to add the Arsis-Thesis wave."*

a) 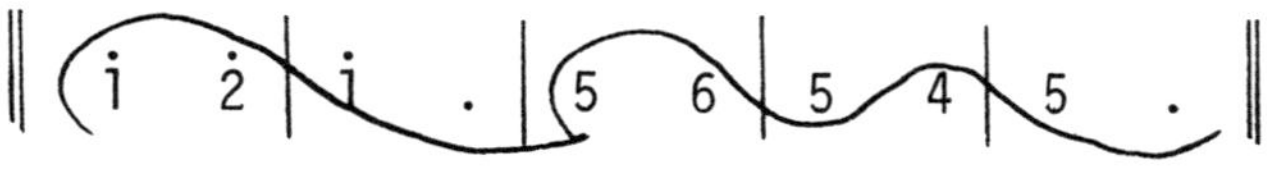

b) 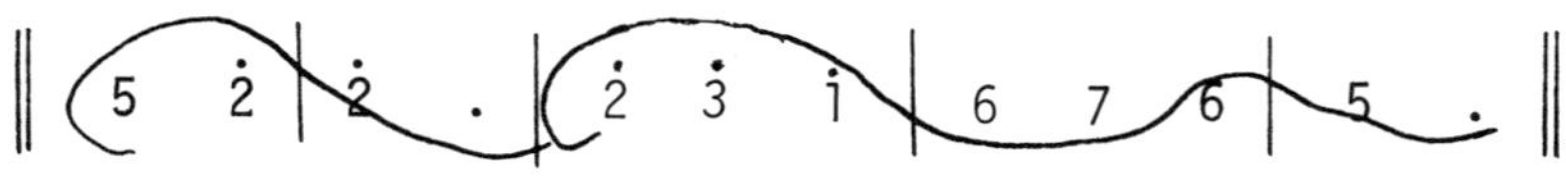

c) 

d) 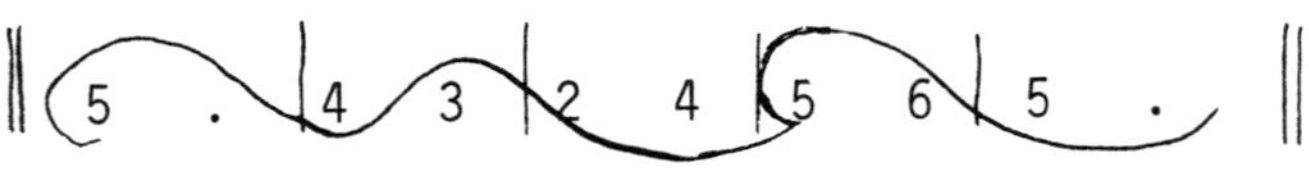

Notation

Transcriptions: DO Clef Ledger Line Below Staff
Sight-Singing Drills
Visual Memory Drills

1) *Transcribe from numbers to staff*

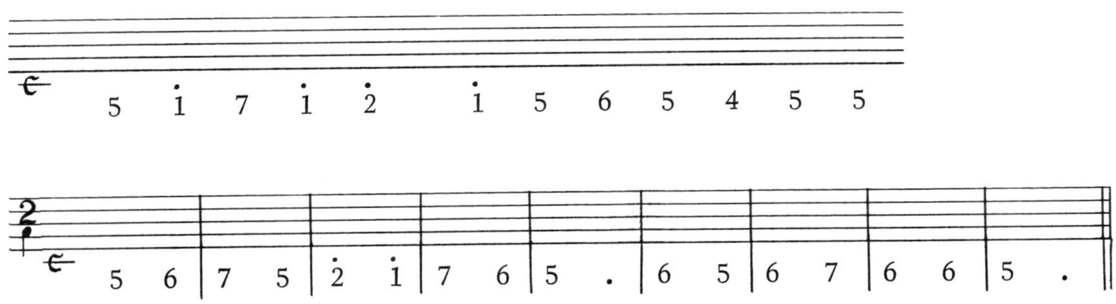

2) *Repeat each segment several times*

1̇ = C
(5 = G)

3) *Visual memory tests. Flash on screen or write on board and erase.*

1̇ = C
(5 = G)

1 = G

1̇ = C

Creative Activity

Discovering Possibility of Rhythmic Enlargement for Changing Binary to Ternary Rhythm

PROCEDURE

1) *Compose tune in Mode of DO, or SOL, for the following text in binary rhythm:*

|| Shé who's | fáir- est | ín my | síght . |
| I'll pre- | sént for | yóur de- | líght. || *Anon.*

2) *Lengthen the note for each accented syllable and rhythm becomes ternary*

|| Shé— who's | fáir- est | ín — my | síght — |
| I'll — pre- | sént — for | yóur — de- | líght. — ||

3) *Repeat procedure for each of the following texts:*

a) Lórd, we thánk thee fór the líght,
Sún- ny dáy and stár- ry níght;
Fór our pár- ents ánd our fríends
Ánd for áll thy mér- cy sénds. *N.H. Dole*

b) Áll the wín- ter trées are báre;
Nót a gréen leaf án- y- whére;
Wínds from í- cy ré- gions blów;
Dówn the híll- side drífts the snów. *N.H. Dole*

Songs

MELODY No. 23 Basque Folk Melody

1 = G (5 = D)

Refrain

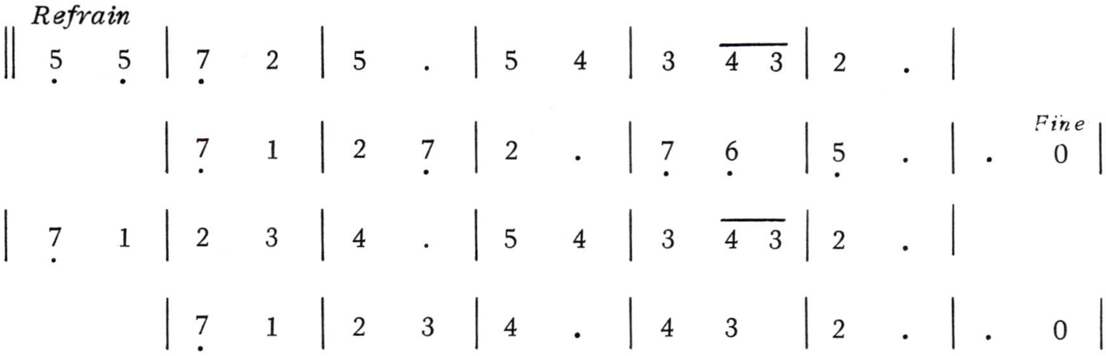

Repeat Refrain

Int. Diagram 12
Phrase repetitions
Half-pulses in binary rhythm
M. G. II

ACCLAMATION: FOR THE KINGDOM From "Order of Mass" TM

i = C (5 = G)

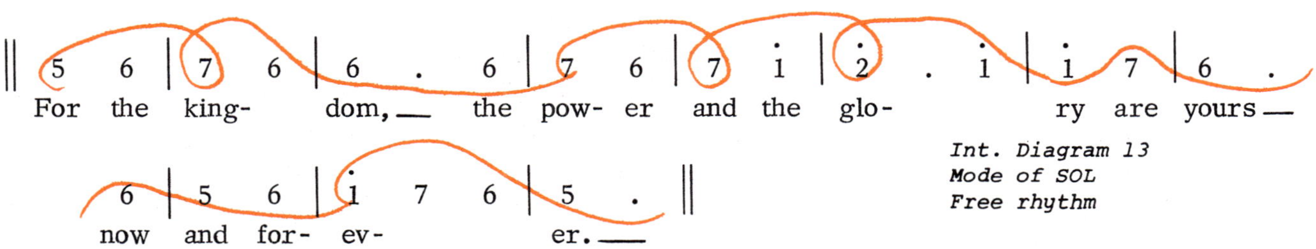

Int. Diagram 13
Mode of SOL
Free rhythm

KYRIE XII Gregorian Chant

i = C (5 = G)

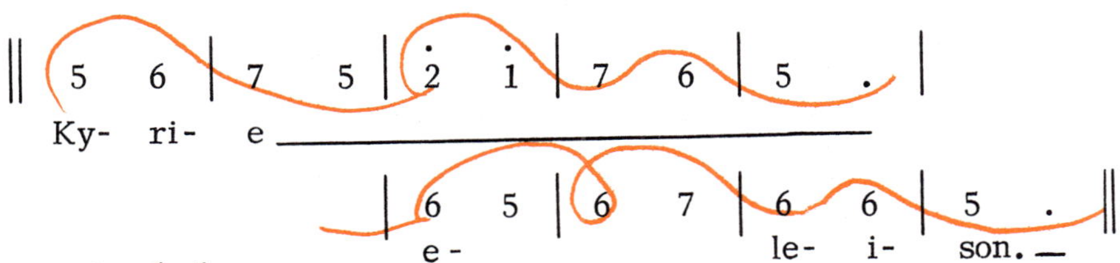

Trans.-Lord, have mercy.

Int. Diagram 13
Mode of SOL
Binary rhythm

SPRINGS OF WATER, BLESS THE LORD TM

i = C (5 = G)

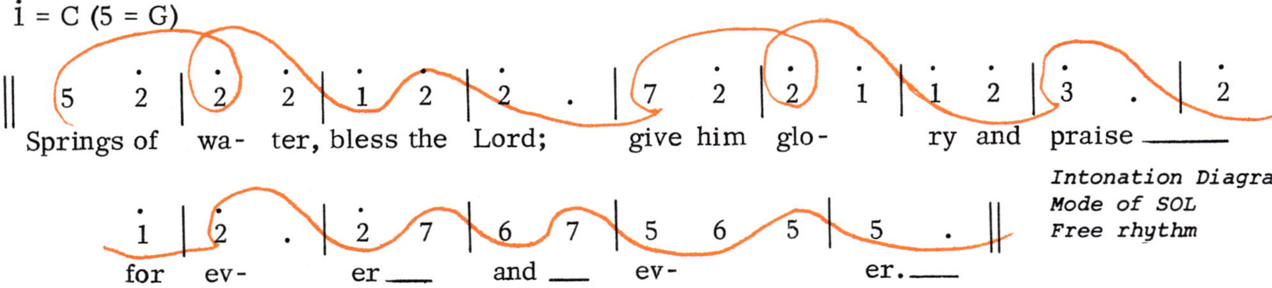

Intonation Diagram 14
Mode of SOL
Free rhythm

AGNUS DEI XVIII *Gregorian Chant*

Intonation Diagram 14, P. 98.
Mode of Sol
Free Rhythm - notice
ternary group in Line 2

i̇ = C (5 = G)

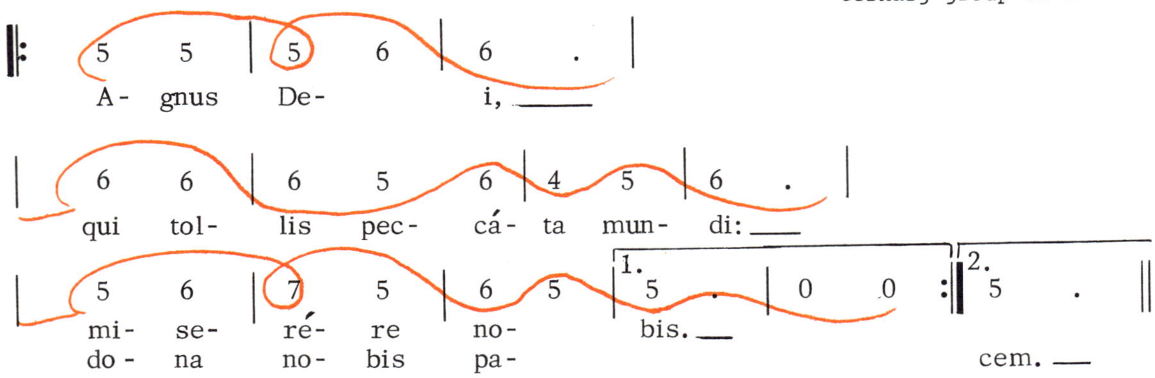

Trans. - *Lamb of God, you take away the sins of the world: have mercy on us: grant us peace.*

GOOD MORNING Basque Folk Song

Prepare with Staff
Diagram 14
Mode of SOL
R.G. II

i̇ = C (5 = G)

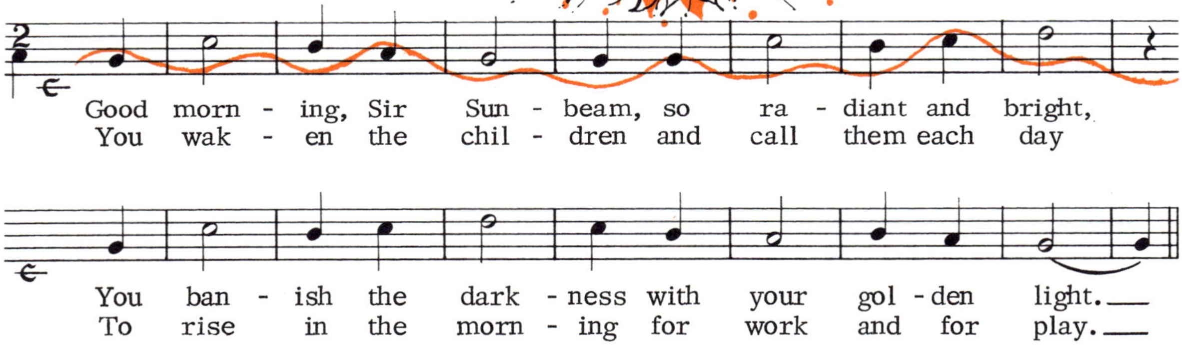

TURNING French Folk Song

Mode of SOL
St. D. 14
R. G. III

i̇ = C (5 = G)

Chapter Eleven

Vocal Training

New Vowels: "e" and "i" ("eh" and "ee")

Vocal Exercise 12a

1 = B♭ — D — G

1 ———————————————
Nu ——— o ——— a ——— e ——— i ———
(Noo ——— oh ——— ah ——— eh ——— ee)

(Pronounced according to pure Latin vowels)

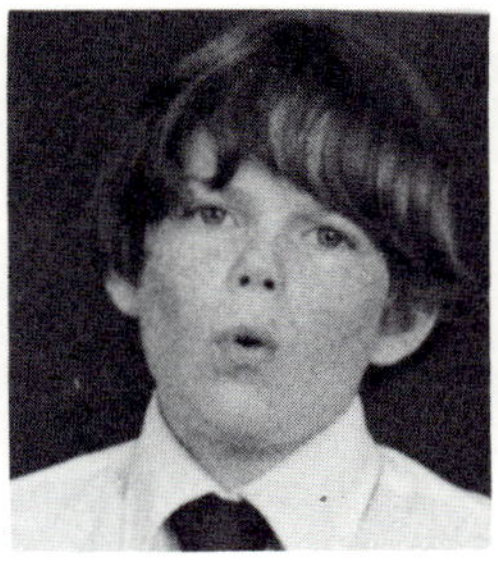
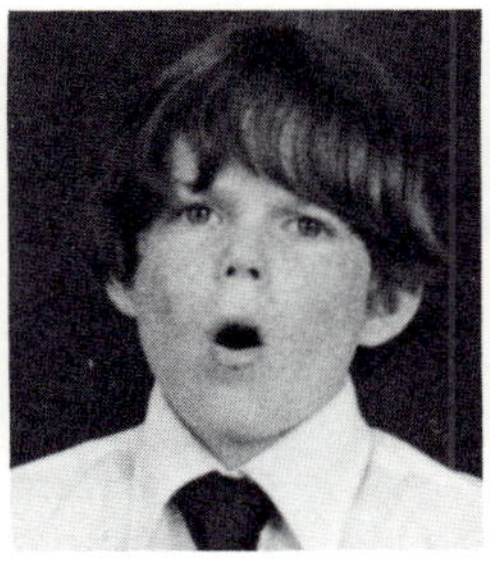
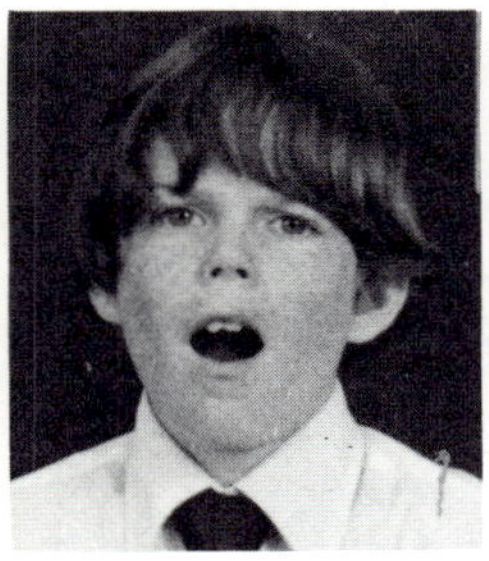

Vocal Exercise 13a

1 = G — Bb — F

Vocal Exercise 13b

1 = G — Bb — F

Intonation

The Mode of SOL: Authentic Range 5̣ - 5 Mode VII

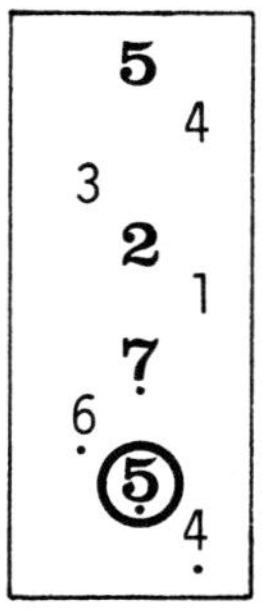

Int. Diagram 12

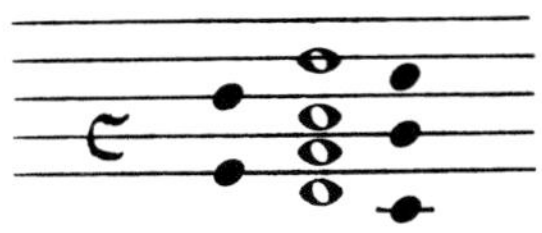

Staff Diagram 12

1 = G (5 = D)

<u>Intonation Exercise 29</u> - *With* Intonation Diagram 12 *and* Staff Diagram 12

| 5̣ 1 7̣ 1 2 3 2   1 2 4 3 2 1 2   2 7̣ 1 6̣ 5̣ |
| 5̣ 1 7̣ 1 2 3 2   2 1 6̣ 1 7̣ 6̣ 5̣   7̣ 1 6̣ 5̣ |
| 2 7̣ 1 3 4 2 2   2 7̣ 1 2 1 6̣ 5̣   6̣ 7̣ 6̣ 5̣ |
| 5̣ 5̣ 7̣ 1 2 3 2   1 3 4 3 2   7̣ 1 2 1 6̣ 5̣ |

Characteristic melodic phrases of the Mode of SOL

<u>Intonation Exercise 30</u> - *With* Intonation Diagram 12 *and* Staff Diagram 12

a)

| 5̣ 7̣ 2   2 1 6̣ 1 7̣ 6̣ 5̣ |
| 5̣ 7̣ 2   2   2 3 4 2 2 |
| 5̣   2   2 3 2 4 3 2   7̣ |
| 1 2 1 6̣ 5̣   6̣ 7̣ 6̣ 5̣   5̣ |

b)

| 5̣ 6̣ 1 1 2 2   1 2 3 4 5 4 3 2 |
| 2 1 6̣ 7̣ 6̣ 5̣   6̣ 5̣ 4̣ 5̣ 6̣ 5̣ |
| 1 7̣ 6̣ 1 2 2   2 1 6̣ 7̣ 6̣ 5̣ |
| 5̣ 2 1 6̣ 7̣ 5̣   5̣ 2 2 4 2 1 6̣ 7̣ 5̣ |

GREEN GAVEL English Folk Song

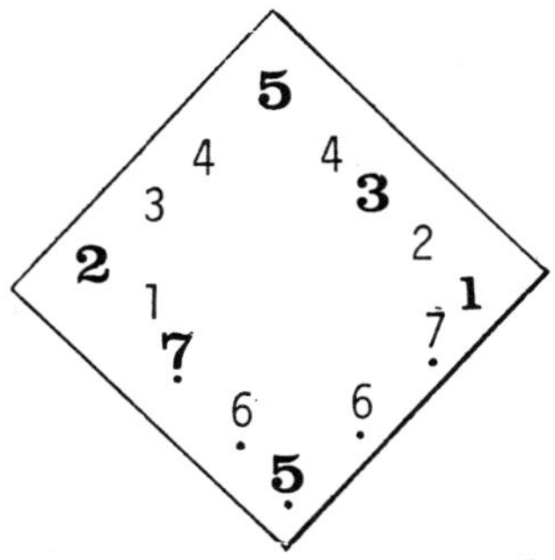

Intonation Diagram 15

1 = G
(5 = 2) *Contrasting 2 7 5 with 5 3 1*

‖ 2 | 7 5 2 | 7 5 6 7 | 1 7 6 | 5 .

5 | 3 1 5 | 3 1 2 3 | 4 3 2 | 1 .

2 1 | 7 1 2 | 7 5 6 7 | 1 7 6 | 5 . ‖

Ear and Eye Tests *1 = G (5 = D)*

"Which family does each one of the following phrases belong to - SOL or DO?"
Teacher sings each phrase on syllable NU while making appropriate rhythm gesture.

a) ‖ 1 5 | 5 . | 1 2 3 | 5 . . | 5 4 3 | 2 . . | 1 5 | 1 . . ‖

b) ‖ 1 2 | 3 4 | 5 . | 5 4 3 | 2 1 2 | 1 . ‖

c) ‖ 1 2 1 | 7 6 | 5 . | 4 5 6 | 5 . ‖

d) ‖ 5 4 3 | 2 . 1 | 2 7 5 | 6 5 | 5 . ‖

With Intonation Diagram 12 *or* Staff Diagram 12 *in view of class*

| 5 6 7 1 2   2 1 2 7 5 | 5 7 1 2 3   3 2 2
| 5 4 3 2   1 2 7 5 | 5 6 5 4 5   5 2

Use also segments of Intonation Exercises 29 *and* 30

With Intonation Diagram 15 *in full view of class*

| 2 7 5   6 7 1 5   5 3 1 | 2 3 4 5 1   1 3 5
| 5 6 7 1 2   3 4 2   2 5 | 2 1 7 1 2   2 5   5 5

Rhythm

Study of Free Rhythm *continued*
Beginning on Up-Pulse
Aural Training - Step 6

1. *Beginning on Down-Pulse. Practise Arsis-Thesis gesture silently before singing phrase.*

1 = G *a)* || 5 4 3 | 2 3 4 | 5 2 | 5 . ||

1 = B♭ *b)* || 1 6 1 | 6 5 4 | 5 6 | 5 . ||

1 = B♭ *c)* || 5 6 | 5 . | 4 5 | 6 | 5 . . | 6 5 4 | 5 . . | 4 6 | 5 . ||

2. *Beginning on Up-Pulse*

1 - B♭

a) || 0 6 | 6 5 | 1 7 | 6 5 | 6 7 | 6 . ||

b) || 0 2 | 1 2 | 7 1 | 6 5 | 4 5 | 5 . |

c) || 0 1 | 1 1 | 1 7 | 6 7 | 6 . | 5 . ||

Rhythmic Dictation

1 = G *a)* || 5 | 1 1 | 3 3 | 5 5 | 3 3 | 4 2 | 1 7 | 1 . | . ||

b) || 0 5 | 1 2 | 3 4 | 5 . | 3 5 | 4 3 2 | 1 . ||

1 = B♭ *c)* || 5 7 | 2 . | 2 1 | 7 1 | 2 3 3 | 2 . . ||

d) || 2 | 7 5 2 | 7 5 67 | 1 7 6 | 5 . ||

Also use lines from songs studied

Aural Training in Rhythm - Step 6 Discovering Rhythm of Unbarred Songs

PROCEDURE - "Guessing Game"

1. *Teacher writes one of the following melodies on board. Bar-lines are omitted.*

2. *Children study melody and sing it. They discover correct rhythm by placing bar-lines as follows:*
   Before last note of each line;
   Before each long note;
   In relation to melodic motifs.

French Folk Song

1 = D *a)*
1 . 1 5 . 5 5 . 5 6 . 4 5 . 5 6 . 6 5 0
1 . 1 5 . 5 5 . 5 6 . 4 5 . 5 6 . 6 5 0
5 . 5 $\dot{1}$. 5 5 . 4 3 . 2 3 . 3 3 . 5 5 . 4 3 . 2
1 . 3 5 . . . . . 6 . 4 2 . $\underset{\cdot}{7}$ 1 . . . . . .

1 = G *b)* *Air 1592*
1 5 5 6 6 5 3 5 3 5 . 3 . .
5 4 4 3 1 5 5 3 1 2 . 1 . .

1 = G *c)* *German Carol*
1 1 . 1 3 . 4 5 . 6 5 .
5 1 . 1 3 . 4 5 . 6 5 . .
5 . 6 5 . 4 3 . 3 1 . .
2 . 2 3 . 2 1 . 2 3 . .
$\underset{\cdot}{6}$. $\underset{\cdot}{6}$ $\underset{\cdot}{7}$. $\underset{\cdot}{7}$ 1 . . 5 . .
3 . 4 2 . 2 1 . . . .

d)

1 = G

Notation

DO Clef on Second Line in Context of
Mode of SOL 5 - 5

1) Transcriptions. *Solutions given are intended only as a guide to the teacher*

a) From numbers to staff

b) From staff to numbers.

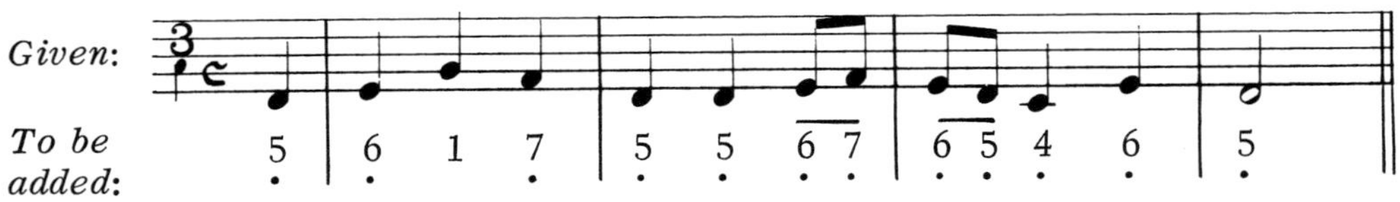

2) Sight-singing phrases. *Repeat each several times.*

1 = G or B♭

3) Visual memory tests
Write on board and erase or flash momentarily on screen. Students repeat from memory.

1 = G or B♭

Creative Activity

Changing Rhythm Design of Text by Adding Notes to Selected Syllables of the Text

PROCEDURE

1. *Teacher writes on board two lines of a poem separating syllables, marking tonic accents and adding measure bars.*

|| Áll the | wín- ter | lóng the | trées are | báre, . |

| Nót a | gréen leaf | flút- ters | án- y- | whére. . ||

N. H. Dole

2. *Students recite lines together and discover binary rhythm.*

3. *Mode of SOL selected in* 5̣ - 5 *range. Students compose a melody for the text.*

4. *Sing note names; repeat melody with words and appropriate gesture.*

(Melody shown is only a suggestion)

|| All the | win- ter | long the | trees are | bare, |
|| 5̣ 2 | 2 7̣ | 1 2 | 3 1 | 2 . |

| Not a | green leaf | flut- ters | an- y- | where. ||
| 2 3 | 2 7̣ | 1 6̣ | 4̣ 5̣ | 5̣ . ||

5. *Change rhythm of second and fourth measures by adding notes to syllables, that is, "filling-in" skips in the melody.*

|| 5̣ 2 | 2 1 7̣ | 1 2 | 3 2 1 | 2 . |

| 2 3 | 2 1 7̣ | 1 6 | 4̣ 5̣ 6̣ | 5̣ . ||

6. *Sing new melodic design with appropriate gesture.*

ADDITIONAL TEXTS FOR SIMILAR TREATMENT

1. || He | práy- eth | bést who | lóv- eth | bést

All | thíngs both | gréat and | smáll. . | . || *Samuel Taylor Coleridge*

2. He is ris-en! He is ris- en!
Tell it out with joy-ful voice:
He has burst his three days' pris- on
Let the whole wide world re- joice. *C. F. Alexander*

> When an attractive melody is composed by someone alone or by several students working together, it should be sung by all every day for a few days. This will be source of great encouragement to all to strive for excellence in their creative efforts.

Songs

Staff Diagram 6
Repetition of motifs
Half-pulses in duple time
Mode of DO ending on SOL
Metrical Gesture II

SOME LOVE COFFEE, SOME LOVE TEA Appalachian Folk Song

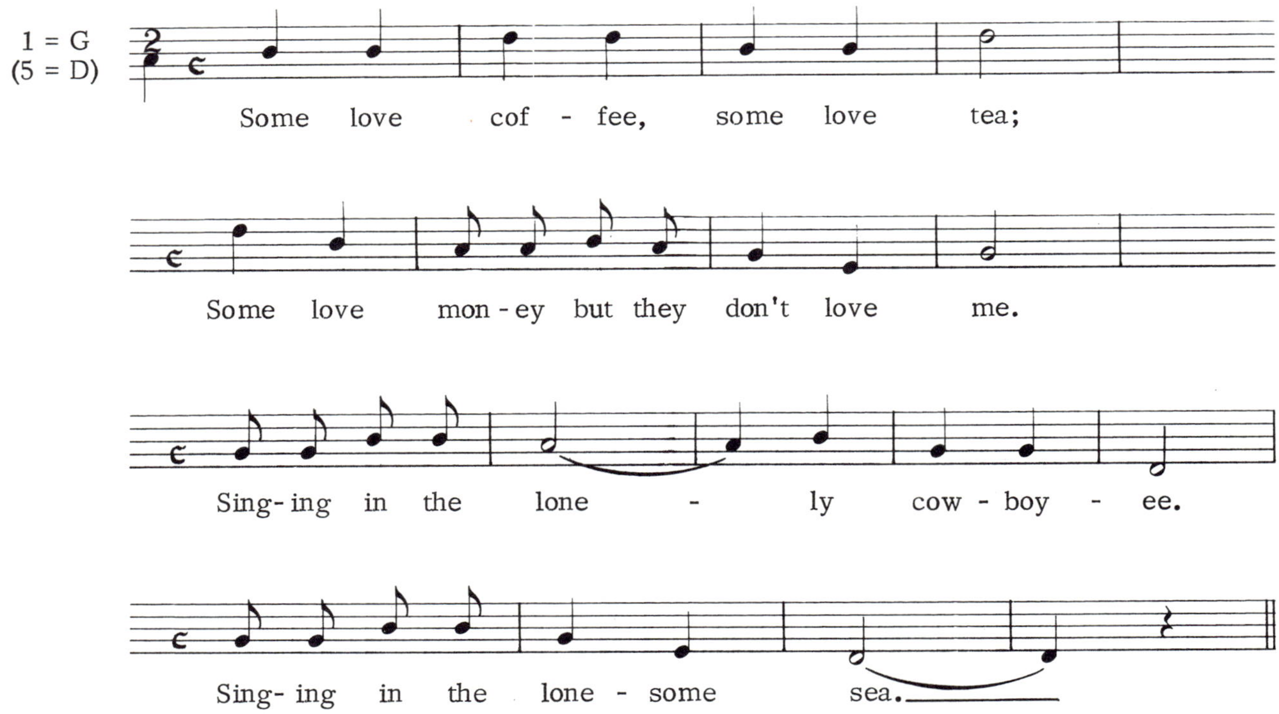

THE MASS IS ENDED Dismissal Response at Mass

1 = G ($\underset{\cdot}{5}$ = D)

|| 0 1 | 1 1 | 1 $\underset{\cdot}{7}$ | $\underset{\cdot}{6}$ $\underset{\cdot}{7}$ | $\underset{\cdot}{6}$. | $\underset{\cdot}{5}$. ||

The Mass is end-ed go in peace.______

|| 1 $\underset{\cdot}{7}$ | $\underset{\cdot}{6}$ $\underset{\cdot}{7}$ | $\underset{\cdot}{6}$. | $\underset{\cdot}{5}$. ||

Thanks_ be to God.________

NOW WITH THE FAST DEPARTING LIGHT *Melody:* Gregorian Chant
Text: "Te Lucis" Trans. anon.

Mode of SOL Authentic Range
R. G. IV Free Rhythm
Int. D. 12

1 = C (5 = G)

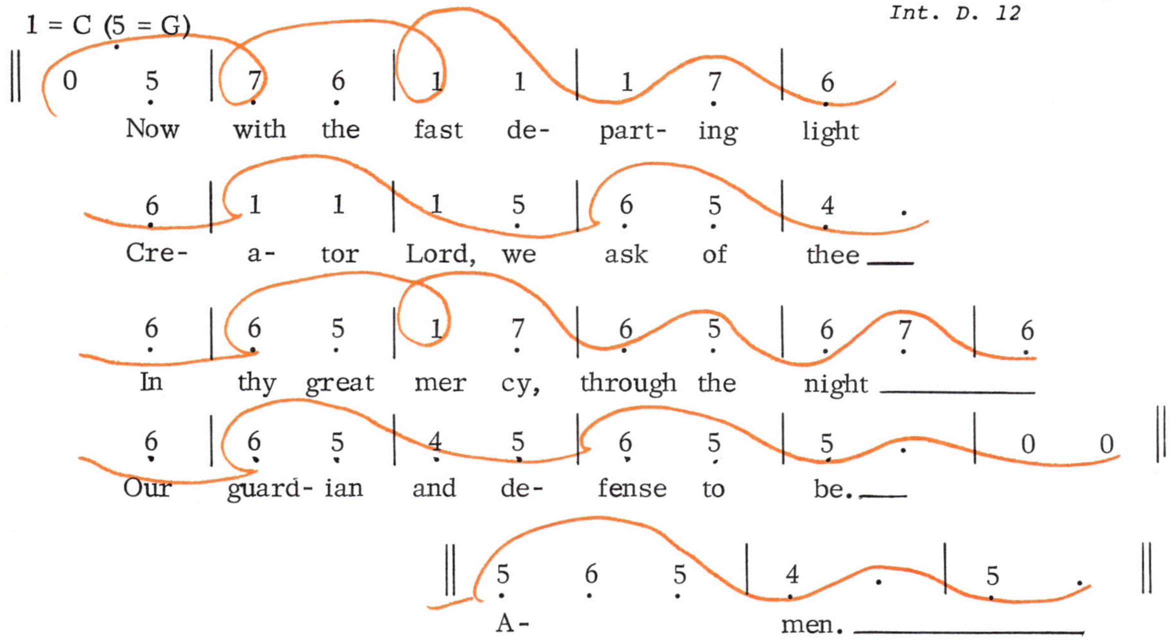

TO THEE WHO MAKEST ALL "Drumcondra" *Irish Hymn*

St. D. 12
Mode of SOL
R. G. II

1 = G
(5 = D)

MELODY No. 24 *Melody:* Gregorian Chant *Text:* "Ecce Panis Angelorum"
by St. Thomas Aquinas Trans. anon.

1 = A (5 = E)

Mode of SOL
Int. D. 12
Free Rhythm
Ternary Rhythms
at end of
Lines 1 and 3

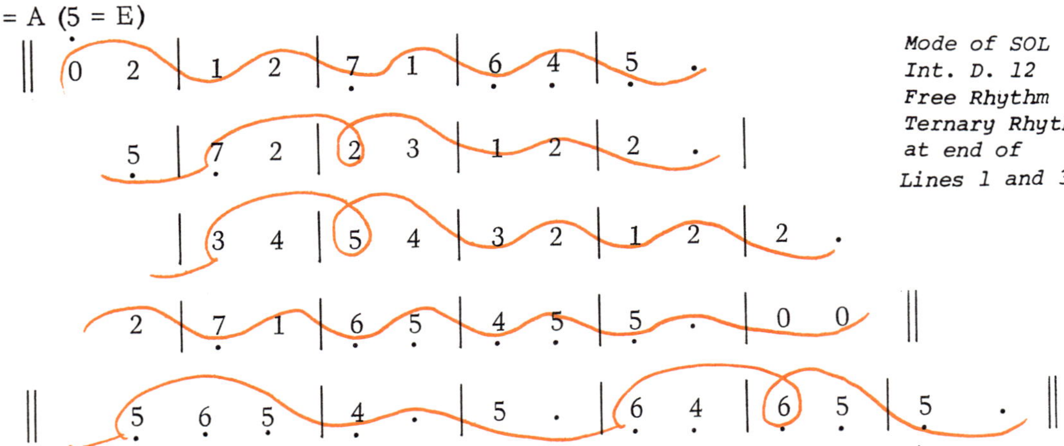

BE THOU A LIGHT *Melody:* Gregorian Chant *Text:* "Lumen ad Revelationem Gentium"
Translation anon.

Mode of SOL Int. D. 12
R. G. IV

1 = C (5 = G or F)

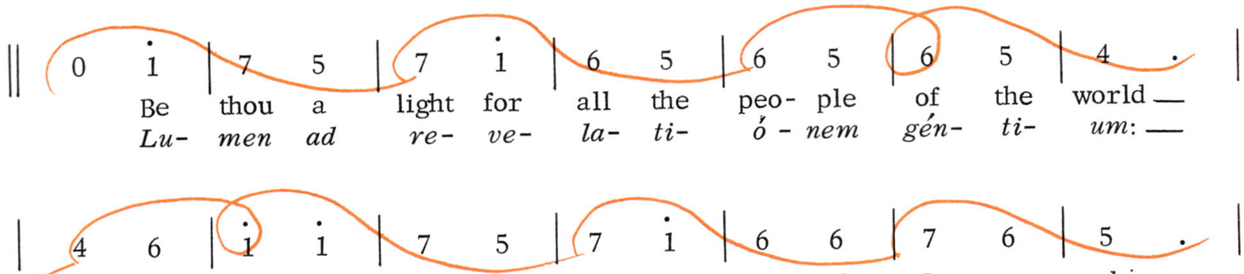

ALLELUIA Gregorian Chant

Int. D. 12
R.G. IV Binary
Mode of SOL

1 = C (2 = D)

Tr. Praise God!

Chapter Twelve

Vocal Training

Study of Latin Vowels u - o - a - e - i Continued

Review Vocal Exercise 12a *Insist on correct shape of lips and position of tongue for each vowel*

1 = Bb ∕ D ∖ F

|| 1 ——————
Nu ——— o ——— a ——— e ——— i
(Noo ——— oh ——— ah ——— eh ——— ee ||

Vocal Exercise 14a *Sing slowly in an even tempo with* Metrical Gesture I. *Use this exercise and the one below after* Plagal Range *of* Mode of SOL *has been presented*

i̇ = C (5 = G)

Vocal Exercise 14b *With* Rhythm Gesture II

i̇ = C (5 = G)

Intonation

Mode of SOL - Plagal Range 2 - $\dot{2}$ Mode VIII

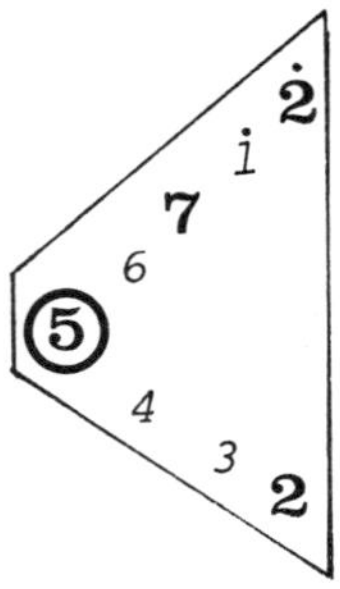

Intonation and Staff Diagrams 16

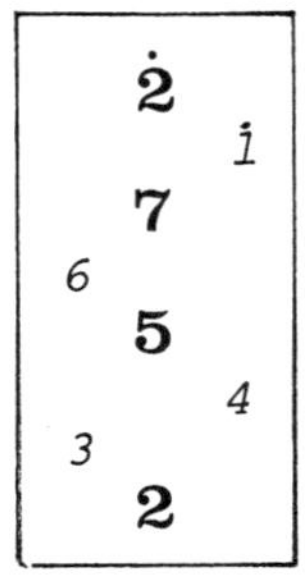

Intonation and Staff Diagrams 17

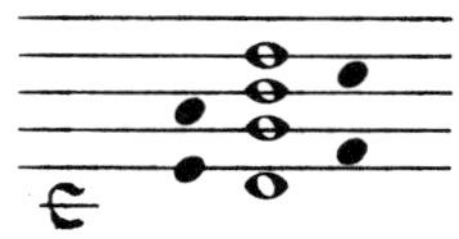

$\dot{1}$ = *C* (5 = *G*)

Intonation Exercise 31 - *With* Diagrams 16 *and* 17

a) ⟶ b) ⟶

| 5 6 7 $\dot{1}$ $\dot{2}$ $\dot{2}$ $\dot{1}$ 7 6 5 | 5 4 3 2 2 3 4 5 |

| 5 *6* 7 *$\dot{1}$* $\dot{2}$ $\dot{2}$ *$\dot{1}$* 7 *6* 5 | 5 6 5 4 3 4 5 |

| 5 7 $\dot{2}$ $\dot{2}$ 7 5 | 5 6 6 5 4 5 5 |

c) ⟶

Pentachord and Tetrachord combined

Intonation Exercise 32 - *With* Diagrams 16 *and* 17

a) ⟶ b) ⟶

| 5 6 $\dot{1}$ $\dot{2}$ $\dot{1}$ *5* 6 $\dot{1}$ 5 | 5 4 3 2 2 3 4 5 5 6 5 |

| 5 6 $\dot{1}$ 7 $\dot{1}$ 6 7 *$\dot{1}$* 5 | 5 *4* *3* 2 2 *3* *4* 5 5 6 5 |

| 5 2 5 6 5 |

| 5 4 *3* 2 5 6 5 |

| 5 4 *5* 6 5 |

<u>Ear and Eye Tests</u> $\dot{1}$ = C for all tests
(5 = G)

1. With Diagrams 16 and/or 17 in full view of class

| 5 7 $\dot{2}$ $\dot{2}$ 7 5 5 4 3 2 | 5 2 2 2 3 4 5 6 5 | 3 2 5 4 6 5 |
| 5 6 5 4 3 2 3 4 5 | 2 5 5 5 4 3 2 3 4 5 | 2 3 2 5 6 5 2 |

| 5 6 $\dot{1}$ 7 $\dot{1}$ 6 7 $\dot{1}$ 5 | 5 2 5 7 $\dot{2}$ $\dot{2}$ 5 |
| 5 $\dot{2}$ $\dot{2}$ $\dot{2}$ $\dot{1}$ 7 $\dot{1}$ 2 | $\dot{2}$ 7 $\dot{2}$ 7 5 2 5 |

2. "To which family, SOL or DO, does each of the following phrases belong?" Teacher sings phrase on syllable NU. Students listen for clue as to which is the correct mode of the melody. Principal clues are the Final and the chord-line tones.

a) ‖ 5 7 | $\dot{2}$. | $\dot{2}$ 7 | 5 . | 5 4 | 3 4 | 5 . | 5 . ‖ (SOL)
b) ‖ 5 6 | 5 . | 5 $\dot{1}$ | 5 . | 5 3 | 1 3 | 5 . | 5 . ‖ (DO)
c) ‖ 5 6 | 5 3 | 2 3 4 | 5 . ‖ (SOL)
d) ‖ 5 6 | 5 3 | 2 4 | 3 2 | 1 . ‖ (DO)

3. Visual Memory Tests. Line by line: LOOK! Turn back to board and sing from memory.

a) ‖ $\dot{1}$ $\dot{2}$ | $\dot{1}$. | 5 6 | 5 4 | 5 . ‖

b) ‖ 5 $\dot{2}$ | $\dot{2}$. | 5 6 | 4 5 | 5 . ‖

c) ‖ 5 . | 4 3 | 2 4 | 5 6 | 5 . ‖

d) ‖ 5 6 | 5 3 | 2 1 2 | 1 . ‖

Rhythm

Study of Free Rhythm Continued
Aural Training in Rhythm - Step 7:
Discover Rhythm of Song by Listening
Dictations

1. *Study Arsis - Thesis silently for each line before singing*

$\dot{1}$ = C (5 = G)

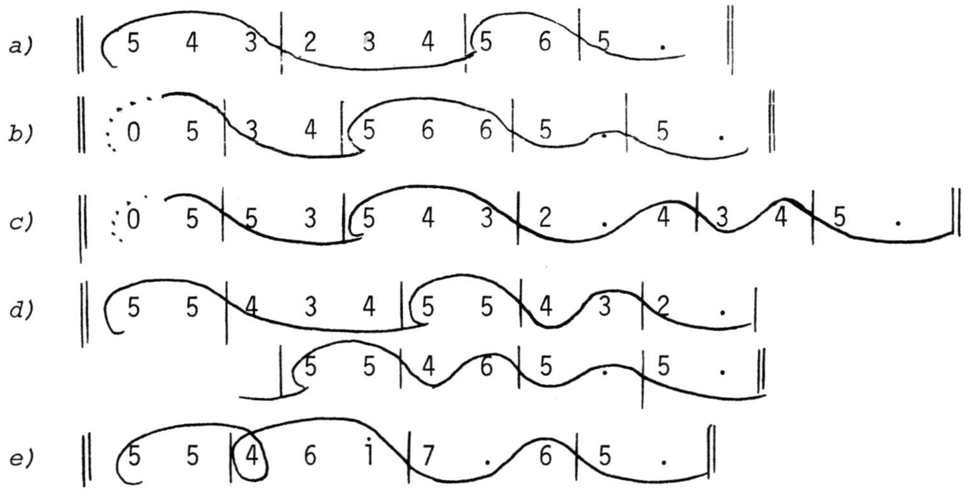

2. Aural Training in Rhythm - Step 7: Discover Rhythm of Song by Listening

Teacher sings familiar song without making rhythmic or metrical gesture
Students listen and repeat song with appropriate gesture
Songs already studied for these tests might include

Chapter Two: AUTUMN LEAVES
Chapter Three: WHEN CHRIST WAS BORN
Chapter Five: THE CIRCUS
Chapter Seven: O WHERE, O WHERE IS MY LITTLE DOG GONE?
etc.

3. Rhythmic Dictations

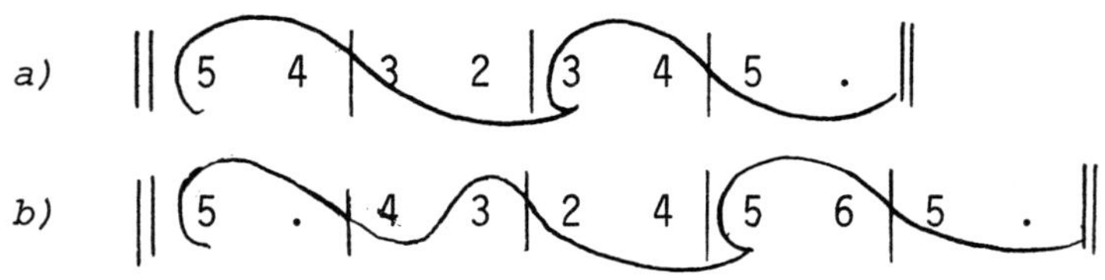

Use lines from songs of this chapter

Notation

Tonic SOL in Three Positions of DO Clef

Transcriptions
Sight-Singing Drills

1. *Transcriptions.* *Exercise for each position of DO Clef.*

a)

Given:

b)

Given:

c)

Given:

2. *Sight-singing Drills.* *Repeat each segment several times.*

i = C
(5 = G)

3. *Visual Memory Tests.*

a)

b)

c)

d)

Creative Activity

Composing in the Mode of SOL

1. *Compose responses for each of the following melodic statements. Responses should follow rhythmic patterns of the statements. Each each response on SOL as shown. A suggested solution is given in italics.*

$\dot{1}$ = C (5 = G)

a) ‖ 5 4 | 2 3 4 | 5 6 5 | 4 5 | 5 . |
| *5 $\dot{2}$ | $\dot{1}$ 7 6 | 7 6 5 | 6 4* | 5 . ‖

b) ‖ 5 5 | 5 . | 3 2 | 5 6 | 5 . |
| *2 2 | 2 . | 2 4 | 3 2* | 5 . ‖

c) ‖ 5 5 | 6 5 | 7 $\dot{1}$ | $\dot{2}$ $\dot{3}$ | $\dot{2}$. |
| *$\dot{2}$ $\dot{2}$ | $\dot{1}$ 7 | 6 5 | 4 5* | 5 . ‖

2. *Compose complimentary melodies for missing lines*
A suggested solution is given in italics

‖ $\overline{5\ 6}$ | 5 7 $\dot{1}$ | $\dot{2}$. $\overline{\dot{1}\ 7}$ | 6 . . | 7 .
($\overline{5\ 6}$ | 5 4 3 | 2 3 4 | 2 . . | . .)
$\overline{5\ 6}$ | 5 7 $\dot{1}$ | $\dot{2}$. $\overline{\dot{1}\ 7}$ | 6 . . | 7 .
($\overline{5\ 6}$ | 5 4 3 | 2 3 4 | 5 . . | . .) ‖

3. *Compose a melody for each of the following texts*

a) ‖ Praise the | Lord in his | ho- ly | place. ‖ — *Psalm 150*

b) ‖ To | Fa- ther, | Son and | Ho- ly | Ghost — *Anonymous Doxology*
All | praise be | ev- er | more. | ‖

c) Who has seen the wind?
Neither you nor I:
But when the trees bow down their heads,
The wind is passing by.

Christina Rosetti

Songs

Mode of SOL Plagal Range - Intonation Diagram 17 - Rhythm Gestures III and IV

MELODY No. 25 Anonymous

$\dot{1}$ = C (5 = G)

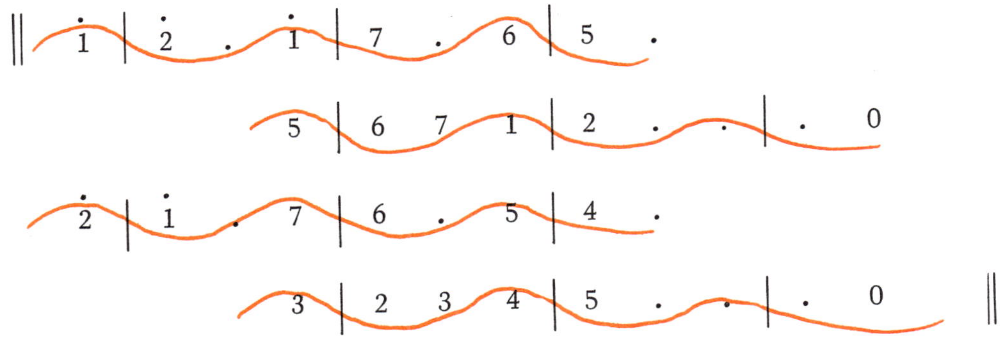

O SWEET LADY *Melody:* 13th Century *Text:* "Notre Dame, toute belle"
Translation anonymous

$\dot{1}$ = C (5 = G)

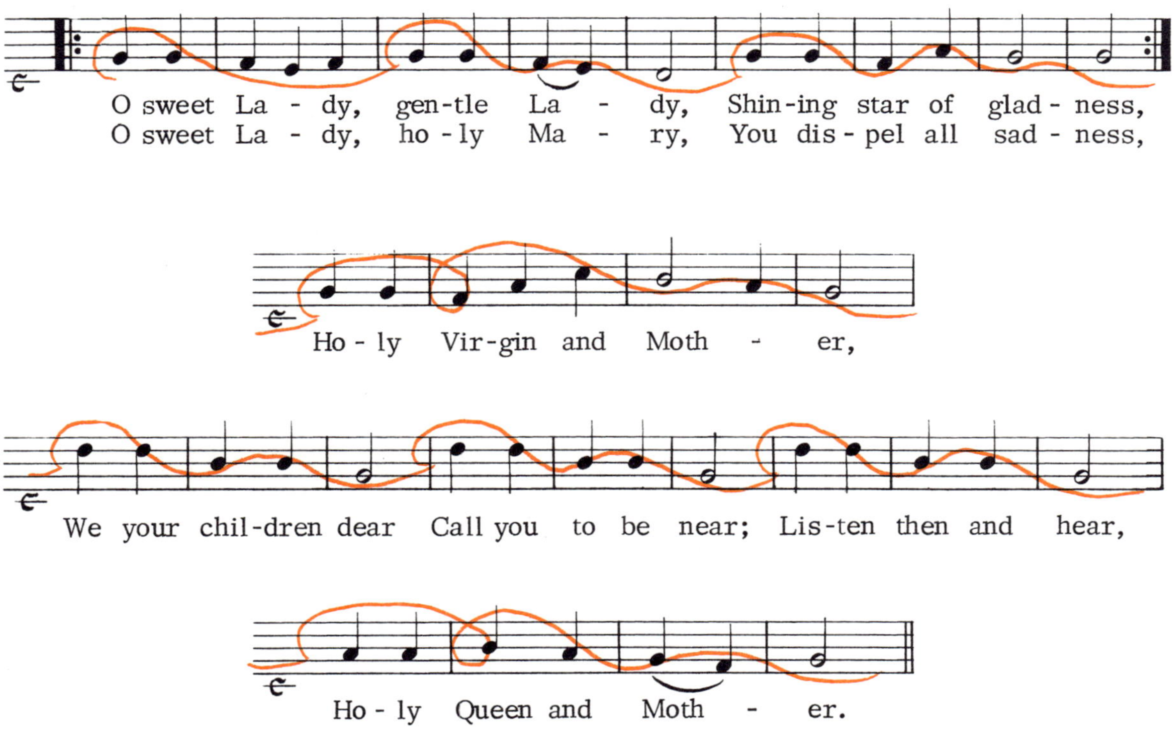

SING WITH JOY TO THE LORD TM

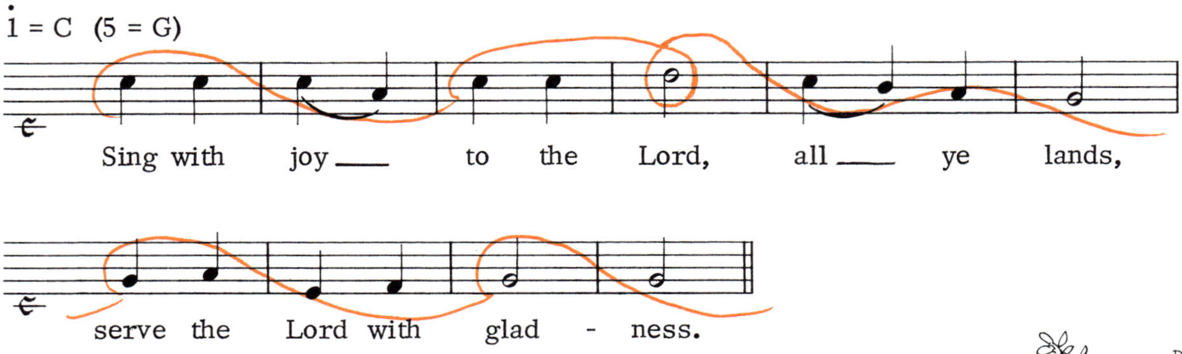

OUR FATHER From "Order of Mass" TM

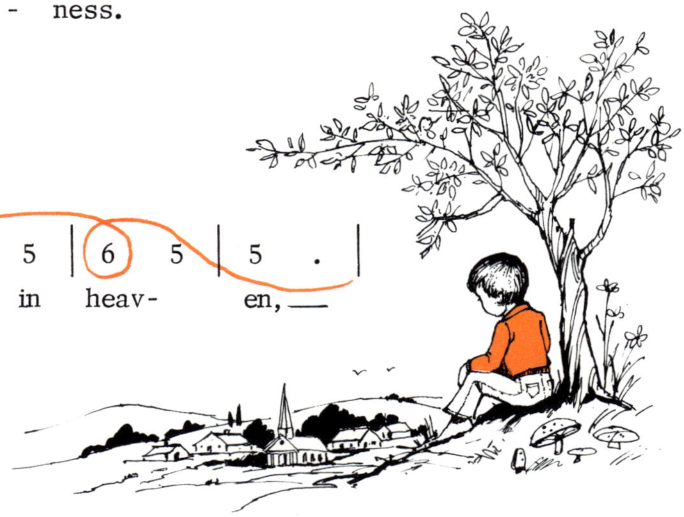

5 = G

‖ 0 5 | 5 . | 5 . 5 | 4 5 | 6 5 | 5 . |
Our Fa- ther, who art in heav- en, ___

| 5 5 | 4 5 | 6 .
hal-lowed be thy name: ___

5 | 5 5 | 6 .
thy king-dom come; ___

5 | 5 5 | 5 5 | 6 . | 6 6 | 3 4 | 5 . | 5 . ‖
thy will be done on earth ___ as it is in heav- en. ___

| 0 5 | 5 5 | 5 5 | 4 3 | 2 . |
Give us this day our dai- ly bread, ___

| 4 3 4 | 5 5 5 | 6 5 | 5 .
and ___ for- give us our tres-pass- es ___

5 | 4 5 | 6 5 | 6 6 | 6 3 4 | 5 . | 5 . ‖
as we for- give ___ those who tres-pass a- gainst ___ us. ___

| 0 5 | 5 5 | 5 5 | 4 3 | 2 . | 2 . |
And lead us not in to temp- ta- tion ___

| 4 3 4 | 5 5 | 4 5 | 6 5 | 5 . ‖
but ___ de- liv - er us from e- vil. ___

KYRIE ELEISON XII Gregorian Chant

1̇ = C (5 = G) (2̇ = D)

|| 5 6 | 7 5 | 2̇ 1̇ | 7 6 | 5 . | 6 5 | 6 7 | 6 6 | 5 . | 0 0 ||
Ký- ri- e ________ e- lé- i- son.__

|| 5 6 | 7 5 | 2̇ 1̇ | 7 6 | 5 . | 6 5 | 6 7 | 6 6 | 5 . ||
Ký- ri- e ________ e- lé- i- son._

|| 0 5 | 5 3 | 5 4 3 | 2 . 4 | 3 4 | 5 . ||
Chri- ste ________ e- lé- i- son.__

|| 0 5 | 5 3 | 5 4 3 | 2 . 4 | 3 4 | 5 . | 0 0 ||
Chri- ste ________ e- lé- i- son.__

|| 5 6 | 7 5 | 2̇ 1̇ | 7 6 | 5 . | 6 5 | 6 7 | 6 6 | 5 . | 0 0 ||
Ký- ri- e ________ e- lé- i- son.__

|| 5 6 | 7 5 | 2̇ 1̇ | 7 6 | 5 . 3 | 5 4 3 | 2 . 4 | 3 4 | 5 . ||
Ký- ri- e ________ e- lé- i- son.__

Lord, have mercy. Christ, have mercy.

MEMORIAL ACCLAMATION: CHRIST HAS DIED From "Order of Mass" TM

RESUME OF CHAPTERS 1-12

VOCAL TRAINING

Long tone, scale and chord-line drills on Latin vowels u, o, a, e, i, (oo, oh, ah, eh, ee) in Modes of DO and SOL, Authentic and Plagal Ranges

Slurs and vowel combinations in upper and lower ranges

INTONATION

Review of DO Mode, Authentic Range with Compass Exercises 1, 2, 3, 4

Discovering Plagal Range and range above Authentic Range of DO Mode

Discovering Dominant Chord line

Discovering Mode of SOL, Authentic and Plagal Ranges

Eye and Ear Tests for all exercises

RHYTHM

Review Rhythm Gestures I, II, III, IV (Arsis - Thesis) Binary and Ternary groupings; up-pulse and down-pulse beginnings.

Review Metrical Gesture I

Drills with Metrical Gesture II

Half-pulse notes

Aural training in rhythm: rhythm determined by long notes; melodic design; repeated notes; discovering rhythm of unbarred songs

Dictations for all exercises

STAFF NOTATION

Review five-line staff; DO Clef on first line; single and two-pulse notes

Moving DO Clef to second line of staff and line below staff

Rests; Ties; Time Signatures; Repeat Signs

Transcription from Number Notation to Staff Notation

Transcription from Staff Notation to Number Notation

Visual Memory Tests and Sight Reading Drills

CREATIVE ABILITY

Review musical conversations; improvising melodies for verbal phrases; melodic applications to rhythm patterns; study of statement-response: repetitive and complementary.

Composition of: two-line songs; missing lines of songs; songs with words; phrases in binary, ternary and free rhythms in Modes DO and SOL

SONGS

See Index. Songs correspond to matter taught in chapters.

Chapter Thirteen

Vocal Training

Vowels in LA Mode Vocalise (Pentachord)

Review Vocal Exercise 12a

1 = A, G, C

1
Nu ____ o ____ a ____ e ____ i
Noo oh ah eh ee)

Review Vocal Exercise 13a

1 = G, A, B

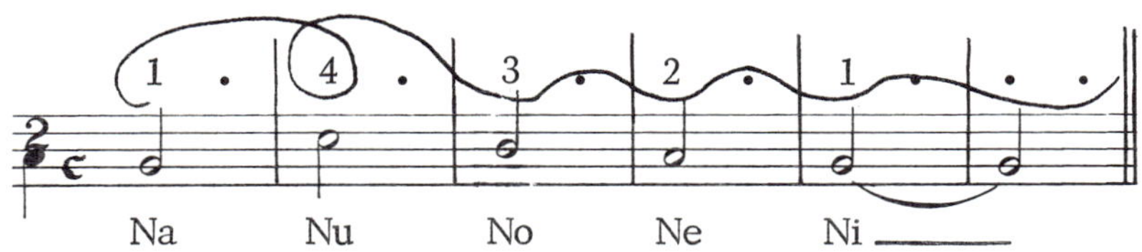

Review Vocal Exercise 13b

1 = G, A, B

Vocal Exercise 15 Vowels in LA Mode Pentachord

1 = C, D

Intonation

Presenting Mode of LA: Pentachord 6 7 1 2 3

Hexachord 6 7 1 2 3 4

Intonation Diagram 18

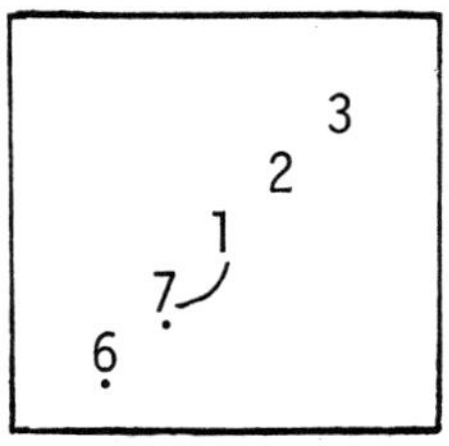

Intonation Diagram 19

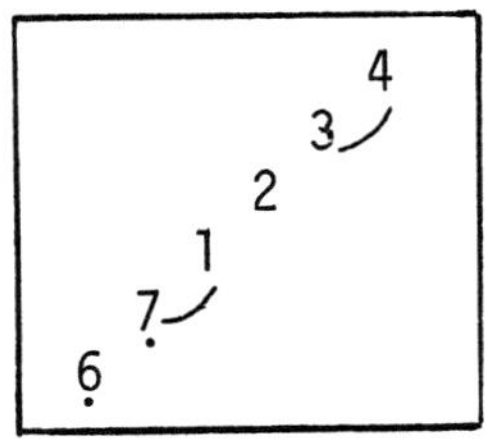

Staff Diagram 18

Staff Diagram 19

1 = C or B♭ throughout all drills
(6 = A or G)

Intonation Exercise 33 — Presentation of LA Mode (Natural Minor) *with* Intonation Diagram 18

1 7 6	6 7 1	1 2 3	3 2 1	1 7 6	*Discovering the Pentachord*
1 7 6	6 7 1	1 2 3	3 2 1	1 7 6	
1 7 6	7 1	1 2 3	3 2 1	7 6	

Intonation Exercise 34 - *with* Intonation Diagram 18 *and* Staff Diagram 18

			Drill on Pentachord Repeating outer notes
1 7 6	6 7 1 2 3	3 2 1 7 6	
	6 7 1 2 3 3 3	3 2 1 7 6 6 6	
	6 6 6 7 1 2 3	3 3 3 2 1 7 6	

Test for accurate pitch at the end of each line. The interval DO - TI (1 - 7) is the danger zone where the "pitch-fall" is most likely to occur.

Intonation Exercise 35 - *With* Intonation Diagram 18 *and* Staff Diagram 18

1 7̣ 6̣ | 6̣ 7̣ 1 2 3 3 2 1 7̣ 6̣ 3 |
| 6̣ 7̣ 1 2 3 3 2 1 7̣ 6̣ 3 |
| 6̣ 7̣ 1 2 3 3 2 1 7̣ 6̣ 3 |
| 6̣ 7̣ 1 2 3 3 2 1 7̣ 6̣ 3 6̣ |

Stop at any point and change direction

Intonation Exercise 36 - *With* Intonation Diagram 18 *and* Staff Diagram 18

1 7̣ 6̣ | 6̣ 7̣ 1 2 3 3 3 3 2 1 7̣ 6̣ 6̣ 6̣ | *Stop*
| 6̣ 7̣ 1 2 2 2 3 3 2 1 7̣ 7̣ 7̣ 6̣ 6̣ 3 | *Repeat* *Continue*
| 6̣ 7̣ 1 1 1 2 3 3 2 1 1 1 7̣ 6̣ 6̣ 3 |
| 6̣ 7̣ 7̣ 7̣ 1 2 3 3 2 2 2 1 7̣ 6̣ 6̣ 3 6̣ |

Intonation Exercise 37 - *With* Intonation Diagram 19 *and* Staff Diagram 19

a)
1 7̣ 6̣ | 6̣ 7̣ 1 1 2 3 3 4 3 3 2 1 1 7̣ 6̣ |
| 6̣ 7̣ 1 1 2 3 3 4 3 3 2 1 1 7̣ 6̣ |

Hexachord drill

b)
| 3 4 3 3 2 1 1 7̣ 6̣ 6̣ 7̣ 1 1 2 3 3 4 3 3 6̣ |
| 3 4 3 3 2 1 1 7̣ 6̣ 6̣ 7̣ 1 1 2 3 3 4 3 3 6̣ |

Ear and Eye Tests *1 = C or B^b throughout all drills*

| 1 7̣ 6̣ 7̣ 1 1 2 3 | 1 1 1 7̣ 6̣ 6̣ 6̣ 6̣ | 1 2 3 3 3 3 1 |
| 1 2 3 2 1 1 7̣ 6̣ | 1 7̣ 6̣ 7̣ 6̣ 6̣ 7̣ 1 | 1 7̣ 6̣ 6̣ 6̣ 6̣ 1 |

| 6̣ 7̣ 1 2 3 3 4 3 | 6̣ 3 2 3 4 3 6̣ |
| 6̣ 7̣ 7̣ 7̣ 1 2 3 | 6̣ 3 2 1 2 3 6̣ |

Rhythm

Presentation of Dotted Rhythm ♩. ♪ (Dotted Quarter Followed by Eighth) in Context of Rhythm Gesture II (Up-pulse Binary)

Rhythm Patterns - Series 10

a)

b)

c)

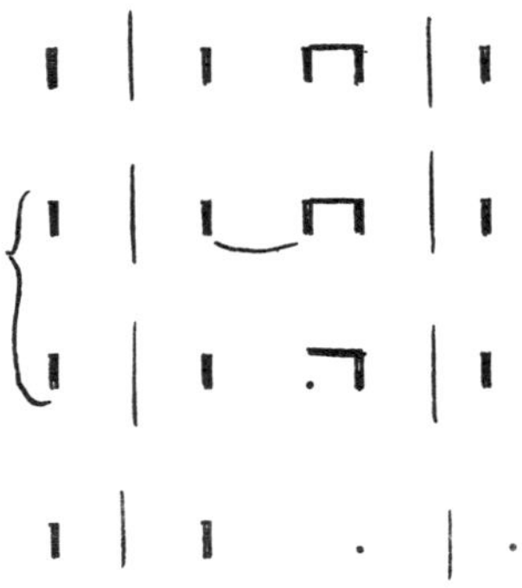

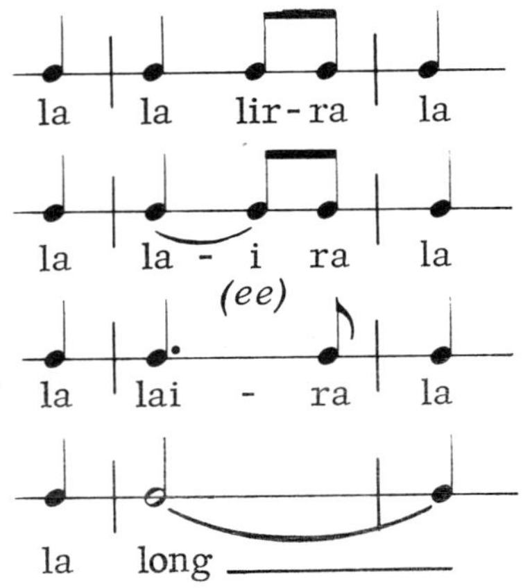

1. *Notice that the two rhythm lines at b) are identical. Practise singing a) + b) as a continuous line on one tone, e.g., A, with* Metrical Language *and* Metrical Gesture I. *There must be no vocal stress on the dot!*

a + b

a + b

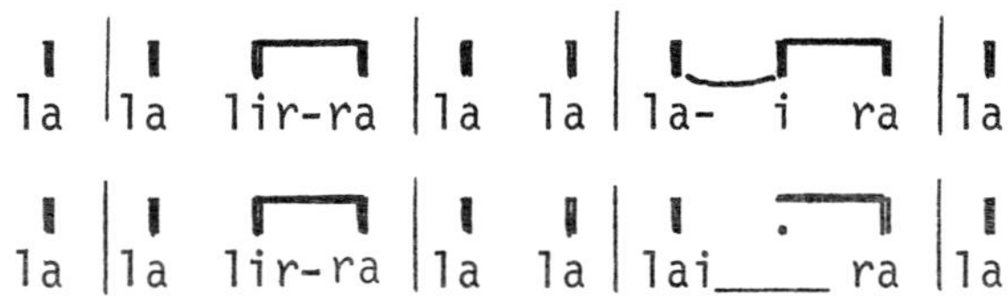

> The letter "i" in the Metrical Language is pronounced as "ee". It forms part of the diphthong "ai" on the dotted rhythm and is not given prominence when rendered.

2. *Sing same rhythm in a melody. Use* Metrical Gesture I

1 = B♭
(6̣ = G)
(3 = D)

a + b 6̣ | 6̣ 6̣ 7̣ | 1 2 | 3 3 2 | 3

a + b 6̣ | 6̣ 6̣ 7̣ | 1 2 | 3 . 2 | 3

3. *Sing the following combination of rhythm patterns on one tone, e.g., A, with* Metrical Gesture I *and* Metrical Language

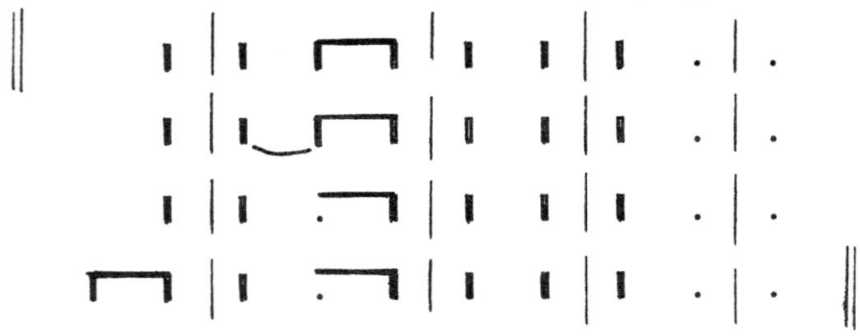

4. *Study* Melody No. 26 *at end of this chapter for melodic application of the dotted rhythm studied above*

Notation

DO Clef on Ledger Line Below Staff for LA Mode
Dotted Rhythm in Staff Notation
Presence of 𝄞 G Clef
Preparation Drills for Staff Songs in LA Mode

1. Transcribe the following to Staff Notation.

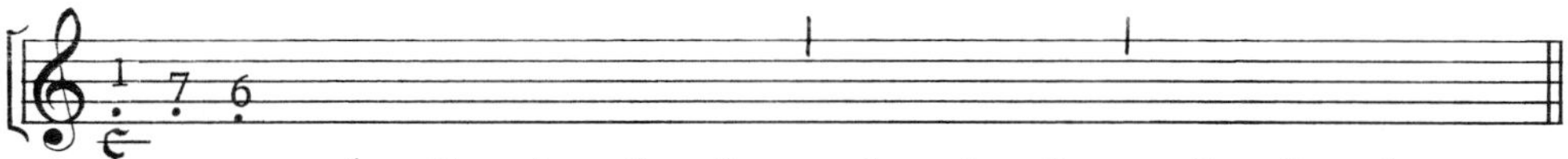

6 7 1 2 3 | 3 4 3 | 3 1 6

2. Transcribe the following rhyhms to Staff Notation.

a) 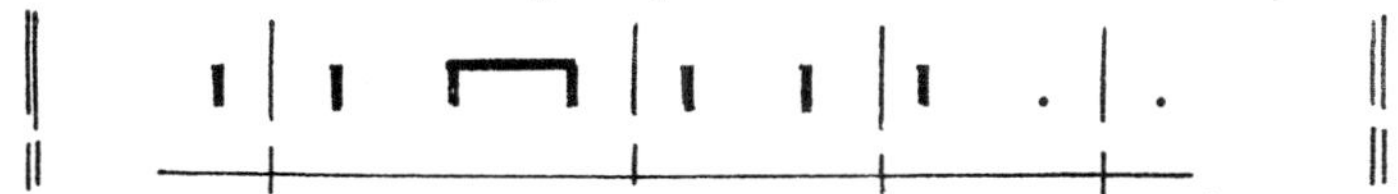

b) 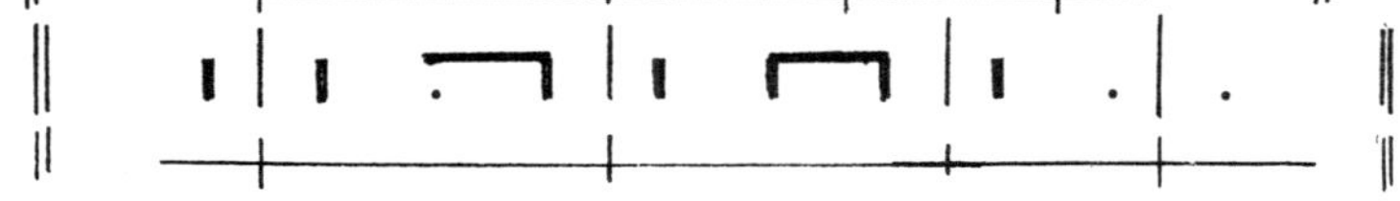

3. Transcribe the following melody to Number Notation.

4. Preparation Drills for Staff Songs in LA Mode *Repeat each segment several times.*

1 = C (6 = A)

N.B. The presence of the G Clef 𝄞 will be noted in the above staff segments as well as in all Staff Notation musical examples in succeeding chapters. Flats (♭) and Sharps (♯) will be added to each staff when applicable. These new signs will be studied in later chapters. It is well for the students to become used to seeing them at this point in their development even if they do not know what they mean for the time being.

Creative Activity

Improvising Melodies to Assimilate LA Mode (Natural Minor)

1. Improvise a response in the same rhythm to each of the following. End on LA.

(6 = G)
(3 = D)
1 = Bb

a) ‖ 3 | 3 . 2 | 3 4 | 3 . | .
| | | 6 . | . ‖

b) ‖ 1 | 6 6 7 | 1 2 | 3 . | .
| | | 6 . | . ‖

2. Compose a complementary missing line to the following melody:

1 = C (6 = A)

3. Compose a melody to the following rhythm pattern. Use tones of LA Mode hexachord. End on LA.

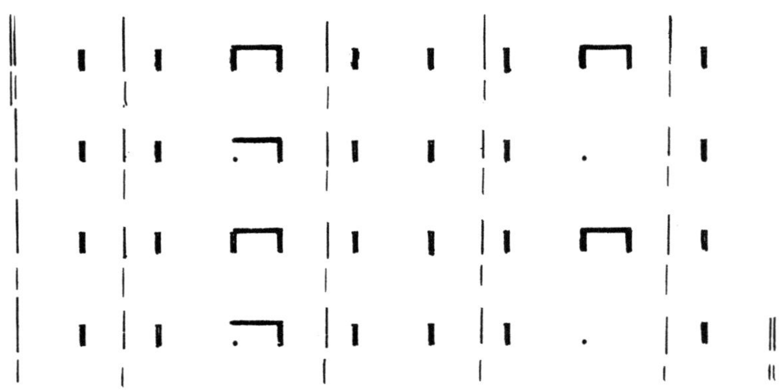

Songs

LA Mode Hexachord - Intonation or Staff Diagram 19 - Rhythm·Gesture II - Metrical Gesture II

MELODY No. 26 Anonymous

1 = B♭ (6̣ = G)

|| 6̣ | 3 3 2 | 3 4 | 2 . 2 | 3
1 | 2 . 3 | 2 1 | 1 . | 7̣
6̣ | 3 3 2 | 3 4 | 2 . 2 | 3
1 | 2 . 3 | 2 1̣ | 7̣ . | 6̣ ||

MELODY No. 27 16th Century Flemish

1 = C (6̣ = A)

|: 6̣ | 6̣ 7̣ | 1 2 | 3 . | 1 3 | 4 2 | 1 . | . :|
3 | 2 3 | 1 2 | 7̣ 6̣ | 7̣ 1̣ 2 | 1 . | 7̣ . | 6̣ . | . ||

MELODY No. 28 Flemish Air

1 = C (6̣ = A)

Mode of DO - Plagal
St. D. 6 P. 34
R. P. 10, P. 128
M. G. II

THE SANDMAN *Melody:* Johannes Brahms *Text:* J. Michael Diack

A BOY IS BORN IN BETHLEHEM *Melody:* Gregorian Chant *Text:* "Puer Natus" Trans. anonymous

1 = G (6 = E)

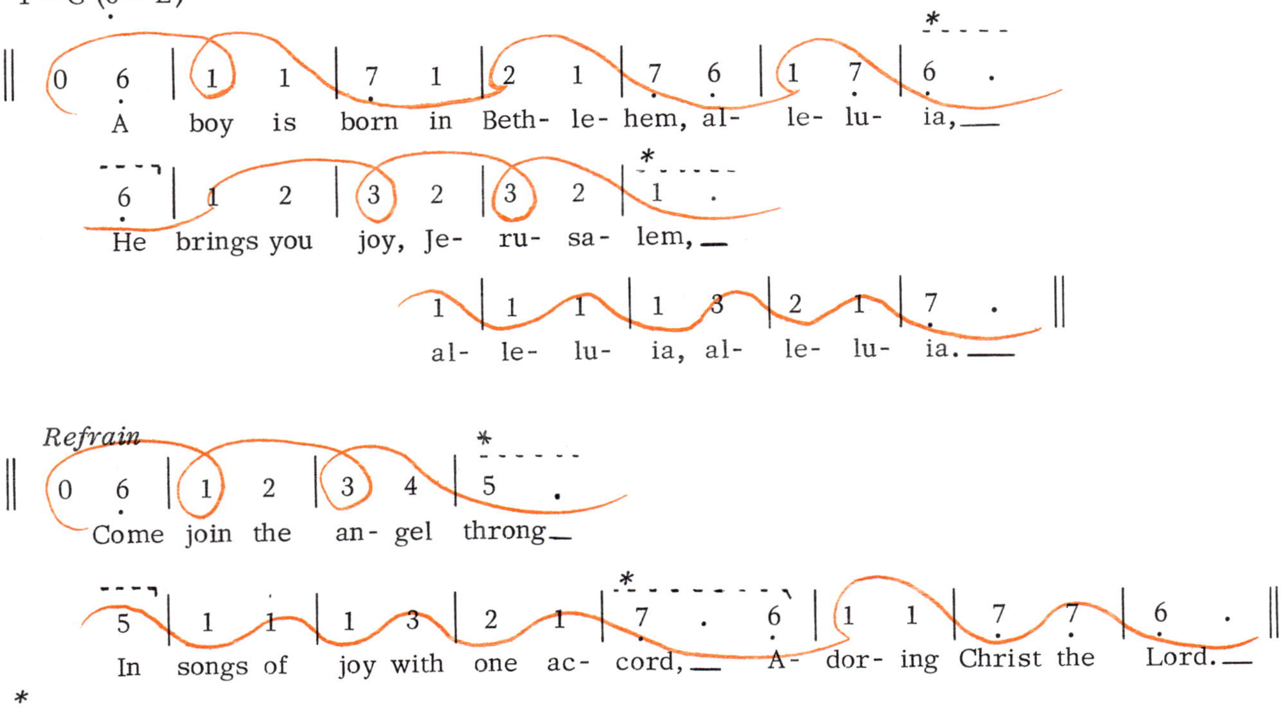

* *Ternary Rhythm*

Chapter Fourteen

Vocal Training

Vocalises on LA Mode Hexachord

Review Vocal Exercise 12a

1 = B♭ \ G / D

| 1 ———————————————————— |
Nu ——— o ——— a ——— e ——— i ——— |
(*Noo* *oh* *ah* *eh* *ee)*

> Listen for clear flute-like quality in all vowels. The most difficult vowel to place in the head is the "ee". Pulling back the corners of the mouth with the muscles of the upper cheek, like a pumpkin smile, will help to send the "ee" tone into the cranium.

Review Vocal Exercise 15 Vowels in LA Mode Pentachord

1 = B♭ or C
6̣ = G or A

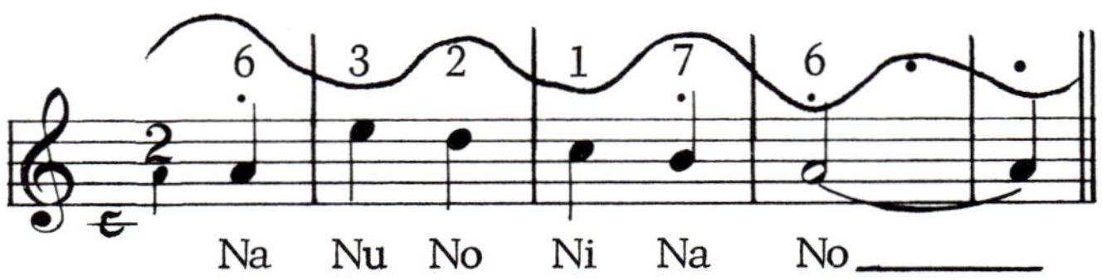

Vocal Exercise 16a Vocalise on Tones of Hexachord

1 = B♭ or C

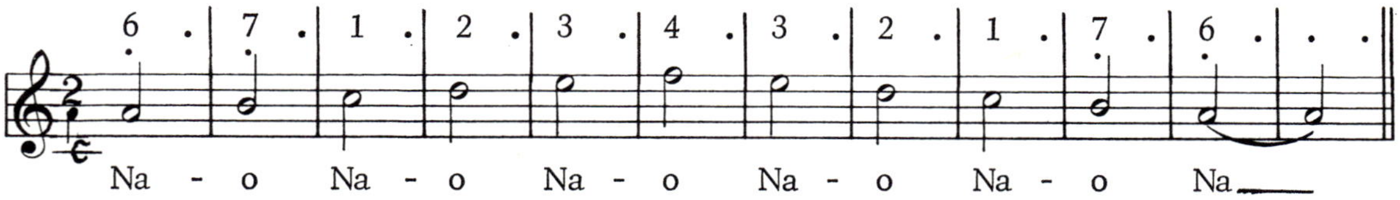

> If any Sparrows remain, they must continue to listen, not sing, during the vocal drills. Periodically, they will be invited to match a pitch or sing a short series of tones. As soon as a child can concentrate sufficiently to succeed in these simple tests, he or she is promoted to the next higher group.

Intonation

LA Mode Continued: Pentachord 6̣ - 3
Hexachord 6̣ - 4

Intonation Diagram 20

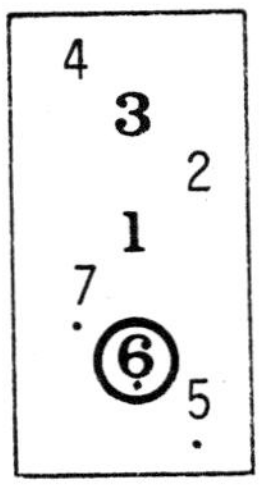

Staff Diagram 20a

Staff Diagram 20b

1 = B♭ Preparation for all drills: 1 7̣ 6̣
(6̣ = G) (3 = D)

Intonation Exercise 38 - *With* Intonation Diagram 18

Drills on minor Pentachord

6̣	7̣	1	7̣	1	2	3	3	2	3	2	1	7̣	6̣
6̣	7̣	1	2	3	2	3	3	2	1	7̣	1	7̣	6̣
6̣	7̣	1	2	1	3	2	3	1	2	1	7̣	7̣	6̣
6̣	7̣	1	2	2	3	3	3	2	2	1	7̣	6̣	6̣

Intonation Exercise 39 - *With* Intonation Diagram 19

Drills on minor Hexachord

6̣	7̣	1	2	3	4	3	3	4	3	2	1	7̣	6̣
6̣	7̣	1	2	1	4	3	2	4	3	2	1	7̣	6̣
6̣	1	7̣	6̣	7̣	1	2	3	4	3	2	1	7̣	6̣
6̣	7̣	1	6̣	7̣	1	2	2	3	2	1	6̣	5̣	6̣

Intonation Exercise 40 - *With* Intonation Diagram 20

Groups and bridges

6̣7̣1	17̣6̣	6̣5̣6̣	6̣7̣1	121	123	343	321	121	121	17̣6̣	6̣5̣6̣
6̣7̣1	1 6̣	6̣5̣6̣	6̣7̣1	121	123	343	3 1	121	121	1 6̣	6̣5̣6̣
6̣ 1	1 6̣	5̣6̣	6̣ 1	21	23	343	3 1	21	121	1 6̣	5̣6̣

Intonation Exercise 41 - *With* Intonation Diagram 20 *and* Staff Diagram 20a

6 7 1 2 3 4 3	3 4 3 2 1 7 6	6 3 6	*Approach by leap to the* 343 *group*
6 7 1 2	3 4 3 2 1 7 6	6 3 6	
6 *7 1 2*	3 4 3 2 1 7 6	6 3 6	
6	3 4 3 *2 1 7 6*	6 3 6	

Eye and Ear Tests

1 = B♭
(6 = G)

6 7 1 7 1 2 3	6 7 7 1 2 3 3	6 1 7 1 2 3 4 3
6 7 1 2 1 3 2	3 1 2 1 7 6 6	6 5 6 1 1 3 4 3

6 1 2 1 2 3	1 2 1 6 5 6 3 4 3
3 2 1 6 7 1 1 2 3	6 3 6 7 6 1 3 2 3

Continue to insist on accurate pitch. Test last note of each line.

Rhythm

Assimilation of ♩. ♪ in Context of Rhythm Gesture II
Study of Free Rhythm Continued

Rhythm Patterns - Series 11

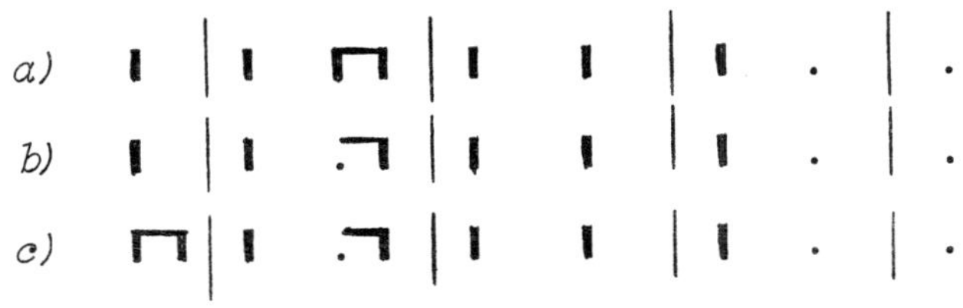

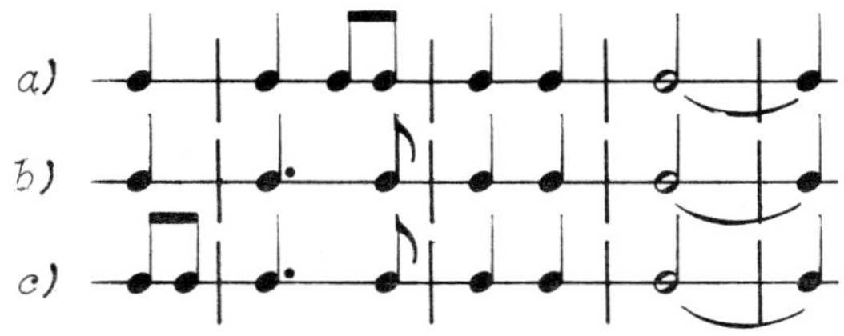

1. Sing Rhythm Patterns with Metrical Gesture I *and* Metrical Language

Repeat using Rhythm Gesture II

2. Derive rhythm pattern of Line 1, Melody No. 30, *placing correct pulse lines beneath the staff notes*

3. Derive rhythm of Line 1, Ave Maris Stella. *"How is this different?"*

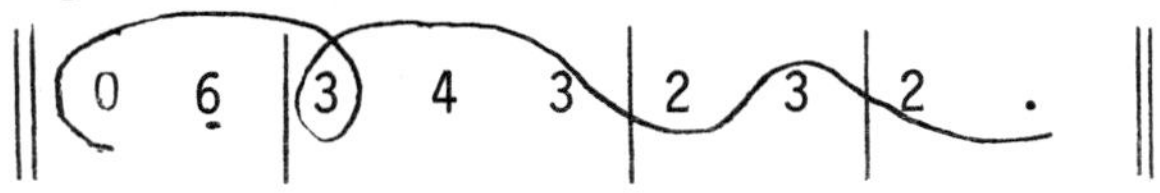

Rhythmic Dictations

1 = B♭
(6̣ = G)

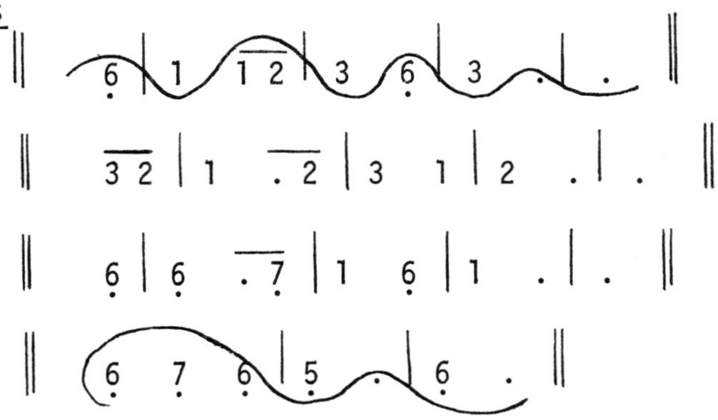

Also select lines from songs being studied

Notation

La Mode on Staff
Assimilation of ♩. ♪ in Staff Notation
Review DO Mode (Plagal Range) 

Review DO Mode 

1. *Transcribe last line of* Intonation Exercise 39 *to Staff Notation*

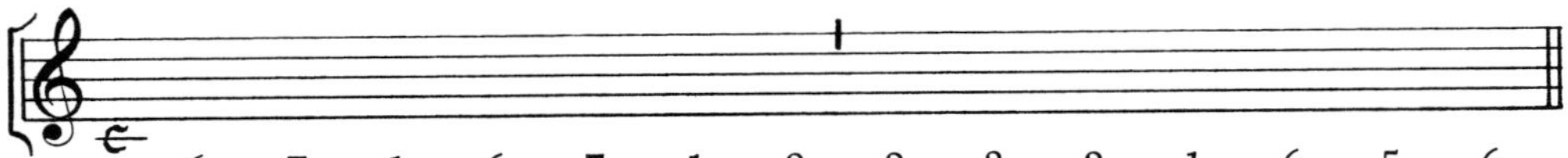

6 7 1 6 7 1 2 2 3 2 1 6 5 6

2. *Transcribe Line 1 of* Auld Lang Syne *to Staff Notation.*

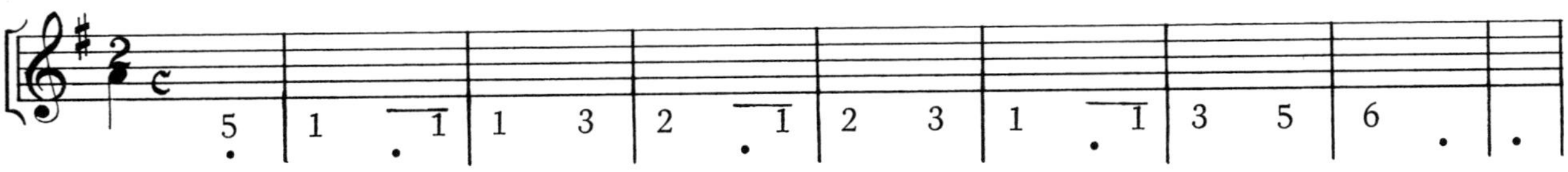

SIGHT SINGING DRILLS

1 = B♭ or C (6 = G or A)

LA MODE - *Preparation for* Melody No. 29

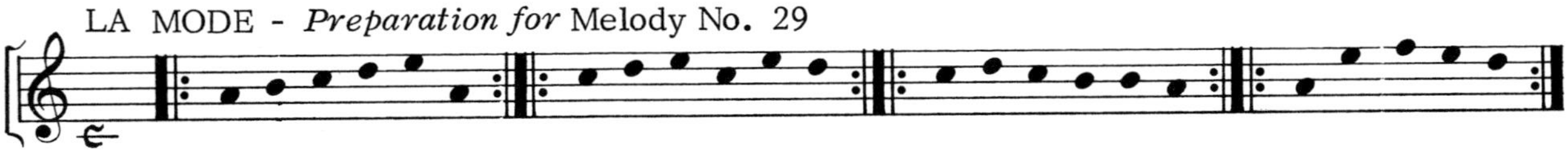

1 = E♭ (5 = B♭)

DO MODE - *Preparation for* Melody No. 30 *(Review)*

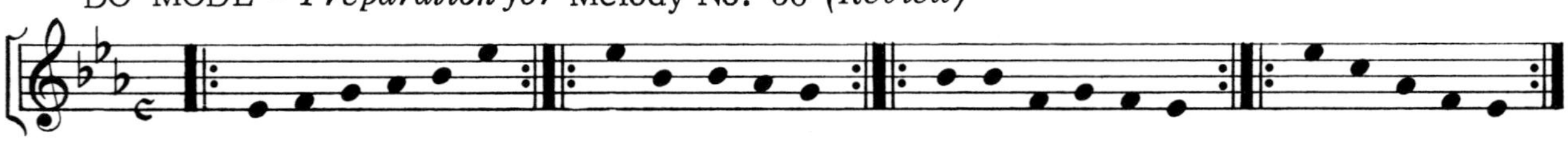

Creative Activity

Non-rhythmic Conversations in LA Mode 6̣ 7̣ 1 2 3 4
Melodic Applications to Rhythm Patterns
Compose Complementary Phrases for LA Mode Melody
Compose LA Mode Melody for Prose Text (Free Rhythm)

1. <u>*CONVERSATION GAME*</u>

A group of three or four students is invited to "converse" in the LA Mode, using five tones each from the hexachord, that is, 6̣ 7̣ 1 2 3 4. First student sings five tones and second student begins with last tone sung by first student. Third student begins with last tone sung by second student, etc.. Conversation ends when a phrase finishes on LA.

2. *Improvise melodic applications to the* Rhythm Patterns - Series 11

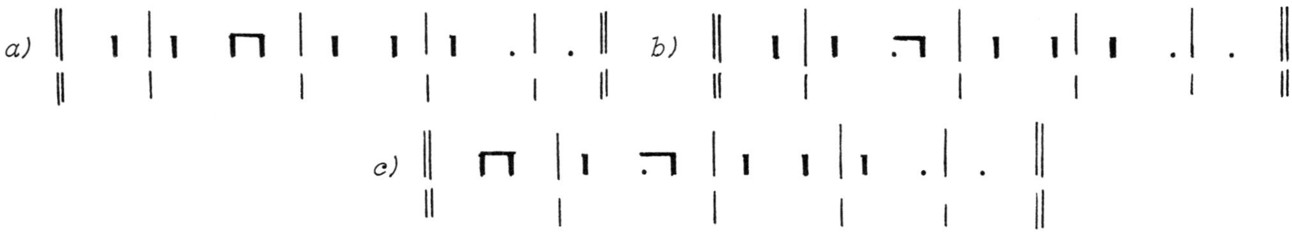

3. *Compose complementary phrases for the lines missing in the following melody:*

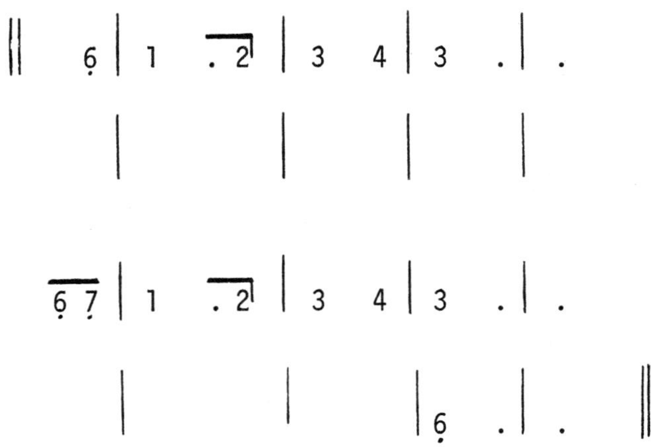

4. *Compose a melody in the LA Mode for the following text. Recite the text aloud to feel the rhythm before writing down the notes. The last note must be a long note. on LA.*

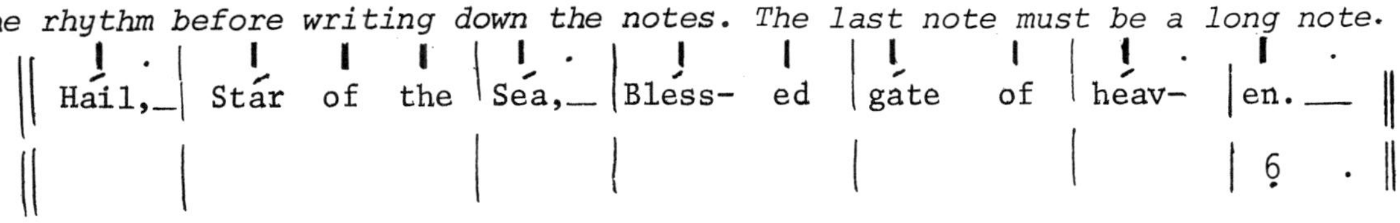

Place a bar line before each word accent

Note the rhythmic groupings of the pulse-lines: all are binary except the ternary group over the words "Star of the".

Songs

Mode of LA Hexachord
Int. D 20 or St. D 20b, Page 135
R. P. Series 11
R. G. II

MELODY No. 29 Anonymous

1 = B♭ (6 = G)

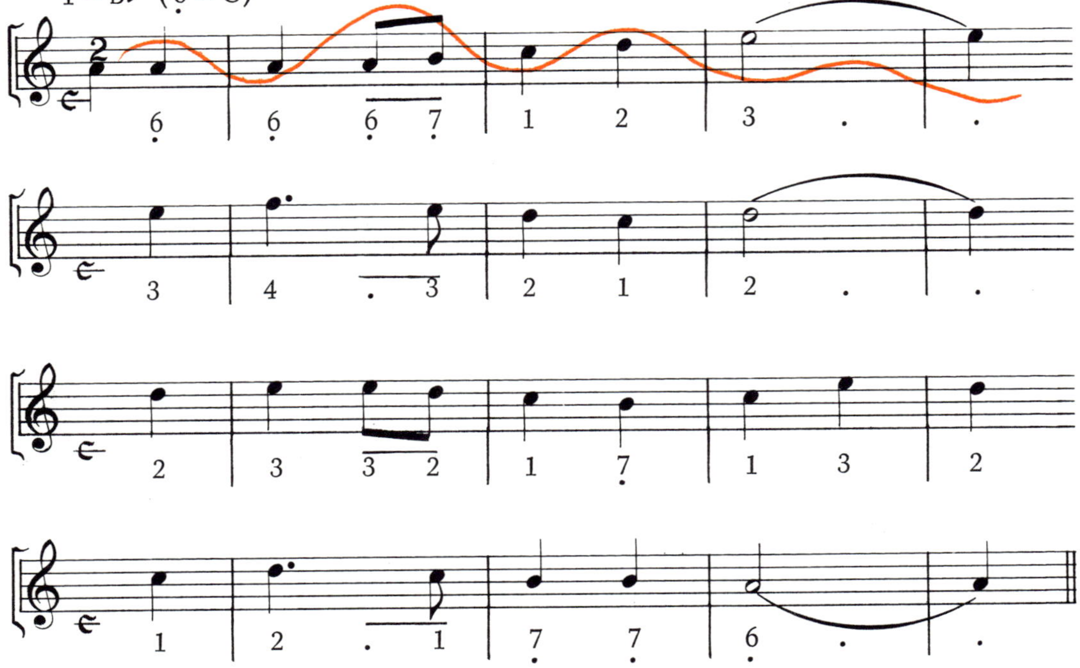

Mode of DO Int. D. 3 P. 14
R. P. Series 11, P. 137
R. G. II

MELODY No. 30 "Gospel" Song *Traditional English*

1 = E♭ (5 = B♭)

AULD LANG SYNE Scotch Folk Song

Mode of DO Plagal Range
Int. D. 6 P. 44
R. P. Series 11 P/ 137
M. G. II

1 = F (6 = D)

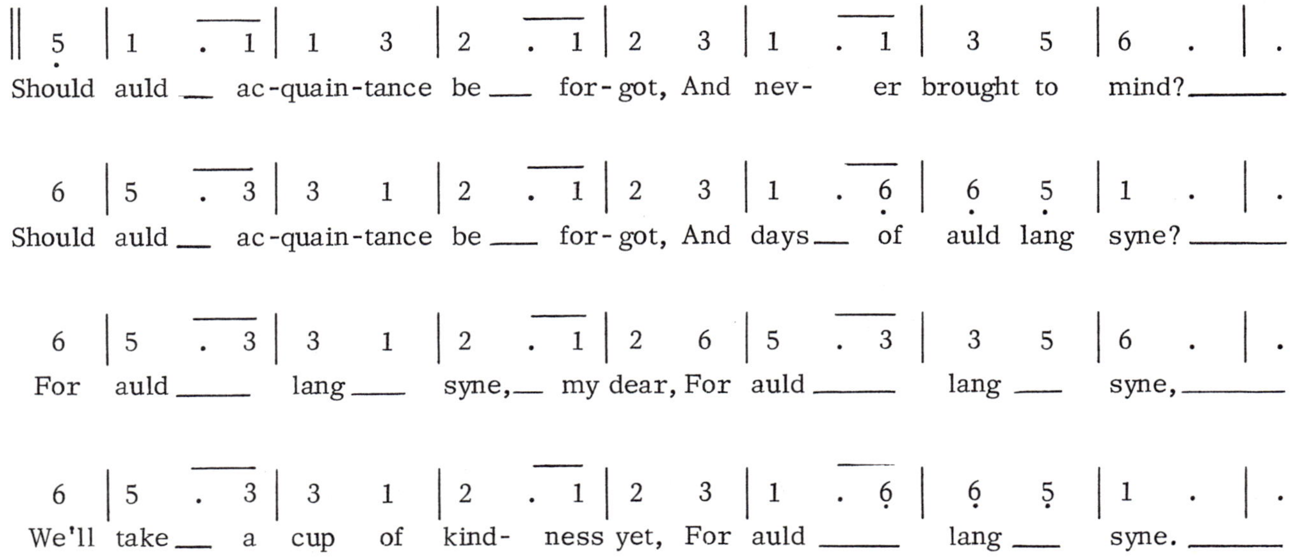

"Auld Lang Syne" means "for old times' sake."

AVE MARIS STELLA Gregorian Chant

Note that the accent of the Latin word often comes before the measure bar, on the up-pulse, whereas in English the accent comes after the measure bar, on the down-pulse.

1 = B♭ (6 = G)

Mode of LA Hexachord
Int. D. 20 P. 135
R. G. IV Free Rhythm

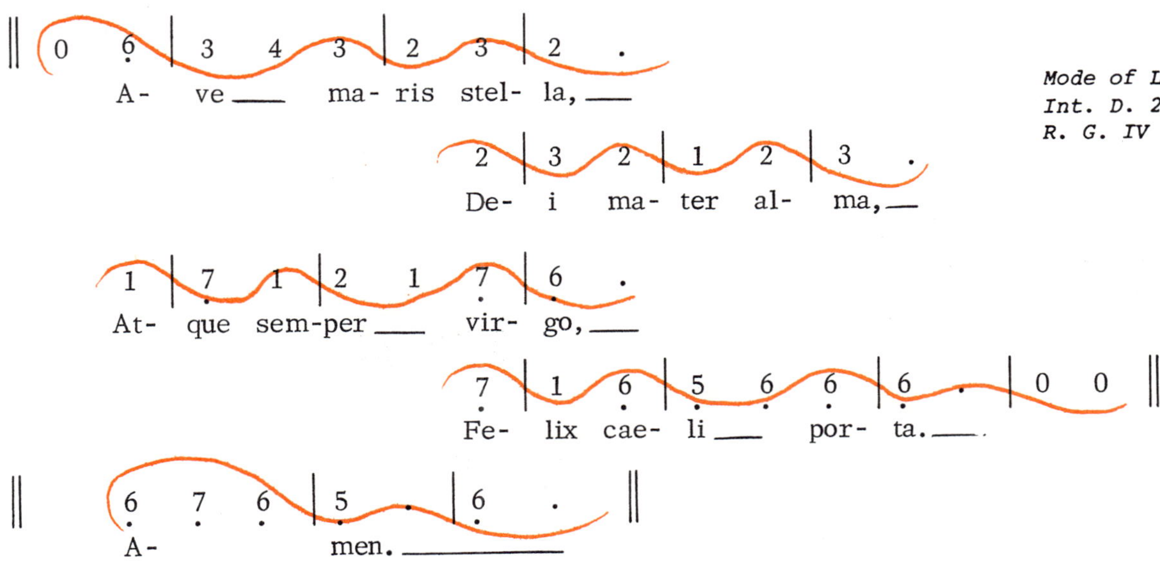

THE GOD OF NATURE AND GRACE *Melody:* J. S. Bach *Text:* JBW

1 = B♭ or C (6̣ = G or A)

Mode of LA Pentachord
St. D. 20a or 20b P. 135
R. P. Series 11 P. 137
R. G. II
Sight-singing Drills P. 138

Chapter Fifteen

Vocal Training

Review of Vocal Exercises 12, 15 and 16

Review Vocal Exercise 12a Sustained Tones at Different Pitch Levels

1 = B♭ / G / D

|| 1 ______________________________ ||

Nu ___ o ______ a _____ e _____ i _____
Noo oh ah eh ee)

> Open tones like "o" and "a" must feel very high in the cranium otherwise they will slip back into the throat and the beautiful clear tone that is characteristic of well-placed head tone will be lost.

Review Vocal Exercise 15

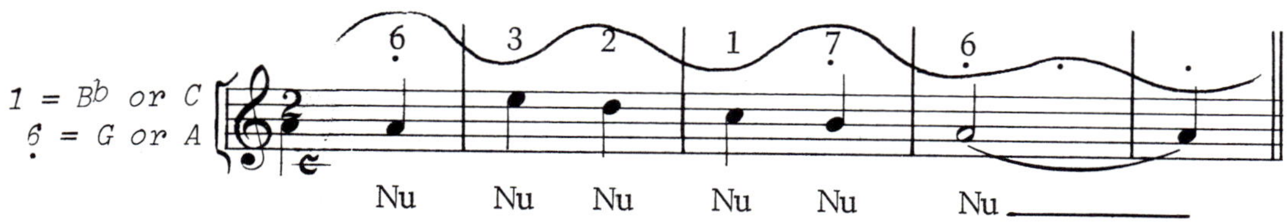

Review Vocal Exercise 16a DO Clef on Line Below Staff

Vocal Exercise 16b DO Clef on Line 2 of Staff

> Link tones carefully in vocal drills for good legato.

Intonation

LA Mode (Natural Minor) Continued
First and Second Compass Exercises
Drills on Characteristic Phrases

Intonation Diagram 20

4
3 2
1
7̣ ⑥̣ 5̣

Staff Diagram 20b

St. D. 20c

1 = B^b or C throughout (6̣ = G or A)

Intonation Exercise 42 - *With* Intonation Diagram 20 *or* Staff Diagram 20b

| 3 4   3 2   1 7̣   6̣   6̣ | *Drill on interval 7̣ - 3*
| 3 4   3 2   1 7̣   7̣ 7̣ 1 2 3 |
| 3 4   3 2   1 7̣   7̣ *1 2* 3 |
| 3 4 3 2 1 7̣ 6̣ 7̣ 1 2 3   3 6̣ 3 4 3 6̣ |

Intonation Exercise 43 - *With* Intonation Diagram 20 *or* Staff Diagram 20b

| 6̣7̣6̣ 6̣7̣1 121 123 343 343 321 121 17̣6̣ 6̣7̣6̣ 6̣5̣6̣ | *First Compass Exercise*
| 6̣7̣6̣ *6̣7̣1* 121 *123* 343 343 *321* 121 *17̣6̣* 6̣7̣6̣ 6̣5̣6̣ |
| 6̣7̣6̣ 121 343 343 121 6̣7̣6̣ 6̣5̣6̣ |

Intonation Exercise 44 - *With* Intonation Diagram 20 *or* Staff Diagram 20b

| 6̣7̣6̣ 121 343 343 121 6̣7̣6̣ 6̣5̣6̣ |
| 6̣*7̣6̣* 1*21* *343* *343* 1*21* 6̣*7̣6̣* 6̣5̣6̣ | *Second Compass Exercise*
| 6̣ 1 3 3 1 6̣ 6̣5̣6̣ |

Intonation Exercise 45 - *With* Intonation Diagram 20 *or* Staff Diagram 20b

| 1 7 6 7 1 6 6   6 5 6 7 1 6 6   6 1 1 7 6 5 6 |
| 6 1 1 2 1 2 1 7 6   6 1 2 1 6   6 2 1 7 6 |
| 6 1 1 2 3 2 1 7 6   6 1 3 2 1 7 6   6 1 3 1 6   5 6 6 |
| 6 1 3   3 4 3 2 3   3 1 6   6 5 6 7 6 |

Characteristic melodic phrases

Intonation Exercise 46 - *With* Intonation Diagram 20 *or* Staff Diagram 20b

| 6 7 6   1 2 1   3 4 3   3 4 3 2 1 7 6   6 5 6 |
| 6 7 6   *1 2 1*   3 4 3   3 4 3 2 1 7 6   6 5 6 |
| 6   6   1   1   3   3   3 4 3 2 1 7 6   5 6 |

| 3 4 3   1 2 1   6 7 6   6 7 1 2 3 4 3 |
| 3 4 3   *1 2 1*   6 7 6   6 7 1 2 3 4 3 |
| 3   3   1   1   6   6   6 7 1 2 3 4 3   3 6 |

Compass Exercise groups combined with scale passages

Ear and Eye Tests

| 6 7 6   1 2 1   3 4 3 | 1 7 6 7 1   7 3 | 6 1 3   3 1 2 3 6 |
| 3 4   3 2   1 2 3 6 | 3 4 3 2 1   7 1 | 6 5 6   1 2 3 1 2 |

| 1 7 6 7 1 6 6   3 6 | 3 3 1 1 6   7 1 2 3 |
| 6 5 6 7 6   1 3 | 3 4 3   6 7 6   6 5 6 |

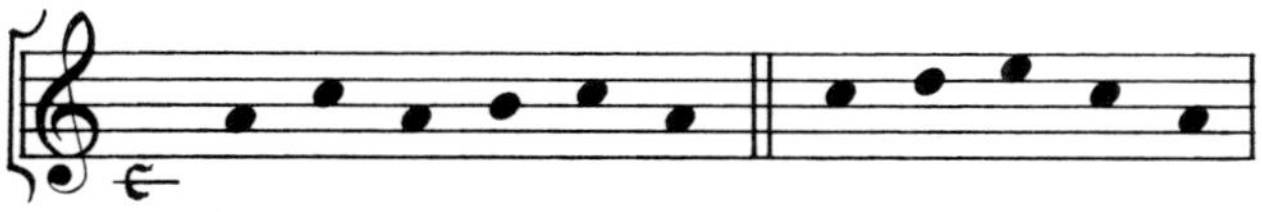

Rhythm

The Dotted Quarter and Eighth in Duple Time
(Down-pulse Beginning)
Arsis-Thesis in Duple Time and in Free Rhythm
Review Metrical Gesture II Beating Duple Time

Rhythm Patterns - Series 12

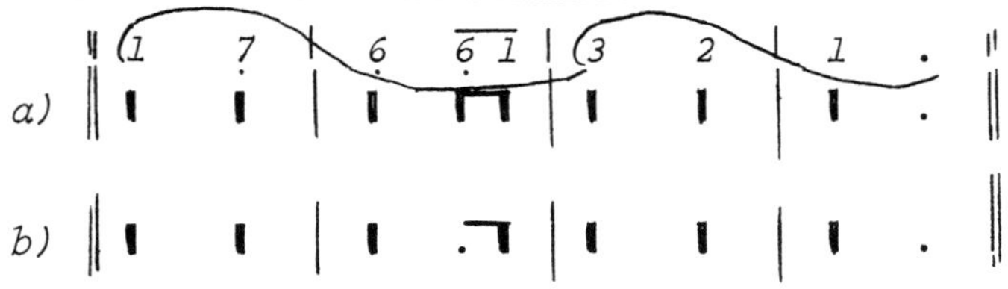

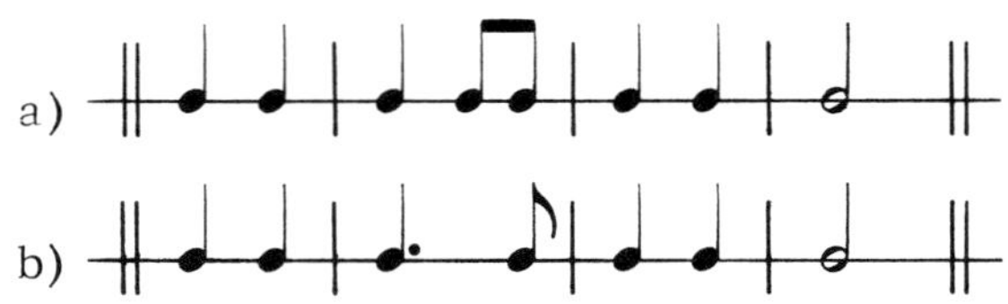

1. *Say rhythm patterns in strict time with* Metrical Gesture I *and* Metrical Language
   Repeat singing note names suggested above pulse lines. Metrical Gesture I

   REVIEW: Arsis-Thesis Gesture in duple time - Rhythm Gesture IV - Binary *(Chapter Two)*

   Repeat singing note names suggested above pulse lines. Use *Arsis-Thesis gesture*

2. *REVIEW: Beating Duple Time* - Metrical Gesture II *(Chapter Seven)*

   a) Sing rhythm patterns above with suggested note names. Use Metrical Gesture II

   b) Teacher sings one of the following songs while children made gestures:
   (Cf. end of chapter.)
   Melody No. 30 *with* Metrical Gesture II
   Ding Dong Bell *with* Rhythm Gesture IV - Binary

3. *REVIEW: Arsis-Thesis Gesture in Free Rhythm* - Rhythm Gesture IV *(Chapter Ten)*

   Practise gestures silently: *a) In Duple Time (Binary Rhythm)*
   b) In Triple Time (Ternary Rhythm)
   c) Alternating Duple and Triple Time
   d) Alternating Triple and Duple Time

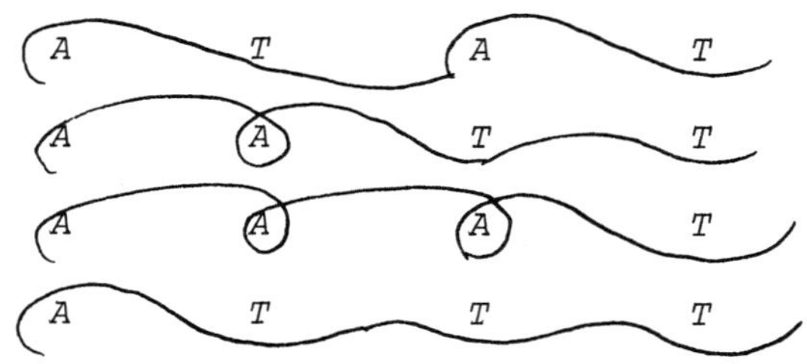

Rhythmic Dictations

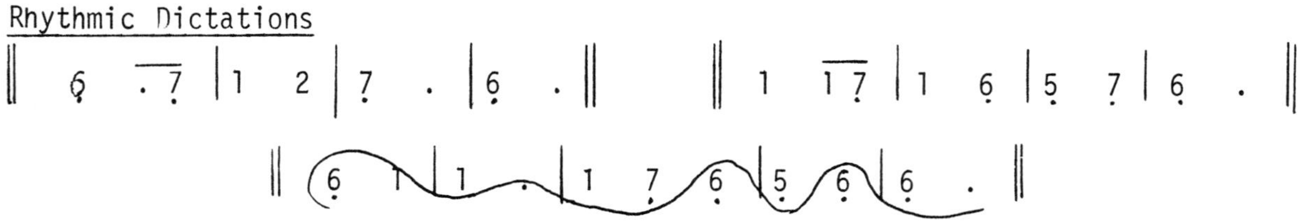

Notation

LA Mode
Transcriptions with DO Clef in Two Positions:
Sight-singing Drills in Staff Notation

1. *Transcribe to Staff Notation the last line of* Intonation Exercise 42

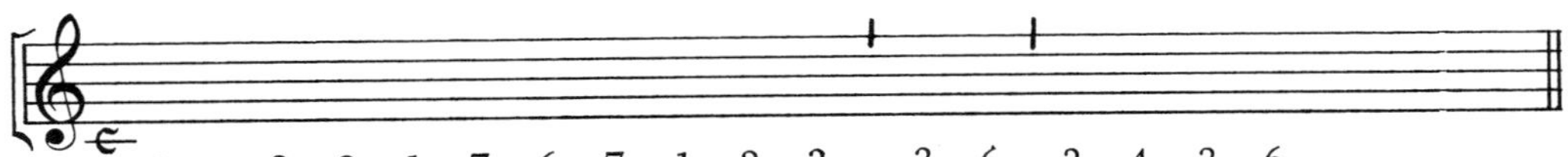

3 4 3 2 1 $\underset{\cdot}{7}$ $\underset{\cdot}{6}$ $\underset{\cdot}{7}$ 1 2 3 3 $\underset{\cdot}{6}$ 3 4 3 $\underset{\cdot}{6}$

3 4 3 2 1 $\underset{\cdot}{7}$ $\underset{\cdot}{6}$ $\underset{\cdot}{7}$ 1 2 3 3 $\underset{\cdot}{6}$ 3 4 3 $\underset{\cdot}{6}$

2. *Transcribe to Number Notation the first line of* Evening Hymn

3. *Transcribe to Staff Notation the last line of* Loving Shepherd of the Sheep

1 $\overline{\cdot\ 2}$ 3 1 2 $\overline{1\ \underset{\cdot}{7}}$ $\underset{\cdot}{6}$ ·

1 $\overline{\cdot\ 2}$ 3 1 2 $\overline{1\ \underset{\cdot}{7}}$ $\underset{\cdot}{6}$ ·

Sight-singing Drills

1 = B^b or A ($\underset{\cdot}{6}$ = G or A)

1 = G ($\underset{\cdot}{6}$ = E)

Creative Activity

Conversation in LA Mode 6 7 1 2 3 4
Composing Answering Statements
Improvising Melodies for Arsis-Thesis Gestures
(Duple Time)

1. *Conversations in LA Mode on rhythm patterns. The teacher selects several individuals to carry on a conversation among themselves while the rest of the class makes the* Metrical Gesture II.

a)
b)

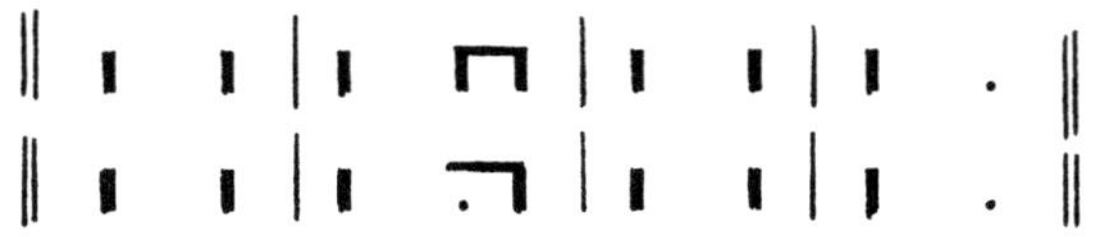

2. *Compose answers to each of the following statements*

a) *By inversion*
‖ 1 7 | 6 1 | 3 4 | 3 . |
| | | | 6 . ‖

b) *By contrast*
‖ 6 1 | 3 34 | 3 . | 3 . |
| | | | 6 . ‖

c) *By repetition*
‖ 67 12 | 3 .2 | 1 2 | 3 . |
| | | | 6 . ‖

3. *Improvise Arsis-Thesis Gestures in LA Mode* - Rhythm Gesture IV (Binary)

‖ A 6 1 | T 7 6 | A 7 1 | T 6 . ‖
‖ A 1 2 | A 3 4 | T 3 1 | T 6 . ‖
‖ A 6 7 | A 1 2 | A 3 4 | T 3 . ‖
‖ A 6 3 | T 2 1 | T 7 7 | T 6 . ‖

N.B. Themes given are suggestions for the teacher should the students have difficulty with these improvisations

Songs

Mode of LA Staff or Intonation Diagram 20
Rhythm Patterns Series 12 - Rhythm Gesture IV Duple
Repetitions, Sequences, Inversions

MELODY No. 31 Basque Folk Song

1 = C (6̣ = A)

‖ 1 7̣ | 1 6̣ | 1 7̣ | 1 6̣ | 1 1 7̣ | 1 6̣ | 7̣ 1 | 2 . |

| 1 7̣ | 1 6̣ | 1 7̣ | 1 6̣ | 1 1 7̣ | 1 6̣ | 5̣ 7̣ | 6̣ . ‖

MELODY No. 32 Basque Folk Song

1 = B♭
(6̣ = G)

LOVING SHEPHERD OF THE SHEEP Anonymous

1 = B♭ (6 = G)

|| 6 . 7 | 1 2 | 3 3 2 | 3 . |
Lov- ing Shep-herd of the — sheep, —

| 3 . 2 | 1 7 | 2 2 1 | 7 . |
Keep — thy lamb, in safe- ty — keep. —

| 6 . 7 | 1 2 | 3 3 2 | 3 . |
Noth- ing can thy pow'r with- stand; —

| 1 . 2 | 3 1 | 2 1 7 | 6 . ||
None can pluck me from thy hand.

DING DONG DELL Folk Song From Lorraine

1 = B♭ (6 = G)

THE FERRY MAN Traditional Round

1 = B♭ (6 = G)

|| + 6 6 | 5 5 6 | 1 7 6 | 5 6 |
Who will fer-ry me o- ver the riv- er?

| + 1 1 1 | 7 1 | 3 2 1 | 7 1 |
Fer-ry man, will you fer- ry me o- ver?

| + 3 . 3 | 3 . 3 | 3 . | 6* . ||
O- ver, o- ver, o- ver? —

**If sung as a Round, this last note is 3.*

Mode of DO
St. D. 6 P. 34
R. P. Series 12 P. 146
M.G. II

EVENING HYMN *Melody:* Old Welsh Air *Text:* Anonymous

1 = G

Mode of LA
R.G. IV Free
Notice frequent
Ternary groups

HOLY, HOLY, HOLY From "Order of Mass" TM

1 = B♭ (6 = G)

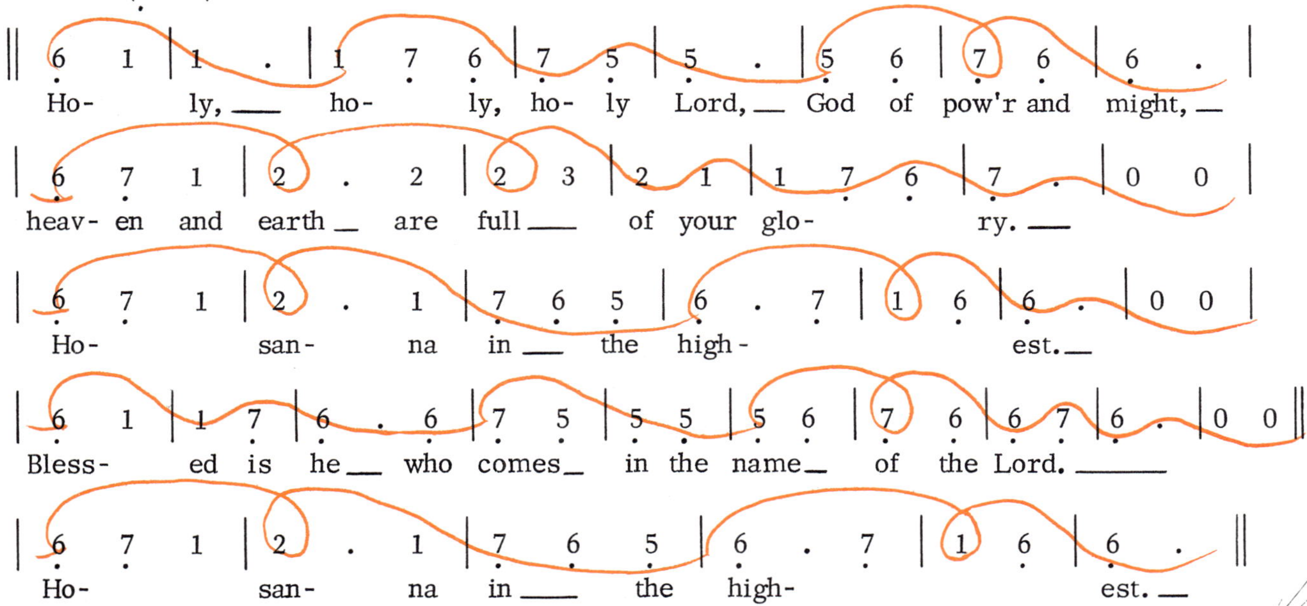

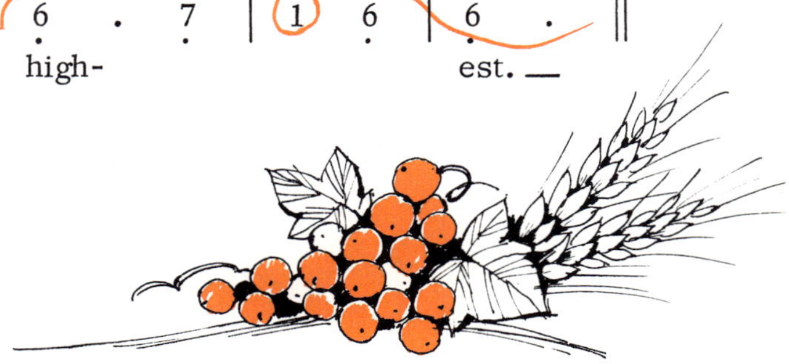

Chapter Sixteen

Vocal Training

Review Vocal Exercises 12a, 15 and 16
as in Chapter Fifteen

Intonation

LA Mode Hexachord Continued
Second and Third Compass Exercises
Strong Tones LA, DO and MI and Surrounding Tones

Intonation Diagram 21

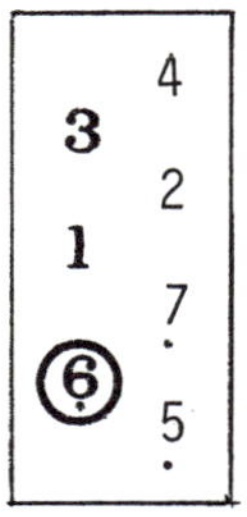

Staff Diagram 21a

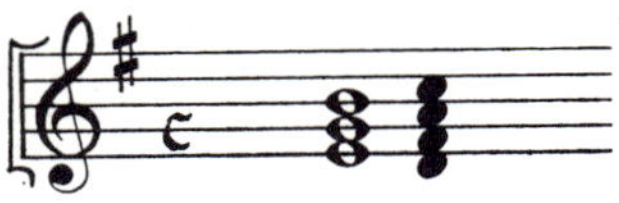

Staff Diagram 21b

1 = B♭
(6̣ = G)

Intonation Exercise 47 - *With* Intonation Diagram 21

6̣	1	3	3	3	3	1	6̣	6̣	6̣
6̣	6	6	1	3	3	3	3	1	6̣
6̣	1	1	1	3	3	1	1	1	6̣
6̣	1				3	1			
6̣	1	1			3	1	1		
6̣	1	1	3		3	1	1	6̣	

Assimilation of Second Compass Exercise

Intonation Exercise 48 - *With* Intonation Diagram 21

6̣7̣6̣	121	343	343	121	6̣7̣6̣	6̣5̣6̣
6̣7̣6̣	121	343	343	121	6̣7̣6̣	6̣5̣6̣
7̣6̣	21	43	43	21	7̣6̣	5̣6̣

Third Compass Exercise

Intonation Exercise 49 - *With* Intonation Diagram 21 *and/or* Staff Diagrams 21a - b

| 6 7 1 2 3   3 4   2 3   3 2 1 7 6   6 7 6 5 6 |
| 6 7 1 2 3   3 2 3 4 3   3 2 1 7 6   6 5 7 1 6 |
| 6 1 3   2   4 3   3 1 6   5 7 1 6 |
| 6 1 3   4   2 3   3 1 6   1 7 5 6 |

Strong tones LA (6) *and* MI (3) *and their surrounding tones*

Intonation Exercise 50 - *With* Intonation Diagram 21 *and/or* Staff Diagrams 21a - b

| 6 7 1 2 3 2 1   1 2 7 1   3 2 1 7 6 7 1   7 2 1   1 7 6 |
| 6 1 3 2 1   7 2 1   3 1 6 1   7 2 1   1 7 6 |
| 6 1 3 1   7 2 3   3 1 6 1   2 7 1   1 7 6 |
| 6 1 3 1   2 7 6   3 1 6 1   2 7 6   6 5 6 |

The note DO (1) *and its surrounding notes*

Intonation Exercise 51 - *With* Intonation Diagram 21

| 6 1   7 6 5   6 6 |
| 6 1   7 5   6 6 |
| 1 6   5 6 7   6 6 |
| 1 6   5 7   6 6 |
| 1 6   7 5   6 6 |

The Final (Tonic) LA (6) *and its surrounding tones*

Ear and Eye Tests

| 6 1 3   3 1 6   6 3 | 7 6 7   2 1   1 2 3 | 1 2 1   7 6   6 5 6 |
| 3 1 3   3 1   3 6 | 7 6   2 1   3 4 3 | 3 4 3   1 2 1   4 3 |

| 6 1 3   2 4 3   4 3 | 6 1   7 1 2   1 3 |
| 3 2   4 3   1 6 | 1 3 1   2 7 1   6 5 6 |

Rhythm

Dotted Quarter and Eighth in Triple Time
(Up-pulse Beginning)

Rhythm Patterns - Series 13

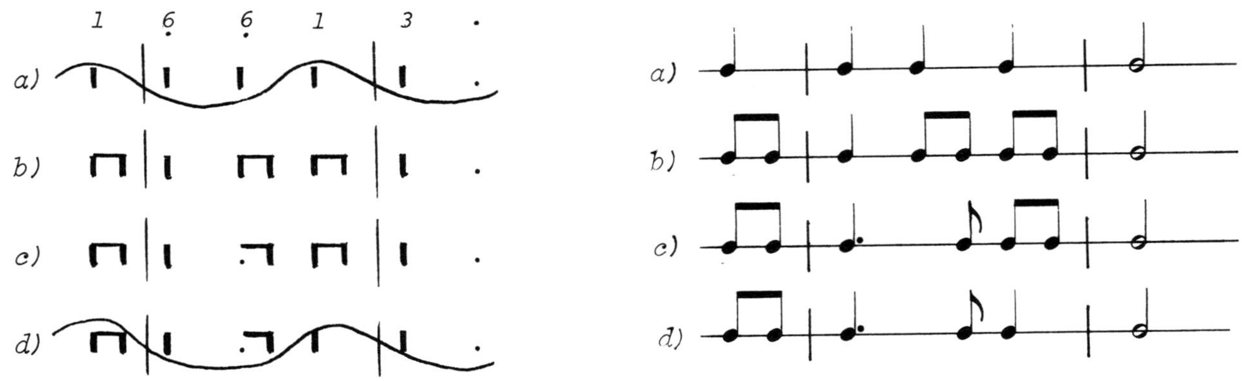

1. *Say rhythm in strict time with* Metrical Gesture I *and* Metrical Language
   Repeat singing note names suggested above pulse lines. Metrical Gesture I

2. *REVIEW:* Rhythm Gesture III *silently. Be sure to control the up-pulse.*
   Repeat singing note names suggested above pulse lines

3. *Derive rhythm pattern structure of the following quotation from* The Silver Moon Is Shining. *Place correct pulse lines beneath notes.*

Rhythmic Dictations

With rhythm patterns in full view of the class, the students:
1. *Identify the combination of patterns used*
2. *Write pulse lines on board allowing space for addition of notes*
3. *Add notes of melody*
4. *Add rhythm wave*

b — d

‖ 1 7 | 6 6 7 1 2 | 3 . 4 4 | 3 . 2 1 | 2 . ‖

a — d

‖ 6 | 3 3 6 | 3 . 4 3 | 2 . 3 1 | 7 . ‖

Notation

LA Mode Transcriptions with DO Clef in Two Positions on Staff  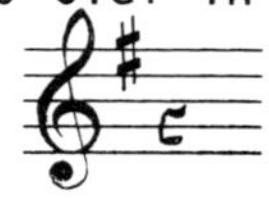

1. *Transcribe last line of* Intonation Exercise 50 *to Staff Notation*

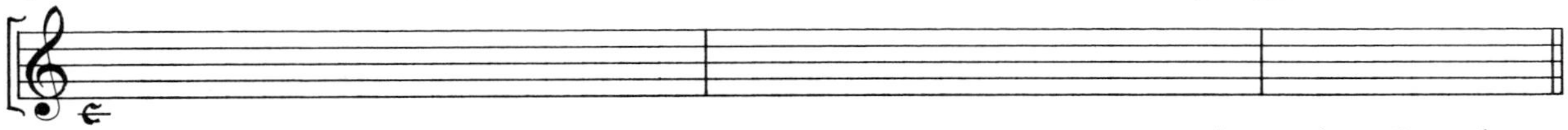

6 1 3 1 2 7 6 | 3 1 6 1 2 7 6 | 6 5 6

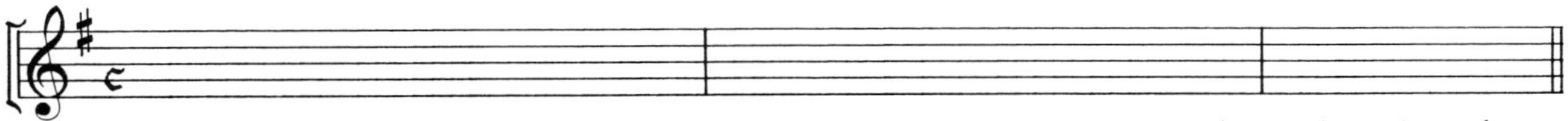

6 1 3 1 2 7 6 | 3 1 6 1 2 7 6 | 6 5 6

2. *Transcribe to Number Notation the refrain of* A Sailor Climbed the Mast on High

3. *Transcribe to Staff Notation Lines 1 and 2 of* The Silver Moon Is Shining

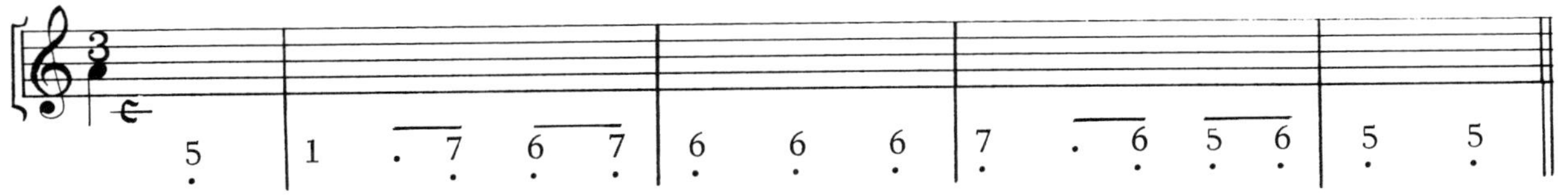

5 | 1 . 7 6 7 | 6 6 6 | 7 . 6 5 6 | 5 5 ||

4. *Transcribe to Staff Notation Lines 1 and 2 of* Melody No. 32

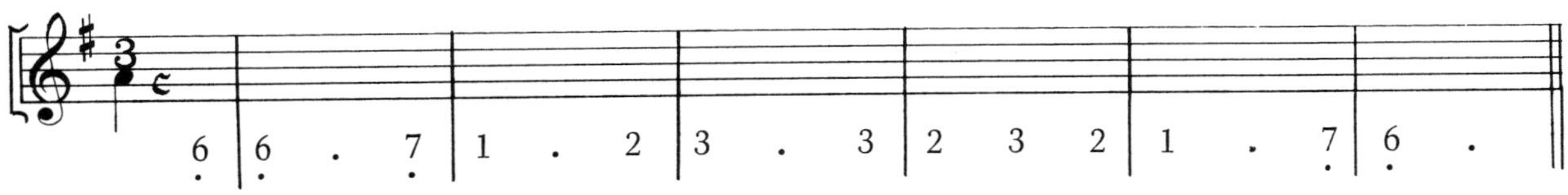

6 | 6 . 7 | 1 . 2 | 3 . 3 | 2 3 2 | 1 . 7 | 6 . ||

Fragments for Sight-singing

1 = B♭

1 = G

Creative Activity

Composing in LA Mode
Ternary Rhythm with Up-pulse Beginning

1. *Improvise melodic applications in LA Mode to rhythm patterns in combination. Use tones of Intonation Exercise.*

a + d

b + b

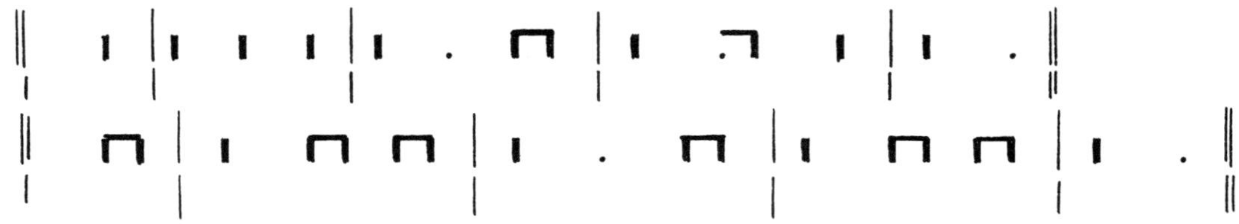

2. *Compose four-line melody on the following rhythm patterns. First line is given. End on LA.*

b)

d)

b)

d)

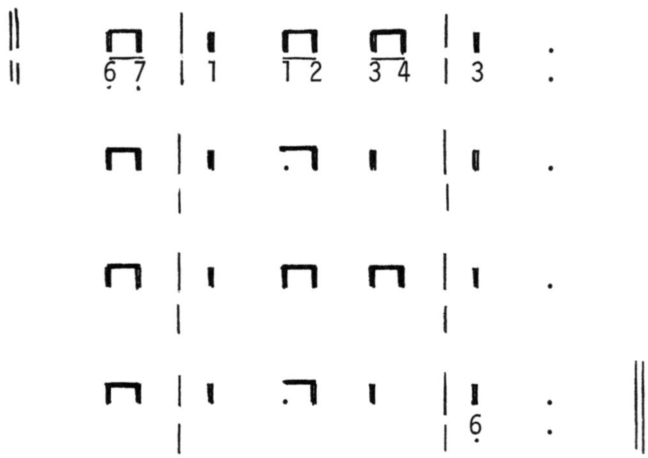

3. *Compose a melody in the LA Mode for the text given below by Robert Burns*

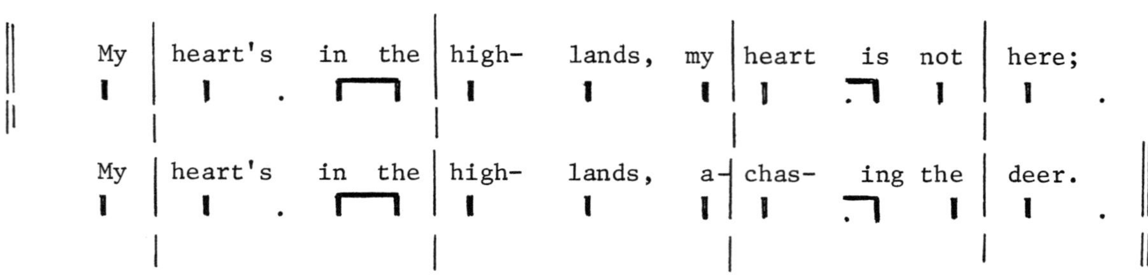

PROCEDURE: Recite the words several times aloud in the rhythm given. Add melody.

Songs

MELODY No. 33 French Folk Melody

Mode of LA
Int. D. 21 P. 152
R. P. Series 3 P. 26
R. G. III

1 = B♭ (6̣ = G)

|| 6̣ | 6̣ . 7̣ | 1 . 2 | 3 .

3 | 2 3 2 | 1 . 7̣ | 6̣ .

7̣ | 1 . 7̣ | 6̣ . 7̣ | 1 . 7̣ | 6̣ .

3 | 3 . 3 | 2 . 3 | 1 . 7̣ | 6̣ . . | . 0 ||

A SAILOR CLIMBED THE MAST ON HIGH *Melody:* French Folk Song
Text: JBW

Mode of LA DO Clef below Staff
St. D. 21a P. 152
R. P. Series 3 P. 26 M. G. III

1 = B♭ (6̣ = G)

MELODY No. 34 English Folk Song

Mode of LA DO Clef below staff
Use for sight-singing and transcription

1 = B♭ (6̣ = G)

THE SILVER MOON IS SHINING *Melody:* Italian Folk Song *Text:* Anonymous

Mode of DO
Authentic Range
Int. D. 8 P. 65
R. P. Series 13 P. 154
M. G. III
begin on up-pulse

i̇ = B♭ (5 = F)

5	1̇ .	7 6 7	6 6
The	sil-	ver moon is	shin- ing
The	night-	ing- gale is	sing- ing
6	7 .	6 5 6	5 5
A-	long ___	the wood-ed	path- way;
With-	in ___	the for- est	shad- ow;
5	6 .	5 4 3	4 4
I	walk ___	a- long the	path- way
I	whis-	tle in the	shad- ow
4	5 .	6	5 3
With	no-	one	near me.
Where	none ___	can	hear me.

Chapter Seventeen

Vocal Training

Review Sustained Tones on All Vowels
Vocal Drill in Upper Tetrachord 6 5 4 3

Review Vocal Exercise 12a

1 = C G E

1 ____________

Nu ____ o ____ a ____ e ____ i ____

Review Vocal Exercise 15

1 = B♭ G C

6 | 3 2 | 1 7 | 6 . | .

Na | Nu No | Ni Na | No ________

Review Vocal Exercise 16b

1 = G B♭

6 . | 7 . | 1 . | 2 . | 3 . | 4 . | 3 . | 2 . | 1 . | 7 . | 6 . | . .

Na - o Na - o Na - o Na - o Na - o Na ____

Vocal Exercise 17a

1 = F G

(6 5 4 | 3 4 5 | 6 . . | . . .

Nu Nu Nu Nu Nu Nu Nu ____________
Na - o - u No - a - e - i ____________

Vocal Exercise 17b In Free Rhythm

1 = F G

0 6 | 5 4 | 3 4 5 | 6 .

Nu Nu Nu Nu Nu Nu Nu ______
Na - o - u No - a - e - i ______

Intonation

LA Mode Upper Tetrachord 6 5 4 3
Extension Upwards 6 7 $\dot{1}$
DO Clef on Bottom Line

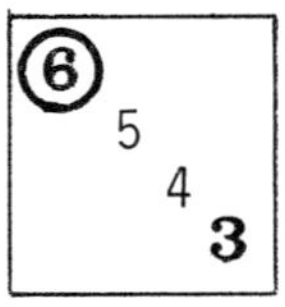

Intonation Diagram 22

Staff Diagrams 22a, b

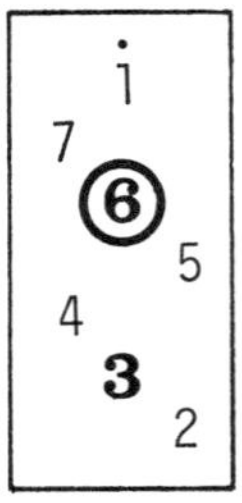

Intonation Diagram 23

Staff Diagram 23

$\dot{1}$ = E♭ or $\dot{1}$ = G (6 = C or 6 = E)

Intonation Exercise 52

Line 1 *with* Intonation Diagram 22
Lines 2 *and* 3 *with* Intonation Diagram 23
Preparation: DO TI LA ($\dot{1}$ 7 6) *on fingers*

| 6 5 6 6 5 4 3 3 4 3 3 4 3 3 4 5 6 6 5 6 |
| 6 5 6 6 5 4 3 3 4 3 3 4 3 3 4 5 6 6 5 6 6 7 $\dot{1}$ 7 6 |
| 6 5 6 6 3 3 4 3 3 4 3 3 6 6 5 6 6 7 $\dot{1}$ 7 6 |

Intonation Exercise 53 - *with* Intonation Diagram 23 *and/or* Staff Diagram 23

| 65676 6543 34323 34323 3456 65676 | *Preparation:* $\dot{1}$ 7 6
| 65676 6543 34323 34323 3456 65676 | *Extended group drills*
| 65676 6 3 34323 34323 3 6 65676 67$\dot{1}$76 |

Intonation Exercise 54 - *With* Intonation Diagram 23 *and/or* Staff Diagram 23

| 1̇ 7 6 6 5 4 3 3 3 3 4 3 3 4 3 3 4 5 6 6 6 | *Repeat outer notes*

| 6 6 6 5 4 3 3 4 3 3 4 3 3 3 3 4 5 6 6 7 1̇ 7 6 |

Intonation Exercise 55 - *With* Intonation Diagram 22 *and/or* Staff Diagram 23

| 6 5 4 3 3 4 5 6 3 6 |

| 6 5 4 3 3 4 5 6 3 6 |

| 6 5 3 5 6 3 6 |

Drill on intervals 5 - 3; 3 - 5

Ear and Eye Tests *1̇ = E♭ (6 = C)*

| 6 5 4 3 3 4 3 6 5 6 | 6 5 6 7 6 6 3 | 1̇ 7 6 6 5 6 6 3 |

| 6 3 6 5 6 6 7 1̇ | 6 3 6 6 7 1̇ 7 6 | 6 5 4 3 3 3 4 3 6 |

| 6 5 5 6 6 3 | 6 5 3 3 5 6 5 6 |

| 6 5 3 5 6 5 6 | 1̇ 7 6 5 6 5 5 3 |

Rhythm

Dotted Quarter and Eighth in Duple Time
(Down-pulse Beginning)
Arsis-Thesis - Free Rhythm

Rhythm Patterns - Series 14

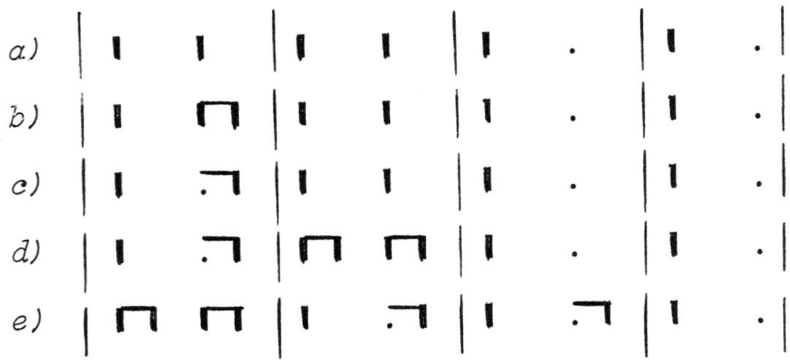

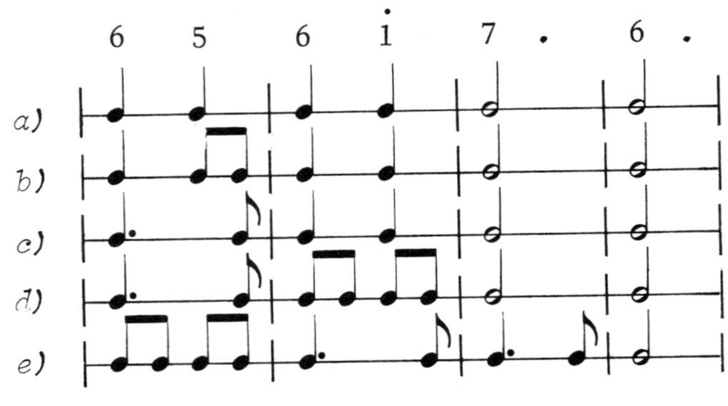

1. *Say rhythm patterns in strict time with* Metrical Gesture I *and* Metrical Language
2. *Sing each rhythm pattern on melody given with:*

   a) Metrical Gesture I
   b) Metrical Gesture II *(Beating Time)*
   c) Rhythm Gesture IV *(As given)*

Rhythmic Dictation (Metrical) *Given with* Metrical Gesture II

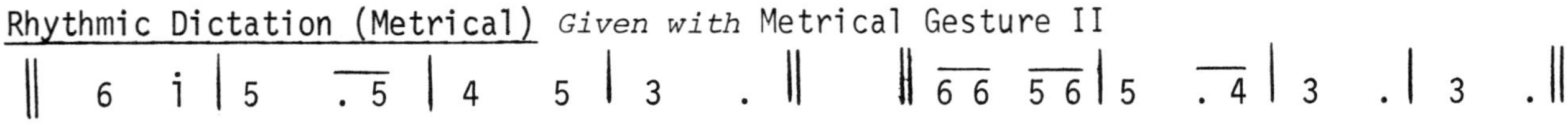

3. *REVIEW* Metrical Gesture IV - Binary and Ternary *as in Chapter Fifteen*
4. *Sing and conduct each phrase given:*

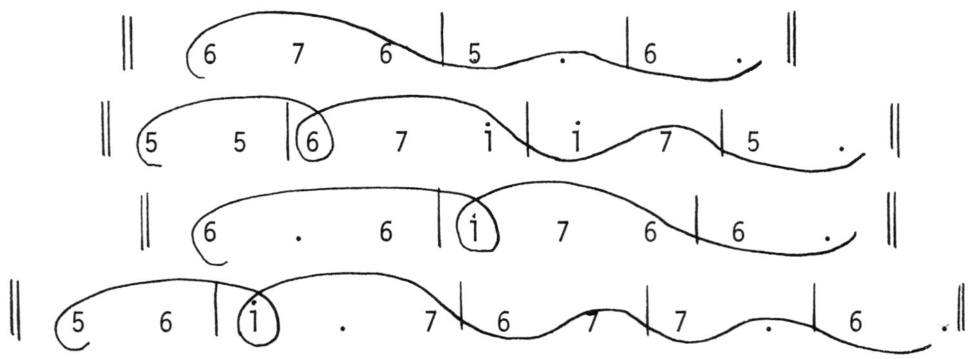

Rhythmic Dictations *Given with Arsis-Thesis shown*

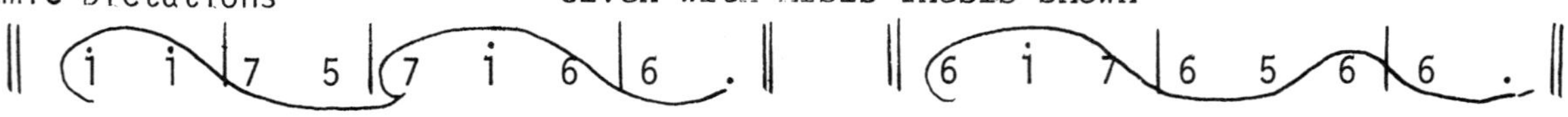

Notation

Key Signature Tells Position of DO on Staff

Up to now we have studied Staff Notation with the DO Clef (C) in three different positions, namely,

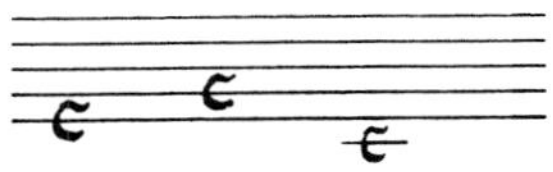

Beginning with Lesson Thirteen, other signs were added to the staff, namely:

G Clef 𝄞 *Sharp* ♯ *Flat* ♭

In one way or another, these signs give us the "key with which we can unlock the secret of the melody." To find this "key", we must first find where DO lives on the staff. These signs will give us a clue. They are called: Key Signatures.

Remember the following rules:

Rule 1. The DO Clef can only be placed on a line, never in a space:

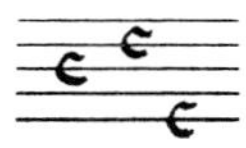 *but never* 

Rule 2. If there is only the G Clef at the beginning of a line, DO is always placed on the line below the staff:

Rule 3. Whenever a sharp sign, or several sharp signs are present, remember the jingle: "If sharps you see, the last is TI."

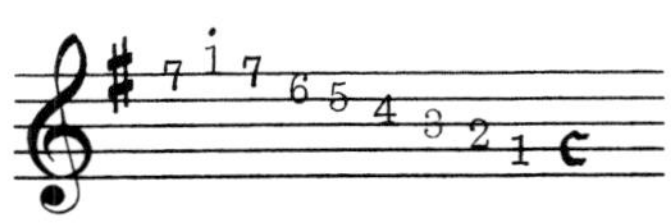

Rule 4. Whenever a flat sign, or several flat signs are present, remember the jingle: "If flats there are, the last is FA."

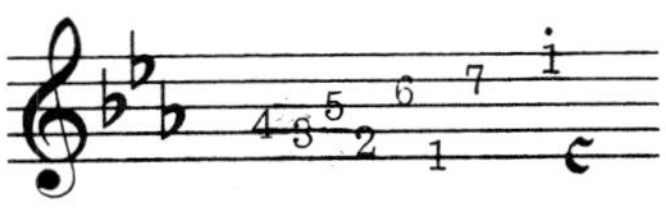

Continued on next page

PRACTISE IN APPLYING RULES

1. Place DO Clef in its correct position on each staff shown below:

2. Name the notes given in each example:

3. Write the notes DO - MI - SOL (1 3 5) in each of the keys shown. (First find the place of DO!)

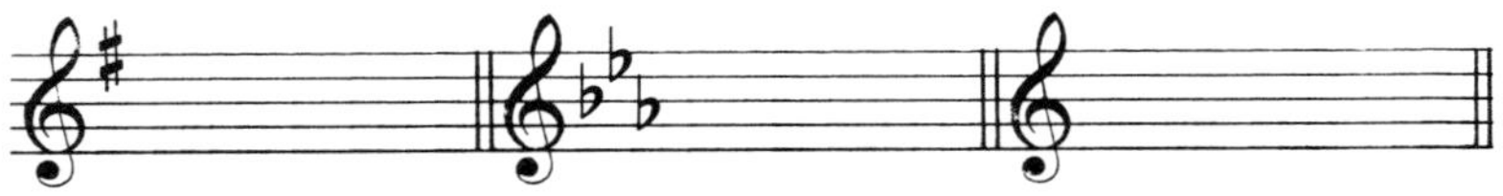

Creative Activity

Compose Two Answering Lines in LA Mode

1. The first two lines of a four-line song are given. Compose two answering lines in contrasting rhythm. End on LA

6 65	6 6	5 4	3 .
6 6	5 . 6	5 6 5 4	3 .
			.
			6 .

2. Improvise melodic applications to rhythms of Rhythm Patterns - Series 14

Songs

Mode of LA
Int. D. 23 P. 160
R. P. Series 14 P. 162

M. G. II
Responses in contrasting rhythm

MELODY No. 35 Anonymous

$\dot{1}$ = E♭ (6 = C) || 6 6 5 6 | 5 . 4 | 3 . 3 | 5 . |
6 . 7	$\dot{1}$ 6	$\dot{1}$.	7 .
6 6 5 6	5 . 4	3 . 3	5 .
3 5 $\dot{1}$ 7	$\dot{1}$. 7	6 .	6 .	

MELODY No. 36 French Carol

Mode of LA DO Clef bottom line
St. D. 23 P. 160 M. G. II

$\dot{1}$ = E♭ (6 = C)

GOD-HEAD HERE IN HIDING *Melody:* Gregorian Chant
Text: "Adoro Te" Trans. by Gerard Manley Hopkins

Mode of DO
Int. D. 1 P. 2
R. G. IV Free

$\dot{1}$ = E♭ (5 = B♭) || 1 3 | 5 5 | 5 6 | 5 . | 4 3 | 2 1 | 1 . |
God-head here in hid- ing__ Whom I do a- dore,__

| 1 3 | 5 5 | 5 6 | 5 . | 4 3 | 2 1 | 1 . | 0 0 |
Masked by these bare shad- ows,__ Shape and noth- ing more._

| 5 5 | 6* 7 $\dot{1}$ | $\dot{1}$ 7 | 5 . | 6 5 | 4 3 | 2 . |
See, Lord, at__ thy ser- vice,__ Low lies here a heart__

| 3 5 | 4 3 | 2 1 | 2 . | 3 1 | 2 1 | 1 . | 0 0 ||
Lost, all lost in won- der__ At the God thou art._

|| 1 2 1 | 7 . | 1 . ||
A- men.______

* Ternary Group

WERE YOU EVER IN QUEBEC? *Melody:* Canadian Folk Song ;
Text: Anonymous

Mode of DO St. D. lb P. 2
R. P. Series 14 P. 162
M.G. II Responses in contrasting rhythm

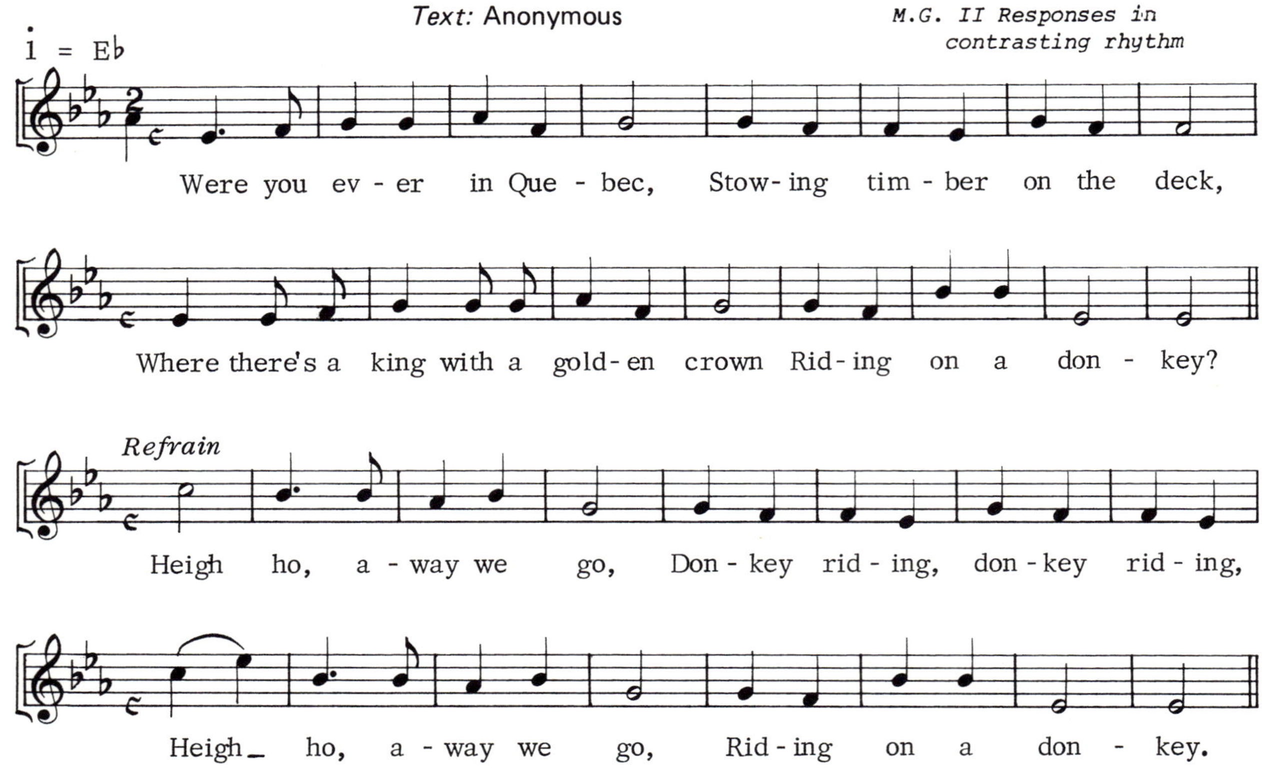

2. Were you ever off the Horn
   Where it's always fine and warm,
   And seen the lion and the unicorn
   Riding on a donkey? *Refrain.*

3. Were you ever in Cardiff Bay?
   Where the folks all shout "Hooray!
   Here comes John with his three-month's pay
   Riding on a donkey." *Refrain.*

PENITENTIAL RITE From "Order of Mass" TM

Mode of LA
Int. D. 23 P. 160
R. G. IV Free

$\dot{1}$ = B♭ (6 = G)

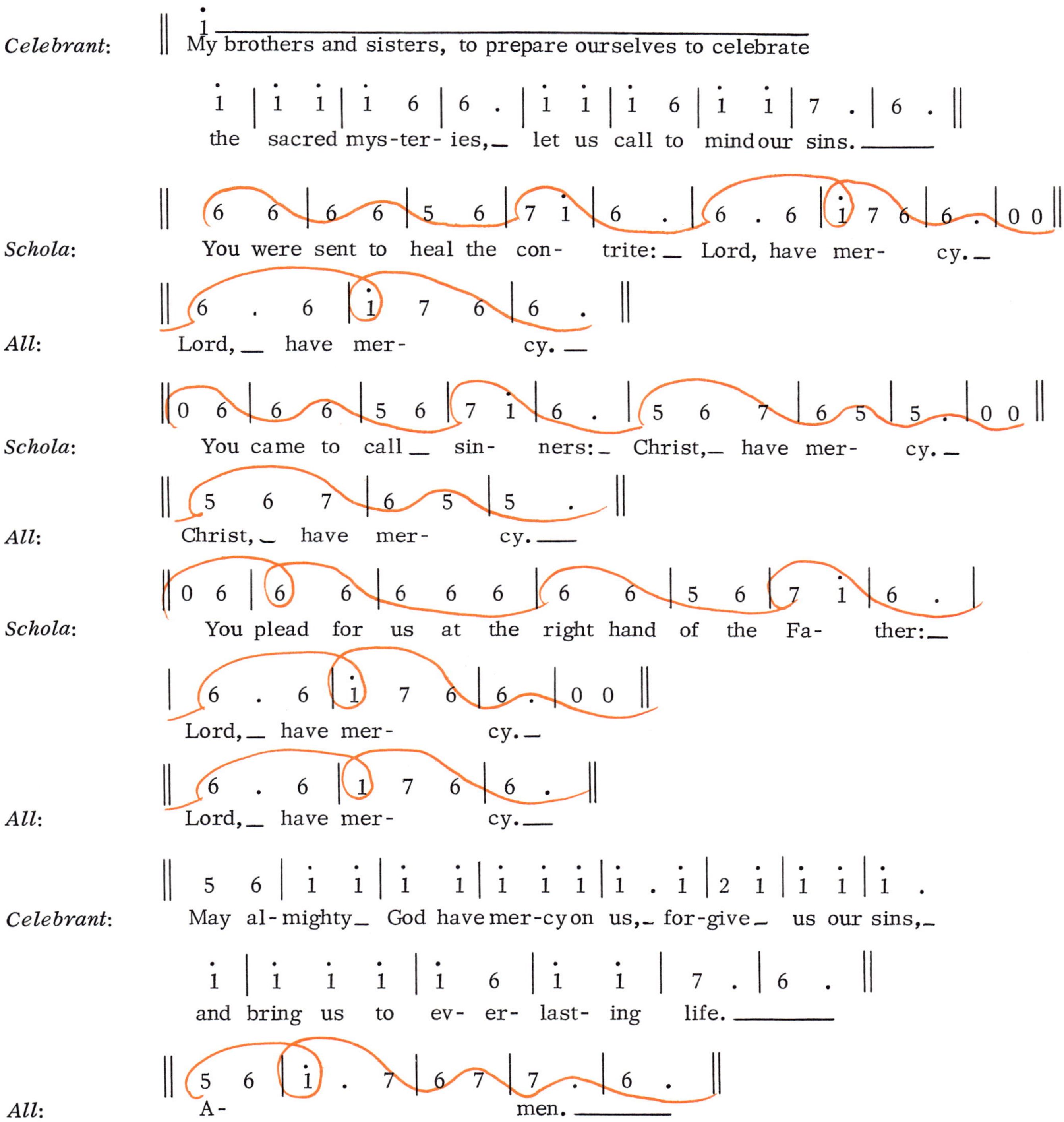

Chapter Eighteen

Vocal Training

Review Sustained Tones on All Vowels
Vocal Drill on Entire LA Mode - Authentic Range

Review Vocal Exercise 12a

1 = B♭ — G — D

1 ——————————————————

Nu ——— o ——— a ——— e ——— i ———

Vocal Exercise 18

1 = G
(6 = E)

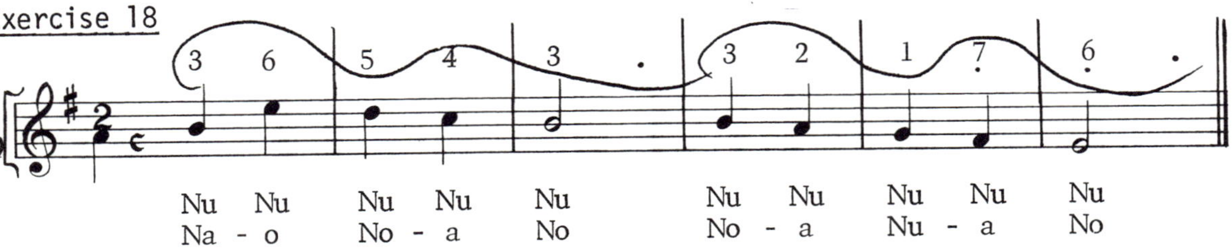

> If the placement of the tone of the open vowels seems to be receding back into the throat, return to practising on Nu with special attention given to the NNNN.

N.B. A pitch-pipe with a C - C range is useful when 6 = E in the Mode of LA

Intonation

LA Mode Authentic Range 6 - 6
First and Second Compass Exercises

1 = G
(6 = E)

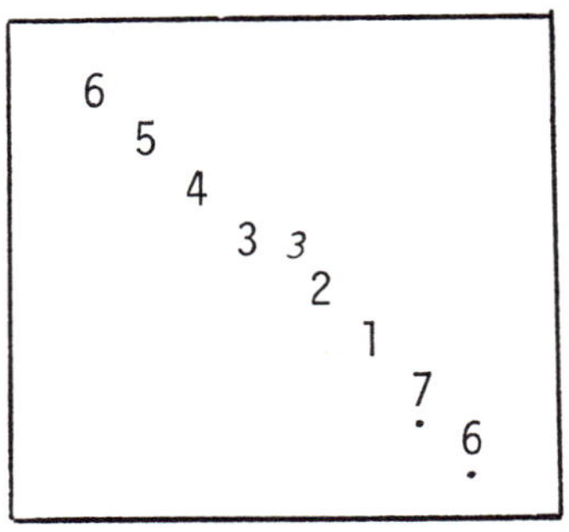

Intonation Diagram 24

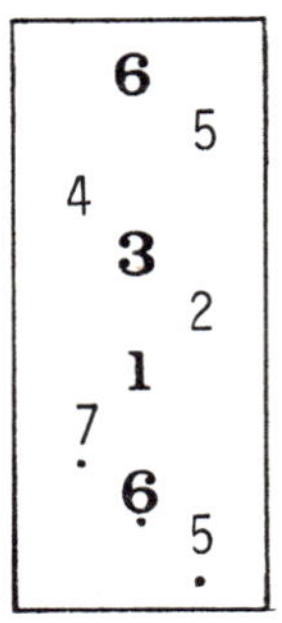

Int. D. 25

Staff Diagram 25

Intonation Exercise 56 - *With* Intonation Diagram 24

| 6 5 4 3 3 2 1 7 6 | 6 7 1 2 3 3 4 5 6 |
| 6 5 4 3 3 2 1 7 6 | 6 7 1 2 3 4 5 6 |

Entire Mode (scale) of LA

Intonation Exercise 57 - *With* Intonation Diagram 25 *and* Staff Diagram 25

676 671 121 123 343 3456 656	656 6543 343 321 121 176 676 656
676 *671* 121 *123* 343 *3456* 656	656 *6543* 343 *321* 121 *176* 676 656
676 121 343 656	656 343 121 676 656

First Compass Exercise

Intonation Exercise 58 - *With* Intonation Diagram 25 *and* Staff Diagram 25

6 7 6 1 2 1 3 4 3 6 5 6	6 5 6 3 4 3 1 2 1 6 7 6
6 7 6 *1 2 1* 3 4 3 6 5 6	6 5 6 3 4 3 *1 2 1* 6 7 6
6 7 6 1 2 1 *3 4 3* 6 5 6	6 5 6 *3 4 3* 1 2 1 6 7 6
6 7 6 *1 2 1* *3 4 3* 6 5 6	6 5 6 *3 4 3* *1 2 1* 6 7 6

Free use of groups

Intonation Exercise 59 - *With* Intonation Diagram 25 *and* Staff Diagram 25

6 7 6 1 2 1 3 4 3 6 5 6	6 5 6 3 4 3 1 2 1 6 7 6
6 *7 6* 1 *2 1* 3 *4 3* 6 *5 6*	6 *5 6* 3 *4 3* 1 *2 1* 6 *7 6*
6 1 3 6	6 3 1 6

Second Compass Exercise

Eye and Ear Tests *"Which family: Major (Mode of DO) or Minor (Mode of LA)?"*

Minor 1 = G (6 = E)

| 6 7 1 2 3 3 4 3 | 6 5 6 3 4 3 6 5 6 | 6 5 4 3 6 7 6 |
| 6 5 4 3 6 5 6 | 6 7 6 1 2 1 3 4 3 | 1 2 1 3 4 3 6 7 6 |

Major

1 = G (5 = D)

| 1 2 1 3 4 3 5 6 5 | 5 6 7 i i 5 3 1 |
| 5 6 5 3 2 1 5 1 | 1 2 3 4 5 3 2 3 |

Rhythm

Dotted Quarter and Eighth in Triple Time
(Down-pulse Beginning)
Combining Triple and Duple Time in Free Rhythm

Rhythm Patterns - Series 15

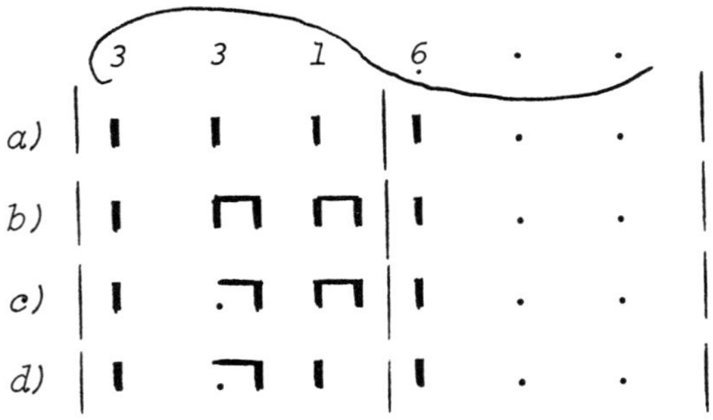

1. *Say rhythms in strict time with* Metrical Gesture I *and* Metrical Language

2. *Repeat singing tones suggested above pulse lines with:*

   Metrical Gesture I
   Rhythm Gesture IV (Arsis-Thesis) Ternary *as given above*

<u>*REVIEW*</u> Metrical Gesture III - Beating Time *(See Chapter Nine)* Triple Meter

Repeat singing rhythm patterns on tones suggested above pulse lines while making Metrical Gesture III

3. *Practise fragments below with Arsis-Thesis as given in preparation for singing* Come, Let Us Make a Snowman

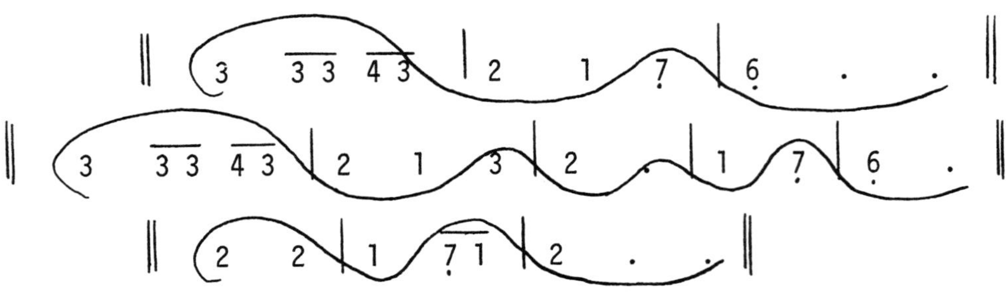

Rhythmic Dictations: Line 1 of Melody No. 37
Last line of "My Country, "Tis of Thee"

Notation

Key Signature Tells Position of DO Clef (Continued)

1. *Review rules for finding the position of DO on the staff. (See Chapter Seventeen).*

   Then place the DO Clef *on the correct* *line* *of each staff shown below:*
   (The DO Clef nevers appears in a space.)

2. *In the Major Mode, DO is the* *Tonic,* *or Final, note. Usually, a song in the Major Mode ends on the note DO.*

   In the Minor Mode, or LA Mode, LA is the *Tonic,* *or Final, note. Usually, a song in the Minor Mode ends on the note LA.*

   To find the *Tonic Note* *of the Minor Mode, sing* 1 7̣ 6̣ *(DO TI LA) from the line on which the DO Clef is located. For example:*

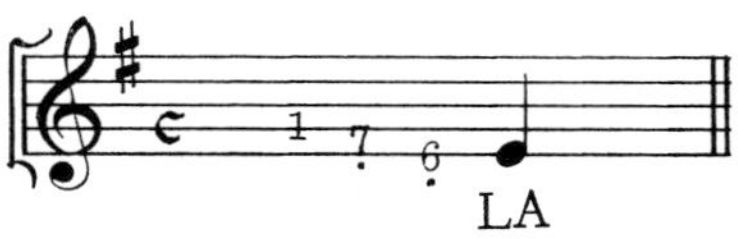

PRACTISE: *Find tonic note of the Minor Mode from each DO Clef given. Place the note LA in its correct position on the staff.*

3. *Add* DO Clef *and transcribe the last line of* Intonation Exercise 57 *to Staff Notation.*

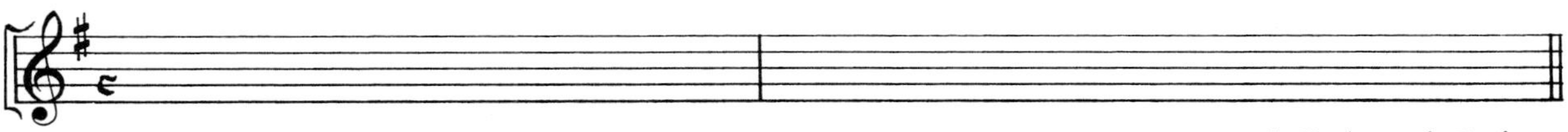

6̣7̣6̣ 121 343 656 | 656 343 121 6̣7̣6̣ 6̣5̣6̣

> For the time being, the students need only to know that the clue to locating the DO Clef correctly on the staff is to be found in the Key Signature. These musical signs are the "key" with which they can unlock the "secret" of the melody.

Creative Activity

Composing Answers to Themes by Classical Composers.
LA Mode and DO Mode
Composing Melody for Text in Free Rhythm

1. *Compose an answer in the* <u>*same rhythm*</u> *to the following statement. The theme is in the LA Mode (Minor) and is by Mozart. End on LA - the* <u>*Tonic,*</u> *or Final, note.*

|| 3 . 4 3 | 3 . 6 | 6 . . | 6 5 4 | 3 . . |

| | | | | 6 . . ||

2. *Compose an answer in* <u>*contrasting rhythm*</u> *to the following statement. The theme is in the DO Mode (Major) and is be Henry Purcell. End on DO - the* <u>*Tonic,*</u> *or Final, note.*

|| 5 5 5 | 5 . 6 7 | 1 1 1 | 1 . 2 3 |

| | | | 1 . . ||

3. *Compose a melody in the LA Mode for the following text. Notice that the first half of the text is in Ternary, and the second half in Binary Rhythm.*

|| Sing to the | Lord a new | song for | ho- ly | is his | name. ||

4. *Compose melodic applications for rhythm patterns of this chapter. LA Mode or DO Mode.*

a + b

c + d

a + c

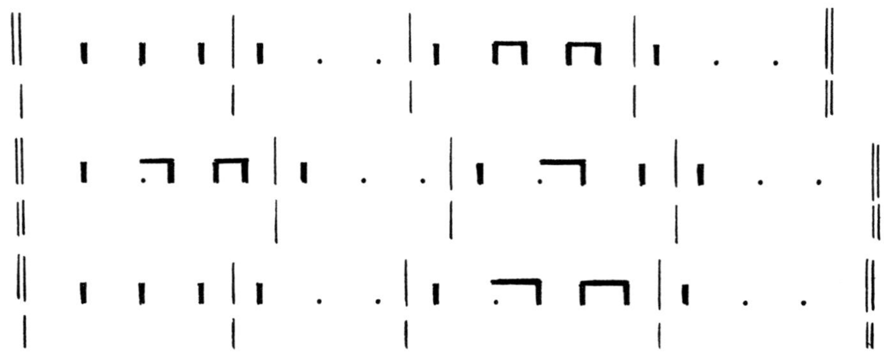

Songs

Mode of LA
Int. D. 25 P. 168
R. P. Series 9 P. 58
M. G. III
Responses in contrasting rhythms

MELODY No. 37 Catalan Folk Song

1 = G
(6̣ = E)

6̣	6̣	6̣	1	.	2	3	.	.	1	.	0
2	4	3 4	5	.	4	3	.	.	.	.	0
3	1	2	3	.	4	2	.	.	1	.	0
6̣	1	7̣ 1	2	.	1	6̣	.	.	.	.	0

MELODY No. 38 "Engadine" *18th Century Folk Melody*

1 = G (6̣ = E)

Mode of LA Authentic Range
St. D. 25 P. 168
R. P. Series 15 P. 170
R. G. IV Ternary
Repetition and contrast

MY COUNTRY 'TIS OF THEE *Melody:* 18th Century English Melody *Text:* Samuel Francis Smith

1 = G (5 = D)

Mode of DO St. D. 6 P. 34
R. P. Series 15 P. 170
Sequence in lines 1 and 3

WE THREE KINGS *Melody and Text:* John Henry Hopkins

1 = G (6 = E)

‖ 3 . 2 | 1 . 6 | 7 1 7 | 6 . . |
We ___ three kings ___ of O- ri- ent are ______

| 3 . 2 | 1 . 6 | 7 1 7 | 6 . . |
Bear- ing gifts ___ we trav- elled a- far, ______

| 1 . 1 | 2 . 2 | 3 . 3 | 5 4 3 |
Field _ and foun- tain, Moor ___ and moun- tain,

| 2 3 2 | 1 . 7 | 6 . . ‖
Fol- low- ing yon- der star. ______

| 7 . 2 | 1 . 1 | 1 . 5 | 1 . 6 | 1 . . |
O ______ star ___ of won- der, star ___ of night, ______

| 1 . 1 | 1 . 5 | 1 . 6 | 1 . . |
Star ___ of roy- al beau- ty bright; ______

| 1 . 1 | 2 . 3 | 4 . 3 | 2 . 3 |
West- ward lead- ing, Still ___ pro- ceed- ing,

| 1 . 1 | 1 . 5 | 1 . 6 | 1 . . ‖
Guide ___ us to ___ that per- fect light! ______

Mode of LA
Lines 1 - 4
Mode of DO
Lines 5 - 8
Int. D 25 P. 108
R. G. IV Ternary
Repetition and contrast

MELODY No. 39 Alsatian Waltz Melody

Mode of DO Plagal Range
Int. d 6 P. 34
R. P. Series 15 P. 170
M. G. III

1 = G (5 = D)

|| 5 . 6 5 4 | 3 1 1 | 2 5̣ 5̣ | 3 1 1 |

| 5 . 6 5 4 | 3 1 1 | 2 5̣ 5̣ | 1 . 1 |

| 2 5̣ 5̣ | 3 1 1 | 2 5̣ 5̣ | 3 1 1 |

| 5 . 6 5 4 | 3 1 1 | 2 5̣ 5̣ | 1 . . |

COME, LET US MAKE A SNOW MAN *Melody:* Folk Melody of the Asturias *Text:* JBW

Mode of LA
St. D 25 P. 168
R. G. IV Free
Repetition

1 = G (5 = D)

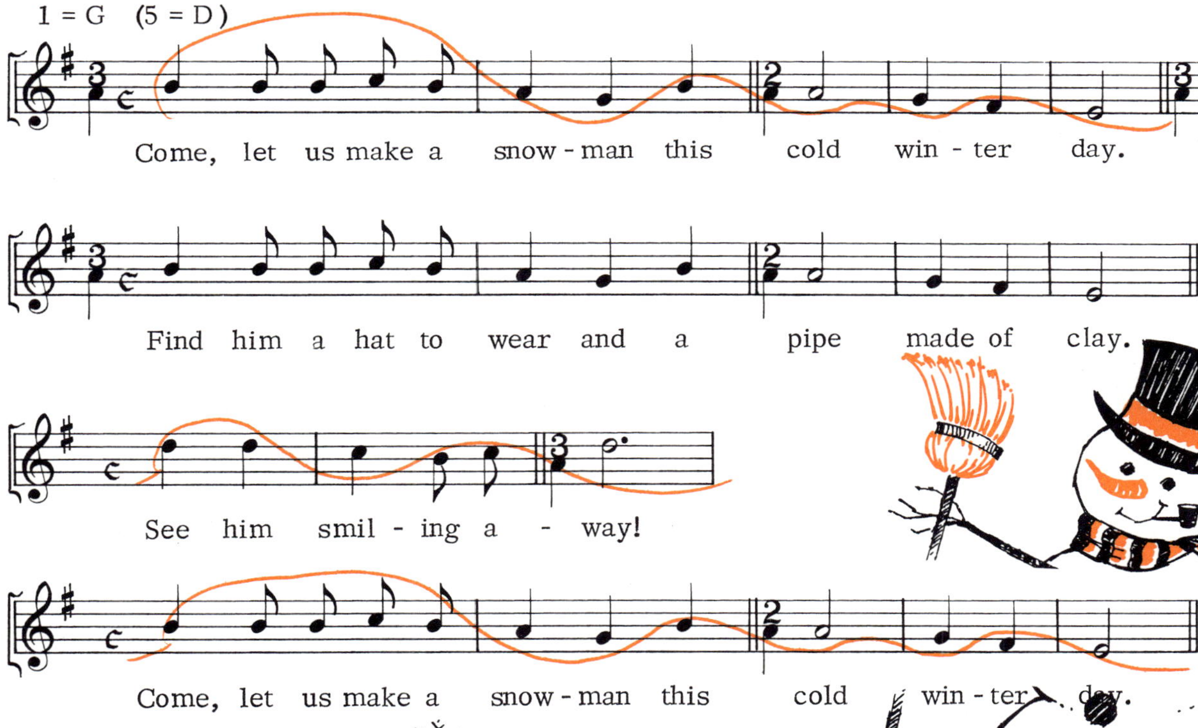

Chapter Nineteen

Vocal Training

Sustained Tones on All Vowels
Introducing Vowels With Consonants N D T
Review Vocal Drill in LA Mode - Authentic Range

Review Vocal Exercise 12a
Vocal Exercise 12b - Introduce Vowel Series with N D T *(Dental Consonants)*

1 = B (*G*, *E*)

1 ______

Nu ____	o ____	a ____	e ____	i ____
Du ____	o ____	a ____	e ____	i ____
Tu ____	o ____	a ____	e ____	i ____

> The consonants D and T are formed by the action of the tongue against the teeth. Sing them gently so as not to lose the head placement of the vowel that follows.

Review Vocal Exercise 18 - *Sing on one breath! Entire LA Mode - Authentic Range.*

1 = G
(6 = E)

Intonation

Tonic Chord Line 6 1 3 6 With Scales
and Surrounding Notes

1 = G (6 = E)

	7
6	5
	4
3	2
1	7
6	5

Intonation
Diagram 26

Intonation Exercise 60 - *With* Intonation Diagram 26

| 6 6 6 1 3 3 3 3 3 6 6 6 | 6 6 6 3 1 1 1 1 1 6 6 6 |
| 6 1 1 1 2 3 3 3 2 3 6 3 | 6 3 3 2 3 6 3 3 2 1 7 6 |

Notes of Tonic Chord LA - DO - MI 6 1 3

Staff Diagram 26a

Staff Diagram 26b

Intonation Exercise 61 - *With* Intonation Diagram 26 *and* Staff Diagrams 26a,b

Notes of Tonic Chord and scale passages

6 1 3 3 4 3 2 1 7 6 3 1 6 6 5 6 7 1 2 3

6 1 3 6 6 5 4 3 4 5 6 3 6 6 6 5 4 3 2 3 3 3 1 6 5 6

Intonation Exercise 62 - *With* Intonation Diagram 26 *and* Staff Diagram 26b

Notes of Tonic Chord with scale groups and sequences

6 1 3 6 6 5 4 3 4 3 3 2 1 2 1 7 6

6 3 6 1 1 7 6 7 1 2 3 2 3 3 4 5 6 6 3 1 6

3 6 6 3 3 1 6 6 7 1 7 1 2 1 2 3 2 3 4 3 4 5 6

3 1 6 6 3 6 3 4 2 3 3 6 3 4 3 2 1 7 6 5 6 7 6

Intonation Exercise 63 - *With* Intonation Diagram 26 *and/or* Staff Diagram 26b

Notes of Tonic Chord and surrounding groups

a)

6 1 1 6 5 6 7 6 6 1 1 3 2 3 4 3 3 6 6 3 4 3 2 3

6 1 1 6 5 6 7 6 6 1 1 3 2 3 4 3 3 6 6 3 4 3 2 3

b)

6 3 3 6 5 6 7 6 6 3 3 1 2 1 7 1 6 3 1 6 7 6 5 6

6 3 3 6 5 6 7 6 6 3 3 1 2 1 7 1 6 3 1 6 7 6 5 6

Ear and Eye Tests

Select note-groups from Intonation Exercises 60, 61, 62, and 63; also, quotations from the songs of this chapter.
Add Major Mode fragments as in Chapter 18.

Rhythm

Dotted Quarter and Eighth in Triple Time
(Up-pulse Beginning)
Introducing the Triplet
Continue Study of Free Rhythm

Rhythm Patterns - Series 16

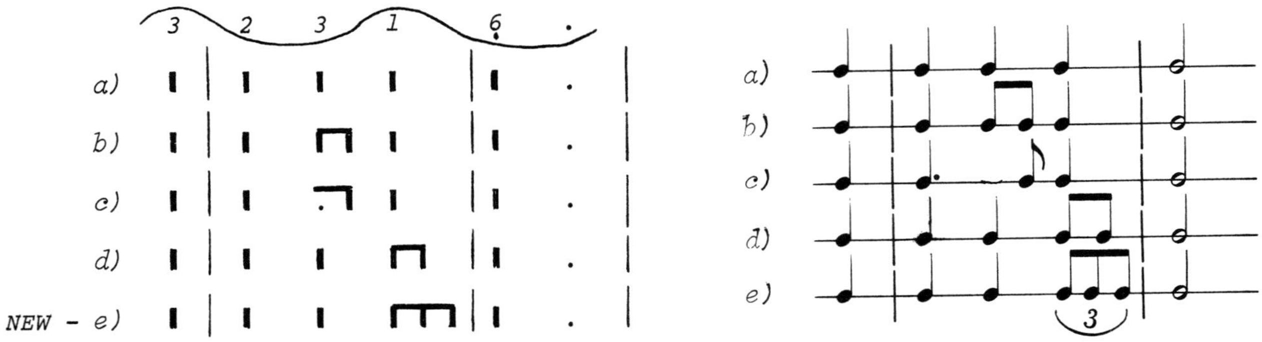

1. *Say Rhythm Patterns a), b), c), and d), in strict time with* Metrical Gesture I *and* Metrical Language

   REVIEW Rhythm Gesture III *silently. (See Chapter Three)*

   Repeat singing same rhythm patterns on tones suggested above pulse lines while making Rhythm Gesture III

2. *NEW PATTERN - the* Triplet. *The Triplet has three notes on one pulse. See* Rhythm Pattern *e) above.*

   Practise singing Rhythm Patterns *d) and e) as follows:*

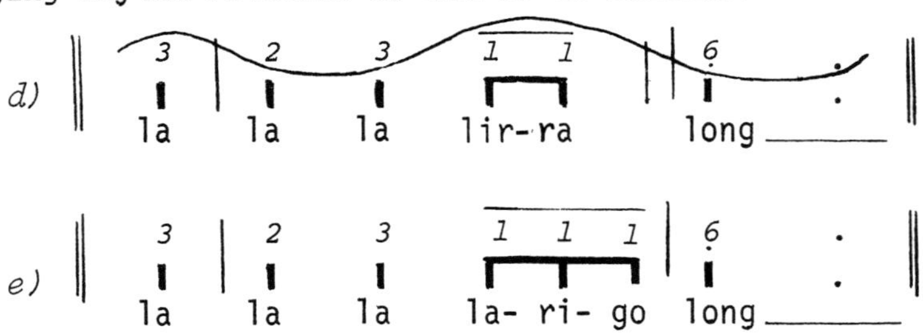

   First sing with Metrical Gesture I *and* Metrical Language *as given*
   Then repeat singing notes suggested above the pulse lines with Rhythm Gesture III

3. *Free Rhythm fragments as preparation for singing* O Come, O Come, Emmanuel

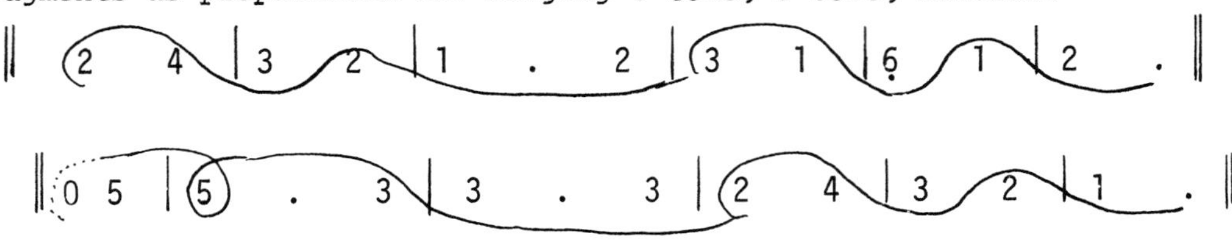

4. *Rhythmic Dictation - Line of* MELODY No. 40; MELODY No. 41

Notation

Continue Finding Place of DO Clef from Key Signature
Continue Finding Place of LA from Key Signature
Notation of the Triplet

1. *Review rules for placing DO Clef on the staff* *(See Chapter Seventeen)*

   Then find the correct place of the DO Clef *for each Key Signature given below*

2. *Find the place of the note* LA *for each Key Signature given below. (Remember: First find DO, then count down to LA.*

Practise in finding the correct place of DO on the staff can be planned whenever a new song is presented and the note names of the song have to be identified.

The Triplet - *A group of three notes sung on one pulse*

In Number Notation (or pulse lines) a bar above the three notes identifies the Triplet *

For example: 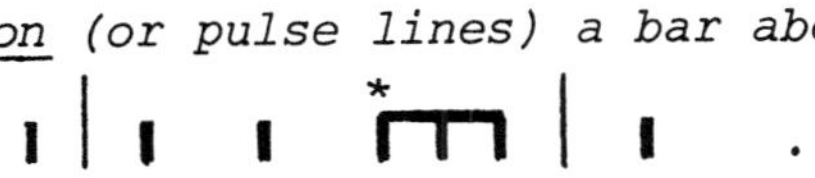 *or* 4 | 5 5 *456 | 5 .

In Staff Notation the figure 3 and a slur, above or below the notes, identify the Triplet

For example:

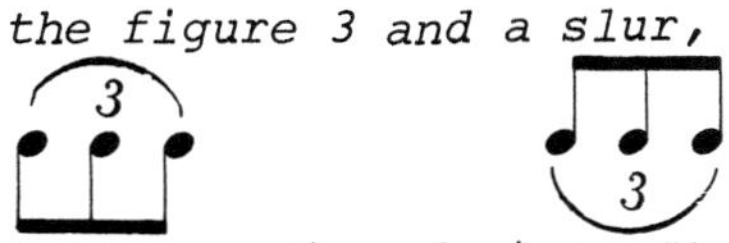

4. *Transcribe Rhythm Patterns d) and e) to Staff Notation note values.*

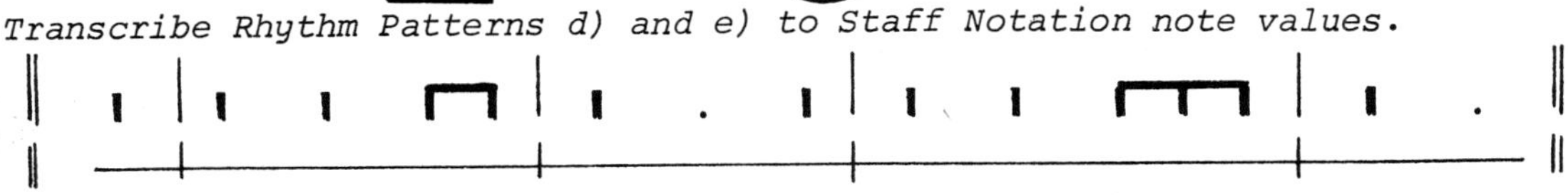

5. *Transcribe to Staff Notation, Line 2 of* The King of Love My Shepherd Is

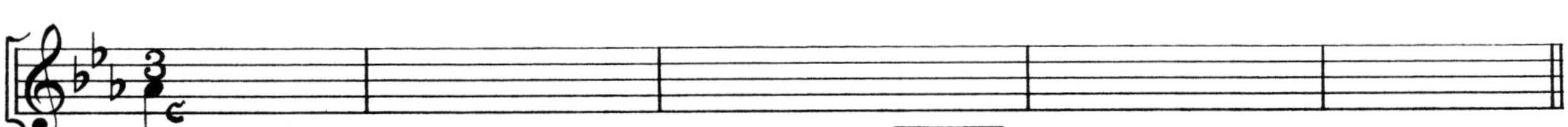

1 2 3 . 4 5 . 4 5 6 5 . . 5 .

Creative Activity

Composing Melody for Poetic Text
Feminine Endings

Feminine Endings

The Feminine Ending occurs when the last accent of a line of text coincides with the the first pulse of the last measure and is followed by another syllable. For example:*

|| 3 5 6 | 4 . 2 | * 1 . 2 ||
|| Rós- es on | híll- side | blóom- ing ||

|| 6 7 | 1 2 | * 3 3 ||
|| Whíle the | trées are | léaf- less ||

To treat the Feminine Ending rhythmically, the last accented syllable may be included in the same measure, as shown in the examples above, or it may be extended to the next measure. For example:

|| 3 5 6 | 4 . 2 | 1 . . | 2 . . ||
|| Ros- es on | hill- side | bloom- | ing ______ ||

|| 6 7 | 1 2 | 3 . | 3 . ||
|| While the | trees are | leaf- | less ____ ||

Compose music for the following texts that contain Feminine Endings.

1. Mode of DO (Last note is Final - DO) Notice the Duple meter of this poem

	Whíle the	trées are	léaf- less,
Whíle the	fíelds are	báre,
Bút- ter-	cups and	daís- ies
Spríng up	hére and	thére.	

Helen Howitt

2. Mode of LA (Last note is Final - LA)

	Ho- ly	Spir- it,	ev- er	dwell- ing
In the	ho- liest	realms of	light;
Ho- ly	Spir- it,	ev- er	shin- ing
O'er the	world with	ra- diance	bright	

T. Reese

Songs

Mode of LA Tonic Chord Line
Int. D 26 P. 176
R. P. Series 16 P. 178
R. G. III

MELODY No. 40 "Intonation Song" TM

1 = G (6 = E)

‖ 6 | 3 . 2 1 | 3 . 3 | 4 . 5 4 | 3 .

3 | 2 . 3 2 | 1 1 7 6 | 7 7 1 | 2 .

6 | 3 . 2 1 | 3 . 3 | 6 6 5 4 | 3 .

3 | 2 . 3 2 | 1 1 2 3 | 2 2 1 7 | 6 . ‖

Mode of LA Tonic Chord Line
Int. D 26 P. 176
R. P. Series 16, P. 178
R. G. III Triplets in Line 2

MELODY No. 41 Anonymous

1 = G
(6 = E)

THE KING OF LOVE MY SHEPHERD IS *Melody:* Irish Hymn "St. Columba" *Text:* Paraphrase of Psalm 23 by H. Baker

1 = D (5 = A)

‖ 1 2 | 3 . 4 | 5 . 4 5 | 3 . 2 | 1 .
The _ King _ of love _ my _ shep- herd is _

1 2 | 3 . 4 | 5 . 4 5 6 | 5 . . | 5 .
Whose _ good- ness fail- eth _ nev- ver; _

5 | 1 . 6 | 5 . 4 | 3 . 2 | 1 .
I noth- ing lack _ if I _ am his _

3 | 5 . 4 | 3 . 2 | 1 . . | 1 . ‖
And he _ is mine _ for ev- er. _

Mode of DO Skips on Chord Line
R. G. III Triplet in Line 2

A DAY IN THE CORNFIELD Folk Song of the Hebrides

Mode of LA
Chord Line Skips
St. D 26b P. 177
M.G. III
Feminine endings
Line 1, 2, 4

1 = G ($\underset{\cdot}{6}$ = E)

O COME, O COME, EMMANUEL Traditional Advent Hymn

Mode of LA
Int. D 26 P. 176
R.G. IV Free
Ternary groups at ends of lines 1, 2, 3, and 5

1 = G ($\underset{\cdot}{6}$ = E)

‖ 0 $\underset{\cdot}{6}$ | 1 3 | 3 3 | 2 4 | 3 2 | 1 .
O come, O come, Em- man- u- el,

2 | 3 1 | $\underset{\cdot}{6}$ 1 | 2 $\underset{\cdot}{7}$ | $\underset{\cdot}{6}$ $\underset{\cdot}{5}$ | $\underset{\cdot}{6}$.
And ran-som cap- tive Is- ra- el

2 | 2 $\underset{\cdot}{6}$ | $\underset{\cdot}{6}$ $\underset{\cdot}{7}$ | 1 . | $\underset{\cdot}{7}$ $\underset{\cdot}{6}$ | $\underset{\cdot}{5}$.
That mourns in lone- ly ex- ile here

1 | 2 3 | 3 3 | 2 4 | 3 2 | 1 . ‖
Un- til the Son of God ap- pear.

‖ 0 $\underset{\cdot}{5}$ | $\underset{\cdot}{5}$. $\underset{\cdot}{3}$ | 3 . 3 | 2 4 | 3 2 | 1 .
Re- joice, re- joice, Em- man- u- el

2 | 3 1 | $\underset{\cdot}{6}$ 1 | 2 $\underset{\cdot}{7}$ | $\underset{\cdot}{6}$ $\underset{\cdot}{5}$ | $\underset{\cdot}{6}$. | . ‖
Shall come to thee, O Is- ra- el.

Chapter Twenty

Vocal Training

Review Vowels Introduced by N D T
Sustained Vowels Introduced by M B P
Review Vocal Drill in LA Mode - Authentic Range

Review Vocal Exercise 12b - Introducing Vowels with N D T *(Dental Consonants)*

1 = B G E

1				
Nu	o	a	e	i
Du	o	a	e	i
Tu	o	a	a	i

Vocal Exercise 12c - Introducing Vowels with M B P *(Labial Consonants)*

1				
Mu	o	a	e	i
Bu	o	a	e	i
Pu	o	a	e	i

> Sing each vowel series on one breath
> Retain head placement of vowel following consonant

Review Vocal Exercise 18 *Sing on one breath. Entire LA Mode - Authentic Range*

1 = G (6̣ = E)

Nu Nu | Nu Nu | Nu | Nu Nu | Nu Nu | Nu
Na - o | No - a | No | No - a | Nu - a | No

> Attack high LA without "scooping". Think the high tone before singing it.

Intonation

Third Compass Exercise - LA Mode
Dependent Tones of Minor Mode

Intonation Diagram 25

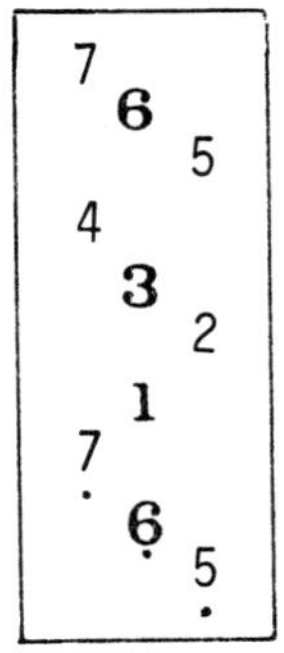

Staff Diagram 25

1 = G (6 = E)

Intonation Exercise 64 - *With* Intonation Diagram 25

Third Compass Exercise

676	121	343	656	656	343	121	676	656
676	*121*	*343*	*656*	*656*	*343*	*121*	*676*	*656*
76	21	43	56	56	43	21	76	56

Intonation Exercise 65 - *With* Intonation Diagram 25

Free use of groups

1 7 6	76	21	43	56	56	43	21	76	56	676
	76	*21*	43	56	56	*43*	21	*76*	56	676
	76	21	*43*	56	56	43	*21*	76	*56*	676
	76	*21*	*43*	56	*56*	43	*21*	*76*	56	676

Intonation Exercise 66 - *With* Intonation Diagram 25

Review of Compass Exercises Mode of LA

676	121	343	656	656	343	121	676	656	*I*
6	1	3	6	6	3	1	6		*II*
76	21	43	56	56	43	21	76	56	*III*

Intonation Diagram 27

6
3
1
6

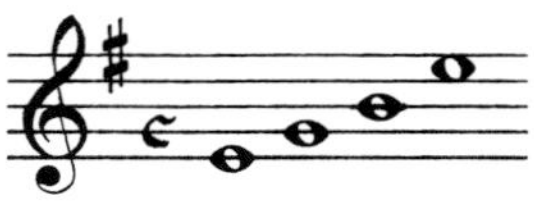

Staff Diagram 27

Intonation Exercise 67 - *With* Intonation Diagram 27 *and* Staff Diagram 27

a)
| 6 1 3 3 6   6 3 3 1 6 |
| 6 1 3 3 6   6 3 3 1 6 |
| 6   3 3 6   6 3 3   6 |

b)
| 6 1 |
| 6 1 3 |
| 6 1 3 6 |

c)
| 6 3 |
| 6 3 1 |
| 6 3 1 6 |

Free use of notes of Tonic Minor Chord

Eye and Ear Tests

| 6 7 6   2 1   4 3 | 6 5 6   4 3   2 1 | 7 6   2 1   4 3   5 6
6 5 6   1 2 1   4 3 | 6 7 6   2 1   7 6 | 2 1   4 3   6 7 6

| 6 1 3 6   6 5 6 | 6 3 6 6 6 |
6 3 1 6   1 2 1 | 6 1 6 3 6 6 |

Intonation Exercise 66 in Staff Notation

Rhythm

Discover Rhythm of Unbarred Songs and Phrases
in Metrical and Free Rhythm
Recognize Rhythm of Songs From Listening

The teacher places a song on blackboard without bar-lines. Students determine rhythm by placing bar before each long note and where melodic motifs suggest.

1. 3 2 1 7̣ 6̣ .

2 1 2 3 3 .

3 6 5 4 3 . 2 .

2 3 2 1 2 . 3 .

3 2 1 7̣ 6̣ .

2 1 7̣ 7̣ 6̣ .

2. 5 6 7 1̇ 7 6 5 6 7 1̇ . 1̇ . 5 . .

3. 3 . 1 2 3 . . 2 1 . . 0

4.

Free Rhythm - *5.* 1 2 1 2 3 . 4 3 2 . 4 3 . 2 1 .

Free Rhythm - *6.* 5 5 . 6 5 . 5 . 1 2 3 . 3 .

<u>Rhythmic Dictations</u> *Fragments of songs are sung by the teacher. Selections should be taken from songs already studied. Dictations are given without rhythm gestures. Students must <u>listen</u>.*

<u>Turning</u> *Chapter Eleven - Last line*

<u>O Lord, I Am Not Worthy</u> *Chapter One - First line*

<u>Some Love Coffee, Some Love Tea</u> *Chapter Ten - Second line*

<u>Sing With Joy to the Lord</u> *Chapter Twelve - First line*

<u>We Three Kings</u> *Chapter Eighteen - First line*

Notation

Transcribe Complete Song in LA Mode With Key Signature of One Sharp

Transcribe to Number Notation Let All Mortal Flesh Keep Silence

1 = G (6 = E)

Creative Activity

Compose Two Answering Lines in LA Mode
Compose Melody for Poetic Text DO Mode

1. *The first two lines are given. Compose two additional lines that develop the dotted rhythm figure. Mode of LA. End on LA.*

‖ 3 $\overline{.\ 2}$ | 3 3 | 1 $\overline{.\ \underset{\cdot}{7}}$ | $\underset{\cdot}{6}$. |

| 3 $\overline{.\ 4}$ | 3 6 | 3 $\overline{.\ 2}$ | 3 . |

| | | | . |

| | | | 6 . ‖

2. *Study the accent patterns of the following poetic text and derive from them a musical rhythm. Compose a melody for the poem in the DO Mode. End on DO.*

‖ The whist- ling post- man swings a- long,
His bag is deep and wide,
And mes- sa- ges from all the world
Are bun- dled up in- side. ‖ *Anon.*

PROCEDURE: *Draw a pulse line over each syllable of the text.*
Mark the verbal accents and draw a measure bar before each.
Look for places in the rhythm where dotted notes could be used.
Is the rhythm Binary (Duple Time), or Ternary (Triple Time)?
Add melody.

Songs

MELODY No. 42 English Folk Melody

Mode of LA
Int. D 25 P. 184
R. P. Series 5 P. 46
R. G. II
Repetition and contrast of phrases

1 = G (6 = E)

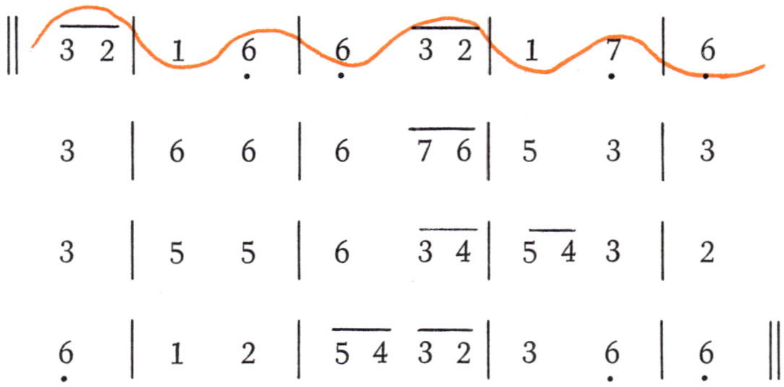

CHRIST OUR LORD IS RISEN *Melody:* Traditional Chant *Text:* JBW

Mode of LA
Int. D 25 P. 184
R.G. IV Binary
Last three phrases begin on on up-pulse

1 = G (6 = E)

LET ALL MORTAL FLESH KEEP SILENCE *Melody:* "Picardy" French Folk Melody *Text:* G. Moultrie

Mode of LA Authentic Range
St. D 25 P. 184
R. G. IV Binary
Repetition Conclusive Response

1 = G (6̣ = E)

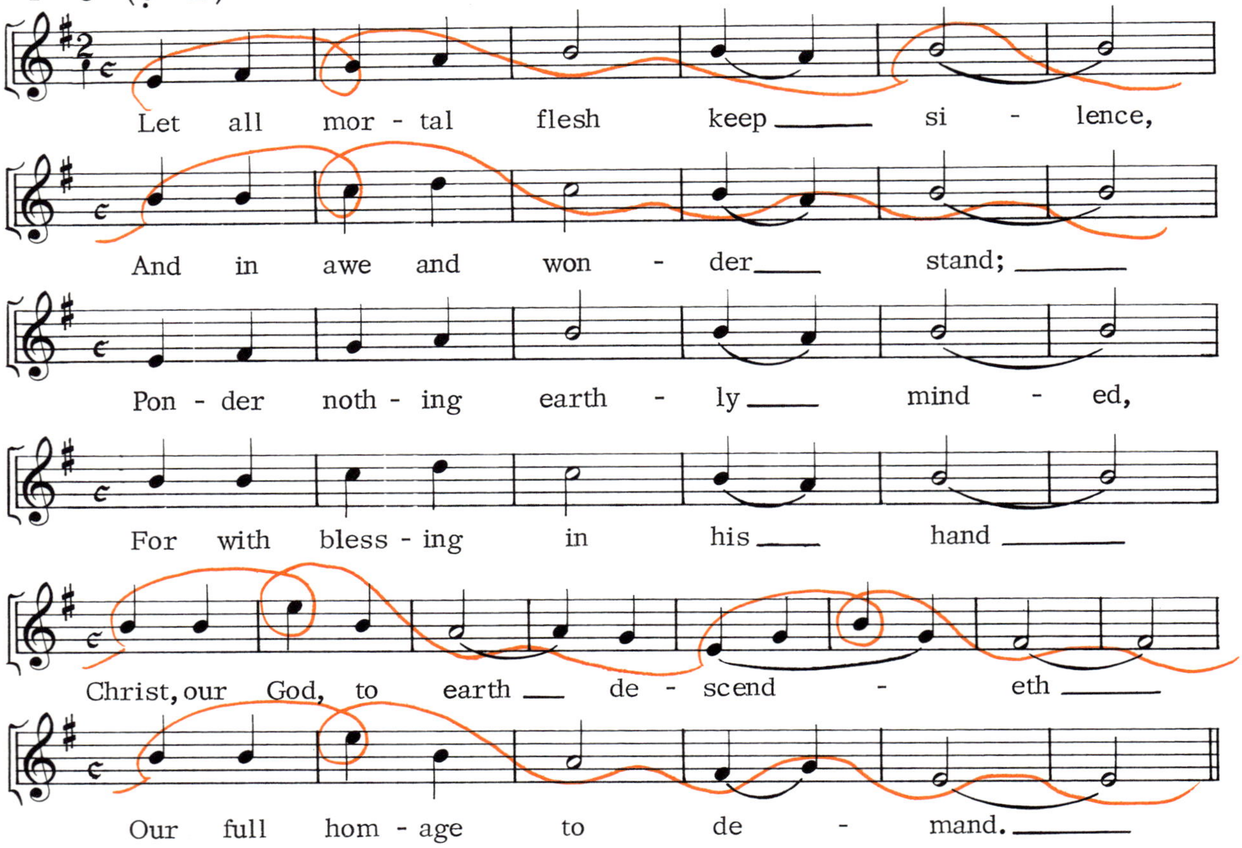

REGINA CAELI, LAETARE Gregorian Chant

1 = G (5 = D)

‖ 1 2 | 1 2 | 3 . | 4 3 | 2 . 4 | 3 2 | 1 . ‖
Re- gí- na cae- li ___ lae- tá- re ___ al- le- lu- ia! ___

‖ 0 1 | 5 . 5 | 6 5 | 4 3 | 1 2 | 3 .
Qui- a ___ quem me- ru- i- sti por- tá- re, ___

4 | 3 2 | 1 . ‖
al- le- lu- ia! ___

JOHN PAUL JONES *Melody:* Dutch Folk Melody *Text:* H. H. Harbour

Mode of DO Plagal Range
St. D. 6 P. 44
R. P. Series 14 P. 162
M. G. II
Repetition - Sequence-Contrast

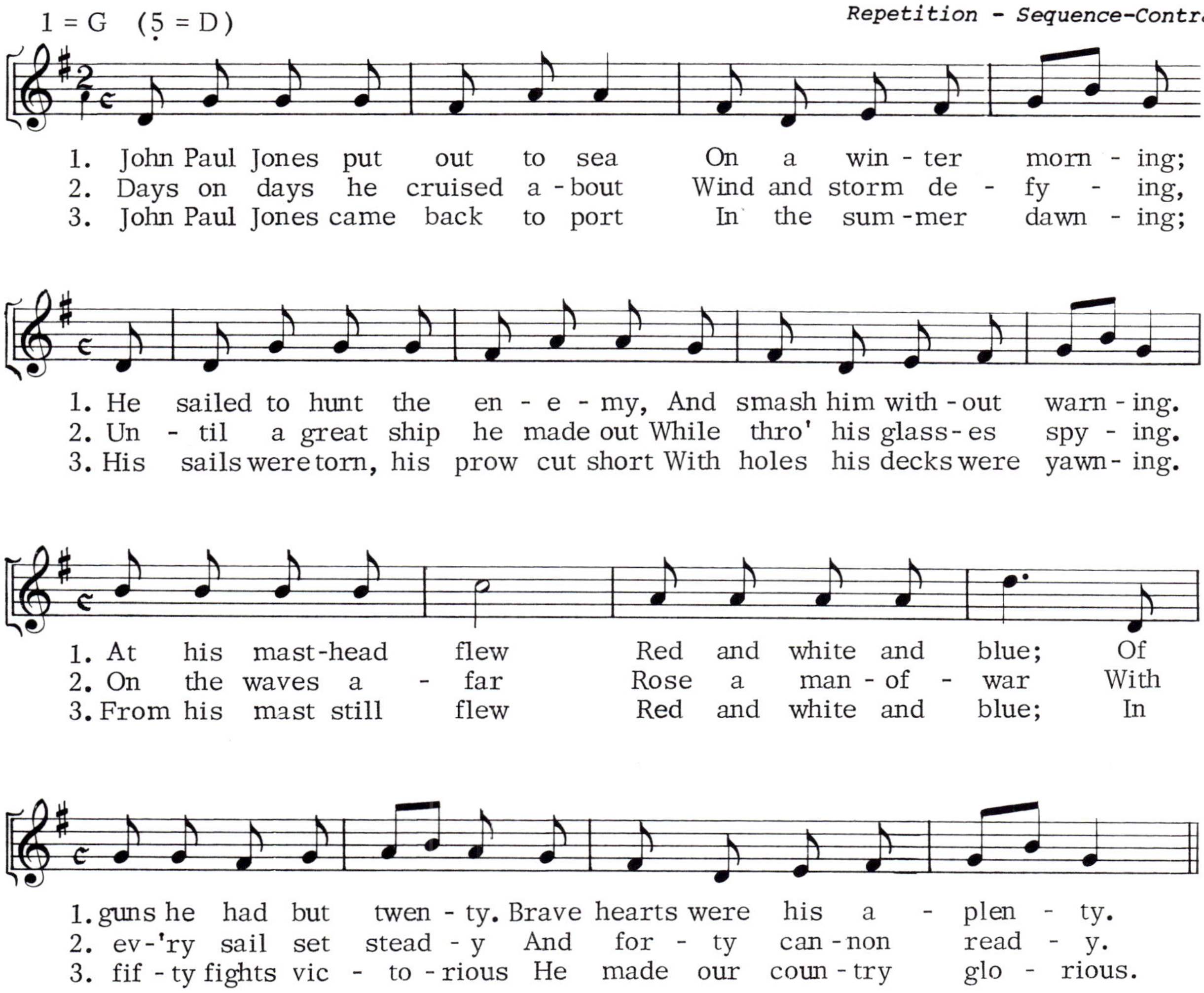

Mode of DO Hexachord
Int. D. 6 P. 44
R. G. IV Free
Notice Latin accent on up-pulse of rhythm

‖ 0 5 | 5 6 | 5 . 5 | 1 2 | 1 . 2 | 3 4 | 5 . | 0 0 ‖
Re- sur- ré- xit ___ sic- ut di- xit, ___ al- le- lu- ia! ___

‖ 5 1 | 2 4 | 3 2 | 1 . | 7 2 | 2 . | 1 . ‖
O- ra pro no- bis De- um, ___ al- le- lu- ia! ___

Trans.: *Queen of heaven, rejoice, alleluia! For He whom you were worthy to bear, has arisen as He said. Pray for us to God, alleluia.*

Chapter Twenty-One

Vocal Training

Review Sustained Vowels with N D T, M B P
Sustained Vowels Introduced by K G

Review Vocal Exercises 12b *and* 12c *(See Chapter Twenty)*

Vocal Exercise 12d - Introducing Vowels with K and G (*Guttural Consonants*)

1 = B (E / G)

|| 1 ________________________________ ||

Nu ____ o ____ a ____ e ____ i ____
Ku ____ o ____ a ____ e ____ i ____
Gu ____ o ____ a ____ e ____ i ____

> Continue drilling with N to introduce vowels. Hold tone placement when using K and G.

Review Vocal Exercises 17a *and* 17b

|| 6 5 4 | 3 4 5 | 6 . . | . . . ||
Nu Nu Nu Nu Nu Nu Nu ________
Na - o - u No- a - e - i ________

|| 6 5 4 | 3 4 5 | 6 . ||

Intonation

Presenting PLagal Range of LA Mode 3 - $\dot{3}$
DO Clef on Ledger Line Below Staff

Intonation Exercise 68 - *With* Intonation Diagram 28 *and* Staff Diagram 28

Intonation Diagram 28

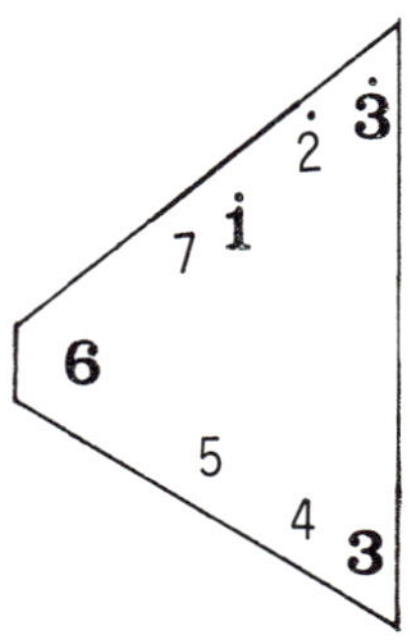

$\dot{1}$ = Bb (C)

Presenting Plagal Range

a)
| 6 7 $\dot{1}$ $\dot{2}$ $\dot{3}$ $\dot{3}$ $\dot{2}$ $\dot{1}$ 7 6 6 5 4 3 3 4 5 6 6 5 6 |
| 6 7 $\dot{1}$ $\dot{2}$ $\dot{3}$ $\dot{3}$ $\dot{2}$ $\dot{1}$ 7 6 6 5 4 3 3 4 5 6 6 5 6 |

b)
| 6 5 4 3 3 6 6 7 $\dot{1}$ $\dot{2}$ $\dot{3}$ $\dot{3}$ 6 |
| 6 3 3 4 5 6 $\dot{3}$ $\dot{2}$ $\dot{1}$ 7 6 |

Staff Diagram 28a

4̇
3̇
2̇
1̇
7
6
5
4
3

Intonation Diagram 29

1̇ = C (6 = A) for all drills

Staff Diagram 29a

Staff Diagram 29b

Intonation Exercise 69 - *with* Intonation Diagram 29 *and* Staff Diagram 29

676	1̇2̇1̇	3̇4̇3̇	3̇4̇3̇	1̇2̇1̇	676	656	6543	343	3456	656
676	1̇2̇1̇	3̇4̇3̇	3̇4̇3̇	1̇2̇1̇	676	656	*6543*	343	*3456*	656
676	1̇2̇1̇	3̇4̇3̇	3̇4̇3̇	1̇2̇1̇	676	656		343		656

First Compass Exercise

Intonation Exercise 70 - *with* Intonation Diagram 29

676	1̇2̇1̇	3̇4̇3̇	3̇4̇3̇	1̇2̇1̇	676	656	343	656
676	*1̇2̇1̇*	*3̇4̇3̇*	*3̇4̇3̇*	*1̇2̇1̇*	*676*	*656*	*343*	*656*
6	1̇	3̇	3̇	1̇	6	6	3	6

Second Compass Exercise

Eye and Ear Tests

6 7 1̇ 2̇ 3̇ 2̇ 1̇ 2̇ 3̇	6 5 6 3̇ 2̇ 1̇ 7 6	6 7 6 1̇ 2̇ 1̇ 3̇ 4̇ 3̇
6 5 4 3 3 6	6 3 3 6 3̇ 2̇ 1̇	6 5 6 3̇ 4̇ 3̇ 1̇ 2̇ 1̇

3̇ 4̇ 3̇ 1̇ 2̇ 1̇ 6 3	6 1̇ 3̇ 3̇ 1̇ 6
3 4 3 6 5 6 3 6	6 3 6 6 3̇ 6

Rhythm

Continue Discovering Rhythm of Unbarred Songs and Phrases in Metrical and Free Rhythm
Identify Rhythm and Mode From Listening to Songs

A song is written on the blackboard. Students study the melody and add bar lines where suggested by long notes and melodic designs. When finished, sing with appropriate rhythm gesture.

1.

Dutch Folk Song

2. 1 1 1 7 6 . 5 . 1 1 2 2 3 .
3 3 3 3 5 5 3 3 2 . 3 . 1 . *Dutch Folk Song*

3. 1 . 2 3 . 4 2 1 2 3 . .
5 . 4 3 . 2 3 2 3 2 . .
5 6 7 1 2 3 2 1 2 1 . . *German Carol*

4. 5 5 . 3 5 . 4 3 2 . 4 3 . 4 5 .
Based on Chant

Dictations — *Fragments of songs are sung by the teacher. Students must identify the rhythm and the mode of the melodies. The clue for the mode is the final; the clue for the rhythm is in long notes and melodic designs such as repetition of notes, sequences, inversions, etc.*

Angel, My Guardian *Chapter Four - Last line*

The Circus *Chapter Five - First line*

Green Gavel *Chapter Eleven-First line*

Melody No. 38 *Chapter Eighteen - Last line*

O Come, O Come, Emmanuel *Chapter Nineteen - Line 5*

Notation

Transcription in LA Mode
Transcription in DO Mode
Sight-Singing Fragments

1. *Transcribe to Staff Notation the first two lines of* Melody No. 43

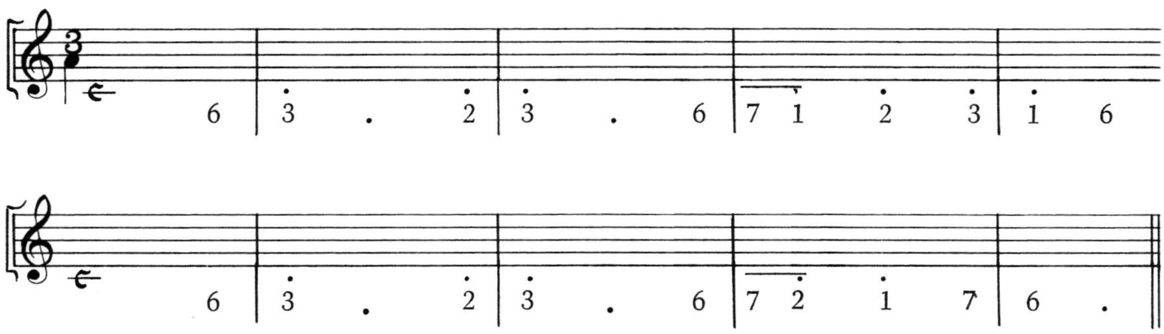

2. *Transcribe to Number Notation the last line of* When I Fetch Water

3. *Sight-singing fragments in LA Mode - Plagal Range* $\dot{1}$ = *Bb or C*

Creative Activity

Compose Melody for Metrical Poetic Texts
Compose Melody in Free Rhythm for Prose Text

PROCEDURE

Recite each line giving special emphasis to the stressed syllables.
Listen for the emerging rhythm patterns.
Place a pulse line over each syllable and a bar line before each accented syllable.
Is the rhythm in Duple Time (Binary) or in Triple Time (Ternary)?
Observe the places where half-pulse notes could occur; dotted rhythms.
If the composition is to be in the LA Mode, be sure to end on LA and to include notes from the tonic chord line of the LA Mode, that is, 6 $\dot{1}$ $\dot{3}$.
If the composition is to be in the DO Mode, be sure to end on DO and to include notes from the tonic chord line of the DO Mode, that is, 1 3 5.

Notice feminine endings.

1. The leaves are green, the nuts are brown;
They hang so high they'll not come down.
Leave them a- lone till fros- ty weath- er
Then they will all come down to- geth- er.

Old Rhyme

2. Stop and look and lis- ten
Be- fore you cross the street.
Use your eyes and use your ears
Then use your feet.

Anonymous

3. Drop down dew from a- bove, ye heav- ens;
Ye clouds, rain down the Just One.

From Advent Liturgy

Songs

Mode of LA Plagal Range
Int. D 28 P. 192
R.G. III
Repeat Signs

MELODY No. 43 "Bouree" from Auvergne

1 = C
(6 = A)

|: 6 | 3 . 2 | 3 . 6 | 7 1 2 3 | 1 6

6 | 3 . 2 | 3 . 6 | 7 2 1 7 | 6 . :| *Fine**

6 | 5 6 5 4 | 3 . 6 | 7 1 2 3 | 1 6

6 | 5 6 5 4 | 3 . 6 | 7 2 1 7 | 6 6 :| *D. C.***

Mode of LA Plagal Range
St. D 29a, 29b P. 193
M. G. III Repeat Signs

MELODY No. 44 Basque Melody

1 = C
(6 = A)

Mode of LA Plagal Range
Int. D 28 P. 192
R. G. IV Binary
Latin accents on up-pulse

AVE MARIA Gregorian Chant

1 = C
(6 = A)

|| 3 5 | 6 6 | 6 . | 6 5 | 6 7 | 6 . |
A- ve Ma- rí- a, — grá- ti- a ple- na, —

| 6 5 | 6 5 | 3 . | 5 . | 6 . ||
Dó- mi- nus te- cum. — A- men. —

**Fine* (Pronounced "fee-neh") means end
***D. C.* Abbreviation of "da capo" means return to the beginning.

WHEN I FETCH WATER FROM THE SPRING *Melody:* French Folk *Text:* JBW

Mode of DO
Plagal Range
St. D 6 P. 134
M. G. III
Repetition
Conclusive
Response

HEIGH HO! NOBODY AT HOME *Melody:* 16th Century Melody *Text:* Anonymous

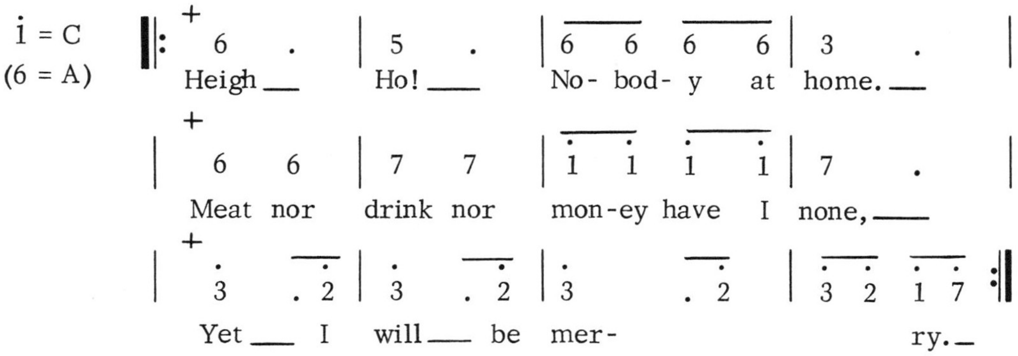

Note: This song may be sung as a three-part canon

Mode of LA 3 - 3 Range
Int. D 29 P. 193
M. G. II
Three contrasting phrases

FATHER ALMIGHTY, POUR ON US THY BLESSING *Melody:* Johann Crüger *Text:* Anonymous

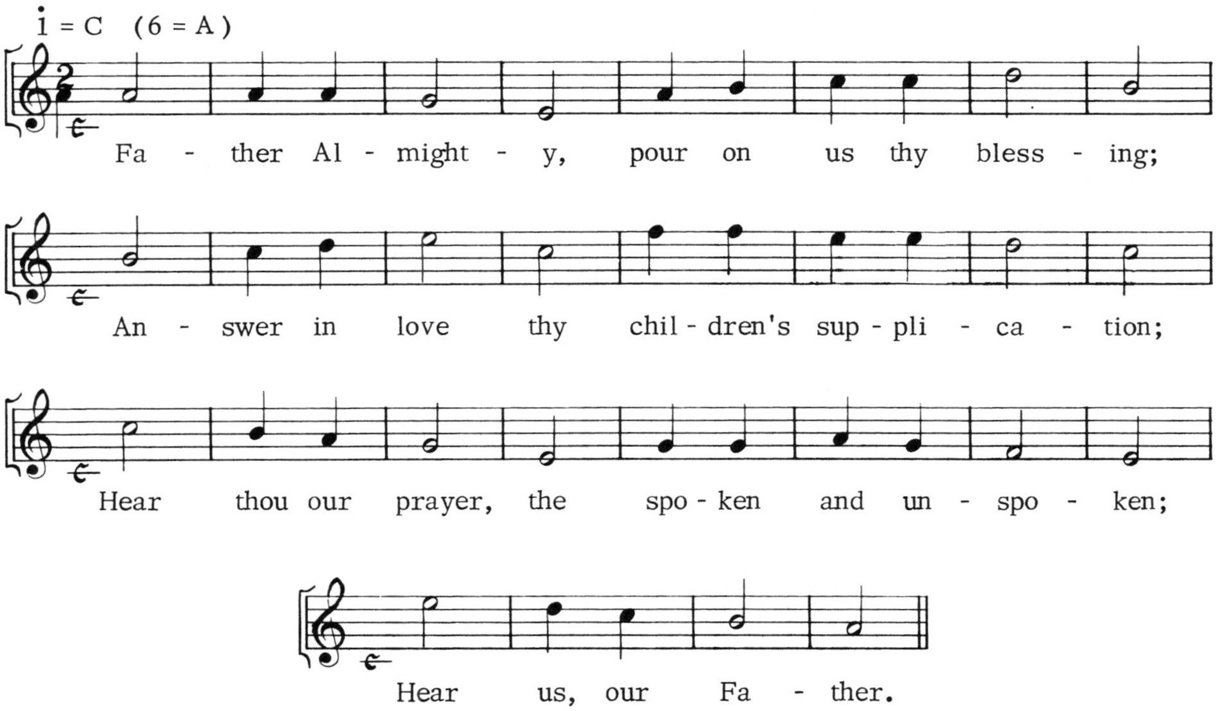

Mode of LA Plagal Range
St. D 29b P. 193
M. G. II
Note symmetry of phrases

Chapter Twenty Two

Vocal Training

Review Sustained Vowels With N D T, M B P, (N)K G
Vocal Drill with N D T in LA Mode, Plagal Range

Review Vocal Exercise 12b, 12c, 12d - Introducing Sustained Vowels With N D T, M B P, K G
(See Chapters Nineteen, Twenty and Twenty-One)

Vocal Exercise 19a

1̇ = B/C
(6 = G/A)

> Sing consonants gently so as not to disturb the placement of the vowel that follows. Check the pitch of MI (3̇) to be sure of its proper height.

Intonation

Tonic Chord and Surrounding Notes of LA Mode - Plagal Range
Contrasting 1̇ 6 3 with 3 5 7

Intonation Exercise 71 - *With* Intonation Diagram 30 *and* Staff Diagram 30

1̇ = C (6 = A)

Intonation Diagram 30

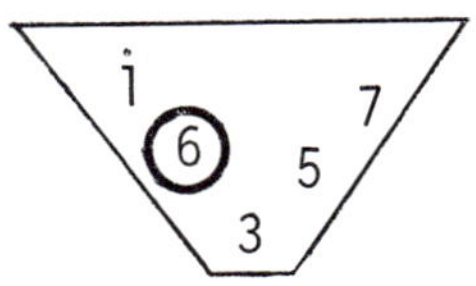

Tonic (Final) LA *with surrounding notes*

a)
| 1̇ 6 3 3 6 5 7 6 |
| 1̇ 6 3 3 6 7 5 6 |

b)
| 1̇ 6 3 6 5 7 5 6 |
| 1̇ 6 3 6 7 5 7 6 |

Intonation Exercise 72 - *With* Intonation Diagram 30 *and* Staff Diagram 30

1̇ 6 3 *contrasted with* 3 5 7

Staff Diagram 30

a)
| 1̇ 6 3 3 5 3 6 |
| 1̇ 6 3 5 3 5 6 |

b)
| 1̇ 6 3 5 3 6 1̇ 6 |
| 1̇ 6 3 5 3 5 7 6 |
| 1̇ 6 3 5 3 6 3 6 |

Intonation Diagram 31

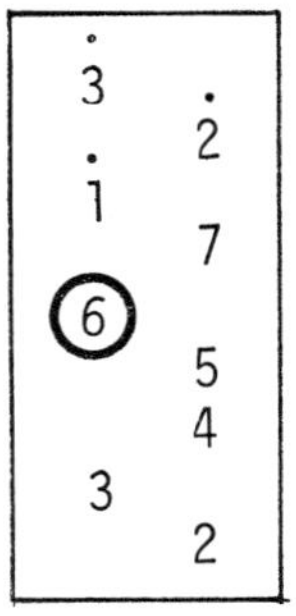

Staff Staff Diagram 31

1̇ = C
(6 = A)

Intonation Exercise 73 - *With* Intonation Diagram 31 *and* Staff Diagram 31

Notes of Tonic Chord and surrounding notes

a)

6 7 1̇ 2̇ 3̇ 1̇ 6   6 7 6 5 6
6 1̇ 3̇ 1̇ 6   7 5 6
6 7 1̇ 7 6   6 5 4 3   3 4 3 2 3
6 1̇ 6 6   3   4 2 3

b)

6 5 4 3   3 4 5 6   6 7 1̇   1̇ 7 1̇ 2̇ 1̇
6 3   6   6 1̇   7 2̇ 1̇
1̇ 7 6 5 4 3   3 6   6 1̇   1̇ 2̇ 1̇ 7 1̇
1̇ 6   3   3   6 1̇   2̇ 7 1̇

Intonation Diagram 74 - *With* Intonation Diagram 31 *and* Staff Diagram 31

Free use of notes of Tonic Chord

6 3   3 6 1̇ 3̇   3̇ 1̇ 6 3
3 6 *1̇* 3̇   3̇ *1̇* 6 3
3 *6* 1̇ 3̇   3̇ 1̇ *6* 3
3 *6* *1̇* 3̇   3̇ *1̇* *6* 3   3 6

Eye and Ear Tests

1̇ 6 3 3 6 5 7	1̇ 6 3 6 5 5 7 6	6 1̇ 3̇ 1̇ 6 3
1̇ 6 3 6 3 5 3	1̇ 6 1̇ 6 3 5 7	6 3 4 2 3 3 6

6 5 4 5 3 4 6 1̇	1̇ 2 7 6 5 6 4
6 3 3 3 6 1̇	6 3 3 3 6

Rhythm

Review Metrical Language With Metrical Gesture I
Determine Metrical Structure of Verbal Texts
Rhythmic Dictations - Quotations From Songs Already Studied

1. *Review* Metrical Language *and apply it to rhythmic phrases given. Sing on one note with* Metrical Gesture I

a)

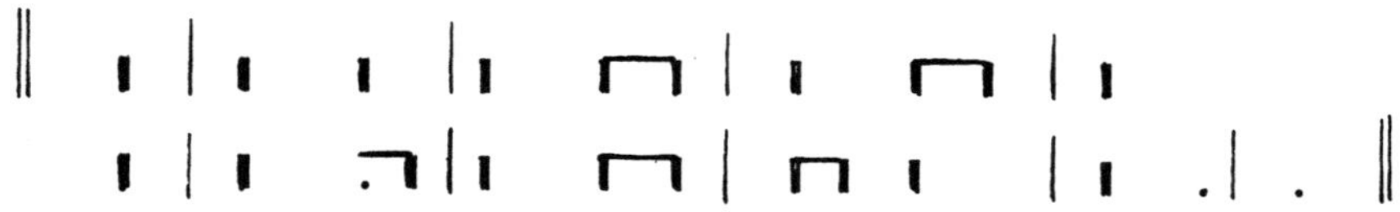

b)

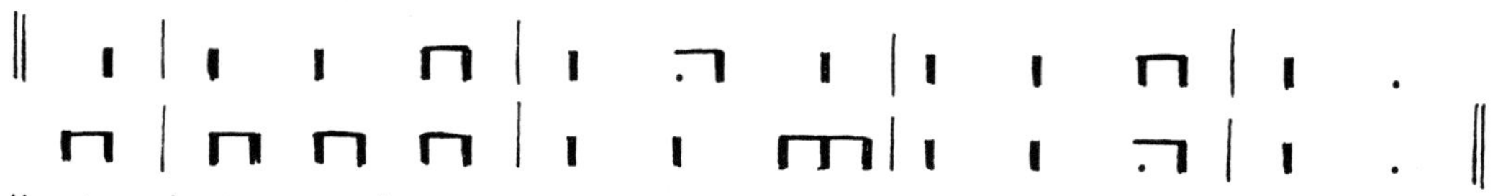

c)

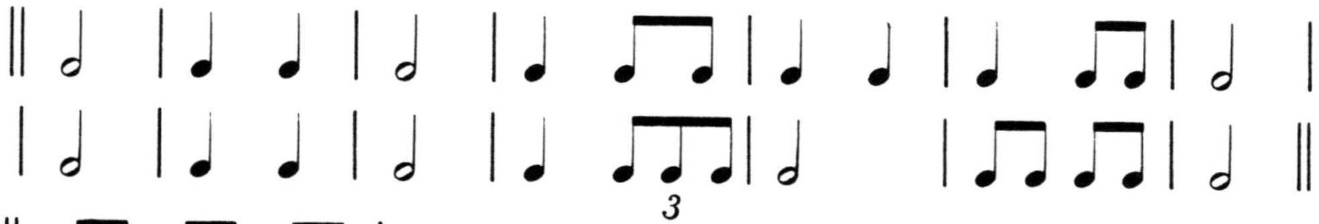

d)

2. *Read aloud the texts given. Determine the accent patterns of the texts and write out the metrical scheme of each poem by adding appropriate pulse lines above the syllables. Melodies will be added in the next chapter.*

Winnie and Minnie
Slept in a shell.
Sleep, little ladies!
And they slept well.

Alfred Lord Tennyson

Jesus Christ, thou child so wise,
Bless mine hands, and fill mine eyes,
And bring my soul to Paradise.

Hilaire Belloc

3. Rhythmic Dictations *Children must identify each line sung by teacher as to: rhythmic structure and mode. LISTEN!*

Christ Our Lord Is Risen *Chapter Twenty - Lines 1 and 2*

Melody No. 38 *Chapter Eighteen - Lines 1 and 2*

The King of Love My Shepherd Is *Chapter Nineteen - Lines 1 and 2*

Notation

DO Clef on Ledger Line Below Staff for Modes of SOL, DO and LA

1. SOL Mode. *Transcribe to Number Notation* O Sweet Lady *from Chapter Twelve.*

Review placement of DO Clef for Mode of Do and Mode of LA. Use flashcards.

2. DO Mode. *Transcribe to Staff Notation* The Silver Moon Is Shining *from Chapter Sixteen. Notice that the melody ends on MI.*

3. LA Mode. *Transcribe to Staff Notation* Melody No. 35 *from Chapter Seventeen (Lines 3 and 4).*

Creative Activity

Review Rhythmic Enlargement
Review Rhythmic Transformation

1. Rhythmic Enlargement *(Chapter Six)*

   a) *Compose a two-line melody for the rhythm given in the Mode of DO. Notice that the second line contains an enlargement of the rhythms of the first line.*

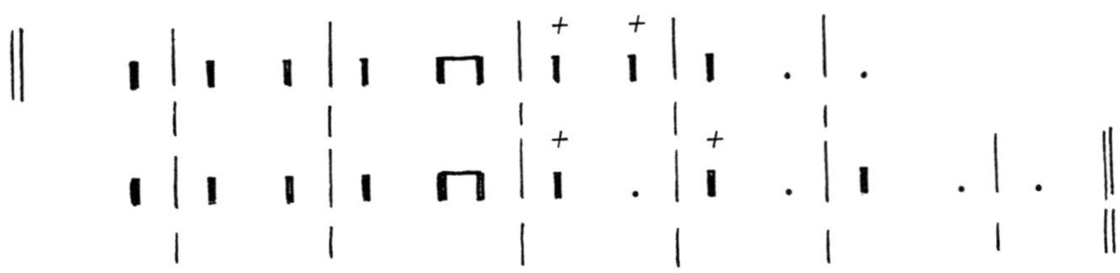

   b) *Compose another melody for rhythms given. Mode of LA. Notice enlargement of rhythm in the second line. Use notes studied in this chapter for melody.*

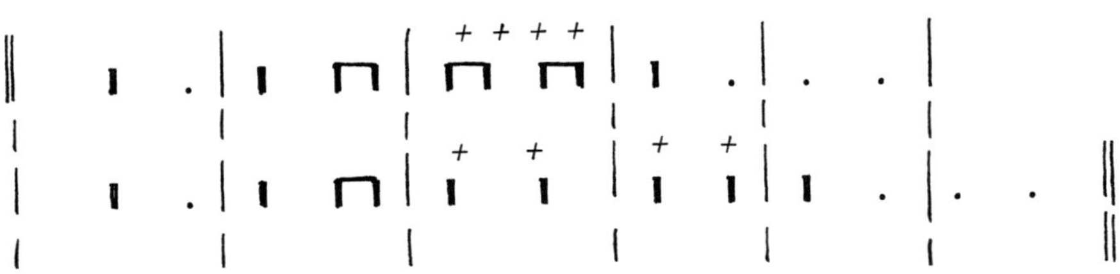

2. Rhythmic Transformation *(Chapter Ten)*

   a) *Compose a melody in Mode of DO for the rhythms given below.*

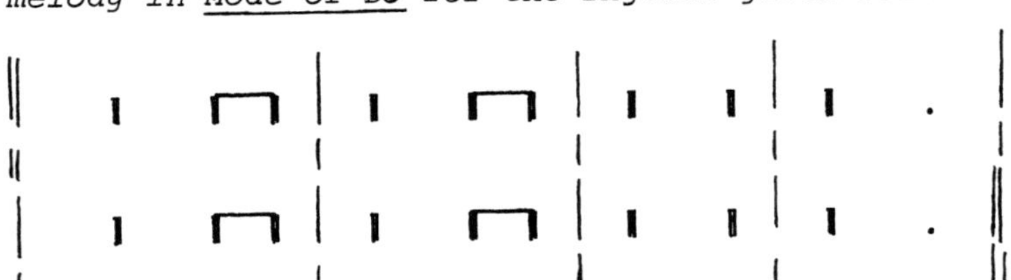

   Re-write the melody but add one pulse to the first note of each measure. The original melody in Duple Time becomes a melody in Triple Time.

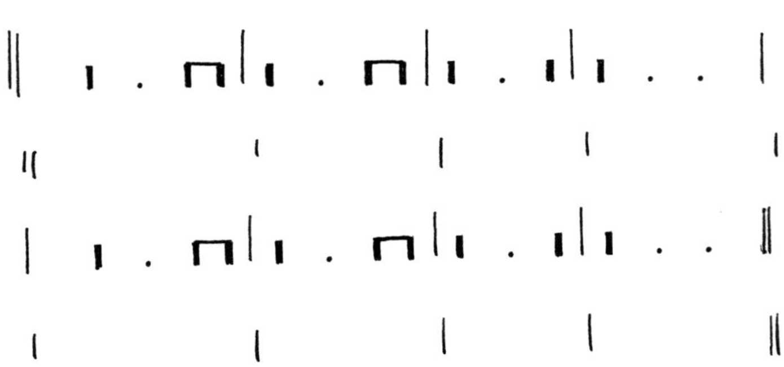

Songs

Mode of LA Plagal Range
Int. D 31 P. 201
R. G. III
Repetition of phrases
Conclusive Response

MELODY No. 45 "Bourée" from the Cevennes

1 = C (6 = A)

|| 3 | 6 7 1 2 | 3 3 3 | 6 7 1 2 | 3

3 | 3 4 3 2 | 1 7 6 7 | 1 6

3 | 3 4 3 2 | 1 7 6 5 | 6 . ||

MELODY No. 46 English Folk Melody

Mode of LA Plagal Range
St. D 31 P. 201
R. G. II DO Clef below staff

1 = C (6 = A)

FAREWELL AND ADIEU Traditional

DO Mode of LA
Int. D. p. 301
M. G. III
Feminine Endings
Lines 1 & 3

1 = C (6 = A)

|| 3 | 6 6 7 | 6 . 6 7 | 1 7 6 | 6 5 3
Fare- well and a- dieu __ to __ you, Span-ish La- dies

3 | 6 6 7 | 6 . 6 7 | 1 2 1 | 7 .
Fare- well and a- dieu __ to you, La- dies of Spain, __

7 | 1 7 1 | 2 1 2 | 3 2 1 6 | 6 5 3
The tide's go- ing out and we're off __ to old Eng- land

3 2 | 1 6 6 | 6 5 3 2 | 3 1 7 | 6 . ||
But we hope in a short_while to see you a- gain. __

FOR THE BEAUTY OF THE EARTH *Melody:* Conrad Kocher *Text:* F. S. Pierpont

1 = G (5 = D)

1	7 1	2	1	4	4	3	.	
For	the—	beau-	ty	of	the	earth,—		
6	7	1	6	5	5	5	.	
For	the	glo-	ry	of	the	skies,—		
1	7 1	2	1	4	4	3	.	
For	the—	love	which	from	our	birth—		
6	7	1	6	5	5	5	.	
O-	ver	and	a-	bove	us	lies:—		
3	2	1	3	5	. 4	3	.	
Lord	of	all	to	thee	we—	raise—		
6	7	1	4	3	2	1	.	
This	our	hymn	of	thank-	ful	praise.—		

Mode of DO Plagal Range
M. G. II
Use for Sight-singing
Notice Mode of LA skips 3 - 6

HORO HARADAL Folk Song of the Hebrides

Mode of LA Plagal Range
Contrasting 6 - i 5 - 3
St. D. 31 P. 201
M. G. II

i = C (6 = A)

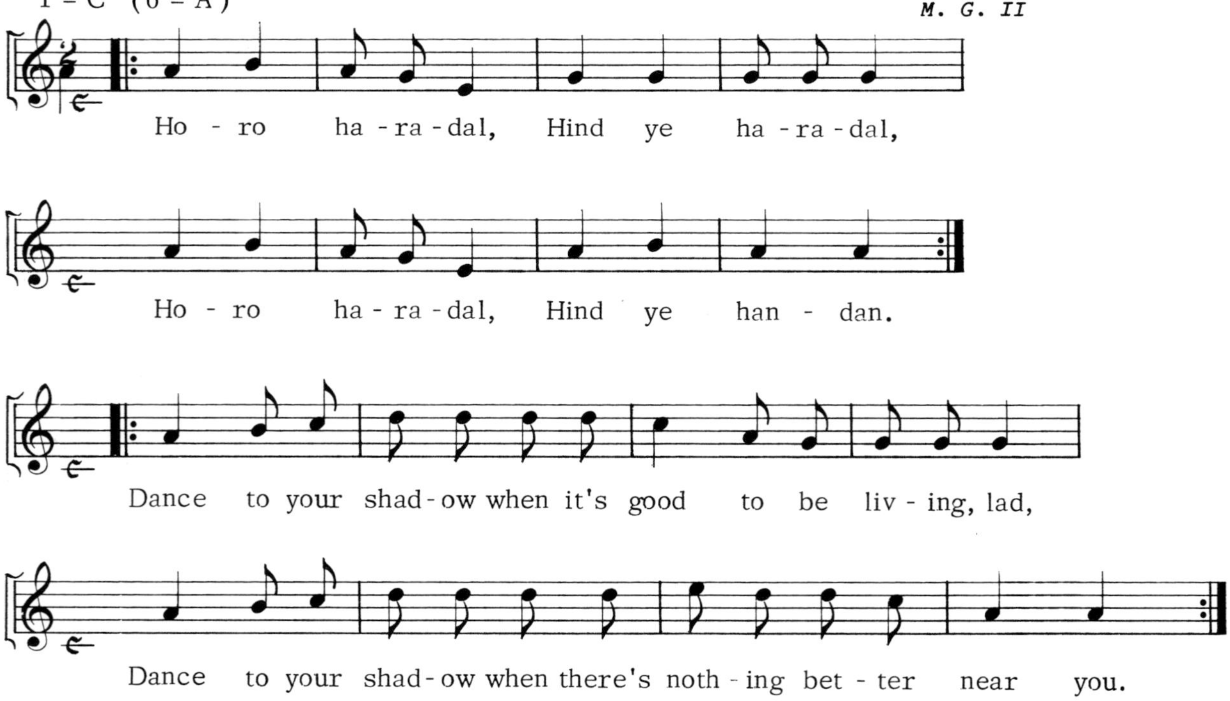

'TWAS IN THE MOON OF WINTERTIME *Melody:* French Carol Melody
Text: Translated from the Huron Indian dialect by T. S. Middleton

Mode of LA
St. D 31 P. 201
R. G. I or II
DO Clef below staff

Commentary: *When the Jesuit missionary Father John de Breboeuf wanted to describe the birth of Jesus to his Indian people, he did so using the Huron dialect spoken by the Indians and employed figures and signs that they would readily understand. For instance, "moon of wintertime," meant the middle of winter because the Indians told the seasons only by the full moon. "Gitchie Manitou" was the Indian word for God. Instead of "shepherds," he referred to "hunters," as those who received the message of the angels. It is doubtful that the Indians would have known the meaning of the word "shepherd," but they surely knew the word "hunter."*

Chapter Twenty Three

Vocal Training

Review Sustained Vowels With Consonants
Vocal Drill With M B P in LA Mode, Plagal Range

Review Vocal Exercises 12b, c *and* d, *as in Chapters Twenty and Twenty-One*

Vocal Exercise 19b

6 1 3 | 2 1 7 | 6 5 4 | 3 4 5 | 6 . .

Mu ___	Mo ___	Ma ___	Me ___	Mi ___
Bu ___	Bo ___	Ba ___	Be ___	Bi ___
Pu ___	Po ___	Pa ___	Pe ___	Pi ___

Intonation

Third Compass Exercises in LA Mode - Plagal Range
Compass Exercises Combined

Intonation Exercise 75 *with* Intonation Diagram 29 *and* Staff Diagram 29c

Intonation Diagram 29

4		
	3	
		2
	1	
7		
	6	
		5
4		
	3	

1 = Bb or C (6 = G or A) *Third Compass Exercise*

676	121	343	343	121	676	656	343	656
676	121	343	343	121	676	656	343	656
76	21	43	43	21	76	56	43	56

Intonation Exercise 76 *with* Intonation Diagram 29 *and* Staff Diagram 29c

Staff Diagram 29c

Compass Exercises Combined

676	121	343	121	676	61316	656	343	656	636
76	21	43	21	76	61316	56	43	56	636

Intonation Exercise 77 - *With* Intonation Diagram 29 *and* Staff Diagram 29c

$\dot{1}76$	6543	$36\dot{1}63$	43	56	$\dot{2}\dot{1}$	76	43	3 6		
$\dot{1}76$	6543	$36\dot{1}6\dot{1}$	43	56	$\dot{2}\dot{1}$	76	$\dot{2}\dot{1}$			
345	$667\dot{1}$	$\dot{1}6\dot{1}3$		$\dot{2}\dot{1}$	76	$\dot{2}\dot{1}$	43			
345	$667\dot{1}$	$3636\dot{1}$	43	56	43	76	$\dot{2}\dot{1}$	$\dot{1}76543$	6	

Scale passages with Second and Third Compass exercises

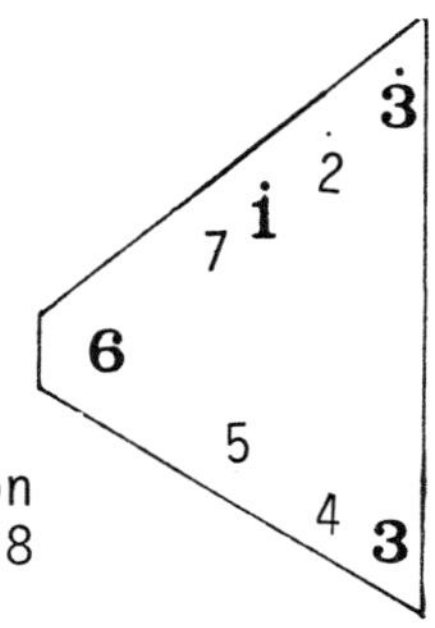

Intonation Diagram 28

Staff Diagram 28b

Intonation Exercise 78 - *With* Intonation Diagram 28 *and* Staff Diagram 28b

a)				b)				
6 5 4 3	6	6 7 $\dot{1}$ $\dot{2}$ $\dot{3}$	6	6	3 4 5 6	6	$\dot{3}$ $\dot{2}$ $\dot{1}$ 7 6
6 5 4	6	6 7 $\dot{1}$ $\dot{2}$	6	6	4 5 6	6	$\dot{2}$ $\dot{1}$ 7 6
6 5	6	6 7 $\dot{1}$	6	6	5 6	6	$\dot{1}$ 7 6
6 5		6 7	6	6	5 6		7 6

Final LA *approached from any note of mode*

Eye and Ear Tests

Select note-groupings from Intonation Exercises being studied.

Rhythm

Review Aural Training in Rhythm
Discover Metrical Structures of Verbal Texts
Rhythmic Dictations – Quotations From Songs Studied

1. *Study each series given below and determine the rhythm structure of each. Sing and conduct each fragment with its appropriate gesture.*

$$3\ 5\ 6\ 4\ .\ 2\ 1\ .\ 1\ 5\ 5\ \dot{1}\ 6\ .\ 7\ \dot{1}\ .\ .\ .\ .\ .$$

$$1\ \overline{\underset{\cdot}{7}\ 1}\ 2\ 1\ 4\ 4\ 3\ .\ \underset{\cdot}{6}\ \underset{\cdot}{7}\ 1\ \underset{\cdot}{6}\ \underset{\cdot}{5}\ \underset{\cdot}{5}\ \underset{\cdot}{5}\ .\ .\ .$$

$$1\ \overline{.\ \underset{\cdot}{7}}\ \underset{\cdot}{6}\ 1\ 2\ \overline{.\ 1}\ \underset{\cdot}{7}\ \underset{\cdot}{5}\ \underset{\cdot}{6}\ .\ \underset{\cdot}{7}\ \overline{.\ \underset{\cdot}{7}}\ \underset{\cdot}{1}\ .$$

2. *Read aloud the texts given and determine accent patterns for each line. Write out the metrical scheme of each poem by adding appropriate pulse lines above the syllables.*

When I was down beside the sea
A wooden spade they gave to me
To dig the sandy shore.

My holes were empty like a cup
In every hole the sea came up
Till it could come no more.

Robert Louis Stevenson

Praise the Lord, ye heavens adore him;
Praise him angels in the height.
Sun and moon rejoice before him;
Praise him all ye stars of light.

Anonymous
Paraphrase of Psalm 148

3. Rhythmic Dictations *Quotations are from songs already studied. Children must identify rhythm structure, notes and mode for each. Solutions should be written on the blackboard.*

Melody No. 15 *Chapter Seven -Last line*

O Where, O Where, Is My Littel Dog Gone? *Chapter Eight - Lines 3 and 4*

Auld Lang Syne *Chapter Fourteen - Last line*

Were You Ever in Quebec? *Chapter Seventeen- Last line*

My Country 'Tis of Thee *Chapter Eighteen - Last line*

Notation

DO Clef on Third Line for LA Mode
Transcriptions
Sight-Singing Drills

1. *Transcribe <u>Authentic Range</u> of LA Mode to Staff Notation - First Compass Exercise*

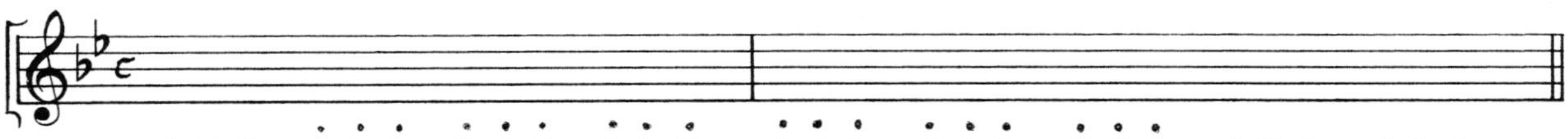

6 7 6 $\dot{1}\ \dot{2}\ \dot{1}$ $\dot{3}\ \dot{4}\ \dot{3}$ $\dot{6}\ \dot{5}\ \dot{6}$ $\dot{6}\ \dot{5}\ \dot{6}$ $\dot{3}\ \dot{4}\ \dot{3}$ $\dot{1}\ \dot{2}\ \dot{1}$ 6 7 6 6 5 6

2. *Transcribe <u>Plagal Range</u> of LA Mode to Staff Notation - First Compass Exercise*

6 7 6 $\dot{1}\ \dot{2}\ \dot{1}$ $\dot{3}\ \dot{4}\ \dot{3}$ $\dot{1}\ \dot{2}\ \dot{1}$ 6 7 6 6 5 6 3 4 3 6 5 6

3. <u>Sight-Singing Drills</u>

$\dot{1}$ = B♭ (6 = G)

Creative Activity

Review Melodic Formation by Repeated Notes and Motifs, Sequences, Inversions
Compose Melody for Poetic Text

1. *Review:* <u>Repeated Notes</u> *(Cf. Chapter Seven under "Rhythm")*

   Example: ‖ 1 1 | 2 2 | 1 . | 5 . | 1 1 | 2 2 | 3 . ‖

   <u>Repeated Motif</u> *(Cf. Chapter Seven under "Rhythm")*

   Example: ‖ 1 2 3 | 1 2 3 | 1 2 3 | 4 . . ‖

   <u>Sequence</u> *(Cf. Chapter Eight under "Rhythm")*

   Example: ‖ 6̣ | 3 2 1 | 2 1 7̣ | 1 7̣ 6̣ | 6̣ . ‖

   <u>Inversion</u> *(Cf. Chapter Eight under "Rhythm")*

   Example: ‖ 3 | 3 1 | 2 4 | 4 2 | 3 5 | 5 3 | 4 6 | 5 . | . ‖

2. *Compose a melody in <u>Mode of LA</u> for each of the following texts. These poems were analysed in Chapter Twenty-Two for their metrical structures.*

Compose melody according to suggestions given above.

a)

Win- nie and	Min- nie
Slept in a	shell.
Sleep lit- tle	la- dies
And they slept	well.

Alfred Lord Tennyson

b)

Je- sus	Christ, thou	child so	wise,
Bless mine	hands and	fill mine	eyes,
And bring my	soul to	Par- a-	dise.

H. Belloc

Songs

Mode of DO Plagal Range
DO Clef on Line 3
Repetition in Lines 2 and 4

MELODY No. 47 "Waltham" 17th Century Hymn Tune

1 = B♭
(5 = F)

Mode of SOL
R. G. IV Free

DISMISSAL CHANTS

1. Throughout the Year in English or Latin

$\dot{1}$ = B♭ (5 = F)

|| $\dot{1}$ | $\dot{1}$ $\dot{1}$ | $\dot{1}$ 7 | 6 7 | 6 . | 5 . ||

Celebrant: The Mass is end-ed go in peace.___
*I- te mis-sa est.*___

|| $\dot{1}$ 7 | 6 7 | 6 . | 5 . ||

All: Thanks be to God.___
*De- o gra- ti- as.*___

2. At Eastertide in English or Latin

|| 5 | 5 5 | 5 5 | 5 5 | 6 . |

Celebrant: The Mass is end- ed go in peace,—
I- te mis-sa est.

| 5 4 | 5 6 | 6 . 6 | 5 $\dot{1}$ 7 | 6 5 | 4 5 6 | 6 . | 5 . ||

Al- le- lu- ia,— al- le- lú- ia.___

|| (5) 5 | 5 5 | 6 . |

All: Thanks be to God.—
De- o gra- ti- as,—

| 5 4 | 5 6 | 6 . 6 | 5 $\dot{1}$ 7 | 6 5 | 4 5 6 | 6 . | 5 . ||

Al- le- lú- ia,— al- le- lú- ia.___

Mode of LA DO Clef Line
St. D 28b P. 209
M. G. III
Sight-singing Drills P. 211

THE JOLLY PLOUGHBOY English Folk Song

1̇ = B♭ (6 = G)

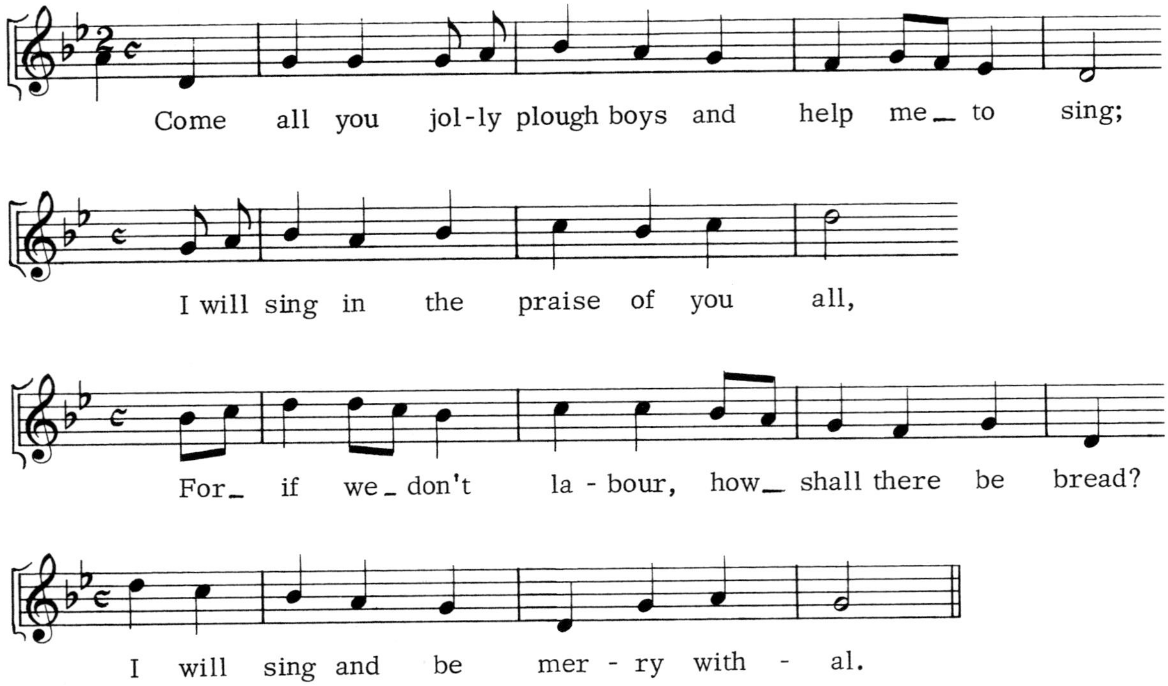

Mode of LA
Int. D 29 P.208

MELODY No. 48 "Compass Song" TM

1̇ = B♭ (6 = G)

|| 6 7 6 | 3 6 | 1̇ 1̇ 2̇ | 1̇ . | 3̇ 4̇ 3̇ | 2̇ 6 | 7 . | . . |

| 6 7 6 | 3 6 | 1̇ 1̇ 2̇ | 1̇ . | 3̇ 4̇ 3̇ | 2̇ 7 | 6 1̇ | 7 5 |

| 3 . 4 | 3 3 | 5 6 | 7 1̇ | 3̇ . 4 | 3 1̇ | 7 . | . . |

| 6 7 6 | 3 6 | 1̇ 1̇ 2̇ | 1 . | 3̇ . 4 | 3̇ 3̇ | 6 . | . . ||

Mode of DO
Int. D 29 P. 208
Dialogue Song
R. G.IV Free

RESURRECTION *Melody:* Gregorian Chant *Text:* JBW

$\dot{1}$ = B♭ (5 = F)

Solo Voice or Small Group:

|: 0 $\dot{1}$ | $\dot{1}$ $\dot{1}$ | $\dot{1}$ 7 | $\dot{2}$ $\dot{3}$ $\dot{3}$ | $\dot{3}$. | $\dot{2}$. |

1.	Three	Ma-	rys	has-	ten	to ___	the	grave, ___
2.	There	they	be-	held	an	An-	gel	bright, ___
3.	"Tell	this	to	Pe -	ter:	he ___	will	see, ___
4.	We	all	re-	joice	on	Eas-	ter	Day, ___

All:

| 0 $\dot{1}$ | $\dot{2}$ $\dot{1}$ | 6 . | 5 . |

al- le- lu- ia, ___

Solo or Small Group:

| 0 $\dot{1}$ | $\dot{1}$ $\dot{1}$ | $\dot{1}$ 7 | $\dot{2}$ $\dot{3}$ $\dot{3}$ | $\dot{3}$. |

1.	Made	in	a	rock,	a	hol-	low	cave, ___
2.	Who	said, "He	rose	by	his ___	own	might," ___	
3.	The	ris-	en	Christ	in	Gal-	i-	lee," ___
4.	And	to	our	ris-	en	Sa-	vior	say: ___

All:

| 0 $\dot{3}$ | $\dot{3}$ $\dot{2}$ | $\dot{2}$ $\dot{1}$ | $\dot{1}$. :|

al- le- lu- ia. ___

All: (Ending for Verse 4)

| 0 $\dot{3}$ | $\dot{3}$ $\dot{2}$ | $\dot{2}$ $\dot{1}$ | $\dot{1}$. | . . ||

al- le- lu- ia. ___

Chapter Twenty Four

Vocal Training

Review Sustained Vowels Introduced by Consonants
Vocal Drill With K G in LA Mode, Plagal Range

Review Vocal Exercises 12b, c *and* d, *as in Chapter Twenty-One*

Vocal Exercise 19c

If well-placed head voice seems to be lost in these drills, return to intensive practise with NNN as the initial consonant.

Intonation

Review First Three Compass Exercises
Study of 3 5 7 in Relation to $\dot{1}$ 6 3

$\dot{1}$ = B♭ (6 = G)

Staff Diagram 29c

Staff Diagram 29d

Intonation Exercise 79 - *With* Staff Diagrams 29c *and* d

676	$\dot{1}\dot{2}\dot{1}$	$\dot{3}\dot{4}\dot{3}$	$\dot{3}\dot{4}\dot{3}$	$\dot{1}\dot{2}\dot{1}$	676	656	343	656
6	$\dot{1}$	$\dot{3}$	$\dot{3}$	$\dot{1}$	6	6	3	6
76	$\dot{2}\dot{1}$	$\dot{4}\dot{3}$	$\dot{4}\dot{3}$	$\dot{2}\dot{1}$	76	56	43	56

Review of Three Compass Exercises

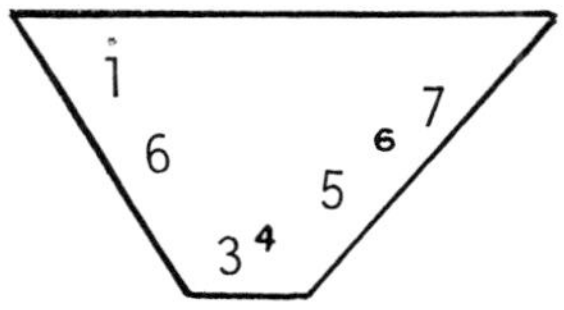

Intonation Diagram 32

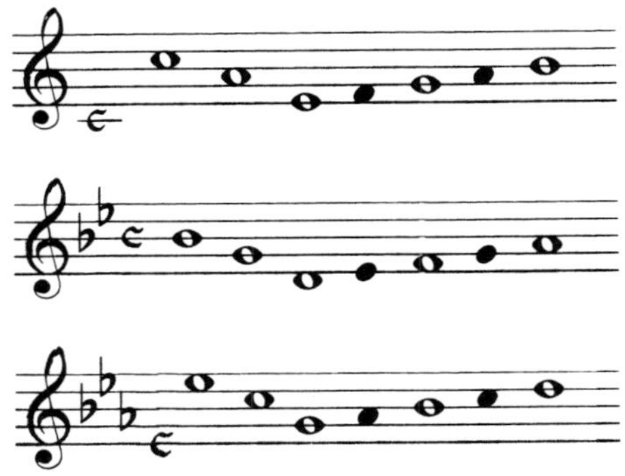

$\dot{1}$ = C a)

$\dot{1}$ = B♭ b)

$\dot{1}$ = E♭ c)

Staff Diagram 32

Intonation Exercise 80 - *With* Intonation Diagram 32 *and* Staff Diagrams 32a, b, c

a)	*b)*	
1̇63 6 5 6 7 5 3 3 6	3 6 1̇ 6 7 6 5 4 3 3 6	MI-LA-DO (361̇) *contrasted*
1̇63 6 5 7 5 3 3 6	3 6 1̇ 6 7 5 3 3 6	*with* MI-SOL-TI (357)
1̇63 6 3 567 6 3 6	3 6 1̇ 6 5 6 7 6 5 4 3 6	
1̇63 6 3 5 7 6 3 6	3 6 1̇ 6 5 7 5 3 6	

Intonation Exercise 81 - *With* Intonation Diagram 32 *and* Staff Diagrams 32a, b, c

a)	*b)*	
1̇ 6 3 3 4 5 6 7 6 5 4 3 6	3 6 1̇ 7 6 5 4 3 4 5 6 7 6	*Drill on interval*
1̇ 6 3 3 4 5 6 7 5 3 6	3 6 1̇ 7 6 5 4 3 5 7 6	MI-TI (37) *and*
1̇ 6 3 3 5 7 3 6	3 6 1̇ 7 5 3 7 6	TI-MI (73)

Ear and Eye Tests

Select note-groupings from Intonation Exercises

and phrases from Songs being studied.

Rhythm

Review of Rhythm and Metrical Gestures

Rhythm Gestures *Describing the Horizontal Flow of Musical Impulses*

Rhythm Gestures I *and* II Up-pulse Beginning of Binary Rhythm *Chapter One*

TWAS IN THE MOON OF WINTERTIME *Chapter Twenty-Two*

Rhythm Gesture III Up-pulse Beginning of Ternary Rhythm *Chapter Three*

FAREWELL AND ADIEU *Chapter Twenty-Twc*

Rhythm Gesture IV - Binary Down-pulse Beginning (Arsis-Thesis) *Chapter Two*

LET ALL MORTAL FLESH KEEP SILENCE *Chapter Twenty*

Rhythm Gesture IV - Ternary Down-pulse Beginning (Arsis-Thesis) *Chapter Four*

WE THREE KINGS OF ORIENT ARE *Chapter Eighteen*

Rhythm Gesture IV -Binary and Ternary Groupings Alternating Freely *Chapter Ten*

REGINA CAELI *Chapter Twenty*

Metrical Gestures *Describing the Time Spacings of Down Beats, or Measures*

Metrical Gesture I Single Pulses - Units of Measures *Chapter One*

Use with any Rhythm Pattern Series

Metrical Gesture II Beating Time for Measures in Duple Time *Chapter Seven*

FOR THE BEAUTY OF THE EARTH *Chapter Twenty-Two*

Metrical Gesture III Beating Time for Measures in Triple Time *Chapter Nine*

WHEN I FETCH WATER FROM THE SPRING *Chapter Twenty-One*

Notation

Review: DO Clef on Bottom Line for LA Mode
Determining Place of DO Clef From Key Signatures
Sight-Singing Fragments in DO, SOL and LA Modes

1. *Sight-singing drills for* *DO Clef on bottom line* *- LA Mode.*

$\dot{1}$ = E♭ (6 = C) (3 = G)

2. *Place* DO Clef *in its correct position for each Key Signature given. (See Chapter Seventeen for rules.)*

3. *Find the place of DO, then name the notes on each staff given below. Identify the* *Tonic* *(or Final) of the mode.*

4. *Transcribe* Intonation Exercise 72 Arrow *a), to Staff Notation in two different keys*

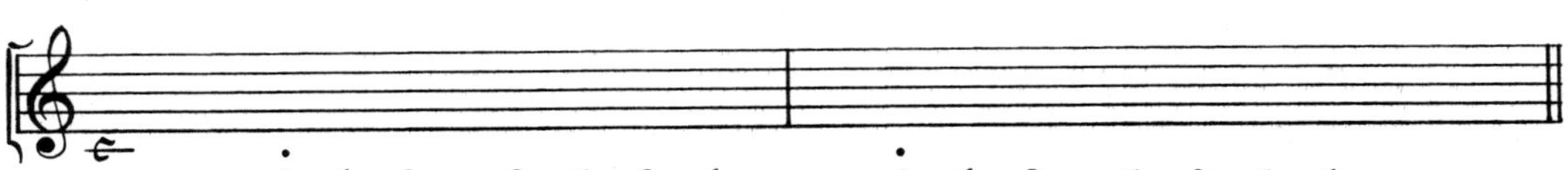

$\dot{1}$ 6 3 3 5 3 6 $\dot{1}$ 6 3 5 3 5 6

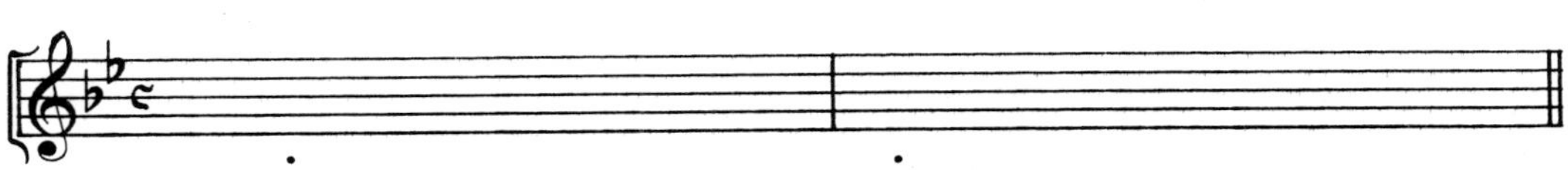

$\dot{1}$ 6 3 3 5 3 6 $\dot{1}$ 6 3 5 3 5 6

Creative Activity

Review Musical Conversation
Compose Melody for Poetic Text
Add Two Lines to Given Melody in LA Mode

1. Musical Conversation *(Cf. Chapters One, Two, Three, Four, and Fourteen)*

PROCEDURE: *A rhythm is given and two students engage in a question-answer dialogue based on this same rhythm. A group of students may also be chosen to take turns in "conversing" on the prescribed rhythm. All others make rhythm gesture.*

Mode: LA Mode Plagal Range

Rhythm: 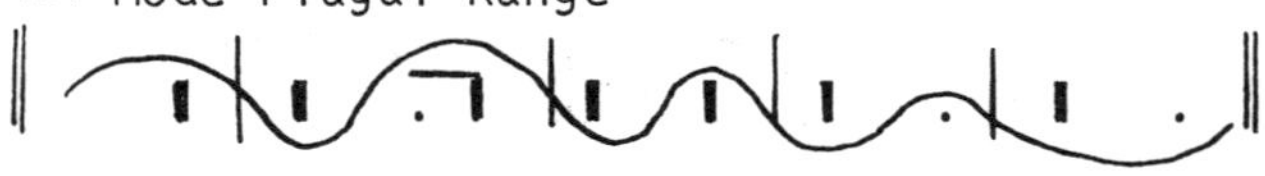

2. *Compose a melody for the poem analysed in Chapter Twenty-Three (under "Rhythm") for rhythmic structure. Use* *Mode of LA* *with notes studied under Intonation, for example,* 3 6 $\dot{1}$ *(or* $\dot{1}$ 6 3*)* *and* 7 5 3 *(or* 3 5 7*).*

‖ Praise the | Lord, ye | heav- ens a- | dore him;
| Praise him | an- gels | in the | height.
| Sun and | moon re- | joice be- | fore him;
| Praise him | all ye | stars of | light. ‖

Ps. 148

3. *Compose two additional lines for the theme given*

A ‖	3	6 . $\dot{1}$	7 $\dot{1}$ 7	6 . .	6 .
B	3	5 . 7	6 5 4	3 . .	. .
A					($\dot{1}$) .
C				6 . .	. . ‖

Songs

MELODY No. 49 Basque Folk Melody (alt.)

Mode of LA DO Clef Bottom line
St. D 32c P. 217
M. G. II Repetition of motif
Sight-singing Drills P. 219

$\dot{1}$ = E♭ (6 = C)

SUNSET ON THE RIVER *Melody:* Slavonic Folk *Text:* N. H. Dole

Mode of LA Plagal Range
St. D 29d P. 216
M. G. II Do Clef Line 3
Repetition - Conclusive Response

$\dot{1}$ = B♭ (6 = G)

THERE WAS A TAILOR HAD A MOUSE Old English Song

$\dot{1}$ = C (6 = A)

Mode of DO Plagal Range
DO Clef below staff
$\dot{1}$ 6 $\dot{1}$ and 5 3 5
St. D 29a and b P. 193
M. G. II begins on
up pulse

Mode of LA
Int. D.28 P. 192
R.G. IV Free

ALLELUIA! YE SONS AND DAUGHTERS OF THE LORD *Melody:* Eastertide Carol
Text: JBW

$\dot{1}$ = C (6 = A)

‖ 0 6 | 6 7 | 6 5 6 | $\dot{1}$ 7 6 | 3 . 7 | $\dot{1}$ 7 | 6 . ‖
Al- le- lu- ia,__ al- le- lu- ia,__ al- le- lu- ia.__

| 0 6 | $\dot{1}$ $\dot{2}$ | $\dot{3}$ $\dot{2}$ $\dot{1}$ | $\dot{2}$ $\dot{1}$ 7 | 6 .
O sons and daugh- ters, let__ us sing!__

| 6 | $\dot{1}$ $\dot{2}$ | $\dot{3}$ $\dot{2}$ $\dot{1}$ | $\dot{2}$ $\dot{1}$ 7 | 6 .
The King of heav'n,_ the glo- rious King__

| 6 | 6 7 | 6 5 6 | $\dot{1}$ 7 6 | 3 . 7 | $\dot{1}$ 7 | 6 . ‖
O'er death to- day__ rose tri- umph- ing.__ Al- le- lu- ia.__

| 0 6 | 6 7 | 6 5 6 | $\dot{1}$ 7 6 | 3 . 7 | $\dot{1}$ 7 | 6 . ‖
Al- le- lu- ia,__ al- le- lu- ia,__ al- le- lu- ia.__

OUR JOY ON EARTH *Melody:* "Jesu Dulcis Memoria" Chant *Text:* Trans. of Verse 5 by W. Shewring

1 = E♭ (6 = C)

Our joy on earth, in Par - a - dise

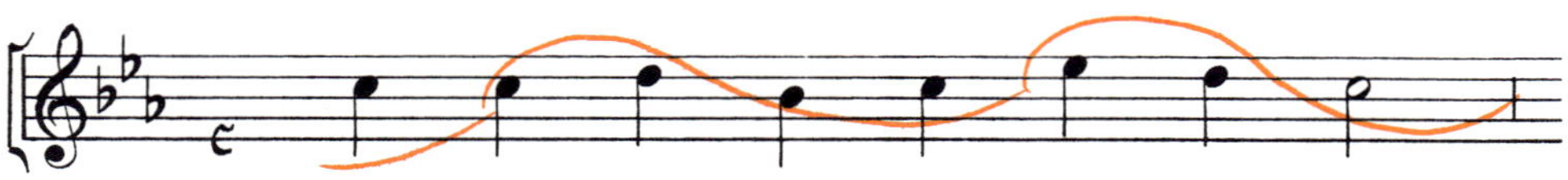

Our dear and ev - er - last - ing prize,

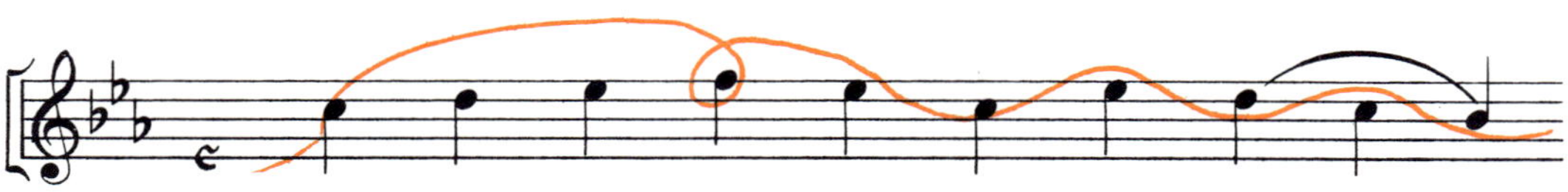

Je - sus, our glo - ry be in thee____

Through time and through e - ter - ni - ty.

A - men.___

Mode of LA
Int. D 31 P. 201
R. G. IV Free

INDEX OF SONGS AND SOURCES

CHAPTER ONE

CHAPTER TWO

CHAPTER THREE

CHAPTER FOUR

CHAPTER FIVE

CHAPTER SIX

CHAPTER SEVEN

CHAPTER EIGHT

CHAPTER NINE

CHAPTER TEN

CHAPTER ELEVEN

CHAPTER TWELVE

CHAPTER THIRTEEN

CHAPTER FOURTEEN

CHAPTER FIFTEEN

CHAPTER SIXTEEN

CHAPTER SEVENTEEN

CHAPTER EIGHTEEN

CHAPTER NINETEEN

CHAPTER TWENTY

CHAPTER TWENTY-ONE

CHAPTER TWENTY-TWO

CHAPTER TWENTY-THREE

CHAPTER TWENTY-FOUR

ALPHABETICAL INDEX OF SONGS

WARD METHOD OF MUSIC INSTRUCTION

CHAPTER SUMMARIES - BOOK II

	Vocal Training	Intonation	Rhythm	Staff Notation	Creative Activity	Repertory
	Numbering sequence for all exercises in Book II begins again with No. 1					
1	**Rev.** Vocal Exercises of Book One Voc. Ex. 1 1 ___ Nu ___ Voc. Ex. 2 1 1 1 1 1 1 Nu Nu Nu Nu Nu Nu Pitches from F to D	**Rev.** Intonation Ex. of Book One Mode of Do Authentic Range Compass Ex. 1, 2, 3, 4 Intonation Diagram 1 and Staff Diagrams 1a and 1b Ear and Eye Tests	**Rev.** Rhythm Gestures I, II Up-Pulse Beginnings in Binary Rhythm Metrical Gesture I Metrical Language Rhythm Patterns Series 1 Combining Rhythm Patterns Rhythmic Dictations	**Rev.** Five-Line Staff DO Clef on Bottom Line Single and Two-Pulse Notes Ties Transcriptions of Rhythms and Pitches	**Rev.** Musical Conversations on Rhythm Patterns Improvising Melodies for Verbal Phrases	S = Staff Notation Song N = Number Notation Song **Rev.** O Cock-a-Doodle Doo O Holy Spirit Melody No. 1a "Scale Song" (S,N) Melody 1b "Compass Song (S,N) Melody No. 2 "O Morning Star" (S) "I Hear You, Wind" (S) "Columbus" (S) "O Lord, I Am Not Worthy"(S)
2	**Rev.** Vocal Ex. 1 Pitches F to D Voc. Ex. 3 (F to A^b) 1 1 2 3 4 5 Nu Nu Nu Nu Nu Nu 5 5 4 3 2 1 Nu Nu Nu Nu Nu Nu	**Rev.** Authentic Range Mode of DO Int. Ex. 5, 6, 7, 8 Staff D.2 Int. D.2 Int. D.3 St. D.3 Ear and Eye Tests	**Rev.** Rhythm Gesture IV Binary (Arsis-Thesis) Down-Pulse Beginnings Rhythm Patterns Series 2 **Step 1** Aural Training in Rhythm Problems in Duple Time Rhythmic Dictations	**Rev.** Notation Values Rests Ties Time Signature 2 Transcriptions	**Rev.** Improvising Melodic Applications to Rhythm Patterns Musical Conversations Melodic Applications to Rhythm Patterns in Combination	Melody No. 3 (N) "Autumn Leaves" (N) Melody No. 4 (S) "This Is Jesus' Birthday" (S) "Flag of Our Nation" (S)
	SIGHT SINGING DRILLS IN STAFF NOTATION INCLUDED AS PREPARATION FOR STAFF SONGS					
3	**New:** Placement of Vowel "O" Voc. Ex. 4 1 Nu ___ o ___ u ___ Voc. Ex. 5 – Slurs 1 1 2 3 4 5 Nu Nu Nu Nu 5 5 4 3 2 1 Nu Nu Nu Nu	**New:** Plagal Range Finger Notation and Arm Gesture Int. Ex. 9, 10 Int. D. 4a Int. D. 4b St. D. 4 Ear and Eye Tests	**Rev.** Rhythm Gesture III Up-Pulse Beginning in Ternary Rhythm Rhythm Patterns Series 3 Rhythmic Dictations	**New:** DO Clef on Staff Line 2 Time Signature 3 Staff Game Transcriptions **Rev.** Repeat Sign Slur	Conversation: Statement – Response 1. Conclusive and Inconclusive Responses 2. Repetitive and Complementary Responses	Melody No. 5 (N) "The North Wind" (N) **Melody No. 6 (S)** **"When Christ Was Born to Set Us Free" (S)** "Halloween Song" (S)
4	**Rev.** Voc. Ex. 4 Voc. Ex. in Plagal Range Voc. Ex. 6a 1 3 2 1 7 6 5 Nu Nu Nu Nu Nu Nu Nu Voc. Ex. 6b 1 3 2 1 7 6 5 Nu Nu Nu Nu Nu Nu Nu	Plagal Range Cont'd Int. Ex. 11, 12 Int.D.5 Int.D.6 St. D. 6 Ear and Eye Tests	**Rev.** A – T in Ternary Rhythm Rhythm Gesture IV Down-Pulse Beginning Rhythm Patterns Series 4 Aural Training in Rhythm: **Step 2:** Problems in Triple Time Rhythmic Dictations	DO Clef on Line 2 of Staff Transcriptions: Pitches Rhythms Melodies Staff and Number Notation	Conversations: Statement and Response in Triple Time Melodic Applications of Rhythm Patterns	Melody No. 7 (N) Melody No. 8 (S) "London Bridge" (S) "Bring a Torch, Jeannette Isabella" (S) "Draw a Bucket of Water" (N) "Angel, My Guardian" (S) **Rev.** "Near to My Woodland Cottage" "Children of Your Heavenly King"

CHAPTER SUMMARIES - BOOK II

	Vocal Training	Intonation	Rhythm	Staff Notation	Creative Activity	Repertory
5	**New:** Placement of Vowel "A" Voc. Ex. 7 ‖ 1 ‖ Nu-o-a-u Voc. Ex. 8a ‖ 1 3 5 4 3 2 1 7 6 5 6 7 1 . . o ‖ Nu Nu Nu Nu Nu Nu Nu Nu Nu Nu Nu Nu Nu Voc. Ex. 8b ‖ 1 3 5 4 3 2 1 7 6 5 6 7 1 . . ‖	Plagal Range Cont'd Assimilation of Compass Ex. 2 and 3 Int. Ex. 13, 14, 15 6 5 3 4 2 1 7 6 5 Int. D. 6 St. D. 6 (Ch. 4) Ear and Eye Tests	**New:** Half-Pulses (Eighth Notes) Binary Rhythm (Duple Time) Beginning on Up-Pulse Metrical Language Rhythm Patterns Series 5 With and Without Final Repose Rhythmic Dictations	Staff and Number Notations for Half-Pulses Transcriptions: Rhythm Patterns, Melodic Designs DO Clef on Line 2	Composing Two-Line Songs From Rhythm Patterns Statement and Response for Balanced Phrasing Composing Missing Line of Song (Inconclusive Response)	"Jesus, the Very Thought of Thee" (S) Melody No. 9 (N) Melody No. 10 (S) "God's Messenger" (N) "The Circus" (S) "Ah, My Castle Fine" (S)
6	**Rev.** Voc. Ex. 7 Voc. Ex. 9a ‖ 1 . | 3 . | 2 . | 1 . | . . ‖ Nu Nu Nu Nu Voc. Ex. 9b ‖ 1 3 2 1 . . ‖ Voc. Ex. 9c ‖ 1 3 2 1 . . ‖ Voc. Ex. 10a ‖ 1 3 2 1 7 6 5 . ‖ Voc Ex. 10b ‖ 1 3 2 1 7 6 5 . . ‖	**New:** Extension of Scale Line Above Upper Tetrachord Int. Ex. 16, 17, 18 Finger Notation for 1 2 3 3 4 2 1 7 6 5 Int. D 7 St. D. 7 Ear and Eye Tests	Half-Pulse Notes ♫ Rhythm Gesture II Up-Pulse Beginning Rhythm Patterns Series 6 Repeating and Combining Patterns Aural Training (Cont'd): Rhythm Determined by Long Note Rhythmic Dictations	**New:** DO Clef on Line Below Staff "Moving Day" on Staff Transcriptions: Numbers to Staff and Staff to Numbers	**Rev.** Study of Rhythmic Enlargements Book One Examples	Melody No. 11 (N) Melody No. 12 (N) Melody No. 13 (S) "Westminster Chime" (N) "All Glory, Laud and Honor" (S) "Coming Back From Fremly Fairground" (N) "Ramponeau Isn't Dead" (S)
7	**Rev.** Voc. Ex. 7 and 10a Voc. Ex. 11a ‖ 1 3 5 4 3 2 1 . . ‖ Nu o Nu o Na Nu o Na Nu	Major Mode 3 – 3 Range Int. Ex. 19, 20 3 4 2 1 7 6 5 4 3 Int. D. 8 St. D. 8 St. D. 9a 9b 6 5 4 3 2 1 Int. D. 9a 1 7 6 5 4 3 Int. D. 9b Ear and Eye Tests	A–T in Binary Rhythm Beginning on Down-Pulse Rhythm Patterns Series 7 **New:** Metrical Gesture II (Beating Time in Duple Meter) Aural Training – **Step 3** Rhythm Determined by Melodic Design: Repeated Notes, Repeated Motifs	**Rev.** Three Known Positions of DO Clef Transcriptions	**New:** Contrast and Repetition Composing Responses to Statements Given	Melody No. 14 (N) Melody No. 15 (S) Melody No. 16 (N) "Hail, Redeemer, King Divine" (N) "Triumph All, Ye Cherubim" (N) "Yankee Doodle" (S) "Shetland Pony" (N) Broom Dance (N)
8	**Rev.** Voc. Ex. 7 Sustained Vowels: u o a u **Rev.** Voc. Ex. 8a and 8b (Chapter 5)	Discovery of Dominant 5 7 2 Triad in Plagal Range Appearance of Dom. 7th Developing Agility in Approaching 5 and 5 Int. Ex. 21, 22, 23 2 1 7 6 5 6 7 1 2 Int. D. 10 St. D. 10 5 3 1 5 4 5 2 7 5 Int. D. 11 St. D. 11 Ear and Eye Tests	Half-Pulse Notes in Ternary Rhythm (Triple Time) Beginning on Up-Pulse Rhythm Patterns Series 8 Aural Training – **Step 4** Rhythm Determined by Melodic Line Rhythmic Dictations	**Rev.** Transcriptions With DO Clef on Line 2 of Staff Numbers to Staff Staff to Numbers	Composition With Words Two Phrases in Ternary Rhythm Two Phrases in Binary Rhythm	Melody No. 17 (N) "If I Get My Pick of the Three of Them" (S) Melody No. 18 (N) Melody No. 19 (S) "The Mill Wheel" (N) "O Where, O Where, Is My Little Dog Gone?" (S) "Altho' at Yule" (N)

CHAPTER SUMMARIES - BOOK II

	Vocal Training	Intonation	Rhythm	Staff Notation	Creative Activity	Repertory
9	**Review Exercises:** Voc. Ex. 7 Sustained Vowels U-o-a Voc. Ex. 6a and 6b Plagal Range Voc. Ex. 8a and 8b Plagal Range Voc. Ex. 9b and 9c	Plagal Range: Tonic and Dominant Chords Octave Interval: 5-5 5-5 Int. and Staff Diagrams 11 (Chapter 8) Int. Ex. 24 and 25 Ear and Eye Tests	Single-Pulse and Half-pulse Notes Beginning on Down Pulse Triple Meter Metrical Gesture III Beating Time in Triple Meter Aural Training **Step 5** Rhythmic Transformation of a Melody Rhythmic Dictations	Transcriptions Interval Drills in Staff Notation Visual Memory tests	Melodic Application of Rhythmic Patterns in Combination Composing Melodies for Texts in Triple Meter	Melody No. 20 (N) Melody No. 21 (S) "Morning" (N) Melody No. 22 (N) "Oh, Dear, What Can the Matter Be" (S) "Holiest Night" (S)
10	**Rev.** Vocal Ex. 7 (Ch. 5) **Rev.** Vocal Ex. 11a (Ch. 7) Voc. Ex. 11b — In context of Mode of Sol 5 7 2 1 7 6 5	Discovering Mode of SOL Pentachord 56712 Special Cadences Int. Diagram 6 (Ch. 4) Intonation Ex. 26, 27, 28 Intonation Diagrams 6, 12, 13, 14, Staff D. 14 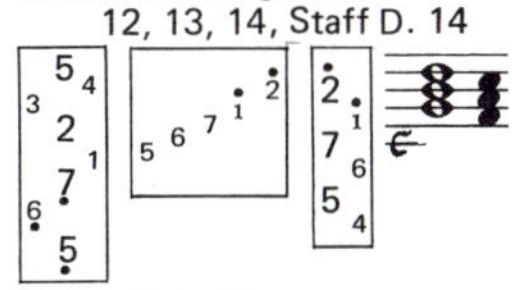 Ear and Eye Tests Visual Memory Tests	Free Rhythm: Irregular Combination of Binary and Ternary Rhythms Arsis-Thesis Combinations Beginning on Down-Pulse Rhythmic Dictations	DO Clef on ledger line Below Staff Transcriptions: Numbers to Staff Notation Staff Notation to Numbers Visual Memory tests	Discovering Possibility of Rhythmic Enlargement to Change a Binary into a Ternary rhythm Composing Melodies for Texts in Modes of DO and SOL	Melody No. 23 (N) Acclamation: "For the Kingdom" (N) "Kyrie XII" (N) (First Kyrie only) "Springs of Water" (N) "Agnus Dei XVIII" (N) "Turning" (S) "Good Morning" (S)
11	New Vowels: "e" and "i" Pronounced as in Latin "eh" and "ee" Voc. Ex. 12a: Sustained Tones: Nu-o-a-e-i Voc. Ex. 13a: 1 · 4 3 2 1 Na_ Nu _ No_ Ne_ Ni_____ Voc. Ex. 13b: 1 4 3 2 1 Na Nu No Ne Ni_____	Mode of SOL — Authentic Range: 5 - 5 (Mode VII) Intonation Ex. 29, 30 Intonation and Staff Diagrams 12 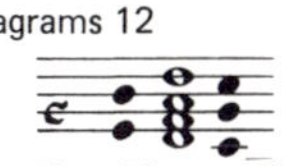 Intonation Diagram 15 "Green Gavel" Ear and Eye Tests	Free Rhythm (Cont'd) Arsis-Thesis (R. G. IV) Beginning on Up-pulse Aural Training — **Step 6** Discovering Rhythm of Unbarred Songs	DO Clef on Second Line of Staff in Context of Mode of SOL 5 - 5 Transcriptions Sight-Singing Phrases Visual Memory Tests	Changing Metrical Design of a Melody to one of Free Rhythm by Adding Notes to Selected Syllables of a Text (or Measures)	"Some Love Coffee Some Love Tea" (S) "The Mass Is Ended" (N) "Now With the Fast Departing Light" (N) "To Thee Who Makest All" (S) Melody No. 24 (N) "Be Thou a Light" (N) (Lumen ad Revelationem) Alleluia (S)
12	**Rev.** Latin Vowels (Cont'd **Rev.** Voc. Ex. 12a Voc. Ex. 14a: Plagal Range — Mode of SOL Voc. Ex. 14b 5 2 1 7 6 5 2 3 4 5	Mode of SOL — Plagal Range Mode VIII 2 - 2 Intonation Ex. 31, 32 Intonation and Staff Diagrams 16 and 17 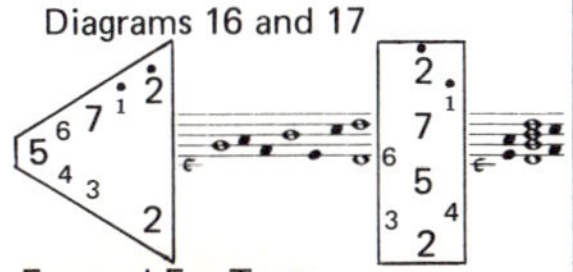 Eye and Ear Tests	Free Rhythm (Cont'd) Aural Training in Rhythm **Step 7:** Discovering Rhythm of Song by Listening Dictations	Tonic SOL in Three Positions of DO Clef 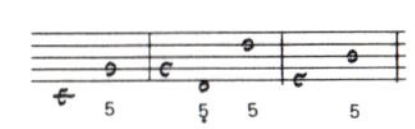 Transcriptions Sight-Singing Drills Visual Memory Tests	Composing in Mode of SOL Responses to Given Statements Composing Free Rhythm Melodies for Given Texts.	"Green Gavel" (N) Melody No. 25 (N) "O Sweet Lady" (S) "Sing With Joy to the Lord" (S) "Our Father" (N) "Kyrie XII" (Complete) (N) "Christ Has Died" (S)

CHAPTER SUMMARIES - BOOK II

	Vocal Training	Intonation	Rhythm	Staff Notation	Creative Activity	Repertory
13	**Rev.** Voc. Ex. 12a, 13a, 13b Voc. Ex. 15 Vowels in Mode of LA Pentachord 6 3 2 1 7 6 · Na Nu No Ni Na No____	Presenting Mode of LA 6 7 1 2 3 Hexachord: 6 7 1 2 3 4 Int. Ex. 33, 34, 35, 36, 37 Int. and Staff Diagrams 18 and 19  6 7 1 2 3 6 7 1 2 3 4 Eye and Ear Tests in Number and Staff Notation	Presenting the Dotted Rhythm in Context of R. G. II (Up-pulse beginning) Rhythm Patterns Series 10 Metrical Language for ♩. ♪ Rhythmic Dictations	Mode of LA with DO Clef on Ledger Line Below Staff The G Clef  Transcriptions from Number to Staff Notation Preparation Drills for Songs in Staff Notation in LA Mode	Improvising Melodies to Assimilate LA Mode Composing Complimentary Phrases Composing Melodies to Rhythm Patterns	Melody No. 26 (N) Melody No. 27 (N) Melody No. 28 (S) "The Sandman" (S) "A Boy Is Born in Bethlehem" (N)
14	**Rev.** Voc. Ex. 12a, 15 Voc. Ex. 16a Tones of Hexachord of LA Mode 6 · 7 · 1 · 2 · 3 · 4 · 3 Na_o Na_o Na_o Na_ 2 · 1 · 7 · 6 · · o Na_ o Na____	LA Mode (Cont'd) 6 - 3 6 - 4 Int. Ex. 38, 39, 40, 41 Int. Diagram 20 Staff Diagram 20a, 20b 4 3 2 1 7 6 5 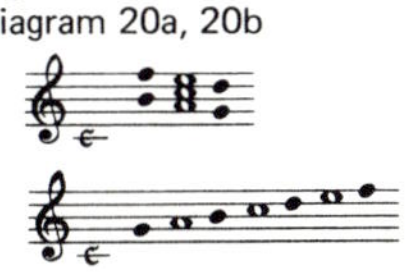 Eye and Ear Tests in Number and Staff Notation	Assimilation of ♩. ♪ in Context of R. G. II Rhythm Patterns Series 11 Study of Free Rhythm (Cont'd) Rhythmic Dictations	Assimilation of LA Mode on Staff 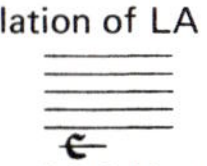 Review of DO Mode  Review of DO Mode – Plagal Range 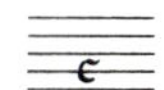 Preparation Drills for Songs in Staff Notation in LA Mode	Conversations in LA Mode Composing Melodies to Rhythm Patterns Composing Complimentary Phrases to Given Statements	Melody No. 29 (S) Melody No. 30 (S) "Auld Lang Syne" (N) "Ave Maris Stella" (N) "The God of Nature and of Grace" (S)
15	**Rev.** Voc. Ex. 12a Voc. Ex. 15 Voc. Ex. 16a Voc. Ex. 16b (DO Clef on Line 2) 	LA Mode (Cont'd) First and Second Compass Exercises Int. Ex. 42, 43, 44, 45, 56 Int. Diagram 20 Staff Diagram 20b (Chapter 14) Staff Diagram 20c 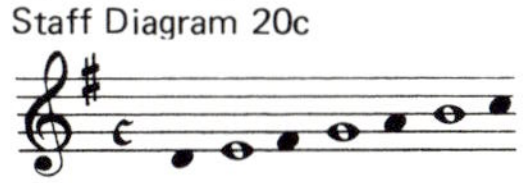 Ear and Eye Tests in Number and Staff Notations	Dotted Quarter and Eighth ♩. ♪ in Duple Time Down-pulse Beginning Arsis-Thesis in Duple Time and in Free Rhythm **Rev.** Metrical Gesture II Rhythm Patterns Series 12 Rhythmic Dictations	LA Mode Transcriptions DO Clef in Two Positions Sight-Singing Drills	Conversations in LA Mode Composing Answering Statements Improvising Melodies for Arsis-Thesis Gestures in Duple Time	Melody No. 31 (N) Melody No. 32 (S) "Loving Shepherd of the Sheep" (N) "Ding Dong Bell" (S) "The Ferryman" (N) (Round) "Evening Hymn" (S) "Holy, Holy, Holy" (N)
16	**Rev.** Voc. Ex. 12a Voc. Ex. 15 Voc. Ex. 16a, 16b	LA Mode Hexachord (Cont'd) Second and Third Compass Exercises Int. Ex. 47, 48, 49, 50, 51 Int. D. 21 Staff Diagrams 21a, 21b 3 4 1 2 6 7 5  Eye and Ear Tests	Dotted Quarter and Eighth ♩. ♪ in Triple Time Up-Pulse Beginning Rhythm Patterns Series 13 Rhythmic Dictations	LA Mode Transcriptions DO Clef in Two Positions (Cont'd)	Composing in LA Mode Ternary Rhythm with Up-pulse Beginning Compose Melody for a Given Text	Melody No. 33 (N) "A Sailor Climbed the Mast on High" (S) Melody No. 34 (S) "The Silver Moon Is Shining" (N)

CHAPTER SUMMARIES - BOOK II

	Vocal Training	Intonation	Rhythm	Staff Notation	Creative Activity	Repertory
17	**Rev.** Voc. Ex. 12a Voc. Ex. 15 Voc. Ex. 16b Voc. Ex. 17a ‖6 5 4 | 3 4 5 | 6 . . . . ‖ Nu Nu Nu Nu Nu Nu Nu___ Na-o—u— Na-a —e—i___ Voc. Ex. 17b ‖0 6 | 5 4 | 3 4 5 | 6 . ‖ Nu Nu Nu Nu Nu Nu Nu___ Na—o—u no—a—e—i___	LA Mode Upper Tetrachord 6 5 4 3 Extension Upwards 6 7 1̇ DO Clef on Bottom Line Int. and Staff Diagrams 22, 23 6 5 4 3 | 1̇ 7 6 5 4 3  Int. Ex. 52, 53, 54, 55 Ear and Eye Tests	Dotted Quarter and Eighth ♩. ♪ in Duple Time Down-pulse Beginning (Cont'd) Arsis-Thesis in Free Rhythm Rhythmic Dictations: Metrical and Free Rhythm	Key Signature Tells Position of DO Clef Notice: 𝄞 ♯ ♭ in Key Signature Jingles for Remembering How to Find Place of DO Practise in Finding DO Flash Cards	Compose Two Answering Lines in LA Mode Duple Time	Melody No. 35 (N) Melody No. 36 (S) "God-head Here in Hiding" (N) "Were You Ever in Quebec?" (S) Penitential Service (Order of Mass) (N)
18	**Rev.** Voc. Ex. 12a Voc. Ex. 18 ‖3 6 | 5 4 | 3 . | 3 2 | 1 7̣ | 6̣ . ‖ Nu Nu Nu Nu Nu___ Nu Nu Nu Nu Nu___ Na—o No—a No___ No—a Nu—a No___	LA Mode Authentic Range 6̣ - 6 First and Second Compass Exercises Int. Ex. 56, 57, 58, 59 Int. D. 24, 25 Staff D. 25 6 5 4 3 3 2 1 7̣ 6̣ | 6 5 4 3 2 1 7̣ 6̣ 5̣  Ear and Eye Tests	Dotted Quarter and Eighth ♩. ♪ in Triple Time Down-pulse Beginning Combining Duple and Triple Time in Free Rhythm **Rev.** Metrical Gesture III Dictations	Key Signature Tells Position of DO Clef (Cont'd) Finding Tonic LA of Minor Mode from Key Signature Flash Cards	Composing Answers to Themes of Classical Composers LA Mode and DO Mode Composing Melody for Text in Free Rhythm Composing Melodic Applications to Rhythm Patterns in LA and DO Modes	Melody No. 37 (N) Melody No. 38 (S) "My Country 'Tis of Thee" (S) "We Three Kings" (N) Melody No. 39 (N) "Come, Let Us Make a Snowman" (S)
19	Voc. Ex. 12b Introduce Sustained Vowels with Consonants D and T **Rev.** Voc. Ex. 18	LA Mode Tonic Chord Line With Scales and Surrounding Notes Int. Ex. 60, 61, 62, 63 Int. D. 26 Staff Diagram 26a, b 6 7 5 4 3 2 1 7̣ 6̣ 5̣ 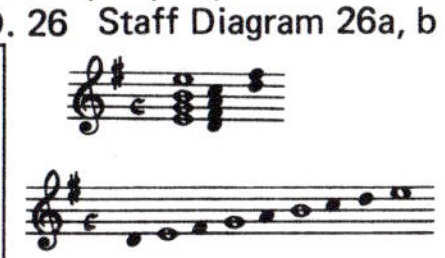 Ear and Eye Tests	Dotted Quarter and Eighth ♩. ♪ in Triple Time Up-pulse Beginning Introducing the Triplet Continue Study of Free Rhythm	Key Signature Tells Position of DO Clef (Cont'd) Finding Tonic LA from Key Signature Notation of Triplet 	Composing Melody for Poetic Texts Feminine Endings	Melody No. 40 (N) Melody No. 41 (S) "The King of Love My Shepherd Is" (N) "A Day in the Cornfield" (S) "O Come, O Come, Emmanuel" (N)
20	**Rev.** Voc. Ex. 12b Voc. Ex. 12c Introduce Sustained Vowels with Consonants M B P **Rev.** Voc. Ex. 18	Third Compass Exercise LA Mode Dependent Tones of Minor Mode Intonation and Staff Diagrams 25, 27 Int. Ex. 64, 65, 66, 67 6 5 4 3 2 1 7̣ 6̣ 5̣ | 6 3 1 6̣  Ear and Eye Tests	Discover Rhythm of Unbarred Songs and Phrases Metrical and Free Rhythm Recognize Rhythms of Songs From Listening Rhythmic Dictations	Transcribe Entire Song in LA Mode with Key Signature of One Sharp 	Compose Two Answering Lines in LA Mode Compose Melody for Poetic Text in DO Mode	Melody No. 42 (N) "Christ Our Lord Is Risen" (N) "Let All Mortal Flesh Keep Silence" (S) "Regina Caeli Laetare" (N) "John Paul Jones" (S)

CHAPTER SUMMARIES - BOOK II

	Vocal Training	Intonation	Rhythm	Staff Notation	Creative Activity	Repertory
21	**Rev.** Voc. Ex. 12b, c Voc. Ex. 12d Introduce Sustained Vowels with Consonants K, G **Rev.** Voc. Ex. 17a, b	Presenting Plagal Range of LA Mode 3 - 3 DO Clef on Ledger Line Below Staff Int. Ex. 68, 69, 70 Int. and Staff Diagrams 28, 29 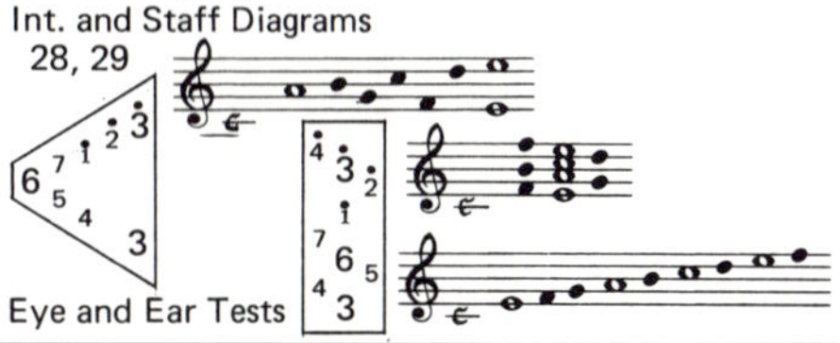 Eye and Ear Tests	Continue Discovering Rhythm of Unbarred Songs and Phrases in Metrical and Free Rhythm Identify Rhythm and Mode from Listening	Transcriptions in LA and DO Modes Sight-Singing Fragments in LA Mode – Plagal Range DO Clef on Ledger Line Below Staff 	Compose Melodies for Metrical and Prose Texts Musical terms: Fine Da Capo (D.C.)	Melody No. 43 (N) Melody No. 44 (S) "Ave Maria" (N) "When I Fetch Water From the Spring" (S) "Heigh-Ho, Nobody at Home" (N) – Round "Father Almighty, Pour on Us Thy Blessing" (S)
22	**Rev.** Voc. Ex. 12b, c, d Voc. Ex. 19a With Consonants D and T 6 1 3 2 1 7 Nu ___ No ___ Du ___ Do ___ Tu ___ To ___ 6 5 4 3 4 5 6 . . Na ___ Ne ___ Ni ___ Da ___ De ___ Di ___ Ta ___ Te ___ Ti ___	Tonic Chord and Surrounding Notes of LA Mode – Plagal Range Contrasting 163 with 357 Int. Ex. 71, 72, 73, 74 Int. and Staff Diagrams 30, 31 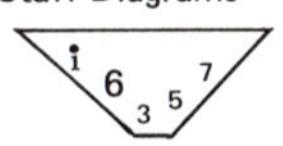 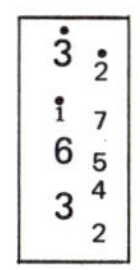  Eye and Ear Tests	**Rev.** Metrical Language with Metrical Gesture I Determine Metrical Structure of Verbal Texts Rhythmic Dictations Quotations from Songs Already Studied Dictations	DO Clef on Ledger Line Below Staff for Modes of SOL, DO, LA  Transcriptions	**Rev.** Rhythmic Enlargement **Rev.** Rhythmic Transformation	Melody No. 45 (N) Melody No. 46 (S) "Farewell and Adieu" (N) "For the Beauty of the Earth" (N) "Horo Haradal" (S) "Twas in the Moon of Wintertime" (S)
23	**Rev.** Voc. Ex. 12b, c, d Voc. Ex. 19b With Consonants B and P 6 1 3 2 1 7 Mu ___ Mo ___ Bu ___ Bo ___ Pu ___ Po ___ 6 5 4 3 4 5 6 . . Ma ___ Me ___ Mi ___ Ba ___ Be ___ Bi ___ Pa ___ Pe ___ Pi ___	Third Compass Ex. in LA Mode – Plagal Range Compass Ex. Combined Int. Ex. 75, 76, 77, 78 Int. and Staff Diagrams 28, 29 (Review) Ear and Eye Tests	**Rev.** Aural Training in Rhythm Discover Metrical Structures of Verbal Texts Rhythmic Dictations Quotations from Songs Already Studied	DO Clef on Line 3 for LA Mode  Transcriptions Sight-Singing Drills	**Rev.** Melodic Formation by repeated Notes, Motifs, Sequences, Inversions Compose Melody for Poetic Text	Melody No. 47 (S) Dismissal Chants (English-Latin) (N) "The Jolly Ploughboy" (S) Melody No. 48 (N) "Resurrection" (N)
24	**Rev.** Voc. Ex. 12b, c, d Voc. Ex. 19c With Consonants K and G 6 1 3 2 1 7 Nu ___ No ___ Ku ___ Ko ___ Gu ___ Go ___ 6 5 4 3 4 5 6 . . Na ___ Ne ___ Ni ___ Ka ___ Ke ___ Ki ___ Ga ___ Ge ___ Gi ___	**Rev.** First Three Compass Ex. in LA Mode Study 357 in relation to 163 Int. Ex. 79, 80, 81 Staff Diagrams 29c, d Int. and Staff Diagrams 32 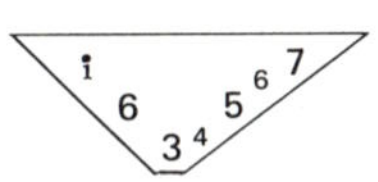 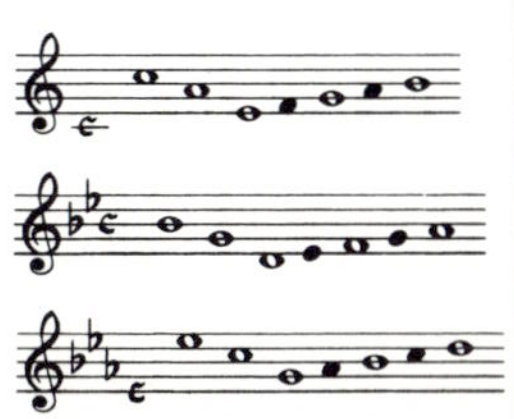 Ear and Eye Tests	**Rev.** Rhythm Gestures I, II, III, IV Metrical Gestures I, II, III	DO Clef on Line 1 for LA Mode  Position of DO from Key Signature Sight-Singing Fragments in DO, SOL, LA Modes Transcriptions	**Rev.** Musical Conversations Compose Melody for Poetic Text Compose Additional Lines for Theme Given	Melody No. 48 (S) "Sunset on the River" (S) "There Was a Tailor Had a Mouse" (S) "Alleluia: Ye Sons and Daughters of the Lord" (N) "Our Joy on Earth" (S)